AMANDA ADAM

MEREWIF

the Mermaid Witch

Copyright © 2021 by Amanda Adam

All rights reserved. No part of this publication may be reproduced, stored or transmitted in any form or by any means, electronic, mechanical, photocopying, recording, scanning, or otherwise without written permission from the publisher. It is illegal to copy this book, post it to a website, or distribute it by any other means without permission.

This novel is entirely a work of fiction. The names, characters and incidents portrayed in it are the work of the author's imagination. Any resemblance to actual persons, living or dead, events or localities is entirely coincidental.

Amanda Adam asserts the moral right to be identified as the author of this work.

Amanda Adam has no responsibility for the persistence or accuracy of URLs for external or third-party Internet Websites referred to in this publication and does not guarantee that any content on such Websites is, or will remain, accurate or appropriate.

Designations used by companies to distinguish their products are often claimed as trademarks. All brand names and product names used in this book and on its cover are trade names, service marks, trademarks and registered trademarks of their respective owners. The publishers and the book are not associated with any product or vendor mentioned in this book. None of the companies referenced within the book have endorsed the book.

First edition

ISBN: 978-0-578-94401-2

This book was professionally typeset on Reedsy. Find out more at reedsy.com

To my Sasquatch, Chris:
It wouldn't have been the same without you. You are a Godsend.

Bear & Dragon:
I wrote this story through both pregnancies;
and while I gave you life, you gave my book life, too.
Inspiration when a little soul is lighting within you is a real thing.

And to Bucky, who finished this story first, and believed in it from the start.

To the sea, to the sea! The white gulls are crying, the wind is blowing, and the white foam is flying. West, west away, the round sun is falling. Grey ship, grey ship, do you hear them calling, the voices of my people that have gone before me? I will leave, I will leave the woods that bore me; for our days are ending and our years are failing. I will pass the wide waters lonely sailing. Long are the waves on the Last Shore falling; sweet are the voices in the Lost Isle calling.

-J.R.R. Tolkien

Contents

Acknowledgement   iii
PROLOGUE   vi

1. Newcomers — 1
2. The Necklace — 8
3. Submerged — 16
4. Clear Moonstone — 21
5. Time Immemorial — 26
6. All Hallow's Eve — 35
7. Unveiling — 50
8. The Letter — 59
9. Royal Cuffs — 74
10. The Saelfen Vault — 102
11. Air — 122
12. Blood Vala — 139
13. In a Tree by the Sea — 150
14. Water — 162
15. Out of Sight — 186
16. Murmuring Madness — 200
17. Morgaine — 205
18. Jonah's Whale — 219
19. Treaties & Promises — 225
20. The Keeper — 237
21. The Academy — 246
22. The Help — 260

23	Droplets of Mist	279
24	Merlin's Cave	286
25	A Taste of Blood	291
26	Breathe, See, Hear	295
27	Pluck, Rattle, Burn	303
28	Squall	308
29	Awakening	316
30	Foreweard	328

Acknowledgement

To my beta readers: you helped me to keep going. Even in the early drafts, you saw what was here and encouraged it.

Chris Adam, my husband: your creativity and insight throughout has made this a joyful process for me, and the journey wouldn't have been with same without you. In those early days I read aloud to you again, and again, and again… And you were patient, and helpful, and *still* excited about it. Thank you for inspiring and helping with many great parts of this story; but most of all, something *more* in the library. My ghostly sea-nymph, Giuliana, is one of my favorite creations. I cannot imagine the book without her!

Susan and David Holmberg, my parents. Your belief in me and in my dreams gives me wings. Thank you for supporting me and this work. It pleased me beyond comprehension when you both read an early draft and how astonished you were that I wrote it.

To my brother, David Holmberg, you were on board and excited about this from the beginning and read early drafts with fervor. I loved how much you geeked out over the story and finished it first when I finally wrote the words "The End." If it weren't for you, the Academy and the SSO would never have been born! It's such a cool element to the story and lends so much to future storyline. What a huge gift.

To Adam and Lauren Sibley: Adam, I'll never forget you

calling me when you'd began reading and how excited you were about it. I was walking aimlessly in a store and listening to you tell me how much and why you loved the story so far, and that conversation is still etched in my mind when I think of future readers. It has helped given me courage to do this! Thank you both for your amazing encouragement. Lauren, I'm lucky to have you as a friend - your creativity and insight is slam dunk.

To my little fireheart and fellow writer, Marie Whipple: your encouragement makes my soul smile, including talking about me and my book in your class at school. I hope others love this story as much as you do, and it gives me a taste of what it might be like to have fans someday. I love it! Thank you for being my first fan.

To my BFF Sarah Hess. You have always, always encouraged my writing. When we'd exchange stories growing up about being shipwrecked with our crushes and into college, when we'd read our poetry out loud (your poetry was far better). And you read an early draft of *Merewif* and have been asking for book two ever since. Much of this novel wouldn't have been written without you to inspire a lot of its content. LYLAS!

To Jeannie Hilderbrand, who first gave me an editorial eye on this thing and brought to light some major story workings that needed fixing! You are not only one of the most talented writers I know, but you are also one of the most talented writers I have read. I remember watching you dance in high school, and how much you stood out; it was written in your face and how gracefully you moved. Your writing feels the same way. I am grateful that I was blessed with your friendship and especially to have you as a critique partner /

beta reader.

I would be remiss not to mention Lisa Edwards, who provided an indispensable editorial development / assessment. If any writer needs a veteran of an editor, with a keen eye and honest feedback, look no further.

Dr. Stanley Williams, author of the Moral Premise: not only did your book resonate and guide my writing, but your early collaboration and advice was monumental and helped me hone my craft entirely.

To Mariah Durst for the amazing cover art and design. I am so happy I found you! You are talented, to say the least! No one could have done what you did - you found Madge. I love this book cover. I hope you have a bright future in your art.

And lastly, to my cat, Papo. You were there with me, in my lap, or resting on my keyboard (that was always fun). Reading with a cat curled up in your lap is much the same as writing with one in your lap; it makes it cozy and magical. In the early, early days of me writing this story and bringing it to life, it was just me and my stripey, soft, three-legged fur baby. I miss my little tiger.

PROLOGUE

When it called, it was at the loneliest part of the night, even when she tried not to listen, no matter how comfortable she was in her bed. Most often it was to sit in the sand and watch, the crashing surf filling her ears, salty mist kissing her face and cooling her mind.

Other times, like tonight, she had a need to be out in it.

Madge had been doing this since she could remember. When Grandpa Ollie was snoring away, she'd slip out her window, inching down the roof, skinning her knees on scratchy tiles as she dangled her legs down to reach the dewy deck banister. From there she'd balance well enough to lightly hop down onto the back deck, tiptoeing across until she reached the wide, embedded wood steps leading down to the sand. She longed for the lonely feeling of swimming in the dark Pacific; the sense of something looming beneath her feet, even if it scared her a little. Her thirst for being out in it alone, drinking up the energy swirling and crashing around her, was a need she couldn't remember *not* having. And somehow Grandpa Ollie had never found out.

Madge relished the ice-cold water that filled her wetsuit, letting her body adjust and warm itself, her long sandy-brown hair tucked into a hood. It was the water that made her feel like anything made sense.

Especially when things didn't.

Like the fact she was going to see the Riveras today, her dead parent's closest friends, people she hadn't seen or even spoken to since preschool. Now, out of the blue, the Riveras apparently had decided to move themselves and their business to her small, cold, wet coastal town. Grandpa Ollie hadn't expanded as to why, and she hadn't bothered asking. She'd given up on these people long ago, so the fact she'd tossed and turned for hours, anxious about seeing them was especially annoying.

She fought past the pounding surf, under and up, and under and up again, until she finally made it past the break. She searched the night sky for the pale spot where the moon was hidden behind storm-torn clouds. And like she always did, she watched it, floating on the swells of the ocean, and imagined her parents looking down on her. Even as she felt her neck prickle with that minty, familiar sensation that someone, or something, was watching her; as all too often when she was out on the ocean at night, alone.

But whatever it was, she knew it wasn't her dead parents.

1

Newcomers

"Pay attention to the road," Grandpa Ollie said, turning the radio down.

"I haven't seen them since…" Madge paused to do the math on her fingers—

"You were five years old."

"Whatever, it's the *nineties* now. Eleven years, grandpa. Did they have to pick my birthday to see us?" Madge huffed, trying to ignore Grandpa Ollie white-knuckling his seat and pumping imaginary brakes as she navigated Taffy, a vintage pink and white convertible Metropolitan on the windy road that edged the Pacific. Towering pine trees, many of them growing sideways from the constant coastal winds bordered the narrow, hilly highway and afforded a peek into the sandy coastline below. Despite last night's gales it was a rare, sunny October morning in Cannon Beach, and Madge drove into town with the top down, eager to drink every drop of sunshine on her too-pale skin before it disappeared again.

"That's exactly why they chose today. And what a day it is," Grandpa Ollie said, raising his bushy white eyebrows skyward.

"I forgot my hat. My hair will be a tangled mess now for my driver's license picture," Madge said, attempting in vain to hold her hair from flapping in her face.

"Not everyone passes their driver's test the first time around. Your mother didn't."

"So you keep saying!" Taffy had been her mother's and would officially be hers today, if she passed her driver's test – the very day she was turning sixteen and was of legal age. "I wish we didn't have to meet these people before I take it."

"You aren't excited to see the Riveras?"

"Not really," Madge lied. She wanted to believe she had dressed nice just to look good for her driver's license picture, if she passed. But she knew better. She wasn't sure which she was more nervous about – seeing the Riveras or flunking her driver's test.

She had laid out her clothes the night before and had run around in a frenzy in the morning to make time to curl her hair and put on makeup. Most days she opted simply for mascara and lip balm. But when she looked at herself in the mirror and felt like a clown, as she usually did when she put on eyeshadow and foundation, she promptly washed her face and settled for mascara. She had serious thoughts about changing again, but she hadn't time when Grandpa Ollie had called up the stairs that it was time to go.

Ollie was never late.

"I just hope their kid is not as obnoxious as he used to be. He used to pull my hair. Hard."

"He's not a kid anymore."

"Well, it would help if they'd ever sent a card. Maybe a picture or two. Or called. You know, the usual stuff close friends and family do."

"I know they've been MIA – and I am sure they've got their reasons – but they are here now. They are as close to family as we've got. Christine was—"

"Mom's best friend since they were thirteen. Yeah, I know."

"I was going to say more like a sister to your mom than anything. And there will be quite a few new folks in town now that they've moved MEI here."

"The Marine Ecology Institute, short for a bunch of nerds and over-achievers."

"Give them a chance. You may be surprised."

Madge slowed as she drove into town, where the entire main drag had been decorated for Halloween. The boutique shops and restaurants were mostly a weathered gray or brown shingle, and the mountains and forests surrounded the quaint seaside town with a rustic and wild flair. She pulled into a parking space directly in front of Grandpa Ollie's coffee shop, the Bear Paw, where they were meeting the Riveras.

But Madge didn't move to get out of the car, or even to take off her seatbelt, but instead stared at the shop window, her stomach dancing a jig. "The display needs more jack-o-lanterns," Madge said, remembering just last week when her and her best friend, Ash, had sat for hours carving all of them. Ash had listened to her complain about the Riveras and their sudden move to town, twisting her tiny diamond nose ring on occasion as she did when she was in deep thought, and absentmindedly getting bits of pumpkin in her russet hair when she'd tuck it behind her ears.

"You and Ash did a fine job. And they're probably inside already—"

"*Okay.* So, I am a little nervous," Madge admitted. "I mean, they never called. Never even a Christmas card. I think they dislike me for making their son cry."

"He did have a nice lump on his forehead," Grandpa Ollie said with a chuckle. "I doubt they even remember that. Auntie Christine and Uncle Dan are excited to see you."

"They aren't my aunt and uncle. And I won't call them that anymore." Madge turned the engine off and removed the keys from the ignition as her stomach tightened.

"Don't grudge them," Grandpa Ollie said, meeting her eyes, an expression clouding his face that Madge couldn't quite place. "I know they've missed you. They'll be in your life *now* and that's what matters."

They entered the café through a heavy wooden door that swiveled open in the middle to the familiar smells of cedar and coffee. On particularly nice days, and today was no exception, the door would be left open, letting the fresh sea air in.

Madge had barely one foot in the door when a voice called out from behind her.

"Madge Farriter! Is that you?"

Madge turned to see a tall, golden haired woman who looked like she'd walked out of an outdoor gear catalogue swoop towards her with open arms. Christine held her by the shoulders and examined her face with bright eyes. "I can't believe it's really you! Look how beautiful and grown up you are!"

"Thanks," Madge managed to say as Christine finally pulled her into a tight hug.

"Happy Birthday," Christine said as she released her, immediately passing her to Dan who hugged her head to his chest. "There she is! Happy Birthday! Madgie, Madgie, pudding pie, kissed the boys and made them cry!"

"Okay. I remember that," Madge said, trying to hide the cringe from her face as she shuffled away from him. Dan was the same as she remembered him, his brown face barely cracked with age, and that huge, contagious smile. Though right now, she didn't allow herself to smile back.

"The song I sang to you because you threw a toy car at Max's head and made him cry," Dan said, howling in laughter.

"Well – he pulled my hair."

"Oh, I'm sure he deserved it!" Dan said as he stepped aside to reveal Max.

Madge's cheeks turned hot and flushed crimson as she tried not to gape at the grown-up version of the little monster she remembered. She hadn't expected *this*. Max was tall, with caramel skin, warm brown eyes and long eyelashes framed by perfect dark eyebrows, and the most beautiful set of lips she'd ever seen. Despite the heat on her cheeks, Madge did her best to hold an indifferent expression, and to her chagrin, Max seemed bent on doing the same. In fact, he was frowning.

"I don't remember crying," Max said as he shoved his hands into the pockets of his jacket. "Hey… Madgie. Happy Birthday."

"Hi," Madge managed to say with a lift of her chin, "Grandpa likes to call me that. No one else does."

"Max!" Grandpa Ollie's voice boomed, interrupting Max's confused stare at Madge and how she was looking at him like some kind of gross worm, "Oh my, what happened to you?" Grandpa Ollie said as he squeezed Max's shoulders. "You work out, kid?"

"They had me working the sails all summer," Max replied with a sheepish grin.

"That explains this shabby haircut," Grandpa Ollie said,

turning to Christine and patting her cheek, "Christine's handiwork?" The familiarity between Grandpa Ollie and Christine made Madge's stomach sink.

"We've been at sea a lot the past eight months," Christine said with a roll of her eyes.

Have you been at sea the past dozen years? Madge wanted to say, but instead stepped aside as the barista set a tray of croissants and gooey cheese Danishes for them to eat, along with steaming hot coffee and Madge's *Black Bear Latte*, which she scooped up before anyone might reach to grab it.

"So… apparently we'll be going to the same school?" Max said, reaching for a croissant.

"We only have one high school in town," Madge said slurping up cold whipped cream topped with dark chocolate chunks before it had the chance to melt.

"You're a sophomore, right?"

Madge nodded. "Yep. What year are you after your semester at sea?"

"Sophomore. I homeschooled on the boat. But I've been homeschooling a long time," Max said, wiping croissant flakes from his shirt. "I hear you and Ollie like to sail."

"How'd you hear that?" Madge said, unable to help the words tumbling from her mouth as her face heated. "I mean, we haven't exactly kept in touch, like… at all."

"Oh – well… We've been out on the boat a lot, going all kinds of places," Max said as he picked up a carving of a bear, trying to avoid Madge's icy stare as he pretended to be interested in it. "This will be my first time since sixth grade that I've gone to a real school."

"The same grade our moms met," Madge said, hastily turning away from him. "Grandpa, we should get going," Madge said, tapping her watch. "My driver's test appointment."

Madge ignored Max's stare and the way he tightly crossed his arms – clearly ruffled that she'd cold-shouldered him – as she smirked with satisfaction.

"We do have to get scooting," Grandpa Ollie said as he looked pointedly at Christine, whose face immediately fell.

"Okay... Well, Madge," Christine said as she inhaled deeply, "we have a little something for you. Don't open it now – open it over lunch or after you take your test," Christine said as she removed a small, tightly wrapped package strung with an obnoxious amount of curly ribbon from her waterproof jacket. "It's from your mom, actually," Christine said softly as her eyes misted over, "and I've been holding on to it for a very long time just to give to you."

Madge stared down at the box in her hand as her heart began to race. "What is it?"

"I can't tell you that, silly. You have to open it. But your mom wanted you to have it."

"She wanted me to have it? But why did you have it?"

Christine's eyes grew large. "She – um – gave it to me to give to you."

"Okay... Wow..." Madge breathed as she stared down at the box in her hand, "Thank you," she said simply, her head pulsing with questions, stuffing fresh waves of anger down deep.

It didn't make any sense. Her parent's death was an accident. So why would Christine have something her mother had wanted *Christine* to give to Madge on her sixteenth birthday?

2

The Necklace

Madge was surprised Grandpa Ollie loved her driver's license picture. She hated it.

"You look fine," he said with his mouth full. "You passed, that's the important part."

Madge frowned out the large window that faced the wide Columbia River with a close view of the towering bridge that spanned it, where freight boats carried timber up and down. The restaurant Madge had chosen was her favorite one in Astoria, along the revamped historical cannery row right on the docks along the river. It smelled like fish and chips and malt vinegar, and had lofty timber ceilings and white tablecloths which added a touch of finery yet was placed near the warehouses where local fisherman sold their daily catch.

"I can't wait to show Ash," Madge said before chomping into a piece of cod dipped in tartar. "She'll be jealous we ate here."

"Okay, now remember, just because I am not in the car with you doesn't mean you don't do all the things we talked about. Clear?"

"Grandpa," Madge sighed.

"I'm serious. You have to pay attention and be hyper-vigilant. Make a full stop at stop signs, go slow when you back up, and—"

"I know, Grandpa. Go slow through neighborhoods."

"I am glad we have this time today. I can't believe you're sixteen. Where did the time go?" Grandpa Ollie's eyes misted over. "Now. Let's open the present Christine brought you." His hand shook as he passed the small box across the table to Madge.

Madge felt her breath hitch in her throat as she pulled at the ribbons she'd wanted to tear open since she'd seen them. Inside was a small box, made of two pieces of driftwood.

"Pretty box," Madge said with a knowing smile. "It looks like one of yours."

"Quite right, because it is. Open it."

Madge opened the box with a slight squeak at the hinge. It was a necklace.

A smooth, rounded, milky white stone held by a tiny silver hand on a delicate silver chain. She blinked several times before she had the courage to take it up in her hands.

"She had it made, just for you," Grandpa Ollie said, his voice cracking. "You like it?"

"No Grandpa," Madge answered, biting her bottom lip so hard it hurt, "I love it."

"It's hard to believe fourteen years have passed," Grandpa Ollie said, shaking his head sadly. "It feels like yesterday – like a blink since she had it made for you. Since I last saw her."

"So… she had it made for me, and intended it for my sixteenth birthday… But why didn't she plan on giving it to me herself? If she'd had cancer, or knew she was about to…"

"I think she didn't want you to find it before it was time," Grandpa Ollie said quickly. "But the important thing is your mother wanted you to have it on this very day, Madgie. She loved you very much. More than anything."

Madge swallowed. And swallowed again at the lump in her throat, trying and failing to fight back the tears that welled in her eyes. Her chest ached with something she'd never felt before; but always wanted. The familiarity of a mother's love.

She sprung up from the table and wrapped her arms around Grandpa Ollie's neck, breathing in the familiar smell of Old Spice, her cheek pressing into the pens that were secured inside the scratchy wool of his shirt pocket. "Thank you, Grandpa," Madge said as she smiled down at the necklace hanging from her hand, while Grandpa Ollie wiped tears from her cheeks with his large, calloused thumb.

"Want me to help you put it on?" he said, grave faced, his voice hollow.

Madge handed him the necklace and turned around, lifting her long brown hair out of the way. Grandpa Ollie's hands shook as he fumbled with the tiny clasp. "I wouldn't take it off if I were you. That way you can't lose it."

Madge nodded her head as Grandpa Ollie placed her mother's necklace around her neck and let go. She let her hair fall as she reached for the smooth stone that now draped at her collar bone, and she didn't take her eyes off it as she sat down to admire its cloudy surface.

"You look beautiful," Grandpa Ollie said with a sad smile, "remember – keep it on you."

"I will. I wouldn't want to take it off anyway. It's a part of me now."

"That's one way to put it," Grandpa Ollie said with raised brows as he looked down to check his watch. "We better get going now if you want to be on time to meet Ash. Where did you say you were going again?"

"We are going for a run down to Indian Beach."

"Your first drive alone and you pick that windy drive?"

"I'll go slow. I promise," Madge said as she placed the driftwood box in her coat pocket.

"Make sure you wear your watch."

Madge turned the music up and drove the windy, forested road north of Cannon Beach to Ecola State Park, where the trail to Indian Beach led from the parking lot. The road climbed around and up, with views of the coasty stretch below and Haystack Rock peeking through large pine limbs, as they talked loudly over the music about Max and the meeting this morning with the Riveras.

"Honestly, I never imagined that spoiled brat kid would turn out like… like *that*," Madge said as Ash sat facing her in the passenger side, eager for all the details. "I don't think he likes me much. I was kind of rude."

"All toddlers can be hell on wheels. I'm sure he'll get over it. Just be nicer next time."

"I don't think I can."

"Why not? You're obviously obsessing," Ash said, rolling her eyes.

"Because he was rude, too. He scowled at me. I'm not going to grovel."

"You must like him then—"

"Stop it!" Madge commanded, slapping Ash's shoulder. "That's him!" she pointed as she rounded a corner, slowing all the way down, where Max was walking along the narrow road with a blonde girl she'd never seen before. Her hair was so blonde it was almost white, and she was entirely too dressy – in all black – to be walking on the side of the road in their small little town where jeans and parkas were the norm.

"That's *him*?" Ash said as her jaw dropped open.

"Hey," Madge shouted, rolling down her driver's side window. "Want a ride?"

Max turned, and as soon as he recognized Madge his face formed into a frown. Not moving an inch, he turned to whisper to the blonde girl, and after what seemed to be a short argument, she approached the car with Max standing stiffly behind her.

"This thing has no backseat," Max said, crossing his arms.

"We can sit on laps," Ash said as she got out of the car and stood with the door open.

"I'm Selene," she said as she bent down to speak to Madge, her pale blue eyes large and assessing. "My dad works for the Institute. I've known Max since we were in diapers."

"I'm Madge," she said with a small wave. "And I haven't seen him until today since I was barely out of diapers."

"My dad was supposed to pick us up," Selene said as she climbed inside next to Madge.

"I'll walk, thanks," Max said, turning on his heels.

"Well, I'm not. I don't like walking home in my favorite pair of shoes," Selene said as Ash climbed in beside her.

"I'm Ash, by the way."

"Is he okay?" Madge asked, watching as Max walked down the street in front of them.

"He's fine. He's been in a mood all day. We live just up this way."

"You all live... together?" Ash asked as they passed Max on the road.

"Families that work for the institute live on the grounds. You can turn here, on the right." Selene pointed to a long driveway that curved left up a hill covered with ferns and pine trees.

"You live *here*? The new place?" Ash asked as her jaw fell open.

"Sorry," Selene said, wincing. "I know it is a stone's throw from where you picked us up. But that driveway is steep!"

"Oh – it's not that," Madge said, exchanging a glance with Ash. "We snooped around here all summer long while it was being built," Madge said as Taffy sputtered up the driveway. "And when it was finished in midsummer and sat empty for a while, it was almost spooky."

It was unlike any of the houses in Cannon Beach and seemed like a medieval castle was being built, with its gray stone exterior, double oak front door thick enough to withstand a siege, and triple turret roofs; but Madge's favorite part was the gargantuan glass-paned dome in the forefront. And when the bright copper roofing and awnings and second story bridges encased in glass connecting the north and south wing to the main house were installed, it got harder to trespass onto the building site.

"Madge tried to convince me Count Dracula was moving here. I almost believed her," Ash muttered, shaking her head.

"We live here but it also houses the offices for the Institute," Selene explained. "The second floor in the main building has a library and some basic lab space for the scientists. Mostly they work from the boats and in warehouses or aquariums on site, that kind of thing. But yeah, the Institute headquarters here."

The driveway at the top of the long gravel drive was laid with brick and grass and formed a circle where in its middle there was a life-sized fountain of a whale's tail. Water slid in a wide berth over the end of the tail and into the pool below.

"Wow. Now that wasn't here before," Madge said as she rolled her window down.

"It's been in front of MEI ever since I can remember," Selene said as she scooted out the passenger side door just as the wide front door to the Institute opened. A slim woman with smooth silver-grey hair past her shoulders came out carrying a pumpkin the size of her torso.

"Hey Pearl," Selene said with a small wave.

"You're home early," said the woman. Apart from the prominent red lipstick and British accent, Madge found it hard not to stare. The woman had a striking face, with a sharp nose and deep-set brown eyes, and though she was older her face was exceptionally smooth for her age. She wore a twill vest with an ornate brooch fastened to it, and jeans tucked into rain boots.

"No, I gave dad the wrong time," Selene said, rolling her eyes as the woman set about rearranging her fall décor by the front door, but Madge kept catching her staring. As if she thought Madge's car was hideous and didn't belong in the driveway. "That's Pearl. She's sort of the boss around here," Selene said, resting her eyes on Madge's necklace. "That's pretty."

"Um. Thanks. It was my mom's," Madge said, casting her eyes away from Pearl and down at the cloudy moonstone hanging from her neck.

"Well. There he is, he made it," Selene said, rolling her eyes as she saw Max reach the top of the driveway. "Thanks for the ride. See you tomorrow?"

"Yeah – see you at school."

As they drove back around the fountain and slowly away, she checked her rearview mirror. Pearl was now standing with Max and Selene, whose argument she was ignoring as she watched them drive away. Apparently, she was done arranging pumpkins.

"Can you believe they live there?" Madge said as she turned out of the driveway and back onto the road.

"I don't know why we didn't think of that when we heard they were moving here."

"That would mean they've known for some time, which is odd," Madge said as the road began climbing up. "They only told Grandpa a week ago or so."

"Or maybe he knew and didn't say anything? Our hand and nose prints are probably still all over the windows!"

"That's an embarrassing thought!" Madge said with a shake of her head.

"You're right about Max though. He's kind of a jerk. A super-hot jerk."

Madge shook her head. "Yeah, who has a super-hot girlfriend who is super nice and who has grown up with them since they were in diapers."

"You think so?" Ash asked, crinkling her nose. "I didn't get that impression – Selene seemed annoyed with him more than anything."

"Maybe a lovers quarrel."

"I don't think so. If anything, maybe he's got a secret crush on her."

"Pitiful," Madge laughed. "We'll have to find out!"

3

Submerged

The paved parking lot at Ecola State Park was mostly empty, and sat atop a wide, grassy bluff with panoramic views of haystack rock. Grey clouds hung high in the sky, but there were small openings over the ocean where golden light spilled through and illuminated the silvery expanse of water. "I like it better up here when the weather is like this. It's easier to imagine a Banshee or a sea monster waiting out at sea."

"DON'T," Ash said, slapping her shoulder.

Madge giggled as she stared out at *Terrible Tilly,* a nickname for the de-commissioned lighthouse perched high on a basalt rock island like a tall thumb poking out of the ocean, left out there like a ship that had wrecked in a storm, rusting away at the mercy of the tumultuous ocean. It was too easy to spook Ash, and Madge was just in such a mood to do it.

"What are you staring at? Don't pretend like you're seeing something. I won't fall for it."

"Terrible Tilly. It's on my bucket list to get in there and take a look around someday."

"Are you crazy? It's condemned. No one goes there. Not who wants to get out alive, anyway."

"Wouldn't want anyone else dying and haunting the place, I guess."

"There really were a lot of deaths – shipwrecks, lighthouse keepers going mad—"

"Grandpa told me it was a crematorium for a while. Who knows, maybe the ghosts wander to shore here," Madge said, giggling as she kicked off towards the trail, leaving Ash behind.

"Stop it!" Ash yelped as she followed Madge, stomping her feet in protest.

The park was indeed quieter than usual, Madge thought. It felt like an enchanted place today. Something felt different, and whatever it was, it gave Madge a chill, despite her body warming up as they fell into a jogging cadence.

Indian Beach trail led north from the parking lot and went for a couple miles, flanked by tall pines, their sprawling roots riddling the often muddy and slippery trail that started in a shallow valley where a small wooden bridge crossed over a clear stream, then moved up and down on a narrow expanse high up over the bluffs on the ocean.

"Seriously, though. It's super quiet here today," Madge said, still feeling a wariness she couldn't quite explain as they crested a hill.

"No more ghost stories, no screaming Banshees and how they haunt the shores at night, or I'm turning around and leaving," Ash said, panting.

"It's just stories Grandpa told me so I wouldn't wander the shores at night as a kid."

"Yeah, a story that made me wet my pants. It wasn't funny."

Madge couldn't help but laugh at the memory. But something in the air today gave her that same chill she would get as a child, when she imagined things wandering the beach at night, ready to snag you from the shore. She sensed every sound and watched the trail with a foreboding that she couldn't quite shake.

Finally, they scrambled down a steep, muddy hill to Indian Beach, where entire trunks of driftwood had been deposited and large chunks of black basalt rock housed tidal pools when the tide was low. A stream of clear freshwater cut through the sand and ran straight into the ocean towards the north side of the small, secluded stretch of beach.

"I can't believe we are the only ones down here today!" Ash called out as she jumped the last bit of trail and headed straight for the expanse of rocks that were exposed due to low tide.

Madge stopped to take off her shoes. She placed her bare feet in the cold sand, and as she did so a tingling shot from her toes and surged all the way to the crown of her head. She stood glued to the spot, as she held her breath and stared down at her feet.

She felt almost dizzy... What was happening?

The tingling didn't relent, and grew in intensity, making her skin even itch.

"Ash?" Madge called out. "Ash!" she screamed again as her heart began to race.

But she didn't see her anywhere.

She moved one foot in front of the other, despite the tingling that continued to course and ebb through her body, getting stronger and stronger until now she could taste salt and metal on her tongue. Panic erupted in her chest and she broke out into a run, as fast as her legs would carry her to the rocks.

As she ran, she was overcome by sensation within herself, but also outside as well. Every sound was alive, and the colors around her so vivid it made her eyes hurt. Finally, she caught sight of Ash, and she stopped to catch her breath with her hands on her knees. Her new necklace hung down in her vision, and she stared at it as it rocked back and forth, as she waited for her heart to stop racing, until she noticed something was different about it. Her eyes widened as she realized the once milky-white stone was now clear as glass.

"What in the…" Madge said aloud as she stood up and waved frantically at Ash to get her attention. "Ash! I have to show you something!" But Ash couldn't hear her and only waved back as a large wave plumed up behind her like a peacock's tail. Madge tried to steady her breath and bite back the terror growing inside her, as she navigated the rocks towards Ash in her bare feet, avoiding sharp barnacles and slippery sea life.

The tidal pools were a glassy pink, a reflection of the horizon that had begun to change color. As Madge dodged landing her foot over a fat orange starfish, hanging above a deeper pool of water where she had been distracted by bright green sea anemones, she lost her footing.

Slip. SPLASH.

She landed in the frigid ocean water on all fours, completely drenched. Gasping from the cold, she tried to stand but immediately collapsed. Her legs ached fiercely, as a deep, burning freeze invaded her bones. It felt like a thousand needles pierced her skin as a wave rushed up over her head. Submerged underwater, she heard a sharp, haunting singing that reverberated in her ears. It felt like a lure. She thrashed and fought against it.

Something is coming.

Madge could feel the pull of something that drew near… a power that tried to pull her towards the sound of the singing like a fish on a line, as it vibrated and echoed in her ears and all the way through her.

Get out of the water. Get out of the water!

Her skin felt tight, and *hard*. Extremely hard.

She grasped onto the rocks to pull herself up but froze when she noticed her arms.

They were covered in coppery scales all the way down to her wrists.

She looked down and her eyes widened at her legs, also covered in scales, and her feet, now two long billowing tail fins, forked at the end.

4

Clear Moonstone

Madge squeezed her eyes shut and screamed… and screamed and screamed, until she heard Ash's voice and opened her eyes.

"Madge! Are you okay?" Ash shook Madge by the shoulders.

"Look at me!" Madge screeched, holding out her arms.

But the scales were gone.

Her legs and feet were normal.

She was drenched, and her knees were red from the fall, but other than that she was herself again.

"We need to get you back to the car," Ash said, helping her up. "Let's go get your shoes."

Madge shook all over as Ash helped her navigate through the maze of rocks and onto the sand. "I'm sorry. I – I just fell. I went head under," Madge said through chattering teeth.

"I heard you scream," Ash said with large eyes. "I've never heard you scream like that!"

"The water was just – *freezing* – and then a huge wave toppled on top of me…" Madge sat in the sand and put on her shoes, fighting back tears, trying to find the words.

How could she explain it? What just happened to her?

"We need to run. You need to warm up. Can you do that?"

"Yes," Madge said, standing on wobbly legs.

"You have everything – your keys?"

"Thank goodness for pockets that zip," Madge said, as she jangled the car keys hidden safely away, before shooting a hand to her chest—

But she couldn't find the stone resting there. "My necklace! It's—"

"Behind your neck." Ash swung the stone around to the front and stared at it curiously before dropping a wide gaze to Madge's bloody knee. "You're bleeding!"

"It is fine," Madge said, turning to trudge up the steep hill leading up to the trail. "Does moonstone go clear when it gets wet?"

"I was wondering the same thing," Ash said, panting for air as they finally reached the narrow trail at the top.

Madge was relieved she hadn't at least imagined *that*. The rest of it she wasn't so sure. But she couldn't get that sound out of her head. That singing.

She stopped and grabbed onto a railing once they ascended the steep hill, her head spinning again. "Did I hit my head? Do you see anything?"

"I don't see anything," Ash said, examining her. "Why, what is wrong?"

She stared back at Ash's concerned face, no longer able to bottle her emotions. What on earth had just happened? Madge's bottom lip curled over, and her face puckered up as fat tears rolled down her face. "I fell in."

"Yes, we know that part."

"It's not just that I fell in, it's... Do you remember me telling you about Banshees?"

"Are you serious—"

"This is not a joke! I swear," Madge said, her expression grave enough that Ash snapped her mouth back shut. "When I was underwater I... I heard something... singing."

"Singing? What do you mean like – like you heard dolphins – or a song in your head?"

"It was a woman's voice. I couldn't understand the words." Madge stopped as a shiver ran up her spine. "It *froze* me. I couldn't move. I felt like it was after me, trying to lure me out."

Ash's eyes were as large as saucers. "Are you trying to say there is a Banshee or that there is someone down there, in the water? A ghost? This isn't funny—"

"I'm serious! When I opened my eyes – Ash, I saw *scales*." Madge took deeper breaths as she looked out at the rock arch in the ocean, bathed in the soft light of the fading sunset, trying and failing to keep her voice from shaking. "All over my body. My legs and arms, and I could feel them, too. They made my skin feel hard, and really tight."

"So you were hearing and seeing things?"

Madge shook her head. "It felt real. I couldn't stand, my feet were – they were like fins. Not just *like* fins – but they *were* fins. And they were huge. I shut my eyes and started to scream, and then you were there."

"Okay. Are you seeing or hearing things now?" Ash's eyes darted up and down the trail, clearly spooked.

"No. When I opened my eyes, it all – it just all went away," Madge said, feeling as though something was truly out there, snapping her into action. "Let's get out of here. This place is giving me the creeps," Madge said, running down the hill as though she was being chased.

"You know," Ash called after her, close on her heels, "it could have been seaweed, or a fish, or some kind of debris stuck to your skin – the cold and adrenaline…"

"I don't know," Madge huffed, feeling her heart race as they ran up another hill. "Let's talk about it in the car."

When they made it to the parking lot, they sprinted for Taffy. And as they climbed inside, turned the engine on and locked the doors, they both loosed screams and laughter as if the car were a safe place against whatever was out there.

"That's the first time I've ever felt what it feels like in scary movies. When people are running from the monsters or the bad guys, and they finally get to the car and it starts, and they can drive off."

"Yeah, but usually the car doesn't start or they drop the stupid keys," Madge said as she rolled her eyes. "It's not the first time. You're scared all the time."

"Never as scared as just now!" Ash said as she watched Madge who sat with her hands gripping the steering wheel, staring out at the darkening ocean.

"Same here."

"Well… I wouldn't mind hitting my head and imagining myself as a sort of… *mermaid*."

"I had thought of that for a minute," Madge said as she put the car in gear, "before realizing how crazy that sounds. But mermaids have tails. Like the body of a fish."

"Maybe mermaids don't have a tail. Maybe they have two."

"They live in the ocean. I'm not a mermaid."

"Maybe they don't. Maybe they – maybe they change during a full moon, like a werewolf. But instead of fur, you get scales.

Really though, what else could a girl want?"

"My legs were *covered* in scales, I didn't... And... No." Madge snapped her mouth shut as she shook her head. "If that's what being a mermaid means, I don't want it."

"Is that... A storm brewing? Look. Out there." As soon as Ash said it, the car shook in the wind, and rain began pelting the windows. A strange voice seemed to whisper; like wisps of mist, curling in Madge's ears. She rolled down the window a fraction—

"Do you hear that?" Madge asked, barely able to breathe. A voice was hissing on the wind, pelting the window as if carried in the rain itself. "I hear – something about a number *nine*? Do you think it's coming from—"

"Just drive!" Ash shrieked, her face a picture of terror as she smacked Madge's arm. "GO!"

And as the voice gushed with a gale of wind that swayed Taffy, she sped away – and looking in her rear-view mirror, she swore she could see a display of light, swirling off the ocean in the direction where she'd fallen in.

5

Time Immemorial

Rubbing her puffy, tired eyes awake, Madge stared at the rain streaking down the large bay window in her room. Haystack Rock was clouded in a misty gloom, the beach awash with grey and beige – and a hint of all things dreadful.

All she wanted to do was close her eyes and find sleep again. To reawake and realize the whole of yesterday had been nothing more than a nightmare – and that today was her *actual* birthday, and everything today was brand new and familiar again. That she wasn't crazy. But there was no relief that it had all been just a dream as her eyes opened wider, and she tucked her arms under the comforter to warm them from the morning cold.

Her old quilt was strewn across the bay window seat where she had sat awake all night, staring out the window. Normally on nights when she couldn't sleep, she'd have crept out her window and gone for a swim; but after what happened, she was terrified of what would happen now. Of her body reacting, becoming something else. But besides recalling her arms and legs knit with scales and feeling powerful fins replace her feet, something else kept her awake that night. Kept drawing her to the window, to check the ocean and watch, until she'd finally given up and sat up in the bay window. That *voice*. It haunted her, even now. *Something was coming...* she remembered feeling it, and hearing it sing to her underwater. Hearing a voice on the wind, in the rain. She had pressed her forehead against the glass in an attempt to cool her mind when she couldn't get it of her head.

At one point, after cracking a window, and considering for a tiny moment to go ahead and swim anyway, she swore she could ever so faintly hear a voice on the wind. She even crawled out and sat on the roof for a moment to hear it better; but a chill ran up her spine that sent her scurrying back inside, locking the window firmly shut behind her, and jumping into bed with the covers over her head as if something would sliver out of the ocean and creep like a foul mist to come for her.

Now her room was filled with the grey light of morning, and she lay awake after barely falling asleep after dawn, the shadows and sounds of the night all gone. Still, she remembered the dark night and it gave her the shivers. All the sounds had kept her awake – everything was so loud – Grandpa Ollie's snoring had never sounded so loud.

She supposed it was due to what had happened yesterday. Maybe someone was playing a trick on them and was playing something off a speaker that was carried on the wind. Or... Maybe she did hit her head. Maybe the icy ocean water cleaned out her ears. Madge resolved herself to believe that must be it – that she'd hit her head hard enough to see things. That the ocean water was so cold she'd felt the prickle from that and not scales. That she'd lost feeling in her feet, and had imagined those billowy things, too.

She kicked off her fluffy down comforter and let her foot hang over the bed, wiggling and stretching her toes. No webbing. Not a cut or a scratch... or anything different at all.

"You awake? Time to get up!" Grandpa Ollie's voice called from her door.

"I'm awake," Madge said, her voice like gravel.

"Leftover birthday cake for breakfast, and hot coffee. Better get downstairs before I eat it all!" Grandpa Ollie laughed.

She hadn't forgotten how wide his eyes had gotten last night, when she leaned over sixteen candles to blow them out – and her necklace – had slipped out of her sweater and hung over the flames. He'd said nothing, but Madge knew he'd seen it. That it was clear. Ever since she'd gotten it wet, it hadn't gone back to what it was before. Maybe it had just been dirty from sitting all those years? Maybe it wasn't moonstone, but something else?

She knew he suspected something – because he'd been trying to get her to talk all last night. More than usual details... how far had they ran? How did she feel? Normally he didn't ask so many questions unless she was in trouble. Still, she'd said nothing to Grandpa Ollie about what had happened yesterday – nor did she intend to. She didn't intend to tell anyone.

In fact, she was going to forget the whole thing, starting today.

"So, did you grow scales and fins last night or what?" Ash asked, climbing into Taffy with a wide grin on her face. "You have dark circles under your eyes. You swam last night, didn't you?"

"No," Madge said with a vigorous shake of her head. "I just couldn't sleep, but I didn't swim. I feel fine, and I don't want to talk about yesterday."

"Okay, but before I fell asleep last night, I asked my mom to help me learn about—"

"Do *not* tell me you told your mom!" Madge hissed.

"No! Of *course* I didn't tell her, I only told her I had a school assignment, and asked what book she'd recommend to learn about… them." Ash said as she fished a book from her pack.

Madge huffed a sigh. "*Them.*"

"She has an Encyclopedia collection on popular Mythology and Folklore. And there is an entire volume about them. *Mermaids.*" Ash held up a large, green book with golden lettering.

"Are you serious?" Madge said as she braked a little too hard for a yellow light.

"I know. I always get stuck at this light."

"No – I mean about the book!"

"This mermaid stuff goes back – way back. Thousands of years – mythology in almost every culture and ancient culture have their own legends. Unrelated, completely their own!" Ash said as she opened the book and flipped through some pages. "Doesn't that prove something already? That is what the introduction talks about. It gave me the chills to think about it – I think it'll be fun – given what happened yesterday, you know."

"You think this is fun? What happened to me was not fun."

"Humor me. I think there might be something to this."

"You are talking about mythology. I need real—"

"Some of the oldest mythologies, actually. Ancient. And wait until you see this," Ash squeaked, holding up a picture of an ink drawing, "a Mermaid with two tails! Or scaly legs!"

"I can't look! I'm driving!" Madge said, though she could see the drawing from the corner of her eye – and it sent goosebumps up her arms.

"This one is called a Melusine. It is French mythology from the 1300's – but the Celts—"

"I just want to forget what happened!" Madge shouted as she pulled into the parking lot at Cannon Beach High. "Why can't you understand that?"

"Geez. I am just trying to help," Ash said, stung.

"Help with what? Mythology? I. am. *Fine*," Madge said, as nausea filled her stomach.

"You never like it when people try to help you," Ash said quietly, rolling her eyes.

"If you want to *help* me, drop it," Madge said, clenching her teeth as her head felt dizzy.

"You okay?"

"I just want to go about my day like a normal person—"

Madge jumped at a knock on her window. Two figures stood on either side of her car, and a blonde woman leaned down, smiling at her. The woman was striking; but despite her beauty, there was something terrifying behind her pale blue eyes. Especially unsettling was the man, who looked in the passenger side window, his creased and muscled face in a trained frown. Madge's gut twisted as she turned her attention towards the woman.

"Morning," the woman said as Madge rolled down the window. "I *love* your car."

"Um, thanks. It was my mom's." Madge felt her heart racing, a cold sweat across her brow. There was something strangely familiar about this woman—

"It's a classic. You new to town?" the woman asked, inclining her head.

"No," Madge said, glancing over at Ash who had gone very still and quiet.

"Oh, just wondering if you were related with MEI. They just moved their headquarters here. Heard of it?"

"Yes. I know some people who moved here with the Institute," Madge said, clutching her stomach in pain. "But we are late. For class." Madge felt like a rock was stuck in her throat.

"Of course. My apologies," the woman said, her face serious. "When you see Pearl, do tell her Viviane says hello."

"Um… I met her only yesterday," Madge said, a warning blaring in her gut.

The woman adjusted the black collar of her pea coat, leaned into the car window, and oddly, *blew* cinnamon breath on Madge's face—

"Hey!" Madge protested, flinching and squeezing her eyes shut.

"Sorry, you had a lash…" the woman said, flashing a grin at her partner who sidled alongside her. He was tall, with thick ears and an even thicker neck.

And as Madge blinked up at the woman, still tongue-tied and flabbergasted about why this strange woman had just blown in her face and was now continuing to smirk at her about it – inexplicably, her nausea ebbed; the putrid feeling in her stomach replaced by cinnamon, still stinging her nostrils.

"You'll be seeing more of her. And please make sure you tell her Viviane dropped by to say hello," the woman said, turning and walking away, the man holding a car door open for her. With one last look, the man walked around the other side, and they drove off.

"That was really, really weird. Who are those people? They aren't teachers," Ash said.

"She looks like a news anchor," Madge said grabbing her backpack, trying to shrug off the fact that she felt it was weird, too. But she couldn't take anymore weird. Not today. Today was going to be normal. "Probably doing an article on MEI and the small little town they've moved to. Let's go, we're late."

A puppet stage had been rolled in and sat at the front of Mrs. Whaling's class, drawn by a curtain, and flanked by two chairs where a xylophone sat, a large piece of sheet metal, and a tin whistle. Every year for the Halloween Faire, Mrs. Whaling held a puppet show. This year she was heading up a rendition of *Sleepy Hollow* and was set to showcase it to the class; and, thankfully, though Madge and Ash were late the show hadn't started yet.

Max and Selene had first period English with them, too, and sat next to each other. Selene seemed to be enjoying all the whispers and stares across the classroom, but Max seemed quiet and brooding as usual and didn't so much as look in her direction.

"What's up with him?" Madge whispered, leaning to Selene.

"Who knows," Selene said, rolling her eyes. "So, tell me. Are there *any* cute guys in this school at all? I haven't seen even one."

Max popped his head up at that, frowning. Maybe Ash *was* right. Or they were a thing and she was trying to torture him.

"It's only first period," Ash huffed, shooting to her feet as she marched towards the front of the class to Mrs. Whaling's desk. Madge's stomach dropped as she noticed Ash had the *book*.

Mrs. Whaling's eyes got big upon seeing it, but Madge stayed glued to her chair.

"Hazel, come take a look at this delightful book Ash brought to show me," Mrs. Whaling said, gesturing to her daughter, a freshman at Cannon Beach High. Hazel was a miniature version of her mother, with the same willowy, slender frame, and large blue eyes; but instead of short, gray curly hair, hers was long and honey blonde.

Madge's stomach sank as she saw Hazel's eyes go wide upon seeing it, too. Desperate to halt any more attention to the book, Madge strode to Mrs. Whaling's desk, trying to hide the look of alarm that was sweeping across her face.

"Um – hey Ash. What are you doing?" Madge asked, trying her best to hide the anger that threatened to flash in her eyes.

"Showing Mrs. Whaling my mom's book," Ash chirped.

"Ash tells me you two are doing some research?" Mrs. Whaling said, eyeing Madge curiously over the rim of her glasses. "About mermaids?"

Madge blinked at Mrs. Whaling – and then over to Hazel, who stared back at her like she'd seen a ghost. "Not *me* – not exactly. Ash wants to – I just—"

"You needn't be embarrassed. It's not just a subject for kids! Mermaid lore has been around since, well, time immemorial. Some of it terrifying, in fact."

"Whoa," Selene said, appearing at Madge's side, as she gawked down at the open book. "I thought I heard that right – you're researching mermaids?"

"No, I am not, Ash is," Madge said through grit teeth.

"You said time immemorial. How long is that, exactly?" Ash

asked, undeterred.

"Mermaid lore has been told in some of the earliest stories around – the Persian Arabian Night's stories were written sometime in the ninth century. Eight or nine hundred years BC."

"That's almost three thousand years ago," Ash said, nodding her head, "and from what I read briefly, there are lots of other ancient myths about them – from different parts of the world."

"Correct. Mermaid lore spanned several ancient cultures, in fact, thought to have no connection at all. Ancient Assyrians, ancient Greeks, Celts, Babylonians – we are talking almost every culture and continent. Native Americans. Russia, parts of Africa, Australia – you name it."

"How do you know all of this?" Selene asked, cocking her head at Mrs. Whaling.

"I studied literature and folklore extensively to earn my degree," she answered, closing the book, and handing it back to Ash. "Now you three take a seat, it's time to begin our show. Any other questions can wait until after class."

"Interesting." Selene said, glancing over her shoulder at Max who was watching with narrowed eyes, especially glaring at Selene.

Why was everyone behaving so *oddly*? Madge was madder than ever at Ash, and felt exposed, like a bad dream where you're caught in public, naked. Why was she so paranoid?

She tried to shrug it off, yet couldn't help but notice the strange, shared look between Mrs. Whaling and her daughter, Hazel, as she turned to take her seat. Or how Hazel openly stared at her the rest of class. As if she *knew* and could see right through her.

6

All Hallow's Eve

Marquis tents made the football field at Cannon Beach High look like the circus had come to town. The student Council had voted for an Edgar Allen Poe theme – which meant fake ravens and skulls were placed in every space available, and banners were hung with words like *"Nevermore"* in old type font to obtain the creepy, Gothic Victorian Poe-vibe.

"I'm starting to wish I hadn't worn this," Madge said, adjusting her wool-felted witch hat again. She'd fallen in love with the mushrooms and leaves on the brim, and the hat's point that rose over a foot from her head before it curled over like an unfurling fern and had bought it in the spring just to wear to this year's Faire. But now, wearing it in public – she'd wished she'd left it hanging from her bedroom door. "Oh, look. Another witch. That's five already."

"Whatever. I'm a mime, basically a clown, and there are plenty of those," Ash said, adjusting her white gloves. "It's freezing and your friend is taking forever. I bet she's dressed as like, Catwoman or something, and piling on red lip liner."

"She is not my friend yet," Madge said, rolling her eyes, staring at the faire map and schedule in her hand. "But if she was, I doubt she'd do what you did, bringing that *book* to class and embarrassing me."

"There's no reason to be embarrassed. Selene seemed mega-interested, anyway."

"I doubt that," Madge said, folding her arms against herself. But Ash had a point. Selene did seem interested.

"Well. I am sorry," Ash said, meeting her best friend's eyes for the first time since their fight. "I was scared, too, you know. And I know that's not hard to do, I am a scaredy cat, I know. But I was like, legit *freaked out.*"

"Well, I was legit freaked out, too."

"I know. I've never seen you that way. And I wanted to help, and I wanted my own answers, and you were kind of a jerk about it, by the way."

Madge felt something loosen inside her chest as she looked back at her friend's shining eyes. "I was a jerk. I was tired. I'm still tired. I didn't get any sleep."

"And?" Ash asked, smirking. "Do we want to do a little digging?"

"No. I hit my head. Music or speakers were carried by the wind. There's a logical explanation. Let's just get on with the night and have some fun,' Madge said, shaking Ash's shoulders. "Please?"

"Yeah – here comes Barbie the Vampire. She's super late, by the way," Ash said, pointing through the crowd. "And Max is with her."

"*Barbie?*" Madge said, giggling and feeling immediately guilty about it as she searched the crowd for Selene's blond head – which she spotted easily, followed by a brooding Max.

"Of *course* he is with her. He's secretly in love with her."

Max followed behind Selene, with his usual gloomy expression, wearing a flannel and jeans and a mask pushed to the top of his head. But Selene walked through the crowd like she was on a stage, dressed as a Gothic Vampire with a pop-up collar and ruby red lips.

"Sorry we are late!" Selene said, immediately drawn to Madge's hat as she grabbed the brim and examined it. "So. You're a witch," she said, exchanging a glance with Max.

Max stared back at her curiously, the corners of his gorgeous, proud mouth turning slightly upwards. Madge blinked at him – it didn't seem natural for him to smile.

"Is it that obvious?" Madge said with frost in her tone, which annoyingly only made Max's ornery smile spread wider.

"I *love* this hat," Selene said. "Max likes witches. Don't you, Max?" Selene asked him, sharing another glance between them that set Madge's blood on fire.

"Is there some kind of joke I'm missing?" Madge asked, trying not to sound upset.

"It's not a joke," Selene said, her eyes suddenly drawn past Madge's face to something behind her. "Ooh. Now who are *they*?"

"Here we go," Max said as his smile disappeared. "Stop it, Selene."

Madge turned to see what Selene was looking at – and knew instantly. Tristan and Drake. The jock twins of Cannon Beach High. And Max was really upset about it, apparently.

"Oh boy," Madge said, swiveling her back towards them again. "The one you're locking eyes with is Tristan – and that's his twin brother, Drake."

"Ugh, *Drake*," Ash looked pointedly at Madge and shook her

head. "Madge has an uncomfortable history with him—"

"A very brief history," Madge said, elbowing Ash.

"Hm. I'll stick to the other twin then," Selene said with an arched brow.

"You won't stick with anything," Max all but growled.

"Don't be a stick in the mud," Selene said, flinging her hair over her shoulder.

"Oh *no*. They're coming this way," Ash complained.

Like Max, the twins hadn't gone through the trouble of dressing up, but instead wore their Letterman's Jackets. They were identical, even with their perfectly coiffed dark brown hair, stiff with too much gel, and the freckles on their faces almost even matched.

"Hey Madge. Ash. You gonna introduce me to your friend?" Tristan said as he smiled at Selene, flanked by his brother Drake who was doing the opposite and wore a frown.

"Selene. Max. Meet Tristan and Drake," Madge said curtly.

"I'm getting in line for some of that apple cider," Selene said as she stepped forward to Tristan. "Want to come with me?"

"Selene, shouldn't we stick together?" Max said through clenched teeth.

"We *are*. The line is right there," Selene said, throwing a flirtatious smile at Tristan.

"Lead the way," Tristan said as he followed her like a puppy dog. But Drake stayed rooted to the spot and staring at Madge.

"Haven't talked to you in a while," Drake said, folding his arms as he sized up Max.

Madge's cheeks flushed. "I've been busy—"

"Dr. Hiromi!" Max interrupted and waved obnoxiously into the air. "He works for MEI," Max said as Dr. Hiromi approached, munching on a bag of popcorn.

"Who have we got here, Max?" he asked as he eyed up the newcomers, settling a stare onto Madge as he silently waited for an introduction.

"Dr. Kento Hiromi, this is Madge. And Ash," Max started, before turning his head to stare blankly at Drake for a moment. "And we just met – sorry, which one are you again?"

"I'm Drake," Drake said as he held out his hand to Ken to shake it.

Dr. Hiromi took his hand. "Please, call me Ken."

Drake looked down at Ken's hand as he shook it, when out of nowhere his eyes widened in alarm as he noticed a small branding just below Ken's thumb—

And wasted no time in promptly releasing his hand.

Madge looked down at Dr. Kento Hiromi's still outstretched hand – and noticed a thick scar there – almost in a shape or a symbol.

"Gotta go. See you around, Madge," Drake said before throwing one last dirty look at Dr. Hiromi, who blinked back in shock.

"Well, that was awkward," Max commented to Dr. Hiromi as he watched Drake, who was now whispering in Tristan's ear, still standing in line for cider with Selene.

"Whatever. They're both jerks," Ash said.

Max shared a strange look with Dr. Hiromi. "Yeah."

"So much for waiting around for Selene," Ash mumbled, rolling her eyes.

"Whatever. I'm starving. Let's get some of that clam chowder," Madge said as she pulled on Ash's sleeve, "Before they run out of bread bowls like they did last year."

Madge was beginning to feel light-headed as they got closer

to the front of the line, and strangely, she was breaking out into a sweat. Ash was droning on and on about something, but Madge couldn't focus. Something was off.

"Is it just me or did it get really hot in here?" Madge took off her felted hat. She was fanning her face with it when she noticed the back of her neck prickling – like she was being watched. But it didn't help – she felt a rising nausea... And fear.

"Can you believe how jealous Max was of Tristan?" Ash said, giggling.

Madge just shook her head. Her neck vein throbbed as though she'd just ran up a hill and beads of sweat formed on her nose and upper lip... and her vision began to swirl. A splitting headache slammed into her, threatening to buckle her knees.

"Madge?" Ash asked, staring wide eyed at Madge who looked like she'd seen a ghost.

"Is it hot in here?" Madge said as she took off her hat, rubbing sweat from her forehead as her vertigo got worse.

"No. Not even a little bit," Ash looked closely at Madge's face. "Whoa, you okay?" Ash asked as she grabbed onto Madge's arm to steady her.

Madge couldn't answer. Her whole body tingled – arms, legs, stomach, back, toes and her head – like it had fallen asleep. And she didn't know how or why, but she felt her body turn towards something. She froze as she locked her vision onto a person that stood nearby, dressed as a raven with a black feathered cloak and a mask with a long beak. Madge couldn't tell, and she could hardly even think straight to begin with, but it seemed as though the person behind the mask stared right back at her. She had thought it was a statue at first it stood so still without as much as a flinch.

"What's going on?" Ash asked shaking her arm.

"Do you see that raven to our left?" Madge asked, peeling her gaze away from it and staring at the ground instead as she tried to steady her breath.

"Where? Which one?"

"It's a costume..." Madge looked up again, ready to point at it, but it had gone.

A chill walked up her spine as the nausea worsened. Was she hallucinating again? Was what she was experiencing now something to do with head trauma from the fall in the water? Or was something more sinister happening?

Her head was spinning. She knew at any moment she might throw up or fall down. "I don't feel so good," Madge said as her knees started to buckle.

Ash held fast to her elbow. "Let's find a place to sit down—" Ash said, looking around for the nearest open seat, until she noticed Max coming towards them. She waved a hand in the air to get his attention. "Max is coming..."

Max reluctantly walked over with a girl dressed as a cat, and someone Madge had never met before, but for some reason seemed excited to meet her. "I'm Akira! I've heard so much about you!" she said with a big smile, waiting for Madge to look up and acknowledge her. "I'm new here, moved with the Institute, and it's my freshman year..." Akira's smile faded as she noticed Madge wouldn't look up. She *couldn't*.

"I'm Ash. Sorry, Madge isn't feeling so good."

"What happened?" Max asked, stepping forward to look into Madge's face. "She was fine five minutes ago."

"I don't know – we were just standing here—"

"We need to find the first aid station," Max said, taking hold of Madge's other elbow.

"I think I'm going to puke," Madge rasped. Her face had gone sickly pale.

"Did she eat something or is she diabetic or something?" Akira asked as they guided Madge through the thickening crowd towards the front of the tent.

Ash shook her head. "She hasn't eaten yet. She said some creepy person wearing a raven's mask was watching her and giving her the creeps, and the next thing I knew she was feeling nauseated."

"Where in the hell is Nico? And *Selene*?" Max growled to Akira, clenching his jaw.

"He'll find us, and *Selene* will be fine, Max. Let's just get her out of here," Akira said, looking over at Ash. "Let's take her to the Institute. We have a doctor there – the first aid station here will just send her home."

"Okay." Ash nodded her head in agreement. "We'll call Ollie from there."

"We parked at the end of the lot – near the tree," Ash huffed, her breath steaming as they exited the marquis tents into the dark parking lot. "This way."

"I don't know if we should be out here, Akira. Where is Nico?" Max spat as they made their way through the darkness. They weaved past dark cars, and further away from people.

"He'll find us," Akira answered gruffly.

"Who on earth is Nico?" Ash panted.

"Stop," Madge grunted, slipping her arms from their shoulders as she fell to her knees.

"Things are going from bad to worse," Max said, looking frantically around in the dark.

"Akira – go find—"

"I think she's going to puke!" Ash squealed, holding Madge's hair back.

Madge felt like her head was splitting in two as the singing she'd heard when she fell in the ocean that day filled her head. *The ocean*. That sweeping cold over her skin that tightened to scales would be a welcome respite from this pain – from this sound in her head...

But then she felt a finger rub across her forehead and the face of a girl with a black nose and whiskers came into view, as the singing ebbed and the world around came crashing in. "Madge, we're going to get you home. But you need to stand up so we can get you to the car. Can you do that?"

Madge shook her head violently. "I need to get in the water," she said, pointing west towards the ocean. She felt Akira's small, cold hands cup her face.

Akira looked up at Max, who nodded silently down at her, while keeping an eye on the dark parking lot surrounding them.

Akira spoke softly, "I'm going to help you, but you need to still yourself, okay?" Akira held her hand to Madge's forehead and whispered, "*Inlīht!*"

Immediately – as if a window had been thrown open – Madge felt the frigid, cold night air fill her lungs. She could hear the distant sound of music coming from the faire, her head empty of the voice that had echoed in her skull... The nausea, gone.

"Let me help you off the ground," Max said, hoisting her up under an arm. The smell of the wind on the sea stung her nostrils. His smell, she realized as her stomach fluttered.

"I'm fine," Madge said, pulling away from his grip as she leaned into a wide-eyed and shaky Ash. Her head still felt hollow – and slightly dizzy now that the singing was gone. But how did this girl do that? One second her head was – somewhere else. But with a word this girl took it all away.

"What language was that?" Madge asked, turning towards Akira. "What you said?"

Akira shook her head. "It's just something my dad taught me."

"But how did—"

"Wait!" Max said, throwing an arm out to hush them. "Did you hear that?"

Madge felt the prickling sensation run up her neck again. That thing, whatever was watching her – it was back. "Do you see it anywhere?" Madge whispered as she turned around in the parking lot, searching the dark. "It's here. I can feel it."

Max's mouth dropped open as he exchanged a panicked look with Akira. "What's here?"

"The raven," Madge answered as her eyes welled with fear. Her entire body, head to toe, was covered in goosepimples, as she pointed into the darkness. "I can't see it – but it's there…" she said as a shock of adrenaline crashed into her. And before she could think why, she screamed, "Get down!"

But it was too late.

There was a flash of light, tinged with electric purple that had come from where she'd pointed in the darkness. Max jumped in front of Akira just in time as it hit him square in the chest, blowing him onto his back as he slammed into the asphalt.

Madge grabbed onto Ash and hit the ground – but Akira was on the move.

"MAX!" Madge screamed, placing a hand on his chest to see if he was still breathing.

"Stay down and keep quiet!" Akira whispered before she ran towards where the light had come from.

"Hey – wait!" Madge rasped – but Akira was gone.

Everything seemed to move in slow motion. Madge could hear footsteps. A burst of red flame erupted from behind a car, then arched and streaked like a comet in the dark towards a dark figure that was on the run. She could make out a cloak, lit by the burn of the fireball aimed towards it: it was the raven.

If anything ever felt like an out of body experience – Madge felt she was having one now. She could hear and feel… but things were happening so fast she couldn't *think*. All she could see was Max, crumpled on the ground in front of her, and she didn't think about rushing to his side – she simply did it, without a second thought, though fire had just launched through the air and some kind of strange light had plummeted towards them only moments ago, slamming Max to the ground like a doll.

Everything seemed to go still and the world went quiet as Madge crouched down beside him and placed her hand on his chest. He was still breathing. The relief that washed over her brought her back – and sound and reality began to set in, when she heard footsteps rushing towards them and Ash's hysterical crying, jolting her with a burst of adrenaline that made her feel like a wild animal backed in a corner.

Madge stood up, ready to fight – or scream for help – when she realized it was Akira sprinting towards them.

"We have to get out of here!" Akira yelped as she grabbed onto Max's arms and tried to drag him towards Madge's car. "Help me with him!"

"Ash, come on, help!" Madge grabbed Max's feet, and Ash

helped Akira with his top half, grabbing his other side and arm as they tried to move him. She could feel her fingers tingle, and a strange sort of energy, sparking and crackling in the air around them. Was this real? She breathed in the cold air as the soles of Max's shoes cut into her palms – he was heavy. *Really* heavy. This was real. Madge was having a hard time carrying him, and felt she was about to drop him when the sound of running footsteps came again – this time several.

"Someone is coming!" Madge squeaked, as she finally let go of Max's feet in a panic, bracing herself for whoever was rushing upon them in the dark.

"Madge, get behind me, now!" Akira yelled as she faced whoever was coming with glowing, red palms. *Fire*.

"Akira?" said a man's voice.

"Daddy!" Akira answered, running towards Dr. Hiromi as several other figures rushed in and surrounded them, wearing strange glasses on their faces. "Max is hurt!" Akira sobbed, pointing to Madge's feet. "He took a hit that I think was aimed for me."

"It's not safe here," said a balding man with wide shoulders, sharp eyes and an even sharper jaw line. "We need to move. *Now.*" Madge stared up at the strange man with wide, disbelieving eyes—

"Madge, this is Nico. Head of security for MEI," Dr. Hiromi said, his face grave. "It's going to be okay, but you and your friend – we need you to come with us now." Dr. Hiromi placed a warm hand on her shoulder as he helped Ash up from the ground. "We'll explain everything when we get to the Institute."

Madge was shaking from head to toe as she watched Nico

pick Max's limp body up like he was a baby. She felt hands grab each arm as she was guided through the dark parking lot, and she could hear Ash's muffling sobs behind her.

A large, dark Suburban had raced up next to Nico, and Dr. Hiromi rushed to get the doors open as Nico laid Max down in the first row of back seats.

Madge froze as she watched the strange men surrounding the Suburban – as she heard another one pull up behind her.

"Get in Madge!" Akira said as tears streamed down her face.

Madge stared at the open door and hesitated – who were all these people? "Where are you taking him?" she said to the tall man standing next to her, who seemed like he was in charge.

"We need to get Max to the Institute as quickly as possible and get you to safety," Nico answered in a gruff voice as he pointed to the Suburban.

"But why the Institute? Why aren't you taking him to a hospital?" Madge didn't hide the suspicion from her voice.

"He doesn't need a hospital," Akira answered. "Hurry, get in. *Please.*"

"Fine. But I'm sitting with him." Madge climbed in next to Max's unconscious body, laying his head on her lap as the Suburban sped away – following another one in the front, and tailed by another one behind them.

Ash whispered from the seat behind her, "what is going on here? I thought they were marine ecologists. This feels military. And did you see Akira's hands?"

Madge shook her head – there was something more than peculiar about *all* of it. It was like they were in a third world country, getting an important political figure to safety. Except something inexplicable was happening, magical things she couldn't explain – and wouldn't have believed had they not happened right before her very eyes. She'd have thought she was imagining it or had hit her head again... But this time, all the others had seen it. Everyone in this very car shared the same reality. *This was real.*

And with a shudder, Madge realized in this very moment, as she held Max's head in her lap, that what had happened to her on her birthday was real, too. A strange stillness washed over her as she stared down at Max's face. And like a stab to the heart, she knew he was in pain. She could feel it, somehow. Could see it, written tightly across his brow.

And an all-consuming thought filled her... She wanted to take the hurt away.

As if in reaction to that thought, her fingertips tingled wildly where she held his head. She drowned out everything else but taking his pain away, and as she did so could feel her heart thrumming in her neck, and her breath sounded like the ocean in her ears... but there was something else she could hear, too: the crackle of electricity *inside* her, as it bubbled and sparked in her fingertips. It almost felt like her hand had fallen asleep, but she knew this was something different. It prickled at her fingertips and coursed through her entire body – she could feel it in her toes, and especially the tip of her nose, until even her hair felt static.

"I can fix this," Madge whispered, barely audible.

She moved her hands – holding one over Max's heart and the other over his clammy forehead, as Akira had done with her minutes ago. His chest rose and fell, but in ragged breaths. Her palms ached as she sensed a sort of black mass that hovered and swam within his chest and head. Like a poison, she wanted to draw it out. She recalled the calm that had come over her when Akira had spoken to her with a palm on her forehead, and she knew what she needed to do.

"Akira, what was it that you said to me in the parking lot?"
"It's Old English—"
"But what was the word?"
"Why?"
"What does it mean? Or what does it do?"
"Well… It's sort of a plea for clarity. I thought you had a migraine. *Inlīht*. It's sort of—"
"*Inlīht!*" Madge screeched.
She heard Akira scream just as a blast of energy surged from Max into her palms.
Madge's body went rigid, and then all went dark.

7

Unveiling

Everything felt cool... liquid... and light. Madge felt like she was floating.

Remnants of a dark dream lingered in the shadows, and as she tried to wake her mind and remember, she noticed heavy, sticky things clinging all over her body. *Sticky things?* Her mind was officially awake now – and alarmed. She was floating indeed – on water.

Slowly, she opened her eyes.

A vaulted, pale stone ceiling arched overhead, and she was in a shallow tub, made of copper. She was still in the black dress from the Halloween Faire... the *faire*. It all came crashing into her mind as she sat up with a start.

"You're awake!" Grandpa Ollie said from a chair behind the copper tub.

Madge swiveled around. "Why am I in a bathtub?" she asked, still slightly dazed – and beginning to feel a panic – the same panic she'd felt the night before slam into her chest.

"Try to remain calm, Madgie. Pearl will be back in a moment," Grandpa Ollie said, standing from the chair as he placed a warm hand on Madge's shoulder. A fountain trickled from a rock wall where Grandpa Ollie knelt beside her. Down by where her feet had been resting was a lip where the water poured out, into a bed of rocks below, and pale flagstone surrounded an aquamarine pool that stretched from the vaulted room they were now in, through a stone archway and into several other vaulted rooms. She couldn't see the end of it. There was a staircase to her right which helped her to realize they were underground. She could tell by the smell, like a cave. And the lack of windows.

"Why am I in a bathtub?" Madge asked as she started to get up – until she saw milky-white, opaque, and translucent jelly-like *things* on her arms – and legs. Madge bit back a scream. They looked like leeches. She knew they were not. Leeches were brown and dark. But they were sure stuck to her skin like leeches.

"Madge – leave those be now—"

"Get them off me!" Madge squealed, stumbling out of the tub. She immediately began dancing around, pulling the gelatinous creatures off as quickly as she could to the ground. They felt slippery and seemed to buzz with electricity, only adding to her horror.

"NO – Madge!" Grandpa Ollie rounded the tub and held his hands out towards her. "Stop!" he said as he held her arms to be still. "They are meant to help you."

Madge stood still and stared into Grandpa Ollie's face, trying to ignore the things that lay on the stones at her feet. "Where are we and where is Max?"

A door opened and footsteps came down the stairs.

"Someone is coming," Madge said with wide eyes.

"It's okay, we are at the Institute. And Max is fine – after what you did to help him. He's upstairs. They all are."

Pearl appeared at the bottom of the stairs with her hand over her mouth. "What have you done?" she yelped, and then frantically began to gather the opaque creatures from Madge's feet, placing them into a tall glass jar full of water that she had set to the side of the basin. "Stand still!" she snipped, placing a warm, bony hand on Madge's ankle. "Don't step on them."

Madge rubbed at the red marks on her arms. "What are those things?"

"Something that cannot be replicated, nor replaced. These were to suck the electricity out of you, and the dark Vala that you decided to absorb from Max," Pearl said as she rose to her feet. "Don't panic, this was a therapy designed to heal you, not hurt you."

Madge's mouth gaped open. This prim and proper English woman, with a perfectly starched and pressed shirt and a big diamond ring on her manicured hand, had just admitted out loud to Madge that magic, or *Vala*, was real. More perplexing was that Grandpa Ollie knew about it, too. "So… it really happened. This is all real," she breathed, staring at Grandpa Ollie with wide eyes. Her head swayed, like she was underwater.

"Why don't you sit down, Madgie," Grandpa Ollie said, helping her into a chair.

"Drink this," Pearl said as she handed Madge a glass of orange juice. "And I wouldn't suggest standing again until you do," she said with a pointed look at Ollie. "I'll let the others know she is awake and quite well recovered. Take all the time you need," Pearl said as she screwed the lid on the jar holding the alien-like leeches and headed up the stairway.

"What is going on, Grandpa?"

"Drink first. Then we'll talk."

Madge huffed as she took a sip of the orange juice, biting into bits of pulp. As she drank deeply, she felt a warmth spread through her, helping her mind to focus.

Grandpa Ollie watched her carefully, silently, until she drank every drop. As he took away her empty glass, he handed her a large, fluffy robe. "We need to discuss some things," he said as he moved another one of the slated teak chairs near the pool next to Madge. "About last night, for starters."

"What did they tell you?"

"What you did for Max. Where did you learn to do that?"

Madge could feel her heart thundering in her ears. "Do what? What did they say I did?"

"You used your Vala," Grandpa Ollie said, his eyes bright.

Madge blinked back at him for a moment as a surge of emotions welled in her stomach. "It all started happening on my birthday and I thought I was... *crazy*. And now the Institute – everything I saw last night – who are these people?" Madge said, her eyes brimming with tears.

"You are not crazy," Grandpa Ollie said, placing a dry, calloused hand on hers. "I knew something was different when your necklace changed."

"This?" Madge stared down at the necklace Christine had given her from her mother.

Grandpa Ollie nodded his head. "When it went clear... I knew something happened. You just weren't ready to tell me. But I need you to tell me everything now, every small thing, since you started wearing this necklace. And then I can explain."

"Everything?" Madge asked, taking a deep breath. She wanted to pour it all out – especially to Grandpa, who was the sanest, most *normal* person she knew. Telling him would make her feel... better.

"Every tiny detail you can think of. Anything you think would be strange and not real, things you think would be in your head and no one would ever believe. I want you to share all of those things, because I am prepared to tell you the reasons why," he spoke softly, as he combed her hair away from her ear and patted her knee.

And that moment brought a spilling point to Madge, as tears rolled down her face, the words tumbled from her lips. All the details she could think of. The day she fell in the water. The sense of tingling in her fingers and the night she laid awake. When she told him about the events at the faire – the last bits of everything she had wound around inside herself – she felt a huge sense of relief wash over her. She finally felt empty of all the worry she'd been carrying around, because if all of this were okay with Grandpa – then it was simply okay to begin with. The way he listened silently, without shock or horror – but understanding and warmth... was better than any outcome she could ever have anticipated.

"But I am sorry I didn't tell you anything. It all sounds so crazy," Madge rubbed her face with the sleeves of her robe. "Who would believe me? It was such a strange feeling – it was more than my imagination. I could *feel* it. The scales felt tight. I felt the power where my feet used to be – it felt fluid. I could feel the length and difference in my feet – or fins or whatever. And somehow last night, I knew I had power within me. And I just went for it. I couldn't hold myself back any more than I can hold back a sneeze."

"That somehow makes sense," Grandpa Ollie said with a chuckle. "Your Vala was hidden from you in this necklace until you came of age on your sixteenth birthday. Your parents thought it was the best way to keep you hidden. That's why all of this has started happening since you began wearing it."

Madge's eyes went wide. "Hide me? Who from? Other people?"

"From your kind, mostly. Because we had to keep you a secret."

"Okay – but why not tell *me*?"

"I wanted every single moment possible for you to feel and live a normal, teenaged life before the change. Had I told you, you wouldn't have believed me."

"I believe everything you say, Grandpa!"

"We also needed your magic, your Vala, to come back naturally. Apparently, that was very important – that you not expect it so that it could do its thing and not be impeded by fear."

"But why was it hidden? I don't understand."

"Because your mother and your father were Royal."

"What?" Madge sat up in her chair. "Say that again?"

"Your father was a King. Your mother became his Queen when they married."

Madge stood up and started pacing. "Okay... Royalty *where*?"

"It's sort of an underground, secret kind of thing, but... your kind segregated this world into realms and each realm is ruled by an ancient line of Royals."

"My *kind*?" Madge paced more wildly now. "You aren't..."

"No, I'm not – I'm human. I don't have a drop of Vala running in my blood. But your parents were... Please sit down, Madge."

"So that means..." Madge sat with a thud and stared at her

feet.

"You are a princess. We had to keep you hidden because there were some bad people after the throne. That's why the Riveras didn't visit, nor anyone else."

Madge felt a shock run through her body. "Anyone else? Do I have more family, or did they have other people that haven't come around my whole life?"

"We couldn't chance you being found. I know it has been hard for you. Lonely at times with only me around."

"I wouldn't trade you for anyone, Grandpa. You know that."

Grandpa Ollie's chin wobbled as he nodded his head. She laid her head on his shoulder and they sat in silence as Madge tried to absorb everything she was hearing. She had some kind of otherworldly power – Vala – in her veins; and it had been hidden, in her necklace. She stared down at it, at the silver hands clasped around the now glassy stone, until her eyes drifted to the strands of aquamarine light that danced on the rough limestone walls. And without warning, she felt a shiver dance up her arms, as if she could feel that aquamarine light reflecting within her…

Madge sat up with a start. She *felt* the power of the water.

"What is it?" Grandpa Ollie asked, his eyes glassy.

"I woke up in the tub because being in the water helps, doesn't it?"

"That's absolutely correct. Your powers are enhanced in water."

Madge felt excitement bubble in her stomach. "You mentioned my *kind*. Who are they? *What* are they?"

"There are many. The people upstairs in the Institute for starters, your grandmother. Your father. Your mother was half-blooded, like you. But you – you are special. You have shared with me something that will shock and awe them all upstairs."

"Half-blooded?"

Grandpa Ollie raised his bushy white brows and fixed a serious look towards his granddaughter. "You're a mermaid."

Madge jumped out of her chair. She felt dizzy.

"Say that again."

"Well, they don't call it that, it's more a human term for what you are. You've got Vala inside you. A sort of... magic, power, not of this world. Though it's been here now for thousands of years, supposedly."

"Not of this world? I'm not human?" Madge's head was swimming again.

"No, your kind are from somewhere not of this world, but you are also human. Like I said, a half-blood. You are extra special. No matter what, you're always going to be *my* Madgie," Grandpa Ollie said, grabbing her in a tight hug that made it hard to breathe. "You may be different, but you are still *you*. Don't ever forget who you are," he said releasing her with a kiss on top of her wet head.

Mermaid.

The word rang in her ears over and over as the memory of scales and fins flashed through her mind. "Wait – does this mean every time I get in the ocean, I'll—"

"No. You have the ability to change or not – you have control. You changed on your birthday because your Vala had just been released from the necklace your mom gave you. That and probably the cold water and the scare of the fall – your instincts probably took over."

"That's another thing," Madge said through knit brows, "you keep saying Mom gave me the necklace. You said before she would have wanted me to have it or intended it – but then you keep saying that she gave it to me."

"Remember I mentioned bad people were after you?"

"Yes. After mom and dad died because someone wanted the throne…"

"Well, they were after your mom and dad, too," he said as he pulled a letter out of his shirt pocket, sealed in a zip-locked bag. Madge noticed her name drawn in big letters across the front, and a lipstick kiss mark.

"Is this from…"

"Your mother and father wrote you this letter when they went away… It was a journey and the reason they left was to secure the throne and your future. They hid your Vala in the necklace and gave it to Christine in case they were to fail… And let me say, they haven't failed, not in the grand scheme of things – because *you* are here," Grandpa Ollie choked out the words as his chin wobbled again. "But they didn't survive the trip."

"What are you trying to say?" Madge felt her pulse quicken.

Grandpa Ollie began to weep. Madge put her hand on his shoulder and wept with him. Though she hadn't heard the words yet, she knew what was coming.

"Your mother and father were murdered."

8

The Letter

Grandpa Ollie hadn't pushed or asked any questions when Madge had said she wanted to go straight home and not see anyone. The minute the letter hit her hand, Madge felt her world unravel – the wonder and excitement had turned to dread upon learning that her parents were *murdered*. By whom, she wondered? Did they know? She hadn't the heart to ask who those bad people were. Not yet.

Madge shut her bedroom door, propped the letter from her parents on her nightstand, and fell into bed. She buoyed herself up on her pillows and stared at the envelope, working up the courage to open it.

She was raised her whole life believing a lie – a lie about herself *and* how they died.

Grandpa Ollie said the letter would explain some things, and Madge feared what it had to say. Would it make her feel better about this path she was on now? What was so important that they'd risk dying – and leaving her behind? Madge felt guilty for the anger that boiled inside of her. They left… knowing they may never see her again.

Maybe the letter would explain why.

Madge popped up and grabbed the envelope and sat on the edge of her bed as she held it in her hands. The envelope was worn and soft… Grandpa Ollie must have taken it out to look at it and hold often through the years. It must have taken heaps of self-control not to open it himself – one of his greatest virtues next to punctuality, Madge knew all too well.

As she imagined him holding the envelope over and over again, all this time, she realized something else like a stab to the gut… to imagine the grief her grandpa must have felt – losing his daughter to then raise Madge, who they left behind in his care, on his own. And that he had to hold onto this secret and this letter for her all these years.

Madge's name was written in indigo blue ink, like it had been drawn in watercolor with deeper blues and lighter blues from where the brush had rested or moved along to form a line, and small stars were painted all around her name. Grandpa Ollie said her mother was an artist – some of her work still hung around the house and Madge had spent a lot of time staring at her sketches and drawings.

Madge touched the lipstick kiss imprint softly… And an idea came to mind.

She jumped from her bed to her desk and grabbed a piece of paper, then fished a tube of lipstick she rarely used from the drawer and made her own lipstick mark to compare to her mother's. It sent a shiver down Madge's spine as she noticed how alike the imprints were – the curve of the top lip, the width of the mouth. Somehow it gave her the courage to finally turn the envelope over.

She couldn't bear to tear it, so she grabbed scissors and

THE LETTER

carefully cut along the seam.

The letter had been written on thick art paper – torn at the edge like it had been ripped from a notebook or a pad of paper, and more indigo stars had been painted along the edges.

Madge took a deep breath and began to read.

November 12th, 1982

Our dearest daughter, Madge,

I write this letter now with tears in my eyes. Just the thought that we might not see our baby girl again breaks my heart and makes me lose courage. If you are reading this, I no doubt have a lot of explaining to do. It's been so difficult, so very difficult, to think of the words to say in this letter to you.

You mean so very much to us, you are our world – the minute you came into it. We do this for you, and for all our kind. Indeed, we do it for the world we live in.

So here goes... Bear with me. I know you'll be briefed but I need you to hear it in your father and my words. Just in case anything gets twisted.

Your Aunt stole an artifact from our vault. It's an ancient head said to have been a voice between realms. You'll no doubt be continuing this journey to find out what exactly this Mimir's Head, as we call it, can actually do. In the years she's been gone, she's grown an army of followers. We've had to keep moving and most importantly – keep you a secret so she would never find out about YOU. She doesn't know you were even born yet.

Your father and I alone know that you have the ability to transform. We do not understand why, we can only imagine it's a part of the Royal Vala in your veins. We have told no one, but no doubt they will find out soon.

We hope that fact alone will bring hope to our kind and the nay-sayers.

And you're probably wondering what we are after and what could be worth possibly dying for. The answer to that is you. And our kind.

If we are to have peace and any future for you, and stop the string of murders of innocents, we must prove that human blood is a beautiful thing – the reborn Vala that comes with it allowing infinite possibilities. It must start with our leaders – with me. With you.

Now onto some further explanations that you'll undoubtedly be wondering:

Your Vala will be withheld, and you will be allowed to live a normal life until your sixteenth birthday to keep you safe. You reading this means your father and I did not succeed.

But we know you will be able to conquer anything. We can see it already that you are special. You are destined for something unlike we have yet ever seen. Everything about you will be more than enough to end the darkness that threatens our kind.

Your Vala resides in a necklace that you'll receive on your sixteenth birthday. Once you put it on, it will come unto you. We are not sure what that will look like, but it was the only way. If your Vala was within you, you'd be found, if not sooner than later. That's a road map to you. We need to give you a head start and keep you hidden amongst humans and away from our kind until the time comes. I truly hope you grasp the reasons why.

We leave you, our most precious daughter, with your grandpa. I trust no one more than him to take the best care of you. He already loves you like his own daughter and dotes on you like only a grandfather could. He had no say in any of this, but he will do whatever he can to keep you safe and to keep his promise to let you reign and follow your destiny as the Saelfen Queen. Though no doubt he'll teach you the love for the simple things in life and what it means to be human!

We love our little Princess. If for some reason we don't succeed... We leave the rest to Grandpa and the Council to guide you. They'll be waiting and ready for you when it is time. The Nine will accept you, especially when they learn of your ability to transform. You will win them over. We know you can do it.

If I didn't say it already, know how much your father and I love you... There are no words to describe it. Until you have your own someday, you probably would never understand. We'll always be with you. Be brave.

All Our Love,
Mom

-Madge, your mother said everything I could ever try to. You're the apple of my eye. You bring me joy unlike anything I could have ever imagined possible. The love between a father and a daughter is very special. I can't imagine any Daddy loving his daughter more than I love you. I love you, so very, very much. Infinitely. Love, Dad

Madge had been pacing, and she stood still when she read the last words, stunned.

Aunt? She didn't know she had an aunt! Let alone an aunt that was the "bad people" that Grandpa Ollie was talking about! And what Council? What was the Council? And what was the Nine? What was a – Madge scanned the page looking for the word – *Saelfen*?

Madge sat at her bay window and read the letter again. Over and over again, until she thought she could actually feel her heart ache inside, spreading through her chest and down her arms and into her stomach. It hurt to read the love her parents had – to find mysterious answers to the question of why they'd left her behind. She still didn't truly understand why, or any of it just yet – but she knew she'd find out soon.

And that was the overwhelming part – that her mother pleaded her to win something she couldn't grasp even a little bit. Become a Queen? Win over the Council? Stop her evil aunt?

But those questions didn't matter as much as the love that sprang from the pages... the carefully painted stars... *daddy's little girl and mommy's whole world.*

She wiped hot tears on her sleeve, careful not to wet her hands so she could continue to preserve those things she'd longed to hear her entire life... now in cold, blue ink.

Madge awoke to a soft knock on her door. She must have passed out, exhausted from crying and sleeping in a bathtub the night before. The sun was close to the horizon, the light already fading in her room. It must have been hours since she'd fallen asleep.

Grandpa Ollie poked his head in. "I looked in on you earlier, you were sound asleep and didn't hear me knocking. Hungry?" he asked as he stepped inside the room and eyed the letter lying open on her lap.

"I'm exhausted."

"I made you your favorite," he said as he placed a mug on her bedside table. "Earl Grey with milk and honey. I'm making a quick trip to the store for some TV dinners."

"Okay."

"I'll get you the one with cherry pie in case you have an appetite later."

"Thanks Grandpa," Madge said as he planted a kiss on her head before leaving her alone again in her room.

Madge sipped her tea and stared out the window from her bay seat.

The sun was low and ready to set, and the sky had cleared quite a bit, showing off deep blues and purples where too often she saw grey these days. Faint reds and orange started to paint the horizon and the ocean below, and Madge felt a thirst to be out in it.

A cutting, insatiable, urgent thirst.

She heard the front door close. With a jolt and without a second thought, Madge popped up, took another chug of her tea, grabbed her wetsuit from its hiding place in her closet, and walked downstairs. This time, instead of sneaking out the window, she walked out the back door.

In her bare feet.

Cold ocean air stung her nostrils and dusted away the cobwebs in her mind, pushing away the shadows and grief she'd felt all day. She loped down the steps and hit the beach, breaking into a run, the sound of sand whipping beneath her feet.

The sun had just sunk into the curve of the ocean in a burst of deep, vivid color, and Madge wanted to be like the sun… to dip into that blue, tempestuous world beyond.

She ran as fast as her legs would carry her, towards the white foam of the waves, their crests saturated with the dim light of the setting sun barely piercing through.

As her feet hit the water, and icy cold ran up her body, she closed her eyes and relished the taste of salty mist that settled on her face from the pounding surf. She thought of what she knew and what Grandpa had said: water was a conduit for her Vala. No wonder she always needed it, to be in it.

With little more than a thought, a pulse of energy shifted

through her.

It was electrifying – and almost scary to feel it. But instead of screaming this time, like she did on her birthday – Madge embraced it and kept walking.

She opened her eyes and held onto the necklace her mother had left her for her birthday and felt a deep affinity to her that she had never quite felt… until now. She felt a sense of awe in *who* and *what* she was, of her lineage. Until now, she had always felt incomplete. She thought it was only because she'd lost her parents at a young age. But now she felt whole, like an answer to a riddle bringing about a calmer mind and a sense of ease, or like an answer to a prayer she'd never uttered, but her heart had known all along.

She felt awake. She felt free. Resolute.

And ready to go for a swim.

After all, she hadn't snuck out since the morning of her birthday – before her Vala had returned to her. Now her favorite thing in the world took a whole new meaning entirely. She had no idea what it would be like as a mermaid, but she could hardly wait to find out.

The tide was high, and all the rocky tidal pools were underwater, only the mountain of Haystack Rock and the two rock columns nearby, called the Needles, rose above the white waves that crashed around them.

Madge took a deep breath. She didn't know exactly what to do to change into mer-form, but she wasn't scared. Quite the opposite. She simply walked into the ocean, though she couldn't feel her toes anymore, until the crests jumped over her head.

She gasped at the freezing cold, smiling to herself as it dawned on her why she had an affinity for swimming in cold water all her life and how she could warm up so quickly and easily, unlike anyone she'd ever heard of or knew: it was her Vala. A part of it that had always been with her, despite it being hidden away in a necklace – remnants must have remained.

When her feet no longer touched the bottom, and freezing water rushed up her neck and over her shoulders, she felt her skin tighten.

Like she had anticipated, on instinct, the *change* took over.

She could feel her flappy, floppy feet – no longer feet but fins – and she could feel them bend and flex, maneuvering her through the water with ease. She looked down at her arms and legs and examined the coppery, tight scales. She could see extremely well, as if it were daylight. But even better and further underwater than she could have anticipated.

And Madge could no longer feel the sting of the cold.

It simply felt *cool* – there wasn't a temperature she could gauge to it, it just felt normal somehow. And even though her scales ended at her neck, her face felt warm, like that stinging warmth on your cheeks when playing in the snow and working up a sweat in the cold air.

Admiring her coppery scaled arms, she turned them over and discovered barely noticeable, sharp fins that extended from her shoulder and tapered just below the elbow and only a quarter of an inch tall. Her tail fins, the rubbery, fluid membrane that were once her feet, transitioned from copper and then bled into a clear, translucent, and almost milky color, and finally, to an opaque, fleshy pink at the ends where the membrane was most fluid.

She could hardly believe her eyes... this was *her*.

When she was done examining this new form, Madge laughed. Turning over and over again in the water – in fits of giggles – she relaxed into the joy of the transformation and the sheer energy that rushed through her from the vast ocean surrounding her.

She'd never felt so alive.

Realizing the possibility of being spotted, she paddled around and behind the rocks, then finally around and behind the large mountainous Haystack Rock. And with one lingering smile up at the waning moon just peeking over the horizon, she swiveled around, took a deep breath, and plunged *down*.

She couldn't breathe below water, and she knew that instinctively. But to hold her breath was no problem at all, like porpoises, who hold their breath and come up for air when needed and can do so for long periods of time. Madge wondered just how long she'd be able to hold it. She'd find out soon enough, she knew, but it felt holding her breath was… *simple*. She hardly even had to think about it.

In fact, she was almost incognizant that she held her breath at all.

She also noticed that her hearing adjusted below the ocean. Usually sounds were muffled underwater, but now they were as clear as a bell. She felt her ears – they felt stiffer, the cartilage rippled, and, she noticed, her ear shape had changed slightly.

Madge homed in on the sounds around her and swam.

It was a world of light and shadows below, in faint shades of emerald-green. She could see things she normally could never see, like tiny specks of gold dancing in the moving water all around her.

Best of all, Madge felt fearless here. No worry of what was lurking, of what she could or couldn't do – she felt the power of it all, surging through her, beckoning her in. So, she pushed ahead as hard as she could to see how fast she could swim.

She knew it was fast – *super* fast, as she felt the power of the water rushing around her, a pulsing energy as she pushed through it, like it was *within* her. That tingling, electric feeling she knew now was her Vala, propelled her forward in the water. She imagined the exhilaration of flight would feel similar, as her belly tickled in the same way when taking off in a plane, or in a dream of flying.

Yes, this was fast indeed.

She could feel the energy of the tides, slight variations in temperature from current and depth, and most fascinating of all was that she could even feel the microscopic plankton.

She surged past creatures hiding in rocky depths, past colorful anemones and star fish clinging to the bottom, and into a deeper expanse.

But Madge kept moving, eager to get to that *beyond* – to that something that pulled her.

Until she stopped abruptly. The sounds of the beyond – that *something* she'd wanted to find since she ducked under the water – filled her ears with a mysterious groaning—

Whales!

Not only could she hear them, but she could *feel* them, sense them. Though they were still a way off, she knew they were close, so she swam faster as the haunting sound sang through the water and vibrated in her ears, rippling past every nerve and scale.

And finally, Madge slammed to a stop.

These were not just any whale – they were huge—

Blue Whales.

Her heart thundered in her chest, and it was hard to keep

her lips pressed together from the smile threatening to widen her mouth open and let the sea water in. The salty ocean carried away the tears that leaked from her eyes. It had to be the single-most beautiful encounter she'd ever had. A calm stillness entered her as she took in their other-worldly presence, and she felt it to her core, as if she were spying on angels gathered in the deep.

She swam closer, moving as slowly as she could, not daring to blink.

They looked like a group of submarines floating – it was hard to imagine she was getting so close to the largest creatures on the planet, being some of the hardest to study due to how far they stayed from shore...

Shore. She had to be out a *good ten miles at least*. Had she really come that far? But Madge was too awe struck to worry how far she'd gone from home.

She swam closer still, stunned more by their size the closer she inched towards them. They were as big as a large plane. Larger than most prehistoric dinosaurs.

As she watched these gentle giants glide through the ocean deep, in awe that a living thing could be so big, all she could do was float and watch, as she listened to the reverberations of their other-worldly singing filling her heart.

She wasn't sure how much time had passed when was shook from her reverie and felt a *nudge*. The air in her lungs had begun to strain. With a sad glance at the host of these otherworldly angels gathered before her, she swam to the surface and took a breath of air.

It was time to figure out just how far she'd come, she realized, as she saw that the moon had risen quite a bit since she'd started her swim. Sparse clouds had opened wide just above her head to reveal a dome of stars. She whipped around in every direction, as she tried to catch a glimpse of light or shore, but she saw nothing.

Nothing but the swell of the ocean in every direction.

Sky and water – water and sky. Panic rose in her throat.

"Think! Madge, think!" she shouted to herself.

And something more magical than magic itself happened: one of the blue whales surfaced for air. She could hear it. But more than that was knowing it was out here with her – and she felt less alone. And they traveled thousands of miles, all the time.

They *knew* where to go.

She closed her eyes and tried to calm herself as she took deeper breaths. She could feel and hear her heartbeat as it thundered in her ears, the kiss of wind on her face. She slowed her breath, breathing even deeper into focus… and as she did so, she felt a tingling sensation and a sort of *tug* to her left, like a turn towards light in the dark, or heat in the cold.

She knew which way was home.

It was as natural as which way was up or down underwater.

She ducked back down, feeling the directional tug even more after she submerged.

And something wonderful happened – something that was beyond her imagination.

Her scales had begun to glow slightly, just at the tips – as if each scale had been dipped in an iridescent glow. Her bodily instincts had taken on a mind of their own in answer to the dark environment she was in, something to help her navigate her way home as she could see even more clearly than before, from the soft glow that emanated from her scales, bounding off her in every direction.

She gazed again at the whales, who now seemed to watch her. Perhaps aware of who and what she was, or simply curious at the light that shone suddenly below in their secret world.

She wanted to stay and watch them – to travel with them... But a thought suddenly struck her to her core: *Grandpa!* Her heart sank. *He must be so worried!* She didn't know what time it was – but judging from the moon, it was later than she'd anticipated.

Madge said a quiet goodbye to her giant angels of the deep, and swam as quickly as she could in the direction she knew was home.

But as she swam, it wasn't worry for Grandpa that occupied her thoughts.

It was time to face all of what she now knew she had been her whole life. What her *parents* were. The words from the letter they had left her burned in her mind, words she'd read over and over. *We know you will be able to conquer anything. We can see it already that you are special... you are destined for something unlike we have yet ever seen...*

Destined. Her destiny felt crystal clear as she marveled at this new reality: she was a mermaid of some kind. And the closer she got to home, the more excited she felt about embracing it and finding out more.

As Madge came up for one last breath of air, where she could see the glowing shoreline, she cast her eyes to the stars... and smiled. She hoped her parents were seeing this – she felt they were. She'd never felt so close to them in all her life until now, whereas before they were a faded, painful memory. And not just for the affinity of what she now was – this Vala they had passed onto her – but because now she felt like they were with her by their words in the letter.

It was their voices ringing in her ears, encouraging her to move forward and *conquer* the legacy they'd left her at her feet.

Or fins.

9

Royal Cuffs

Madge sat up and wiped drool from her cheek. She'd slept hard and awoke disoriented. In fact, she was almost surprised that she was in her room. She'd wondered for a split second if all that had happened last night – even the past few days – had been real. She touched her head as a smile spread across her face – ocean water had dried in her hair and left it a tangled mess, and she could still smell and feel salt on her skin.

She checked her alarm clock – it was six a.m. and entirely too early for a Saturday. A dull, grey morning yawned outside her window. It was hard to imagine she was looking at the same sky and ocean she'd swum in only hours before. The starry dome from last night was replaced by a wall of fog and clouds, and the sheer exhilaration she'd felt was completely gone as she realized she hadn't faced Grandpa yet. She wasn't sure she had it in her to do it now, either – she was exhausted, and it felt like she had sand in her throat.

She opened her bedroom door slowly to see if Grandpa was up already, and she froze when she heard his voice carrying up the stairs, along with the bang and clang of pots and pans. *Who would he be talking to at this hour?*

Grandpa Ollie hadn't said much to Madge last night. When she'd gotten home, he'd stood up and informed her that a large search party had been out looking for her from the Institute. He seemed disappointed and scared more than angry. All Madge could do was apologize. With a face full of worry and hurt, he'd sent her up to bed. She tried to explain, but he wouldn't allow it. "Get to bed," was all he had to say.

Madge wanted a hot shower, but her stomach growled and felt like it would burn up if she didn't get some food in it. She felt dizzy and weak. She had gone to bed with nothing to eat, she'd hardly eaten yesterday, and she'd just swum something around twenty miles, at least.

Madge remembered that swim with a half-smile – how far she'd gone, what she'd seen – what she was capable of… What she now was. But the light of morning reminded her things were about to change. Drastically. As her parent's letter, still propped on her bedside table where she had left it, reminded her like a blaring horn. She kissed the letter and put it away in a drawer before heading down the stairs to face Grandpa Ollie.

The smell of sausage wafted up the stairs, aggravating the hunger burning in her belly, and Grandpa Ollie was still on the phone – the cord stretched to capacity as he flipped an egg with one hand. Madge tip-toed to the fireplace to warm her bones and wait – where she noticed with a cringe Grandpa had laid her wetsuit before it to dry – shivering as the heat from the fire warmed her back and still-damp hair.

"Yep, she's awake now," he said, glancing over his shoulder at her with a frown, "we'll be over around eight then… Okay, see you then. Bye-bye now." He hung up the phone and pulled a platter out of the oven with a hot pad piled high with sausages, toast, and fried eggs. "Pearl said you'd be especially hungry after your swim last night."

"Who was that?"

"Pearl – we're going to see her after breakfast."

"But – I was going to—"

"Eat," Grandpa Ollie barked as he slid open the back door with a mug of coffee in hand. "You and I will talk on the way, after I've had my coffee and my walk."

What are they doing here? Madge wondered, closing the front door behind her as she saw Dr. Kento Hiromi, Christine and Dan Rivera standing on the driveway talking to Grandpa Ollie, who was already sat in his truck, steam billowing from the exhaust pipe. They were all geared up in rain boots, rain jackets and wool caps – and covered with icy morning mist. A pang of guilt hit her already nervous stomach as she realized they were likely in the search party last night.

Christine turned and immediately walked towards Madge, but instead of Christine's hallmark smile, her expression was unusually grim. Madge's heart sank. But instead of saying a word to her, Christine wrapped her in a huge, wet hug.

"Have you been out here all night?" Madge asked, noticing the purplish bags beneath Christine's eyes.

Christine nodded and said, "We had to secure a few things."

"I'm so sorry. I had no idea—"

"I'd have done the same thing. That ocean can be magnetic. And for you, this is all so new – I'd imagine the pull was unbearable. Besides," Christine shrugged and finally smiled, "how else are you going to figure all of this out?"

Madge felt a smile tug at her face. If Christine only knew how often she'd actually been out there, alone at night… "I'm glad someone understands."

"Are you encouraging her?" Dan asked with an incredulous look on his face.

"But it's also something *we* should have anticipated," Christine said, waving him off, "and we should have warned you – shown you why you can never do that again. Today we'll be doing just that."

Madge felt her stomach sink. "What do you mean – never go on a night swim again?"

"Day or night, never go on a swim *alone* again. Not while people want you gone."

Hearing Christine say that felt like a hot knife piercing her heart. How on earth would she manage keeping herself inside when she knew what she was now missing? "Sounds like I have a lot to look forward to," Madge huffed, trying to breathe past the lump growing in her throat.

"No need to get upset now – you're safe. That's all that matters."

"Ollie is tapping his watch, but I need you to do one thing before you go," Dan said as he pushed over a wheelbarrow full of gray pea gravel.

"So, I'm to do hard labor now as punishment?" Madge asked, glancing at Grandpa Ollie who had on several occasions made her do yard work when she got into trouble.

"No," Dan laughed, "though I'd love to say otherwise. "We use rocks – gravel driveways, and such all the time. A simple incantation to charge the rock puts up an invisible barrier."

"But I don't know how…"

"It's easy. I'll walk you through it, but you have to be the one to do it."

Madge blinked, unsure what to say. Was this some kind of test?

"This is your house. Only you – or your grandfather – have the right to protect it. And since you have Vala and Ollie does not, I'll need you to do this. Place your hand on top of the gravel here."

"Okay, this is weird…"

"Now, when you say the incantation, just think about and understand what you are saying. You are declaring this ground as yours and that nothing shall pass over these stones that can do harm."

"Does this have something to do with my aunt?"

"Pretty much," Dan admitted.

"It's not just your aunt," Christine said, putting a gloved hand on Madge's shoulder. "You'll hear all about it from Pearl. But for now, just focus on the incantation to protect your property, yourself, and Ollie."

"Grandpa is in danger, too?" Madge's breath caught in her throat.

"Not exactly—"

"Everyone is," Dan interjected with a fold of his arms, ignoring his wife's glare. "No need to candy coat it, we cannot protect her if she doesn't know everything."

"What if it doesn't work?" Madge asked with wide eyes as she stared at Grandpa sitting in his truck, picking at his teeth with a toothpick, oblivious to the conversation at hand.

"An incantation is a lot like a prayer. You ask. It's that simple," Christine said as she placed Madge's hand on the gravel. "Now, you're going to say two simple words. *Munda Eard.*"

"Okay, simple enough," Madge said as she patted the gravel feeling strangely awkward.

"Honey – you're forgetting to tell her the most important part," Dan said. "Remember to focus on what you're asking as you say it – that no one shall pass who intends harm. The intention is the most important part."

"Okay," Madge said.

"*Munda Eard*," Christine repeated, rolling her eyes at her husband.

"*Munda Eard*," Madge said, her tone like a question.

Immediately a shock of light shot up from the gray gravel, like a flash from a camera – causing Madge to jump and pull her hand away as she felt the heat of it, like a candle passing under her palm. She blinked down with her mouth open. The gravel had changed.

"Did it work?" Madge breathed, adrenaline still coursing through her body.

"Well done," Christine said with a nod of her head. "As you can see, rocks change color when enchanted – in this case, white and bright."

"What would happen to – something – if it tried to pass?"

"You're going to see birds exploding, feathers flying—"

"Stop it, Dan," Christine said with a shake of her head. "Only things that intend you harm. It's like an invisible wall. Nothing gets through."

Grandpa Ollie had the heater on high and the news blasting as they turned onto the main road, barely visible through the still thick fog. As Madge stared at the wet road ahead, hoping maybe he'd forego their conversation – he turned the heat down and the radio off.

"Streets are sure quiet today," he said as he cleared his throat.

"Well, I'd rather be home in front of the fire. Or still in bed. And not on the way to see a bunch of people I don't know, who were up all night, supposedly searching for me."

"Not supposedly, they were. Max will be there. You know Max."

Madge felt her stomach sink. *Max.* Had he been out searching for her, too?

"Your grandma used to love night swims, you know," he said, changing the subject.

"Seriously?" Madge asked, her stomach tumbling with excitement at the thought of her grandmother – who she never knew but from stories and pictures – in mer-form.

"I'd sometimes gear up and go swim with her. I couldn't keep up with her in the water, especially with the heavy gear we had back then, so it was rare I went along."

"I'm having a hard time imagining that!" Madge laughed.

"The point is, I have an idea, you know, of what drew you out there. Grandma used to do that sometimes – middle of the night and all. But it was safe back then," Grandpa said, throwing an icy sideward glance before focusing back on the road. "She loved it. More than anything."

"Sounds like Grams and I had more in common than I ever knew," Madge muttered, feeling pieces of a jigsaw puzzle coming together in her heart. "And you said Christmas was her favorite thing in the world."

"Okay, not more than Christmas. But close."

"It was *amazing*, Grandpa," Madge smiled widely, suddenly feeling the rush of her swim come back to her and the sheer bliss she'd felt. "What about Mom and Dad? Did they go for night swims?"

"It wasn't only at night. If they were in a secluded area, daytime was great, too. And your mom didn't. She was only half-blooded, remember."

"So? I'm only half-blooded. I don't get it."

"Half-bloods aren't supposed to be able to transform. Vala, yes. Mermaids, no. They are essentially a witch. But they have a unique Vala full bloods cannot have."

"So... I'm a half-blood. And a mermaid?"

"They actually have different words for all of this," Grandpa Ollie said, turning off the windshield wipers that were now screeching across the truck window as they drove through town, past storefronts glowing dimly in the thinning fog. "A half-blood, and unlike anyone else, you can transform into a mermaid – but your kind don't call it that. They call it *Saelfen*. A Saelfen is a full blood, which you are not. And that makes you an anomaly."

"Saelfen? That means mermaid?"

"Yes. Full-blooded. And half-bloods, like your mother, she was a *Merewif*."

"Why do they have different names?"

"Some old, dead language. I'm not sure which or where it came from, but I do know what they mean, literally," Grandpa Ollie said as he raised his bushy white eyebrows, chuffed with himself. "Saelfen means Sea Elf. Some argue Sea Fairy. Merewif means Sea Witch."

"So, elves and witches? I can't believe those words are coming from *your* mouth!"

"I learned everything I could, so I knew what to expect once Rachel was born," Grandpa Ollie said as his eyes grew distant.

The driveway to MEI was up ahead – and Madge thought quickly about the one lingering question she wanted to ask him before meeting Pearl. "My aunt murdered them, didn't she?"

"I wondered what was in that letter," Grandpa Ollie said with a shake of his head as he turned up gravel driveway. "She would have gotten the throne upon your father's death if it weren't for you. And she didn't know about you back then."

"So... the answer is yes?"

"Likely, her or her spawn, and likely at her behest, yes."

"Great. I have an aunt. And she murdered my parents and she likely wants me dead, too."

"It's a lot all at once, I know. And after learning what happened to your mom and dad last night... You have every right to be scared."

"I am scared, but..." Madge started as Grandpa Ollie took the key from the ignition, and they sat for a moment in the now silent truck, both staring out the front window. The fog was lifting, and she could faintly see a glimpse of the ocean, which oddly felt like what was happening in her mind. "All my life I had bad dreams of them drowning at sea. I never felt settled about it. They always just felt lost to me. And somehow, as shocking as the news was last night... To know my parents were taken rather than lost... actually it makes me angry."

"It makes you feel like something can be done instead of feeling hopeless. Anger can be a healthy emotion, if handled correctly."

"It's enough to push me to meet with Pearl and whoever else is waiting in there for me."

"Well, let's not keep them waiting."

"There she is!" Selene said as she opened the wide oak door.

"We were looking *all over* for you last night. How was your first swim?"

Madge opened her mouth to answer – and snapped it shut, noticing Max had appeared quietly behind Selene. He said nothing, but stared at her with a wide, serious expression; and if Madge didn't know better, he almost seemed... upset. Or angry. Madge's stomach sank. She was not exactly expecting a thank you – but a hello would at least be nice.

"I know. Sorry," Madge said, feeling her knees begin to wobble at the knowing way they were both smirking at her.

"Oh, please." Selene rolled her eyes. "I would have done the exact same thing."

"Would you now?" Grandpa Ollie snapped disapprovingly as he brushed past them into the house. Selene smirked, grabbing onto Madge's arm conspiratorially and whispered, "Next time you won't go alone is all."

Madge's stomach flip-flopped as she was led by Selene past Max, who still smelled like the wind on the sea as he stood by to close the door behind them, and her head was spinning with the fact that they knew what she was, and they were what she now was... But the minute she stepped foot in the foyer, her mouth dropped open as she looked up at a glass-domed ceiling overhead, flooding the entrance with natural light.

"Everyone is finishing breakfast," Selene said, letting go of Madge's arm and resting her hand on the doorknob to the right, which led into the dining room. "Ollie, Pearl wants a word with you if you don't mind," Selene said, opening it just enough for Grandpa Ollie to step inside. Madge caught a glimpse of a long table, and a room fit for a castle hall – and quite a few faces staring quietly back at her. "Max, take Madge to the living room—"

"Thanks Selene, I think I got it."

Selene rolled her eyes as she shut the door behind her, and Madge felt her stomach churn. The last thing she wanted right now was to be alone with…*him*. Max watched her warily, his brow furrowed in deep thought as he led her through the foyer. They passed under the double grand stairway arched above them, and into a huge living room area where floor to ceiling windows revealed the tall pines and ferns behind the house, with a view of a huge glass atrium that looked like a glass cottage in the woods.

Madge knew that atrium. It was the one they'd come out of after exiting the underground pools, through a hidden hatch in the floor. And instead of going into the house that day – which unbelievingly she realized was just yesterday – she'd rounded the outside and had gone home to read her letter where she could be alone.

"I can't believe there is a secret underground pool under there," Madge said, breaking the awkward silence as she stared at the atrium. "I can believe it's under this house. But there? Nope."

"Technically, it *is* under this house – but the entrance is through there."

Madge looked down the length of the room to the right, where oversized leather chairs and couches sat amongst low-lying shelves full of books and sculptures. To the left, a fire blazed in an open fireplace, the other side open to the kitchen where Madge could partially see a heavy wood table sat beside it. A large world map hung on an easel before the north wall.

"So… I wanted to see you before the meeting today," Max said, clearing his throat. "I haven't had the chance yet… to thank you. For what you did for me."

She caught herself staring at Max's mouth, unable to look up at his eyes – because if she did, she felt she'd melt into a puddle. "Thanks. You," Madge stammered. "I mean thank you," she said, finally meeting his gaze.

"What we all want to know," he said, his eyes searching hers, "is who taught you? To use your Vala?"

"No one," Madge breathed, trying to keep her voice from shaking. "I just felt… when Akira helped me in the parking lot, I knew I could do what she'd done for me. Somehow I just knew what to do – I felt it."

Max's eyes narrowed, and he held her stare until he finally shrugged and shook his head. "*Inliht* – the word you hijacked from Akira, means to enlighten. It's for clarity of sight and mind, so it's useful for Vala headaches or to help reveal hidden things."

"Sounds… useful."

"Old English can be kind of tricky to translate. Saelfen – and some Merewif study it from the time we can speak and learn to access our Vala, so you'll have some catching up to do."

"So, are you Elf or Witch?"

"Elf," Max answered with a crinkle of his nose. "But we never use that word. We do use witch when referring to Merewif. But that's just the English speaking of us – there are other words in other parts of the world by our kind," Max said, glancing up at the world map.

"*Right*," Madge said. "How many of us are there, then?"

"We are a very small percentage of the world population – but we exist in every part of the world," Max said, sweeping a hand over the map, which had various colored circles drawn over lands and oceans.

"What is the map here for?" Madge asked as she examined it closely.

"Looks like Pearl wants to teach you about the Nine."

"The Nine?"

"The land and oceans within these circles are the nine realms. The territories of the Royal Council of the Nine."

The Council. "My mom mentioned the Council in a letter – but she didn't elaborate. So, who are they? Or *what* are they?"

"That's what today's meeting is for," Pearl said, appearing behind them, looking as well-groomed and stately as could be, her long silver hair as if it was cut and styled hours ago.

"Madge, this is—"

"We met, more or less, yesterday," Pearl interrupted Max as she stepped forward and brushed a hand over the United States. "The Nine Realms – and ours here is the eighth realm." Pearl stood and assessed her with a cold, blank expression.

"The United States. Makes sense," Madge squeaked.

"And Canada, Greenland and Iceland," Pearl corrected before she pointed to the yellow circle below. "Mexico, Central and South America are the Ninth Realm."

"Nine realms... I get it. So, what makes up the Council?"

"The *Royal* Council of the Nine. Some just call it the Nine. Some, simply, call it the Council. Each of the nine realms has its own royal leaders, and the leaders form the Council. Royalty dictates leaders by birth rather than election," Pearl said, gesturing at Madge with an almost disapproving look. "It is a destined position and royal bloodlines are powerful and unique. Other positions, like the Regent, of course, are elected."

"Pearl is Regent here – *your* Regent. And President of MEI," Max added.

"Are Regents a part of the Council?" Madge asked, wondering with slight horror if Pearl was one of the people she was supposed to win over.

"Not officially, no – not in the way that matters. I sort of stand in until someone of the royal bloodline returns to the throne. I think I am the longest standing Regent in history. We've been waiting for your return for fourteen years."

"Did you know me when I was a baby?" Madge asked, her breath hitching in her throat.

"No. You were kept a secret, but I did know your parents rather well. They had me elected, after all. When I'm not acting as Regent, I act as Chief Advisor."

"She was Chief Advisor to your parents. They become Regent if anything happens…" Max said carefully as he shared a look with Pearl. "They chose her – as you would choose yours when you become queen."

Madge frowned at the word. She'd barely gotten used to mermaid yet – and queen was a whole other title she felt would be even more difficult to wrap her head around. She blinked up at Pearl, who watched her almost too closely, and thought about how her parents must have trusted this woman who oddly didn't seem to like her very much.

"Getting started without us?" Grandpa Ollie's said as he walked into the room, followed by Dr. Hiromi.

"Max was starting without us," Pearl said, arching a brow at him.

"She was asking," Max answered with a shrug.

"I was. My mom's letter mentioned the Council, and how I'll have to win them over. Now I know they're the leaders of the other realms – but why do I have to win them over, if it's my birthright and not won by election?"

"Yes," Pearl said as she let out a deep sigh. "The answer is complicated, I'm afraid. Your mother was queen – but she hadn't been accepted to the Council yet," she said as she pointed to the red circle. "The Hawaiian Islands, the Islands of the South Pacific, Australia and New Zealand make up the sixth realm. They were in favor of your mother being on the Council. Some realms accepted her, others did not."

"Okay… like a majority rules kind of thing. What about this one?" Madge pointed at the purple circle.

"The continent of Africa, and the islands of Madagascar and Mauritius and other outlying islands. The second realm. They're one of the older links in the chain. And no, they did not accept her. Not one little bit."

"Older links?"

"The Council is like a chain ring. Each link adds something, and your royal powers become connected. As time progressed since our kind came here – we have established new realms and so new links in the chain. It's been nine since not long after the new worlds were established – or rather, populated by Europeans."

"New worlds – you mean the Americas?"

"And Australia and New Zealand, of course," Pearl said with a sidelong glance at Madge. "Though our kind had been in those locations for a long time, we slowly established realms later on as the world progressed."

"That explains the ancient mermaid mythology," Madge said with enthusiasm as finally some things were starting to make sense.

"Quite right," Pearl said with a curt nod. "And this is the oldest of the realms," Pearl said in an exasperated tone as she pointed to Europe, circled in green. "Once our kind decided to start dividing power into realms that is. All Western, Central, Northern and Eastern Europe. And don't forget the far northern islands of Svalbard. The first realm."

"Did Europe – I mean, the first realm – want my mother on the Council?"

Pearl shook her head slowly, turning towards Grandpa Ollie who had made his way behind them. "They were the first to speak against it. She was the first Merewif that married into royalty, and they were afraid she'd be a weak link, so to speak."

"That's what she was working on," Grandpa Ollie said with a stony expression. "She was trying to win them over and prove herself. And look where that got her."

"Yes, but don't forget how many supported her. This realm here – the fifth realm," Pearl pointed to Antarctica, circled in pink. "They were all for it."

"So was the Ninth realm. But it's still not a majority," Grandpa Ollie grumbled.

"The Middle East, Turkey – and all countries between including India and Sri Lanka make up the fourth realm," Pearl said as she traced a finger over the orange circle. "They were against it. However," Pearl stabbed a finger at the countries within the black circle. "The seventh realm was the last to chime in. Russia, Kazakhstan, and Mongolia. They were on the fence, in a matter of speaking."

"That leaves China, Japan, Indonesia and the rest of Southeast Asia," Grandpa Ollie countered, pointing to the brown circle, leaving Madge to wonder why he was challenging Pearl. "And they certainly don't agree to a Merewif being on the Council, either."

"So doom and gloom, Ollie," Pearl said with a fold of her arms. "But true."

"Well, she needs to know what she is up against."

"I still don't understand why this feels like I have to win an election! I mean, didn't you say it wasn't an election – but a birthright?"

"Royal Leader of the realm by birth, but that doesn't get you *linked* to the chain. It doesn't get you a seat on the Council. The Council, I'm afraid, is by majority election of its members, unfortunately. It's a safeguard against tyrannical rulers – and our history has seen a good few of those, believe me."

"So why does the Council matter so much, then?" Madge wondered, hoping the answer would be simple enough for her to be able to blow the whole endeavor off entirely.

"If you aren't on the Council, you won't have the power for very long to hold off another thirsty royal Council member from unseating you. Any of their offspring – as long as the bloodline is royal – can take over power here. You're safe if you're on the Council. That's the simplest explanation I can offer, for now."

"Pearl has royal blood," Grandpa Ollie said as the thumped the map where the first realm stood. "And she hasn't unseated you. She was a deliberate and careful choice of your parents. She could have taken this realm for herself. And she's kept others from doing just that."

"The point is, once you are inducted into the Council, your powers grow. The power in your blood – between all Council members – becomes *linked*. Their powers become yours and your power becomes theirs. That is why many realms voted against your mother. Because she was a half-blood."

"Merewif," Madge whispered.

"Precisely. And she was particularly gifted in Earth Vala, which only human blood can access. Full-blooded Saelfen don't have that gift."

"Earth Vala?" Madge asked, turning towards Grandpa Ollie.

"Slow down a bit there, Pearl, she's only known her Vala was real for a day and you're moving into the elements. Let's stick to the Council today," Grandpa Ollie huffed, taking a seat.

"Come on, Ollie. It's simple," Dr. Hiromi said, stepping in front of the map as he waved four fingers in the air. "Earth, Air, Fire, Water. The Four Elements. But we have a more important matter to discuss," he said turning towards Pearl. "We think Madge may have been sighted by the Daeds last night."

"What do you mean? How do you know?" Grandpa Ollie said as he shot up from his seat. Madge didn't know what Daeds were, but from Grandpa's response – they must be bad.

"Because I saw it, and as you all know, I think I know a Daedscuan when I see one."

"Daed – what?" Madge asked as her head began to whirl.

"Daedscuan. We call them Daeds for short a lot of the time. They're Viviane's followers," Dr. Hiromi answered, though he was still making eye contact with Pearl as though in a silent conversation.

"Viviane?" Madge asked, her heart thumping in her chest.

"Your aunt," Grandpa Ollie answered, watching Madge's face closely.

"Is she blonde? Blue eyes?" Madge asked, feeling her eyes welling up as Grandpa Ollie silently nodded. "She… told me to tell Pearl hello."

"What." Grandpa Ollie said, barely above a whisper, his face drained of color. "You *saw* her? Your aunt Viviane?"

"She approached my car at school. Her and another man—"

"Malcolm," Pearl said in a low voice, her eyes wide. "Did they try anything? Hurt you?"

"No. She asked if I was new in town, a part of the Institute, and just said to tell Pearl hello. I didn't know she was my *aunt*. That I was talking to... *her*." Madge felt rage boil in her stomach. Especially when she remembered how the woman smiled at her. "What a *snake*."

"Oh, you have *no* idea. When did this happen? Where were you?" Pearl asked, locking her blazing eyes on Madge.

"It was the day after my birthday. At school. In the parking lot. She asked about my car... Said she liked it."

"She knows it was your mother's car. That is how she found you. And she had the nerve to say she liked it?" Grandpa Ollie smacked a hand on the couch. "That rotten, evil woman."

"She asked if I knew Pearl and to say hello. I felt sick, and she blew in my face—"

"She used her Vala to rid you of your nausea?" Pearl guffawed. "Wow. How charitable."

"I did feel better afterwards. And then... She just walked away and left. It was *weird*, and I had put it out of my head until now, when I heard her name," Madge rambled and her voice shook, and she felt like sand was in her throat.

"Pearl, this should have never happened," Grandpa Ollie said, his eyes on fire. "You came to town, brought the attention of the Daeds with you and my granddaughter like a flopping fish out of water."

"Please, let's all sit," Pearl said, gesturing to the tufted chairs and couches nearest the fireplace. "We'll double security efforts. That was an oversight, and it won't happen again. We never anticipated them to be here – to have found her so soon, and I have no clue why she and Malcolm left you – well, why they didn't hurt you. Because believe me, if you hadn't been at school…"

"That explains Madge being followed," Dr. Hiromi said. "They've been following her – they know where she is, where she lives, and it all happened a heck of a lot sooner than we imagined. But why they haven't done anything to her yet is beyond me."

"So tell us about this Daed you spotted then. Anyone you recognized?"

"It was a young woman. She had long dark hair. I don't know who she is, but her black scales were as dark as any I've seen. She deflected my attack towards her, and I was almost hit in the process. She disappeared after that."

Madge felt a chill crawl up her spine as she realized with a gulp that someone – maybe the same person at the faire, she wasn't sure – had been following her last night.

Maybe even her aunt. Or that man.

"Any sign of my estranged wife?" said a tall, bearded man who bounded into the room and sidled up near Pearl's chair with his arms folded. He reminded Madge of a Lumberjack, with a faded flannel shirt folded to the elbows and large, hairy forearms, one a faded tattoo of a pin-up Sailor girl.

"Well, I suppose now is as good a time as any, Robert," Pearl said to him with a shake of her head. "Madge, meet Robert Olander. Your Uncle."

"My – my what?" Madge gasped, staring at Grandpa Ollie for confirmation, then back at the burly lumberjack – her *uncle* – and saw that Selene now stood behind him, glaring at Pearl.

"And this is my daughter Selene. Your cousin," he added apologetically.

"We would have told you sooner, but…" Selene's voice trailed off as she sat with a thud. "For obvious reasons, I couldn't exactly tell you about us. Until you, you know, *knew*."

Madge took a deep breath and tried to organize her thoughts. She looked over at her *cousin* and her *uncle*. Her *family*. All her life she'd wanted family. But these were *strangers*.

"Grandpa, how did I not know about this?" Madge asked with a high-pitched voice.

"We didn't even know you were born, your mom kept you such a secret," Robert answered instead. "My wife didn't know, thankfully – I'm sure you've heard about her by now."

"I met her, apparently," Madge said, feeling heat rush to her cheeks.

"What? How?" Robert said, eyes flashing.

"She's not hurt, nothing happened, but she paid Madge a cheeky visit at her school, but I'll fill you in later, Robert," Pearl said, waving a hand in the air. "And Madge, they didn't know about you," Pearl said, gesturing to Robert and Selene, "Not until after your parents died did anyone say a word about you. You were being hidden from Viviane when your mother's belly started to show she was with child."

Madge tried to let that sink in – *the evil aunt*. This was her estranged husband and *daughter*. This woman had a child of her own? Madge couldn't help but stare aghast at Selene.

"Well I have never met her – well, not since I was a toddler… And believe me, I wanted to tell you we were cousins. It took a lot of effort not to spill the beans, trust me," Selene said under Madge's stare, looking awkward for the first time possibly ever. "But obviously that was impossible and not a good idea until you were told or figured out who you were."

The room grew quiet. Everyone seemed to be staring at the floor – apart from Max, who was watching Madge carefully as though she might break at any moment. She felt like she could.

"Selene and I have our thoughts about how Madge could win over the Council of the Nine," Max said as he sat forward in his chair. "Saelfen don't contain earth Vala. But a sitting Royal in the circle of the Nine – a Merewif who does have it – would give the Royal Saelfen Vala that power."

"Yes, we know that – that's what Rachel tried to convince them of," Pearl said softly as she cast a glance towards Grandpa Ollie.

"But from what we have been told, and unknown to everyone until now, she has full Saelfen power but she's not full-blooded. Rachel did not have that ability," Max countered. "No one *ever* has."

"Full Saelfen power – you mean the ability to transform?" Madge asked, wondering what was sparking behind Max's eyes.

"That, and what you did for Max," Dr. Hiromi spoke as though he'd seen the light with a snap of his fingers. "Your ability to heal him – without the use of a potion. That marks a distinct Saelfen ability. I wouldn't be able to do that, for example, because I am only half."

"But… Akira – your daughter was able to heal me without a potion, and if you're half-blood, then she would be too, right?"

Dr. Hiromi shook his head, his eyes still flashing with that same epiphany light as before. "I adopted her from her mother who is no longer with us. Akira is full-blooded. I am not."

"So, I'm a half-blood, but I'm able to do things only full-bloods can do – transform and… whatever," Madge said, rubbing at her temples. "And that will win the Council over?"

"Well – it's that and more," Pearl said in a surprised tone. "Your Vala, by what we've seen in just a few days, is… well it's shocking. Your ability to do things with no training especially – and yes, the fact you can transform though you are not full blooded. You contain distinctly Saelfen abilities. Now if you can also perform Earth Vala… which those with human blood have, and Saelfen do not – you'll truly be one of a kind." Pearl's eyes glazed over as she thought deeply on what she said. "What you are – what we are discovering about you – it's true. This gives us new reasons to hope."

"Holy Moses," Robert said. "When Viviane finds out…"

"Hope for what, though?" Madge asked, ignoring her uncle.

"Hope that you win the Council, which should be near impossible, seeing your mother could not," Grandpa Ollie said with a fold of his arms.

"Did your mother or father mention anything about this in their letter to you? About what their plan was that was worth risking their lives for?" Pearl asked.

The words from their letter rang again in her mind. "I must have read it a thousand times last night. I practically memorized it. But she didn't say what their plan was. Only that I'd probably win the Council over because I could transform."

"Yes, we get that part – but did the letter mention anything about what they were doing or what they were after when they left home?"

"No. None of you know?" Madge asked as she stared at Grandpa who shook his head.

"No one knows," Pearl said with a lift of her chin, looking between Madge and Grandpa Ollie. "We have theories… But

I find it hard to believe they didn't tell *one* of you."

"I had assumed it would be in the letter," Grandpa Ollie looked at Madge with a bewildered expression. "She didn't write anything? Nothing at all as to what their plan was?"

"No…" Madge breathed. "Just that I could."

"Her plan might not matter anymore," Dr. Hiromi said, looking at no one in particular, as he paced near the map of the world. "She was trying to prove herself, not you. You have things she did not, as we've all agreed here today. What you have to focus on now is proving yourself to the Nine. You need your own plans, and that means Vala training, princess." Dr. Hiromi turned and faced her with his hands behind his back. "It has been agreed that I will begin your training in Air Vala. I like to think of it as the foundational element."

"Earth, Air, Fire, Water…" Madge said with a half-smile.

"Yes, one you are already familiar with as you used it unknowingly to help Max. Air Vala. So, this part of your training will likely go quickly."

"When I heard about what my niece did for Max the other night," Robert said with raised brows, "and with no training – it made the hairs on my neck stand up," he said as he held his large forearm in the air. "Thinking about it now… I get goosebumps."

Madge felt heat rise to her cheeks upon hearing the word niece. "I'd heard Akira use a word, so I used the same one," she said with a shrug. "I knew it was for healing because she'd just used it on me. I just felt a need to do it, so I did – and it just happened to work."

"It's not just the word, Madge," Dr. Hiromi said as he shook his head and flashed a smile. "It's the focus and intention that matters – and how much power you have to back it up, of course. There are a lot of words and incantations, but their job is only to help formulate intention and clear focus. In fact, focus and intention will a big part of your training in Air Vala. Something you appear to have a good grasp of already."

"But is there a timeline? When exactly do I need to convince the Council?"

"When you officially come of age and I can no longer officially be your Regent," Pearl answered with a tap of her finger on the arm of the couch. "When you're eighteen."

"Oh. Well, that gives me plenty of time!"

"Time runs differently in the eyes of the young," Pearl said with a sigh.

Dr. Hiromi cleared his throat. "You have a lot of catching up to do especially if one of your appealing talents will be Earth Vala – that element takes the most time and is the most difficult," he said as he removed his glasses to clean them. "Earth Vala is… untidy, if not even a bit chaotic; it's potions and spells, and, depending on your giftedness at this craft, abilities become exponential with practice. Add an ingredient here, take it away. Mash or chop. Strain? Drink? Make it into a powder? There are infinite possibilities."

Pearl lifted a finger in the air. "And a truly gifted Witch can create new spells not yet discovered. The abilities of a Merewif are something any Saelfen would love to have. The power to create something new," Pearl said as her eyes flashed with excitement. "We all benefit greatly from it – throughout history. Merewif Vala explodes with possibility. Earth Vala is raw, creative, and unruly. The Royals – they fear it. But they want it."

"So… if I join the Council, and our Vala is linked, they'll get Earth Vala abilities, too? Because I'm partly human, I'll have this ability no matter what. Is that right?"

"We *assume* you'll have it – but we have yet to see," Dr. Hiromi said, looking pointedly at Pearl as though it was something they hadn't yet considered. "Because you are showing Saelfen power and yet you're a half-blood – so we cannot be sure. No Saelfen has Earth Vala, so why would you?"

"Oh, she will," Pearl said with a casual wave of her hand. "She must. To be on the seat and connected to the Nine heightens and strengthens your Vala – for all of you. The gift of one becomes the gift of many. So, to answer Madge's question, yes. And the more gifted you are with Earth Vala, the better."

"That's why everyone is so against my mother becoming queen," Selene said with an antagonistic and angry tone, her eyes lined with silver. "Let's address the elephant in the room, shall we? The fear is that if Viviane were ever to find her seat on the Council, that her dark Vala would infect the entire globe and Saelfen existence, because her dark Vala would affect the other Nine and the royal Vala chain would never be the same!"

"Your mother wouldn't stop there," Robert growled. "She's never liked humans – barely tolerates half-bloods. She'd aim towards a new sort of world dominance over humans, mark my words, and I'm not the only one who thinks so."

"She's evil and everyone hates her and blames her for all the bad things that have ever happened!" Selene screeched, shooting out of her chair. "Russ and Rachel are not to blame at all – oh no! They just did what they pleased, no matter the cost! Love for each other came before all – ALL OF THIS!"

"Selene! That is enough!" Robert's voice boomed.

Max got up from his seat and tried to put a hand on Selene's shoulder, which she promptly shoved off.

"If this is all going to work, and she is so *special* and destined to be our queen, why have the cuffs not returned? Ask them about the cuffs that disappeared with your parents," Selene said before she stomped away, slamming the door behind her as she disappeared around the back of the house in a flash of white-blonde hair.

"I'll talk to her—"

"No, Max, sit down. She is not your responsibility," Robert said, rising to chase after her, but Pearl held out a hand to Robert—

"Let her be," Pearl said before turning a tired expression towards Madge.

"Cuffs?" Madge squeaked.

Pearl pinched her nose and sighed. "They are the Vala objects that link the Royals to the Council. Your parents both wore one – all the royal leaders of the Nine realms do."

"But I thought you said my mom wasn't on the Council."

"Even without a connection to the Nine the royal cuffs have other protective properties, and those worked for her," Pearl said, twisting the giant ring on her bony finger. "Objects can be charged with Vala, but to link powers or entities together through an object requires greater Vala… one that the others linking it all together have to agree to and enact. Hence, there is a ceremony involved that inducts the wearer of the cuffs into the Royal Chain, hereby known as the Council, which fuses your Vala together. Your father was linked. But… they never gave your mum that chance."

"In short, what your cousin was trying to warn you about was that not only do you have to convince the Council to let you in – but you need at least one of the cuffs to do it," Robert said.

"But Selene said they're lost – how am I supposed to get one?" Madge asked, frowning.

"The cuffs are lost for now in some kind of magical limbo. They will return to you – when it is time. You may have to do a little digging."

10

The Saelfen Vault

All Madge associated the Royal Vault with up to now was her aunt stealing an ancient relic. So, when Pearl said it was housed beneath the atrium, hidden in the back of the secret pools – Madge imagined something the size of a closet – perhaps a large walk-in closet. But as she followed Nico and Pearl through the steaming aqua underground, where water slipped down in wide silvery berths into the pools below each chamber they breezed past, she wondered what exactly she was in for.

They reached the far end, stopping in front of one of the waterfalls, and the hair on Madge's arms prickled when she followed them into a hidden pathway circling behind it.

Pearl faced the wall, flipped up a hidden keypad concealed within the rock and entered a code.

"We use technology and Vala to protect this place. Double whammy," Nico explained as he watched Madge's perplexed face.

"It's impossible to know anything is even back here," Madge said, turning to face the cascading water behind them, "I mean, no one would be able to see us back here. And even if you were to see us or even the pathway – there isn't any sign of a door, let alone a keypad."

"Precisely," Nico said, ushering Madge towards the heavy rock wall grating slowly open that Pearl stepped through the minute there was enough room to squeeze past.

"Quickly, it closes immediately after opening. Nico will wait outside."

Madge stepped through with trepidation – wondering what was back there that had to be kept so secret. And as the wall sealed shut, blocking out the sound of cascading water pouring into the pool behind it, she turned to face the vault.

But this room was practically empty – until Madge realized that whatever was back here was hidden behind a heavy, red velvet curtain that was drawn closed, open just a crack peeking into a cavernous room beyond it...

But Madge didn't have time to register anything through that peep through the curtain, because a ghostly figure with long dark hair and a dress that flowed all around her like she was an angel descending from the heavens was floating towards them from the other side.

Trepidation turned to terror as Madge paced backwards until she slammed into the rough stone wall behind her. "What is that?" she squeaked.

"That is Giuliana. She is a Sea Nymph," Pearl said through a smirk as though holding back a laugh at Madge's horror.

Giuliana squeezed between the curtain like a wisp of cloud, and apparated before them.

Madge wanted to run but there was nowhere to go—

A wake of minty, cool air breezed onto Madge's face. It was familiar somehow, but... terrifying. Her presence felt as powerful as the ocean itself.

This thing – this Sea Nymph – had her shimmering, indigo eyes locked on Madge's, and she was frozen under their stare.

Fathomless eyes... Like staring into the Pacific, like they saw straight through her.

Madge blinked, and blinked again, and tried to swallow but she seemed to forget how. Giuliana was the most beautiful, terrible thing she'd ever seen. And up close, rather than a ghost the sea nymph looked like a woman suspended in water, as even her hair floated around her face and her white gown flowed behind her as she moved. She was a phantasm of watery light, and as she moved the light spilled through her, like a body of water nearest the surface, a dance between light and the depth of water it tried to penetrate.

"Madge." Giuliana said, as if she knew her.

"Giuliana, this is the royal heir of the eighth realm. Madge Ferriter—"

"I know very well who she is. Welcome, Princess," Giuliana said as her essence seemed to calm, as if the water all around her, holding her in the air had gone still, her hair settling around her shoulders. Then the curtains drew back on their own, as if by a phantom hand.

"A sea nymph's Vala flows from a deeper well than you or I could fathom. It's what she's made of, and that makes her formidable and unstoppable if the wrong person were to step through here. Follow me," Pearl said, stepping past the curtains.

Madge squeezed past the sea nymph as quickly as she could without running – and almost tripped as she took in her surroundings. The massive cavern located somewhere below the Institute extended further back – and *up* – than she could have imagined.

"This looks like a *cathedral!*" Madge said, craning her neck to the ceilings.

Rough, square-cut stone columns ran the length of the vault on each side, making it seem it had simply been carved from the rock and the columns left standing. Chandeliers bathed stone-arched ceilings with golden light. Between the columns and beneath each arched ceiling were intricately carved cabinetry, leather armchairs, and artwork lining the walls, each section separated by the same red velvet curtains in the entry, drawn in by a hook on the wall.

"We told the builders that we were building a private chapel and fallout shelter down here, hence its Cathedral-like design. Those shelves there were built to resemble a shrine, or an altar you'd see in a church for that reason as well," Pearl said, gesturing to the far end of the vault, where books spanned the entire back wall, framed in by intricate corkscrew columns and arched nooks. A floating staircase spiraled up to a lofted walkway in the middle to access the shelves, and sliding ladders were on each floor to reach the higher stacks.

"That's a lot of books..." Madge breathed.

"Yes, and we'll get to that. First, I want to show you what's hidden in the cabinets."

"Relics and artifacts?" Madge said with a sharp look towards Pearl. "Like the head?"

"Yes."

"So why is this so secret – is this stuff worth a lot of money or something?"

"Nothing is down here because it is valuable monetarily. It is down here because it contains power or an important historical record to our kind and needs to be protected. But

Giuliana does more than protect this space – she's also your card catalogue, so to speak. She knows the material in here better than anyone."

"Giuliana?" Madge asked with a shiver as she glanced sidelong at the sea nymph who was floating alongside them silently, every move like she was swimming underwater, her gowns flowing around her like a painting of a goddess.

"Yes. Now, each cabinet holds relics of a similar nature. One in particular I want to show you," Pearl said as she gestured towards a cabinet against the wall in the middle of the vault. "This is where we shelf the *mysterious.* Things we know have power, but we do not know exactly how," she said as she opened it on each side. "The relic your aunt stole was here," Pearl said, indicating to an empty spot on the very top shelf, where a placard read *Mimir's Head*. "We have left this spot empty in the hope that we will get it back. Someday."

Madge took a step closer to get a better look at the curious objects within the cabinet, and as she did so the hair on her arms shot immediately up as she felt an otherworldly, strange power humming from inside. She searched the shelves, trying to pinpoint where it was coming from, when she realized everything in here could be culprit. A large stone tablet with rune symbols… a silver comb and matching mirror… a black jeweled necklace hanging from a marble bust… until finally her eyes settled on a large golden quill with a glass pot of deep red ink. But looking closely she knew it wasn't just ink as she pointed to it and asked, "Is that – *blood?*"

"Yes. Unfortunately, all these items are from sinister creators or have been confiscated for sinister reasons, so we haven't tried nor wanted to uncover what these items can do. Some we can imagine or guess – like the quill and blood ink. We suspect it's a form of dark Vala used to write curses. The pages it was confiscated with were burned in the hopes it would release its victims. We do not know whose blood it is, nor have we ventured to find out," Pearl said as she closed the cabinet, quieting the humming that had entranced Madge. "You'll need to learn how to deal with the power that emanates from these things before you spend significant time with any of them," Pearl said through a raised eyebrow before pointing to another cabinet about ten feet away. "Especially that one, which I will not show you until you familiarize yourself a bit more with your Vala and how to protect yourself. That one houses dark Vala items in which we do know their function, and we rarely open it. Those were confiscated with a clear knowledge of what they do."

Madge looked at the closed cabinet and shivered. "How do you keep track of all of this? I mean – if someone comes down here, how would they know what these things do?" she asked, wondering what had possessed her aunt to steal the head from the vaults. If Mimir's Head was shelved in the mysterious section – how did her aunt know it was worth stealing? Her mother had written it was said to be a voice between worlds. Whatever that meant.

"We keep a ledger with a brief description and notes as to where to locate books – historical records and journals – to research each one. A quicker way, however, would be to ask the resident Sea Nymph."

"These are organized by year, and then are organized in a number of ways. Anything you want to find, any subject, any spell, any ingredient – I can get it for you," Giuliana said with a small incline of her watery head. "To the left are historical journals and records, and some secret, important or official documents, perhaps. To the right we house spell books and tomes from former royals, or anyone who sees a vision of particular importance, or notable new spells and potions, for example."

"Spell books? I want to see one!"

"You'll have plenty of time to look at anything you wish – but let me conclude my tour with you up there, where you'll find by far the best view of the vault," Pearl said as she headed up the stairs.

The steps wound up and up, and looking up the spiral from the bottom reminded Madge of the inside of a conch shell. The oak banisters were smooth, and she was grateful they were there to hold onto because by the time she got to the top, she was almost dizzy.

"You see, this is the best spot in the place," Pearl said with a sweep of her hand.

Looking out over the vault was worth the climb, even if the height they were at kept Madge clinging to the shelves behind her. They were eye level with the chandeliers, and somehow the vault looked even bigger from here.

"Careful what you touch, please. Remember, the books are organized by year and then alphabetically, so the ones highest up are also the oldest," Pearl tutted as Madge released her grip on the shelves behind her.

"How old is the oldest book here?" Madge asked with her head cranked up, balancing her hand on the sliding ladder that reached almost to the ceiling.

"As old as the sixteenth century," Giuliana answered. "There weren't many books before then, as things were more commonly recorded on scrolls and in other primitive ways. Those items are in some of the cabinets below, but we do have even older, ancient books."

"They aren't traditional books like you're probably imagining," Pearl said.

Giuliana shook her head, as her long dark hair trailed around her ivory neck. "A fine example – not to mention the oldest in our collection – dates back to somewhere around six-hundred BC. It contains six sheets and are all made from twenty-four karat gold in which the letters and images were pounded, not written or drawn. The Etruscans that made it were wiped out by the Romans when they were expanding their empire."

"Who were they – and what is their book about?" Madge asked as she tried to imagine what a book made from pure gold would be like.

"I can answer this question, if you don't mind," Pearl said as her eyes flashed with excitement. "The Etruscans were an ancient civilization that depicted mermaids in their rare artifacts because they suspected or knew of our kind. They are just one of many if not all the ancient cultures that believed in mermaids in some form or another. Mesopotamians, Sumerians, Greeks, Aborigines, Inuit, many Native American tribes, Aztecs, Assyrians, Egyptians, Celts. I could go on and on. In many civilizations, mermaids were even treated as deities. Which we are not, but a little show of *magic*, as humans call it, and there you have it."

"You say mermaids. But I thought we are supposed to call ourselves Saelfen?"

"We use the modern English word humans do when we talk about what they *believed* us to be, especially when depicted with the tail of a fish and a naked torso. But who knows what they did in the ancient world – maybe they were often naked when they came from the water."

"It wasn't only the ancients," Giuliana said as she floated over with a large modern book. "Take a look at this painting of the first Queen Elizabeth, who heavily relied on the British Armada to strengthen her reign. Do you see anything peculiar in this painting?"

Madge studied the depiction of the powder-faced queen, in her huge dress with puffed sleeves, sitting in a chair in front of images of a warring armada. Her red hair was coiffed behind a pearl-like crown, her hand placed on a small globe of the world. Finally, Madge's eyes darted to the gilded figure of a mermaid in the bottom right corner of the royal chair she was sat on. "There's a mermaid on her chair! Was Queen Elizabeth Saelfen?"

"Yes," Pearl answered with a lift of her chin. "And one who tried to wipe out half-bloods and discourage breeding with humans – by accusing them of witchcraft in order to turn the human populace against them. One popular test was to submerge those accused in water. If they floated, they were a witch. Merewif cannot hold their breath underwater as a Saelfen can. If they sank, they were innocent. It was meant to suss out those caught doing magic to differentiate between them."

"She reminds me of my aunt," Madge commented, earning a snort from Pearl.

"Undoubtedly," Pearl said with an arched brow.

Madge ran her finger along the spine of a book with a green cover, titled *Greek Mythology and Saelfen Influence of the Hellenistic Period*. The historical records were standard old books, some with beveled spines and often dark colors and gold printed titles, but the books on the right – the spell books and tomes – were books of every size and color imaginable.

"I've got to see one of these spell books," Madge said, reaching out to grab one, but Pearl stopped her with a light touch on the shoulder.

"Giuliana can help you in the future with these on the higher stacks. For now, you can handle any you can reach from the ground floor," Pearl said as she began the descent back down the stairs. "There is one in particular I want to show you."

Madge skipped the last steps to the bottom floor, eager to see what a real spell book would look like. As she stood before the shelves at the bottom, she noticed many of the books appeared to be leather or canvas journals – and there were even what appeared to be regular lined composition books. Some had feathers, bone, sticks… One seemed to *move* on the shelf, even.

"The tomes we keep here are the most gifted spells and discoveries of their time, and your mother created some of the best I've seen in my lifetime," Pearl said as she handed Madge a heavy leather-bound book. A long, braided strap was wound around it, partially concealing the raised leather oak tree with a face in the middle which had two amber stones for eyes.

"Was this…" Madge's heart was racing so much she couldn't finish her sentence.

"Your mother's tome, yes. The stones protect it – if in the wrong hands, it won't open."

Madge froze as she held it in her hands. She couldn't even begin to formulate the thoughts that raced through her mind. Her mother had enchanted this book. Why would she do that? And what kind of spells were within?

Madge swallowed against the lump that rose in her throat.

"I can't wait to read them," she breathed, unable to peel her eyes up to look at Pearl.

"Take your time. I will take my leave now, but should you need anything, Giuliana will assist you," Pearl said as Madge heard the click of her heels walking away. "And feel free to look around. There are some masterpieces hanging on the walls."

Madge waited until she could hear the grate of the rock wall as it slid open, then the sound of water as it echoed from the pools and the wall grating shut again, before she began to unwind her mother's tome book with shaking hands.

"Not that I ever sit in them – but I'm told the chairs are extremely comfortable. Why don't you go have a seat?" Giuliana said as she gestured towards one of the leather armchairs behind her. "I'll be right back."

Madge plopped down in the giant armchair, brushing her fingers over its leather cover, pausing on the raised stones in its middle. The vaults were chilly – but the stones somehow felt slightly warm. She had just begun to unwind its leather strap when Giuliana returned.

"Before you try to read your mother's tome, I wanted to show you this," Giuliana said, holding what appeared to be a large scroll, wound around two wooden holders. "You won't be able to comprehend her work if you cannot read the runes in this scroll. I promised your mother I would deliver it to you – and to tell no one."

Madge blinked at Giuliana as she tried to process the words she'd just heard. "She told you? About what she was working on?"

"Her work began after she was pregnant with you, and then

they went into hiding and she only came back to the vault once – and it was to get this to you if anything were to happen."

"Was the work in her tome anything to do with winning over the Council or does it point to why she left or what she was after, by any chance?"

"Perhaps. But first things first, we have to see if you can decipher this scroll," Giuliana said, handing it to Madge. "Don't worry about its age and how delicate it should be. Merlin used a Vala charged vellum, so this scroll is not fragile like other scrolls from its time."

"*Merlin*? Are you talking about *the* Merlin from Arthurian Legend? The Wizard?"

"Yes, *that* Merlin. Although most legends peg him wrong."

"NO WAY!" Madge couldn't help the excitement that escaped from her lips. "I'm just – a huge Arthurian legend fan!"

"So, you know some of the theories as to where his power came from?"

"Yes – there are a few, but I think what you're about to say – I mean, I could imagine if he had magic abilities – famous ones in his time, seeing he was a very powerful wizard," Madge blabbered excitedly before she looked up at Giuliana, "he must have Saelfen blood in his veins somewhere," Madge breathed, meeting the nymph's swimming indigo eyes.

Giuliana nodded, and said, "One popular theory is that he was born to a human woman, probably a nun, sired by an Incubus."

"Sired? Like, made a knight? And what is an Incubus?"

"Sired by in this instance indicates procreation – the father. And an Incubus is sort of a daemon, or some say a vampire. The victim would be called the succubus, in this case the female. But it's all wrong."

"Who were his parents? Or *what* were they?"

"Merlin's mother was, in fact, a human woman. And she was not a succubus – not a victim. And Merlin's father was no daemon, or vampire. He was Saelfen. A Royal Saelfen who had his fun before marrying his queen."

Madge gaped at the scroll in her hand and her mother's leather-bound tome, sitting in her lap unopened. "What does Merlin have to do with my mom's work? And why is it a secret?"

"Your mother had reason to believe that Merlin found a way to allow a Merewif to transform and earn Saelfen abilities. That was her work. If the information were to fall into the wrong hands, it could be squashed and lost forever."

"Do you mean to tell me that was her *plan*? To find a way to transform? That was how she wanted to win the Council?" Madge's jaw dropped open. "But I do – *transform*. Apparently, that is what will win the Council for me. But she knew that, too."

"Her work wasn't just for her. It was something to prove that Saelfen bloodlines would not be bred out. That Vala would not eventually fade from this world. That was what she wanted to do to stop Viviane, to ensure your future and a better future for *everyone*."

"But didn't she figure it out? Is that how I transform?"

"No. You were born to be what you are," Giuliana said, her tone serious. "The matter at hand is what you will do with her work. Will you continue it? What will *your* plan be?"

"I have no idea – you haven't told me *how* she intended to… what the spell in this scroll entails. If she couldn't do it, why would I be able to? And why was she traveling thousands of miles away to accomplish a spell?"

"I cannot say. She didn't have the chance to tell me everything."

"Why didn't she tell anyone else? Pearl? Or Grandpa?"

"To protect them, I imagine. For the record, she told me because I am the Royal's Keeper of Secrets. I am her safest choice if she wanted something well protected. But – she told me she'd be writing you and her father a letter."

"She did!" Madge snapped her fingers as what her mother wrote came to mind. "She wrote they may have found something that would negate being a half-blood. She didn't elaborate – but I guess… Merlin's work is what she was alluding to. My question now is – seeing you're the *keeper of secrets* – where are these royal cuffs that are lost somewhere in magical limbo?"

Giuliana cast a strange look towards Madge, and said, "If you figure out what your mother was working on – perhaps they will return to you. All I can tell you is she left specific instructions to get you the scroll. Open it."

Madge's hands shook as she unrolled the vellum on her lap. The text was written neatly in gold and sectioned in columns, but she couldn't read it. The characters and letters were strange.

"What language is this?"

"It's written in runes. It was a secret runic alphabet and symbology that Merlin enchanted. If you're meant to read it, you'll be able to."

Madge stared at the gold text. Her eyes darted around the page as she tried to at least make out a letter, but she saw nothing she recognized. Nothing that could look like it might be an H, or a Q, or any possible letter in the English Alphabet.

"I don't get how I am supposed to be able to read this."

"Focus, breathe, relax… the runes will appear—"

"It's a language I can't read. I don't think high school Spanish is going to cut it here," Madge said as she felt a drop in the pit of her stomach and was about to give up—

When the runes began to blur – and *rearrange*.

"Wait! It's moving!" Madge squeaked.

The gold symbols stirred and danced, making her feel dizzy, until she noticed line by line and letter by letter… *words had formed*. Madge gasped and held her hand over her mouth, dropping the scroll as though it could bite her.

"So, you *can* read it?"

"Yes. It looks like a poem," Madge said as she stared down at the ancient parchment, the text now plain before her eyes. "And Merlin really wrote this?"

"He did. Would you like to read it out loud?" Giuliana asked, flashing a smile that danced like sunlight on water.

Madge's stomach bubbled with excitement as she took a deep breath and began to read.

Light shall illuminate thee
Angels sing from Heaven
Waters quench thirsty Earth
Green sprouts, new Life
Moon and Sun, gaze upon thee
And all the Creatures of the waters, air and earth
Sing, call, and listen
And on this day, he stood
And He rested between Light and Dark
It was Good, it was Wondrous
Dawn of a new day
She listened to his call
She rose to help him

But Evil bit from the Tree
Fruit left to decay
Banished they were
Those that sing
Those that listen
A voice calls from the heavens
The blood of an innocent
Heals old wounds
Rise!
Behold, she comes to help
Singing from the deepest waters
A new creation rests within
Blood shall be one, sing, listen!"

Madge blinked at the page as she finished reading. "How is this... a spell? Where's the eye of newt and cauldron bubble?"

"You'll find many spells rhyme or seem poetic. They're easier to chant and remember that way, for starters. Some were even sung. But I never said it was actually a spell."

"Well, what is it then? Is it a prophecy of some kind?"

"Your mother thought it was. Until she read the history of our people from that time, and how Merlin was working on a spell... one that would make him like his father. He was an illegitimate son, after all."

"To be like his father – Saelfen."

"Study your mother's tome, and you'll find hidden notes on this scroll. She drew pictures and enchanted them so they would be revealed only to you."

"Kind of like what just happened with the runes, then?"

"Perhaps," Giuliana said as she floated away, "I'll just be in the painting if you need me."

"In the painting?" Madge called after her, as Giuliana drifted across the room towards a twenty-foot rendition of a storm-thrashed sea... And Madge watched wide-eyed as the nymph *melted* into the canvas. Disappearing.

Madge shot up from her chair and approached the painting, depicting a titanic wave smashing into a rocky shoreline. Giuliana was barely a watery shimmer, frozen within the squall's crest, her hair splayed out amongst the splash and sea foam. Even more unnerving was that Madge could see and feel her sea nymph eyes watching her.

After gaping at the picture until her eyes burned, Madge turned back to go finally unravel and read her mother's tome. She tried to ignore the feeling of being watched, which she knew was just Giuliana in the painting. But when she unwound the braided leather, staring once more at the image of the magnificent tree on the front – she wondered if its amber eyes were somehow watching her, too.

Madge took a steadying breath and opened the front cover.

Her face cracked into a smile upon the very first page, where *Rachel Ferriter* was written amongst a jungle of leaves and flowers. Its pages were a heavy, textured paper, and spells had been meticulously recorded with vivid images of ingredients – such as elderflower, fire, smoke, cauldrons and alembics, the spells neatly written out in small handwriting next to the images – colorfully recorded with a few in black and white using pencil or charcoal.

Madge finally stopped when she felt her fingertips tingle on a drawing of parched earth, with a sprig of green shooting up and a drop of water suspended above. It was the same tingling she'd felt when she'd helped Max. The same tingling she'd felt in her feet when her Vala returned on the ocean just days ago. Something tugged at her, deep in her gut.

Giuliana had said there were *hidden* notes… Was this drawing hiding something?

Madge scanned Merlin's scroll until the lines jumped out at her—

Waters quench thirsty earth… Green sprouts, new life.

Her heart was pounding as she stared at the drawing again, the tingle growing within her fingers as she touched the page. But nothing seemed to be happening. No words appeared – nothing moved on the page…

She was about to call out for Giuliana when out of nowhere a thought struck.

Max had said that *Inlīht* was a plea for clarity – not only for healing magical migraines, though staring at the picture was about to give her one – but it was for *revealing hidden things.*

Last time she'd used the word, however, things had gone terribly wrong. She felt Giuliana's watchful eyes and bit her lip – if anything happened this time, hopefully the sea nymph would come to help…

She spread her fingers wide over the page, squeezed her eyes shut and blurted – "Inlīht!" – like it was a dirty word. And when she was brave enough to open her eyes…

Nothing had happened.

The drawing was just the same as it was before.

Madge threw her head back in the chair and grumbled. "Giuliana, you can come out now! I can't do this!" she yelled across the room at the painting. "Giuliana?"

But Giuliana didn't stir. Perhaps because the nymph could see she was on to something?

So why didn't it work?

Madge chewed angrily on her lip until she recalled what Dr. Hiromi had said was most important when tapping into one's Vala – *focus* and *intention*. And what Dan had said – it was like a prayer and as simple as asking. She'd said the word, scared to say it, without thinking of what she'd wanted it to do.

Letting out a big huff as she closed her eyes, Madge asked for clarity and for whatever was hidden to reveal itself. *"Inlīht,"* she whispered, and slowly opened her eyes.

Now something was moving!

Like the text had moved earlier in Merlin's scroll, she saw the drop of water swirling on the page, as small handwriting popped up inside it: *Water Sings.*

Madge felt her heart race as the drop of water splashed down to the parched earth, not daring to so much as blink, as fractures began to appear... and formed words: E*arth Listens.*

She waited for more to reveal itself; but just as quickly as it started, the movement on the page ebbed away until it stopped altogether.

"Giuliana!" Madge squeaked, sprinting over to the painting Giuliana was residing in with the tome still in her hands. "Um... If you can hear me, I found something!"

Apparently, that was what Giuliana had been waiting to hear, as the water in the painting sparkled and the nymph rose from it right before her very eyes, like a drop of dew that drips from a leaf, her ghostly shimmer floating as she craned her head in question. "Pray tell?"

"A picture," Madge said as she held up the drawing for Giuliana to see. "Words formed. It said *water sings* and then it said *earth listens*. I stopped on it because I could sense there was something there – and then it reminded me of a line in Merlin's scroll."

Giuliana reached a watery hand to Madge's chin that sent a

chill through her body, the wet feeling leaving a minty touch behind that lingered long after. "That's a good start, and there are many more drawings. But that's probably enough for today."

"What? Why?"

"Vala works up an appetite and besides, you'll need time to absorb, think and figure it all out. There's too much to uncover this afternoon. And you're new to all of this, remember."

Madge's stomach growled, as if agreeing with the nymph. "I'm starving, actually."

"You have strong instincts. I was surprised you were able to do what you did so quickly," Giuliana said, assessing her with curious, fathomless eyes. "You are able to unravel your Vala without instruction."

"I feel like *I'm* coming unraveled."

"Well, I urge you to continue to let it happen, Madge Ferriter."

11

Air

Three minutes to go.

She had been counting the minutes since she'd sat down, her eyes sliding between the clock on the wall and the window, streaked with rain. Today would be her first lesson with Dr. Hiromi after school, and though she'd started the day feeling excited and a little nervous about it, ever since second period history class, when Madge was reminded how much she had to study for tomorrow's history test, her excitement had turned sour.

When the final bell rang Madge was the first one out as she whooshed past students pouring into the dimly lit hallway. She skidded to a stop at her locker and as she heaved her gargantuan history book into her backpack, she felt a tap on the shoulder –

"Hey," Selene said with a small smile as Madge blinked back at her, tongue tied, seeing it was the first attempt she'd made to talk to Madge since she'd erupted that day when she'd been told they were cousins. "Good luck today. Not that you need it."

"Thanks," Madge said, trying to hide the surprise from her tone. "You want to ride with us?" she asked as she glanced over Selene's shoulder at Tristan and Drake, who waited in the wings like they were her bodyguards.

"I told Tristan I'd go kayaking with him and Drake after school. But don't tell anyone. I'm studying with them if anyone asks."

"You're not grounded anymore?"

"No, I'm still grounded, so… I just stopped to say good luck," Selene said as she turned away to join the twins. "We are on for that swim soon, by the way."

"How about now?" Madge shrugged, half serious. "If we could get past Nico that is."

"Oh, there are ways," Selene said with a mischievous grin, turning back towards her.

"It's not my first… it wasn't my first swim, alone – the other night. I used to go out, *sneak out*, all the time. Until now. They watch my house around the clock."

"*Nice.*" Selene smirked at her conspiratorially. "But… Yeah, ever since you mentioned my mom paid you a visit they won't let you out of your sights until this blows over. Pearl can be strict, and Nico can be… overbearing. But like I said – there are ways. Trust me."

"Don't tell anyone. It's sort of a secret."

"I won't. I get it, I understand that ocean thirst more than you can imagine. We will go, *soon*. Speaking of overbearing – I heard Max has to ride home from school with you?"

"He never said he *had* to. He just asked for a ride," Madge said, feeling her stomach sink. "Why does he have to ride with me?"

"Because they don't trust me to, that's why."

"But they follow me everywhere now. I mean, *everywhere*. So how does it help if he's riding in the car with me when Nico is following me around anyway?"

"Nico is paranoid," Selene said as she turned and grabbed Tristan's hand and waved goodbye. "*Swim*. Soon!"

Madge slammed her locker shut, watching her cousin's blonde head disappear down the hallway. Now she really felt a fool – when Max asked her for a ride after school, she was happy about it, somehow. He was even nice about it. But to know he had done it because he'd been told to… She had a bone to pick with Max.

Madge pushed past the double doors and bee lined towards Ash's rusty brown Honda. She saw Max leaning against it, with a bored expression, and it agitated her even more. She wished she had her own car – so she could drive off without him. But it was the first time her best friend had driven them to school since Madge had passed her driver's test and inherited Taffy. They'd hoped it would throw the black sedans that followed them every time they went anywhere these days, but as sure as rain there it was, idling on the street curb. And Nico was there, waiting as usual, his eyes on Madge the minute she'd exited the building.

She could hardly wait to take that swim with Selene and risk being grounded and everything else, because she was watched every second of her life now. It was maddening. "And there he is," Madge grumbled as she waved at Nico, when she'd rather throw him a middle finger. "I'm surprised the school allows them to wait there every day – he looks like he's ready to kidnap someone."

"More like he's ready to escort the President," Ash said,

rolling her eyes.

"Selene finally talked to me – wished me luck for today," Madge said to Max before climbing into the passenger seat.

"I told you Barbie would come around," Ash remarked with a roll of her eyes.

"Don't call her that," Max said, shaking his head.

"So, her and Tristan are a thing, huh?" Madge asked, watching Max carefully as he tried to move papers, shoes, garbage and books away from where his feet were supposed to be. She wanted to ruffle him, and it seemed mentioning Tristan was a good way to do it.

"She doesn't last long without a boy toy," Max said, his expression angry. "And come to find out his parents used to support Viviane."

"Say WHAT?" Madge screeched, turning all the way around in her seat to watch the red Jeep and Selene fading from view.

"We found out the night of the Halloween faire – but yeah. They're Saelfen, never Daeds though, and we aren't sure where they stand now – but they've been quiet a long time, so…"

"I – I've known them since junior high!" Madge shrieked.

"And dated one," Ash chimed in.

"Not *really*," Madge said, her cheeks flushing as she slapped Ash on the leg. "But she's still allowed to hang around them?"

"Not exactly. But Selene doesn't do what she's told to – or what she's told not to, for that matter. She's acting out worse than ever lately."

"But why? Because she's forbidden to see Tristan?"

Max was quiet a moment, his face a storm of thought. "That and all the reminders lately that her mom's such a monster."

"Reminders *lately*? What's that supposed to mean?" Madge

swiveled around in her seat again to look at Max, who shook his head like he didn't mean to say that part. "Come on, Max! You owe me. You asked for a ride today and come to find out you're babysitting me on the car ride home. You could have just told me that, you know."

"I didn't want to make you feel... I needed a ride home anyway."

"Max, come *on*," Madge said through gritted teeth. "What are these *reminders lately* about Viviane supposed to mean?"

"There was talk about some new case that could be linked to her mom," Max said with a shrug, but continued when Madge kept her steely gaze fixed on him. "She was sort of kept in the dark when anything came up about Viviane and the Daeds – no one talked about it around Selene. But lately things are heating up a bit and it's hard to keep everything from her."

"Kind of like the way everyone is keeping things from me," Madge said, meeting his eyes – and shame flickered in his expression as she turned away from him to face the front.

"Speak of the devil," Ash said as she drove past Selene, who was hugging Tristan around the neck by his red Jeep. "Barbie seems fine to me."

"Fine," Max grumbled, finally seeming to give in a bit. "Viviane recently has been taking out Saelfen who don't live by the old laws and leaving clues that leave a trail so we know it, but without leaving hard evidence behind so it can officially be linked to her."

"Old laws?"

"The old laws were enacted by the realms and agreed to by the entire Council. They were enforced to forbid romantic relationships between humans and Saelfen. They loosened the laws in the sixties, but they think she's doing it because she knows you're back and she's trying to stir things up... amongst other things."

"She's stirring things up because of *me*? What other things?"

"Isn't that what this is all about? Why you're being followed all the time?" Ash said.

"Exactly, Ash. Madge is back – and the only thing really standing in Viviane's way. She's always been in her way, because she's the rightful heir to the royal seat."

"Killing my parents wasn't enough?" Madge said as her hands form into fists. "What did she do this time?" Madge asked, feeling sick that bad things were happening because her aunt wanted her out of the way.

"I don't know specifics," Max said almost too carefully. "I only pick up bits and pieces. But that's why my mom and dad have been gone a lot."

"You said they were away for work and I hadn't thought to ask what for – I just assumed it was for MEI. You know, marine ecology stuff – not *Saelfen* stuff. So, they're investigating something, then?"

"They found a body somewhere around Mount Hood – and a couple in the San Juan Islands not long ago, and they're traveling around following leads."

"They're sure it's her?" Madge asked with eyes like saucers.

"Oh, yes."

"But how do they know?"

"She bleeds and brands her victims – the brand is always fresh. It's the same firebrand they were giving Merewif when we battled her the first time around."

"Branding?" Madge asked with an incredulous expression. "She *bleeds* them?"

"Bloodletting is used in dark Vala – who knows for what

purpose she's using it from dead victims, though. They're finding pricks – like fang marks on various parts of her victims. They aren't completely bled out, but she's taking some, for some reason."

"I can't believe she's Selene's *mom*. I can't imagine what that would feel like," Madge said, feeling nauseous that she was even related to this woman.

"I'm trying very hard not to like her, but I feel sorry for her in that way, too," Ash said as she turned into the driveway of MEI. "I'd be angry at the whole world if I were her."

As Ash pulled her rusty brown Honda to a stop, they sat in silence a moment, staring out the window. The Institute glowed in a premature dusk, the cloud cover so heavy that the sunset looked like a thick blanket had been hung over a lamp, and the outdoor lights were haloed in heavy mist that not only fell from the sky but was also blowing in from the ocean.

Max set a warm hand on Madge's shoulder, and Madge almost flinched at the touch. "We are not keeping things from you, for the record. But there's only so much you can learn at one time. And I'm here because I want to be here, not because Nico told me to. Selene is not the only one who doesn't always follow the rules."

As they followed Max into the kitchen, Madge felt more nervous than ever as she saw Dr. Hiromi was there, sat at the long table by the blazing fireplace, holding a cup of tea in one hand and a book in the other. "Pearl whipped up some scones for you guys. They're still warm from the oven, help yourselves," he said, barely looking up from his reading.

Porcelain teacups, silver spoons and fine China had been

laid out next to a platter piled high with golden scones, kept warm with a teacloth laid over the top.

"That horrid weather outside called for a bit of cheer," Pearl said as she breezed into the kitchen, dressed in a crisp brown and gray tweed vest, "so I also whipped up some clotted cream, and steeped some proper tea in the teapot there."

"What she means by *proper* tea is a brand she buys in the UK," Max said with a roll of his eyes. "And she says the *only* way to drink it is with milk and sugar."

"Yorkshire Tea," Pearl said as she patted Max's cheek. "These have been Max's favorite since he was a lad. Better get some before he eats them all," she said, arching a brow at Max who was already scarfing one down without a plate.

"Say – Madge," Dr. Hiromi said as he got up from the table, "once you're finished here, we'll have our lesson in the atrium. Akira will be joining us."

"Kento and I need to have a quick meeting," Pearl said, brushing Max's crumbs from the table into a palm while throwing him a glare that had him quickly grabbing a plate.

"Perfect," Madge lied, glancing at her watch as her stomach flip-flopped.

"Can I sit in, too?" Ash begged with her hands folded under her chin.

"Not today," Dr. Hiromi said with a shake of his head. "She will need concentration and no distractions. Sorry."

As Pearl and Dr. Hiromi disappeared from the kitchen, Madge finally plopped down in a chair near the fire, relishing the smell of burning cedar mingling with Pearl's fresh baked goods. Max placed a scone piled high with clotted cream onto her plate, which she promptly shoved into her mouth. "Divine," she said through a mouthful, savoring the warm buttery flavor that mingled with the sweet cold cream.

"I wish your lesson could be here," Ash sighed.

"That makes two of us," Madge agreed, remembering the damp and earthy atrium, as she readied another scone. "I just want to study for my history test – and ignore all of… this!"

"Ignore what?" Max said, taking a break from stuffing his face as he turned in his chair to level his eyes on Madge.

"All of the expectations. Being followed every step I take, anywhere. Starting… in a few minutes," Madge said as she looked down at her watch, "I'll be judged as to how well I can perform Vala and how quickly I can make up for lost time."

"You don't *perform* Vala. It's there. You access it, use it. Performing it sounds like magic tricks."

"Yeah, we'll see. I might have to pretend and use magic tricks by the time all of this is over," Madge huffed as she shoved off from her seat.

"I thought you'd be excited," Max said, his perfect brow knit with confusion.

"I thought so, too. But… Nothing feels *normal* anymore, and I'm about to dive into more – *abnormal*. It feels like a rug is being swept from under my feet."

"You're calling us – me – abnormal?" His face swept into a rare smile as he chuckled and shook his head. "Today will be easy, *lunita*."

"Lune-what-a?" Madge asked, feeling her face heat even more.

"Lunita. It means little moon," Max chuckled, shrugging his shoulders.

"Why are you calling me that?"

"Your skin – it's as white as the moon."

Madge stomped away to the sound of Ash choking on her

tea – and when she was out of their eyesight, her frown spread upwards, and it stuck like glue all the way through the back of the house and out the back door. Whatever Max had just done – whether it was flirting or truly making fun of her pale skin – it had taken her mind off her nerves for what laid in front of her: her Vala lesson in the glass atrium, steamed up from the cold rain.

She stepped inside, walking past plants stood in neat rows, the smell of wet dirt and flowers in the air. Dr. Hiromi sat with Akira at a long, heavy wood table in front of alembics, mortar and pestles of different sizes, books, metal bowls, and glass alchemy sets bubbling away, and above their head herbs and seaweed hung from hanging racks.

"I'm so excited you're here! I made something for you," Akira said, hopping up from the table and handing over what looked like a diary with a heart-shaped lock on it.

"Thank you – what is it?"

"Notes I compiled for you to learn about Air Vala. It's short. Don't worry. But only you can open it. It *looks* like you need a key, but you need only say *onspen*, and it will open for you and you alone. Try it!" Akira said, unable to withhold her excitement.

"Owns. Pen?" Madge said, as the book flew open in her hand. "Whoa!" Madge laughed as she dropped the book in surprise.

"It's spelt *o-n-s-p-e-n*. It means open – not only to open something literally but to open something that is hidden," Dr. Hiromi said, making Madge think of her mother's work – the tome and the scroll… the hidden notes.

"Does it work on other tomes – or books or like, hidden notes, for example?"

"It depends how well protected the hidden thing is. But it's a fine first example of some of the uses of Air Vala – willing the energy surrounding something to your will," Dr. Hiromi answered, casting a curious gaze on Madge. "Why do you ask?"

"Oh, just curious! Last time I was in here I was rushing through it," Madge said as she ogled over her surroundings, trying to quickly change the subject as she took a seat.

"Ask away! These first days of training are important. You're building a foundation for the rest of your learning!" Dr. Hiromi said as excitement flashed in his eyes. "The foundation of your Vala lies in your ability to harness it – to reach in and *grab* it," he said, placing a fist in the air, "no matter the element you are conducting! But it's important not to overthink it and to allow yourself to *feel* your way through this. Does that make sense?"

"I think so, yes." Between healing Max and asking her mother's tome to reveal hidden words – so far all of it had been following a feeling.

"Now, let me ask you, what *is* energy? Do you know?"

"Not really…" Madge answered with a shake of her head.

"Energy is heat!" Dr. Hiromi said as his face exploded in a smile. "All matter contains heat energy. Energy cannot die – it's a *source*. To harness your Vala is the same as harnessing energy – which is in all matter, all around you – and doing something with it. You can't see it – but it's there."

"So Vala is in the air," Madge said, as she thought of the tingling she felt when her power had prompted her so far.

"Precisely!" Dr. Hiromi said with a clap of his hands. "Sometimes using Air Vala, you can call on the wind – there's nothing solid there that you can see. But you can feel that wind, can't you? The basis is energy itself in this element. It's the beginning, the spark, the foundation. Kind of like the spirit inside you."

"That makes sense," Madge said as she thought about her soul and how it exists though she couldn't see it.

"But you can't create something from nothing. Nothing creates nothing – you need something, matter, energy – to conduct your Vala," Akira said, lighting a match in front of her face. "Heat needs fuel to generate, like fire needs wood to burn. Fire cannot burn without it. Energy needs fuel to generate, in the same way heat needs fuel to generate."

"That's my kid!" Dr. Hiromi said, beaming.

"So, in order to call on Air Vala, or energy – I need fuel?" Madge asked.

"Exactly!" Dr. Hiromi slapped the table with excitement. "And *you* are that fuel."

"Is that why I get hungry and tired when I use my Vala?"

"That's precisely why!" Dr. Hiromi said, sharing an impressed glance with Akira. "Which brings us to the fundamental part. Think of your Vala as a well. It's there inside you. A normal human cannot draw from it because it is not there. They don't have the fuel, but you do. And your ability to draw from the well will be the deciding factor in how far you get," Dr. Hiromi said with a nod towards his daughter. "And Akira had a great idea to illustrate this point."

Akira pushed forward a tall glass of water that had been layered inside with raspberries on the top, blueberries in the middle, and a layer of crushed mint at the very bottom of the glass.

"Think of this glass as a well. When I draw water from the top," Akira said as she dipped a spoon into the very top and drank it, "I only taste the flavor of the berries and mint in the water."

"She can taste those things, but she didn't actually eat those things because she didn't reach far enough down to scoop them up with the spoon. The water and the ingredients in the glass represent your well of Vala. By drinking the water at the top, infused with the flavors from the other layers, she has reached an *essence* of Vala. This is the first tier in the well."

"If I go deeper, I can reach a raspberry," Akira said as she plucked out a raspberry with her spoon and ate it. "That is the second tier."

Madge wondered which tier she'd gotten to so far. "So, there are four tiers?" Madge asked as she sat up in her chair. "So – how far did I get when I helped Max?"

"It's not exactly a measurable science," Dr. Hiromi said with a wave of his hand. "And we aren't sure because we haven't experimented with your particular capabilities yet. But we want to help you figure that out – how deep you can draw from your well. It takes practice and focus and breathing. When you breathe in deeply, as far as you can go, you can feel that well, like you're standing on the brink. Then call your Vala. Try it."

"You want me to hold my breath and call my Vala? To do what with it?"

"Just hold your breath and focus on the well you feel inside as you stand at the brink."

"Okay, here goes," Madge said before sucking a deep breath in. She kept her eyes locked on the glass ceiling overhead… And held it… And kept holding it until—

"What's supposed to be happening?" Madge said, releasing her breath in an exasperated woosh. "I am not feeling anything other than dizziness."

"What did you feel when you helped Max?" Akira asked, her dark, upturned eyes fixed on Madge. "You've already done this. *Think*."

Madge felt a rush of warmth hit her cheeks. "I just thought about how... sad I felt... and how I needed to help him."

"Yes – but did you feel anything physically? Any changes in breathing?" Dr. Hiromi asked, cleaning his glasses from the condensation steaming the lenses.

Madge looked down at the table as she recounted that horrific scene – of Max's drawn face on her lap that looked like he was in pain. And then she remembered the tingle she'd felt all over her body – even on the tip of her nose. Lightning, heat, energy... *Vala*. She had felt it in her fingers when looking at her mother's tome, too. "Tingling. Like when your hand or leg falls asleep. But all over."

"Bingo! Access that and try again, but this time go ahead and close your eyes."

"Okay," Madge said apprehensively as she did as he asked.

"Now, picture yourself at your well, whatever that looks like to you... and when you're ready, take a deep breath and hold it, stare into that well and call your Vala up to you... Until you feel it. Once you find it, you can let your breath go."

As Madge kept her eyes squeezed shut, sitting with so much air in her lungs she felt she could lift off her chair – she imagined herself standing not at a well but before a dark ravine. Wherever *this* was, it was cold. She couldn't make out a moon, but bright stars were peeking through the clouds, and she could smell and faintly hear the ocean somewhere not far away... But it was the sound of rushing water in the ravine that drew her attention – and though she couldn't see how far down it went, she felt the light, tickly feeling of standing on its edge, giving her a sensation that it was a long way down.

As she felt her chest growing tight, she stepped closer to the edge to try to see the bottom of the ravine – to find her Vala and call it up. As she stepped on its edge, the fear of falling into it intensified the tickling in her belly… until she realized that feeling in her stomach was it. It was her Vala, saying hello. Struggling to hold her breath just a tad longer, she leaned further down, the tickling swirling in tighter circles until it her skin was tingling all over…

And then she was falling.

She didn't know if she'd slipped or simply leaned too far – but she was going down. As she fell, she could faintly hear Dr. Hiromi's voice asking her to open her eyes…

But his voice cut out as she hit the water – and her body pushed down until her elbow scraped a rock. It was freezing, frigid water, and immediately she felt her body transform as her skin became tight, coppery scales and her fins pushed her back to the surface, where she gasped for air.

And somehow – she was still *here.*

The walls rising around her were slated, dark rock, much of it covered in thick moss, and a natural arch stood above her head upstream, where a small cascade of water poured through, revealing a tall waterfall behind it.

It was beautiful here… but something was coming.

She'd felt this way before – the day she'd gotten her Vala back and fell into the water at the tidal pools… And she remembered what had accompanied that horrible feeling that still haunted her at night. *Singing.*

As if in answer to that thought, the same lament-filled sounds could be heard in a far-off distance somewhere, until it swept down and touched her ears like a breath of wind. As Madge's heart began to race, the singing grew... echoing off the steep rock walls around her as if the voice and whoever sang it was coming closer—

And it had Madge in its thrall.

As the beautiful, terrifying song flooded out even the sound of the waterfall behind her head, Madge felt her neck prickle. She knew that feeling and knew she was being watched... that someone was there now with her.

She wanted out – why couldn't she wake up?

Madge wanted to scream for help, but she couldn't move, let alone make a sound. She managed to crane her neck up to search the cliffs above her head when—

SPLASH!

Whatever it was – it was *here*.

In the water... with her.

The only sound now was the sound of rushing water. It was quiet – too quiet.

She squeezed her eyes shut – willing herself to wake up, too afraid to see what was in the water – honing her ears to hear the faintest sound coming near –

But she felt it before she heard anything.

Someone – or something – stood right by her, so close she could feel breath on her face.

Cinnamon.

"Open your eyes, *Merewif*!" hissed a familiar voice, one that sent shivers up Madge's spine—

"*Munda Eard!*" Madge screeched a second later, recalling the first incantation that came to mind and was supposed to keep bad things away, her whole body tingling with Vala it felt like her skin was on fire. "*Inlīht*! Wake up!" she screamed as she thrashed her arms out to push away from the living nightmare she was in.

Her arms were hitting something hard behind her – and she stopped thrashing when she realized she was on *solid ground*. She slowly opened her eyes.

Madge was on her back – on the floor of the atrium.

Tears streamed down the sides of her face as she looked up at Dr. Hiromi and Akira who were both leaned over her, looking as terrified as Madge felt. And as she tried to catch her breath, she realized that her hair and clothes were wet – as if she'd actually been *in that place.*

And then Madge *screamed*.

"Akira – go get Pearl," Dr. Hiromi said through pale lips as Akira immediately obeyed her father in a flash of dark hair.

12

Blood Vala

Violent shivers had taken over her body and hot tears streamed down her face.

A vile of something had been forced down her throat – something so salty it had sent her into dry heaves. But whatever it was, at least she was *here*... she was *back*.

But that haunting singing was back, ringing in her ears like a relentless echo...

Madge chanced squeezing her eyes back open – as sight and sound came rushing back into focus. Max and Ash were here now, too – and Max was sitting on the floor with her, holding her tightly against his warm chest.

"The revivification potion won't be enough. She seems to be in a little bit of shock," Dr. Hiromi said to Max as he reached for Madge's hand and pressed his fingers into her wrist. "I'm not a medical doctor, but—"

"What are you a doctor of, then? Should we take her to a hospital?" Ash demanded.

"I'm a marine veterinarian, but it's not conventional medicine she needs," he said as he pointed his head at Max.

"She needs a Saelfen healer."

Max shook his head and said, "Akira is bringing Pearl—"

"You can do this, Max. Before we do need conventional medicine and a hospital."

Max's heart was racing – Madge could feel it on her cheek. She felt his chest rise and fall with a deep, steadying breath. "I've got you," he said, gathering her in an even tighter embrace. Another deep breath as Max placed his mouth by her ear – "*Friðospéd*," he whispered, his breath tickling her ear.

Heat radiated from his hands and spread, battling back each and every shiver that crawled up her spine and wound around her stomach. Max's scent of wind on the ocean breezed through her as slowly warmth made its way up her arms and neck, until she felt it flush her cheeks and forehead, finally reaching the crown of her head, seeping into her bones, the tremors gone...

Her head clear.

And Max's arms tighter than ever around her.

"Thank you," she mumbled into his chest, biting back a sob. She wasn't ready to let go yet, or even lift her head – no matter what the others were thinking, she didn't care – and she wasn't sure she could stand yet even if she tried. She felt Ash's arms wrap around her back as she heard the door open and the click of feet rushing in – Pearl.

"What on earth?" Pearl gasped, seeing Madge soaking wet and everyone gathered on the floor around her.

"She's coming to now – thanks to Max."

"You can call it even now," Max said, still pressing his cheek into her hair. "And before you ask, Friðospéd is an incantation that begs for the protection of peace."

"Not just peace," Dr. Hiromi said with an approving smile,

"but an overwhelming abundance of it. I'm not Saelfen so I can't heal without use of a potion – but if I could have, I couldn't have thought of a better word to help relieve her shock. Well done, Max."

"Get her inside and into some dry clothes," Pearl said, shaking her head. "And then we'll sit and have hot tea by the fire while you all explain to me how she is on the floor, soaking wet."

The fire was almost too hot, and Madge's tongue was burnt slightly from the hot cocoa Max had brought her in lieu of Pearl's tea.

"Madge was asked to access her well of Vala, just the basics. And I think she went there – traversed somehow – but I don't know. I've never seen this before," Dr. Hiromi answered Pearl, whose mouth was in a thin line.

"It wasn't a well," Madge said as she put down her mug of cocoa and discarded the blanket across her lap. "It was a steep ravine. And I *was* there."

"So – what happened?" Pearl demanded with an almost slight reprimand in her voice.

"I fell in, and then… *she* was there with me," Madge said as she remembered the horror with a shiver up her spine.

"Who? Who was with you?" Pearl asked.

"At first whatever it was felt… like a demon in a bad dream, when you can't move. It… *sang*. The song was… it was beautiful, but it terrified me. It's as if the words were what kept me there, unable to move. I kept my eyes squeezed shut—"

"What was she – or it – singing?" Pearl asked, her brown eyes narrowed.

"I couldn't make out the words, but... she did say something. She told me to open my eyes and called me... a *Merewif*. Like it was a bad name."

"You say she like you know who it is, Madge." Akira said, her voice steady and gentle.

"I can't be sure it was *her*. I don't see how it could be. I heard the same haunting singing underwater when I fell in and realized I was a mermaid – when my Vala came back. I don't see how that could be..."

"Viviane?" Pearl asked, her eyes flashing in alarm.

Madge nodded, biting her lip. "I am not sure what's worse. Being stuck in my Vala with her there, the one who murdered my parents, or a demon that sings and makes it so you can't move. It was like... She was *both*."

"I just don't understand how she could have gotten to you," Dr. Hiromi said, his expression puzzled. "We've never seen or heard of anyone actually travelling to that place where we are meant to imagine our well of Vala residing in," Dr. Hiromi said, half in wonder and half in contemplation. "Who's to say what that person or thing could be if it too, was able to step into your consciousness... Able to step into *your* Vala?"

"I barely had time to look around before I felt her coming for me. I could feel it – I felt the same thing when I fell in and my Vala came back, and the singing came with it. Like something was coming. Something bad, something... wrong."

"You may not know what the words were saying – but can you describe what it sounded like?" Dr. Hiromi asked as he sat forward in his chair.

"It echoed... like it was coming from many places all at once. It sounded... beautiful – but also sad... and... *terrifying*. Like it was the voice that rooted me to the spot."

"There are stories…" Pearl said carefully, "ancient legends, if you will, from our kind – of creatures that sing and lure victims to their death."

Dr. Hiromi nodded his head in fervent agreement. "Sirens. The closest comparison in human literature – that I know of – exists in the tales of the Odyssey, when creatures called sirens sang to lure sailors to their deaths. But our kind recorded sirens to be far worse than what the Odyssey described."

"Great!" Ash exclaimed, grabbing onto Madge's arm, "You're saying these Sirens are real and they sing—"

"It's not a siren," Selene said loudly as she entered the front room, with Tristan and Robert on her heels. "It's my mother," she added.

"What is *he* doing here?" Max asked he shot up from his chair, pointing at Tristan.

"Believe me, I was about to run him off the property," Robert said with a hand in the air, "but, you're all going to want to hear this."

"Go ahead," Selene said as she squeezed Tristan's hand.

Tristan shifted on his feet, his face flushing crimson as he answered, "Viviane told my mom about some kind of blood Vala she uses to find Madge."

Madge felt her stomach tighten into a knot as Tristan's words echoed in her ears.

"And?" Selene said, nudging Tristan. "The potion?"

"And my mom was asked – by Viviane, I mean – to get a local witch – I mean, healer, to brew her a potion. A potion to help your Vala when something is sucking it dry."

"A *warding* potion? Against what?" Pearl asked, her tone clipped.

"I don't know."

"You're admitting your mother is in cahoots with Viviane and the Daeds?" Dr. Hiromi asked, his jaw clenching.

"Not by choice," Tristan answered, staring down at his feet. "She's threatened my mom, and my dad. Says she'll hurt me and Drake if we don't do as she says, basically."

"A little hard to believe, considering Vince and Scarlett Abano were on our local watch list as Daed sympathizers," Pearl said almost too softly, staring back at Tristan's shocked face that she knew his parent's names. "Why not come to us sooner, if that's the case?"

"Most sympathizers no longer support her after she went into hiding as you well know," Selene said, flicking her long ribbon of white-blonde hair over a shoulder, her chin in the air as she spoke to Pearl. "Apparently, mother dearest knows how to scare people into submission. They're terrified. It took a lot to get him to come here tonight, so give him some credit."

"It's not that I'm terrified. I don't want anything happening to my brother, or my parents is all," Tristan said, shuffling his feet.

"You seem to hate half-bloods, judging by the way you behaved towards me at the faire," Dr. Hiromi said, meeting Tristan's shocked eyes.

"That wasn't me. That was Drake. And… I'm sorry. For the way my brother treated you. We have been taught to – I mean—"

"That's his apology to make, not yours," Dr. Hiromi said, waving his apology away. "Was it him, at the faire? The one who hurt Max?"

Tristan's eyes grew wide as he shook his head. "No – no! We wouldn't – we were with Selene the whole time. But I did hear that one of their Daeds – a younger chick, I think, was tasked with spying at the faire. She was dressed as a raven—"

"Chick?" Pearl said, nostrils flaring.

"That creepy mask!" Madge exclaimed, remembering how the presence of just one Daed had made her stomach turn and her head foggy. "It was following us around!"

"We did tell mom – who told Viviane – where Madge would be that night, though. And I'm sorry for that, too – but—"

"She basically threatened their lives," Selene cut in. "They're not reporting to her anymore, though, on Madge's whereabouts—"

"Yeah, right!" Max said, glaring at Tristan—

"Not truthfully, anyway. What we're here to tell you, if you'd stop interrogating and picking on poor Tristan," Selene said, throwing an icy glare at Max, "is they'd found Madge before the Abanos were forced to spy. That's how they found the Abanos – was because my mom, Viviane, found Madge using blood Vala – but it's a *familial* blood Vala, which is how she found me one day, too."

"Found *you*?" Robert barked, looking as though his eyes would bulge from their sockets. "Are you out of your damn mind? And you're just telling us this – after *everything* your mother has been doing lately?"

"Yes. We were kayaking. She found me," Selene said, her face paling.

"And I don't suppose Tristan and Drake—"

"No! I just told you. She can find me anytime, or Madge, using familial blood Vala. Can't you listen to what I am saying for once?" Selene looked so frustrated she could cry.

"Let her talk. What did she do?" Max said softly, his face crumpled with worry.

"She had the relic. She dragged me down from the kayak... Tristan and Drake were up ahead..." Selene paused as she watched Max's expression go dark, his jaw clenching as he glared at Tristan. "They were racing, Max. It's not like they have to make sure I won't drown or anything."

"Fine. I don't care about them. What happened with your mom?"

"She had the relic," Selene said, shivering. "And she tried to tell me that I would be princess soon, and a bunch of other garbage. She's crazy. It was... horrible—"

"How long have you known about all this?" Madge shot up, feeling rage boil in her stomach. "Viviane found *you*, and you haven't had the nerve to tell anyone about it?"

"I just found out she knows how to find you! I didn't know until now—"

"Let me guess, you were hoping to rekindle a relationship with that *monster*?" Madge fired back, her adrenaline pumping so hard her hands were shaking.

Selene's face tightened, but she shook her head. "*No. Simmer down, princess*—"

"Hey," Tristan cut in, placing a hand on Selene's shoulder. "You said you were going to try, remember?"

"Don't call me princess, *cousin*. And besides, sounds like you are the one who wants to be one. I could care less." Madge said, and she meant it.

"Alright you two. We are getting off point here," Pearl cut in, her voice ringing in warning as she fixed eyes of steel on Madge. "Why don't you sit down and let Selene finish telling us what she so bravely came to tell us about?" Madge remained standing with a fold of her arms but kept quiet, even though she wanted to scream.

"I'm *sorry*," Selene said, laying her palms open in her lap as she sat with a thud. "You and I aren't exactly close enough... yet... for me to tell you about how my mom found me one day and how horrible it felt to meet her acquaintance for the first time since I can remember."

Something loosened in Madge's chest. She met Selene's eyes – and saw it. The sorrow and pain. The fear.

Selene rolled her shoulders and continued with icy calm. "Look. Dad just told me what happened to you before I could walk through the front door. He wasn't going to let us inside, but we were already coming here, to tell you all about the blood Vala and Viviane, and it's obviously only a coincidence that this is all happening all at once but – I *know* it was her. It had to be."

Everyone sat in shocked silence for a moment, staring at Selene who still locked eyes with Madge – neither seeming to want to back down.

"It doesn't add up," Madge said with less edge to her voice, her hands flailing. "Why didn't she come after me before, then?"

"Your *Vala* is the link – without it she couldn't find you," Tristan answered. "Apparently she found you the day your Vala returned."

Madge's breath felt like it was knocked from her chest as she remembered the singing she'd heard, plunged momentarily into the tidepools the day she'd transformed. She'd had her Vala return. And just now – she was in her Vala, when she heard it again. She sat with a thud as a shocked look passed over her face. "But it felt like something was with her, that singing... I don't think it was *her* voice."

"She's using the relic," Selene said with a shake of her head, as she looked around the room at all the scared, shocked faces.

"The one she stole? Mimir's Head?" Pearl asked, her voice a mask of calm.

"Yes. That face of nightmares with snakes for hair and fanged teeth. She showed it to me the day she found me. It's more than a relic. It's… alive… somehow. The snakes on its head tried to bite me, and she seemed to want to let them. I barely got away," Selene's voice shook, and she rubbed the goosebumps from her arms as she looked at Madge with wide, terrified eyes.

Madge felt her heart sink. The pain in Selene's face was almost unbearable.

"Your mom has a head with snakes on it, that was sitting in the vaults and supposed to be a golden relic, and she wanted to let it bite you?" Max said, his face purple. "Just when I thought I couldn't hate her more."

Selene's face crumpled, and her eyes welled with angry tears. "Point is, cousin. It's… it's got a voice. I heard it, whispering. I couldn't understand it, but… she *lets* it bite her – repeatedly. I saw it. It's like a drug. She *likes* it. Wants it. I think it's giving her dark powers somehow."

"She's channeling it, maybe, or it's using her somehow," Robert said, his face almost as pained as Selene's as he looked at his daughter. "The woman I knew has been gone a long time. Maybe that's got something to do with it. I'm sorry this happened. But I am more sorry you didn't come to me about it."

Dr. Hiromi shot to his feet, snapping his fingers. "She's not channeling it, that *head* is. The relic Viviane took from the vaults – we thought was a golden sculpture, a depiction if you will, of the head of a siren. Perhaps infused with Vala, yes… but… if Viviane is using blood Vala – that's some pretty serious, powerful, dark Vala – and of everything Madge has said about its voice… you must be right. It's channeling a siren. That's the voice between worlds. That's what the legend means."

"You better find those cuffs and quick, kiddo," Robert said. "If that's true, you're going to need all the help you can get. We all will."

13

In a Tree by the Sea

Saturday was just as cold and dismal as the days leading up to it. There wasn't a crack in the late November sky to reveal anything resembling a sun – or that it was still even up there to begin with. Madge had started her dark and stormy Saturday making chocolate chip cookie dough and was sat in front of the fireplace while they baked in the oven.

Thanksgiving was in five days – which meant weeks had swept past and she still didn't have any inkling how to piece the clues together that her mother had left her in the tome. Between Vala training, looming finals and all the rest of it – she simply didn't have time.

Or so she told herself.

In reality, she was too scared to access her Vala again, and mercifully she was asked not to, until they found more answers as to what happened – what she was up against. How a siren could possibly be involved, how Viviane was using it to get to Madge in her very own mind.

So Vala training was funneled instead into study and theory.

History, even.

But today, she'd resolved, would be different. She needed those cuffs, if nothing else – and according to the sea nymph, unraveling her mother's work might lead to their return.

By the time the cookies sat on the rack to cool, Madge was bundled up and out the door and on her way to the Institute – because she had to be there, in the chilly underground vaults to find answers – not sitting by the fireplace, still wearing her pajamas, and eating all the cookies.

"Back to study the tome?" Giuliana asked as the stone wall ground shut behind her.

"Finally, yes! But I wish we could turn the heat up in this place," Madge said, pulling her cardigan tightly around her waist as she followed in Giuliana's wake, feeling a cold, minty kiss on her face.

"If only it wouldn't jeopardize books and relics that are centuries old," Giuliana said, turning her head slightly as her dark hair streamed behind her. "You've been busy, I take it?"

"I had my first lesson on Air Vala," Madge said loudly so Giuliana could hear her as she disappeared to fetch Merlin's scroll and her mother's tome, "and was told to imagine my well of Vala, which was supposed to be a well but wasn't. I sort of got stuck there… And haven't really wanted to – well, visit or even *imagine* it since—"

"You traversed to your well of Vala – and it wasn't a well? Where were you?" Giuliana asked, reappearing with the tome and scroll and placing it before the same chair Madge sat in last time, nearest the stacks and across from the painting Giuliana had melted into.

"It was a dark ravine – and no one seems to be able to tell me how to not do that next time, or how I got there in the first place. But you say I *traversed* there as if it's a word to describe what happened," Madge said, meeting Giuliana's sparkling indigo eyes that seemed alight with understanding. "And I saw you float in and out of that painting, which tells me you might know more than the others do."

"It's *your* place. All you have to do this time is not fall in, which you couldn't have done without leaning too far, so it wasn't an accident, really. More a subconscious choice."

"I did lean to see the bottom," Madge said, sinking down into the chair, "and I wondered how I'd fallen. I didn't slip or anything… but I didn't exactly jump in, either."

"Plunging into its water is what traversed you there. Next time simply stop at the edge. There's plenty of Vala standing before it – no need to immerse yourself in it. Imagining your Vala place with your eyes open should help, too – it helps root you to the world you're in."

"How do you know all of this?"

"I am made of the very fabric of Vala. I know how these things work."

"Well, what if something was there with me? It can't get to me if I don't – traverse there, is that right?"

"Right – but what do you mean, something was there with you?"

"My aunt got to me somehow…"

"She was there?"

"Yes, in a matter of speaking, I think so."

Giuliana's indigo eyes went frosty. "Sounds to me like you have a deep, ravenous fear injecting itself into your psyche," Giuliana said through knit brows, though her expression seemed disturbed and inquisitive.

"You're saying I imagined it?"

Giuliana shook her head. "Don't be afraid of your own Vala, and you won't be afraid of your ravine. And just keep your eyes open this time! If she really was there, she can't get to you if *you* aren't traversed there. You know where I am if you need me," she said as she trailed away towards her painting, and in a sparkle and a flash, she was gone.

"That's it?" Madge said into the now empty room, though she knew Giuliana was watching her from the painting as usual. "Why does she keep doing that?" Madge sighed, glancing down at the table in front of her where her mother's tome and Merlin's scroll sat.

Ever since she'd learned the incantation at her first Vala lesson – *one that might illuminate hidden things* – she had been chomping at the bit to use it on her mother's tome, but devastatingly scared to try, hence the weeks that had passed in visiting the vaults at all. "If I fall down or seem stuck – you better come get me out!" Madge called out across the room, knowing Giuliana could hear her.

"Just keep your eyes open!" Giuliana's voice called out *from the painting* – sounding like the ocean in a conch shell when you lean your ear into it.

Madge grumbled.

Apparently, Giuliana was the push them in the deep end, so they learn to swim type.

She grasped the tome with shaking hands and took a deep breath. She'd read the letter from her parents again that morning – just before baking cookies. It was their letter that ramped up the courage to do this again – to access her Vala and imagine that dark ravine.

She unwound the tome and opened it to the sketch of dry earth… Better to test what she already knew, first.

"Just keep your eyes open. Stand at the edge. Don't fall in. Keep your eyes open!" she told herself, balling her hands into fists... and took a deep breath in.

Filling her lungs with air as far as she could go and her eyes as wide as saucers so she wouldn't chance a blink – she let herself imagine that place – *her place.*

Fear tickled in her belly as she stood near the edge, but she pushed it away this time.

Don't be afraid of your Vala, Giuliana had said. *Don't be afraid.*

While still holding her breath and her eyes burning from remaining open, Madge allowed her imagination to have a look around.

It was not as dark as it had been before. A full moon illuminated a hilly landscape, and a wind swept across her face, rustling her hair that sent goosebumps rising on her neck. She could feel the ocean not far away and could faintly hear it even – and she felt her Vala swirling in the dark chasm at her feet – a gentler nudge this time. Finally, she peeked down into that large crack in the earth and tuned into the water running through it... and felt her fingers tingle.

Madge held onto that vision and the Vala coursing through her as she stared down at the drawing of dry earth, willing it to reveal itself without uttering a word or releasing her breath.

Words formed and the picture moved, and Madge finally let go of her breath, left the ravine, and allowed herself to blink. Fingers still tingling, the incantation she'd learned from Dr. Hiromi teetered on the tip of her tongue.

It was time to use it – to find *more.*

With the tome open in her lap, she took another deep breath

in as far as she could, focusing on the intention of finding more clues to reveal Merlin's spell. And when she could breathe in no further – with eyes wide open, she stood again before the chasm of her Vala and finally said the word out loud.

"Onspen!"

The wind kissed her face as she stood before it… and the pages of the tome fanned open, as if also carried on the phantom breeze of her imagination, until a wide drawing taking up two pages laid open on her lap.

Her eyes widened at the detail – how had she missed this before? She couldn't have breezed past it without noticing it – this was new. It had been hidden somehow.

A great tree spanned past the edges of the pages – suggesting a massive size Madge couldn't fathom. It was dripping with crimson fruit and rooted into a rock crevice above a sea, and a great wall was behind it, made of pale rock – visible through the branches. A woman's head and torso were afloat in the water below with a coppery, scaled arm stretched towards the tree – a piece of the fruit aloft in her hand. *Saelfen.*

And blood trailed down her hand and wrist – or was it juice from the crimson fruit?

Madge stared blankly at the page as her heart raced. There was something bigger here… She could feel it in her gut – this drawing was the greatest clue of all.

But what was it? She chanced closing her eyes, focusing on allowing her mind to clear – for whatever she was feeling to come into focus…

Madge loosed a gasp as her eyes snapped back open—
The fruit!
Was it the fruit she needed to complete Merlin's spell and

allow a Merewif to transform and become what this woman in the drawing was – a Saelfen?

There had to be more. There was Vala still hidden here, Madge could feel it pulsing against her fingers, *waiting*. It made her heart race when she wondered what would happen if it revealed itself – and instantly a light came on.

She knew why it wasn't able to come forward yet...

Her fear.

Fear of her own power was what was holding something back. The difference between peeking through a crack in a door – or fully opening it wide.

Madge sucked in a breath, ready to unleash herself. *To unravel.*

Her whole body tingled wildly now – so much her skin felt *itchy* – and continuing to hold her breath, she focused again on the intricately detailed drawing, spanning two pages in the heart of her mother's tome.

The drawing began to shimmer, and blur... Madge refocused her eyes...

Color and dimension intensified until the drawing looked almost real – infinitely more detailed than before. Madge dared not loose her breath as she examined the new detail.

An enormous snake was now visible, wound around the trunk over and over again, as if it tried to squeeze the life from the tree itself. She almost dropped the tome when she saw the tail of the snake slither up the trunk... and when a face appeared in the shadows, barely visible, in the branches higher up, she felt a shiver run up the back of her neck and back down again, as she felt like it stared back at her from the page. Though it was hard to make out, she could tell it was a haunted and tortured looking creature – neither Saelfen nor human, with a crown of snakes writhing around its head, reaching out from amidst the branches.

Madge finally dropped the book into her lap and allowed herself some air – though she kept her eyes on the page. She didn't dare touch the drawing as it seized her with a deep foreboding as though it might come to life from the page – and come for her.

There was a sparkle – something was moving again...

The sea was pulling back from the page, from the shore where the tree hung in the rock, until out of nowhere, a tsunami-sized wave swept over the scene, and a word formed on the churning water...

Blood.

And when she saw the creature from the tree peering back at her from the water – as though it really watched her – she slammed her mother's tome shut and finally loosed a blood-curling scream, squeezing her eyes shut as she threw the book across the floor and away.

This time, Giuliana knew to respond.

The wave in the massive painting across the room sparkled as Giuliana emerged and streaked towards her, bringing in the smell of the sea in her wake and cold, fresh air.

"I – I found something," Madge said with a shudder. "A hidden drawing."

"One that compelled you to throw your mother's tome across the room?" Giuliana asked as she floated over to pick up the disheveled book.

Madge's hands were shaking as she peeled herself from the chair to unravel Merlin's scroll. "Blood – it had to be *blood*," Madge answered as she waited until the golden runes formed to words that she recognized, her eyes scanning the columns until she found the word she was looking for. *"The blood of an innocent... Heals old wounds."*

"Are you going to tell me what you saw that's to do with blood?"

"A tree – and some kind of monster was inside it, hiding – and then a tsunami hit, and the word blood appeared. And there was a woman in the water – she had fruit in her hand, and I couldn't tell if she was bleeding, too…" Madge bit her lip as she frowned at Giuliana. "But what does the blood of an innocent have to do with any of that? Or healing an old wound?"

"Blood of an innocent? What does that sound like to you?"

"Sacrifice of some kind," Madge admitted. "But to heal an old wound?"

"Merlin's mother was said to have been a Nun, so alluding to sacrifice might have meaning," Giuliana said as she watched Madge continue to scan the scroll.

Until — "Oh, wow," Madge gasped, gaping at the golden writing on the page, written in a hand centuries ago. *"But Evil bit from the Tree!"* Madge squeaked. "There was that freaky thing in the tree! And a woman – a Saelfen – she had blood on her hand… And another line in Merlin's scroll mentions fruit – *fruit left to decay*. The woman had fruit in her hand – blood-red fruit, from the tree!"

"Keep reading," Giuliana said as her brow deepened.

Madge felt goosebumps rise on her arms as she read to the end. *"Rise! Behold, she comes to help, singing from the deepest waters."* Madge read, looking up at Giuliana with huge eyes. "It mentions *singing*…"

"It does," Giuliana said as she inclined her head at Madge.

"It's got to be a siren. But aren't they monsters? How would a siren help—"?

"What makes you think he's writing about a siren?" Giuliana interrupted, her once composed face turned stormy.

"He mentions that she sings from the deep."

"The singing mentioned here does not allude to the call of the siren."

"But how do you know? I've heard one – and when I read sings from the deep—"

"What?" Giuliana's voice was a high, threatening pitch. "Pray tell, what *on earth* makes you think you've heard one?"

"It wasn't just my aunt, inside my Vala place with me. When I got stuck – when I came up from the water there, I heard it singing – pulling me towards it, and I couldn't move. That's what got me stuck – it wouldn't let me leave, wouldn't let me move."

"You said it was your aunt – it can't be both. Describe this singing to me."

"Selene said it was my aunt, that she's using familial blood Vala to find me. The singing was horrible and beautiful all at the same time, and—"

"It's impossible," Giuliana said, her watery gaze serious.

"I heard it the day my Vala returned, too – apparently my aunt is using familial blood—"

"She's not a siren," Giuliana's face flashed anger. "Believe me princess, your aunt cannot be something she is not. She is not that."

"I didn't say she was. But the relic she stole is a golden sculpture of one… and according to Selene, it has a voice and the snakes on its head move – and the picture my mom drew—"

"*Mimir's Head*," Giuliana whispered as a haunted expression flashed across her face.

The nymph turned and flashed towards the shelves – so swiftly Madge could hardly track her with her eyes. She breezed along the stacks until she removed a book, and in a streak of light she returned to Madge as quickly as she'd left.

She held it open to a page that made Madge's blood run cold. "This is a Saelfen depiction of a siren – drawn from legends of a world long since lost." Pale winged creatures flew around a ship, their faces horrible, long claws ripping men and ship to shreds – and the worse part: serpents crowned their heads. "I can assure you, even this is far from an accurate depiction. If one of these had been there, inside your Vala with you, you would not have made it out," Giuliana said as she snapped the book back shut. "They are horrible, demonic creatures – besides wings their lower half is serpentine, and instead of hair—"

"Snakes!" Madge screeched. "That's what was in the painting! I didn't realize it until you mentioned the lower half is serpentine – like a snake – it was wound around the tree."

For the first time since Madge had met her, the formidable sea nymph looked frightened. Giuliana's watery eyes grew distant and she breathed, "Your mother drew Eressëa."

"I'm lost now. What is Er – whatever you said?"

"Eressëa is the Old World. Where your kind were cast out from. Sirens have infiltrated the outer walls and linger by the Treoliffruma – the tree your mother drew in her vision. Its fruit is the only cure for the bite and thrall of a siren, so they guard it so none can be helped."

"She drew this from a vision? What does that mean?"

"That's the only way she could have depicted this. Your

mother had a vision that led her on this whole quest to find Merlin's spell – until now, I didn't know what it was. When she had it, she was in the ocean – pregnant with *you*, as a matter of fact. Saelfen and Merewif access visions most powerfully when submerged. And certainly while pregnant."

"Why is this the first time I'm hearing this?" Madge asked, throwing her hands up into the air. "So, what now, I'm supposed to find fruit from a tree from the Old World? It's the fruit, not a spell that I need?"

"I'm not sure – but possibly…" Giuliana said, lost in thought. "I'd be a little more concerned at the moment that your aunt is using blood Vala to get to you inside your Vala place, and that she's using the voice of a siren, somehow."

"Doesn't that mean that the legends are true… the relic is a voice between worlds? If sirens only exist in the Old World?"

"Legend states that those who seek to be unstoppable conquerors use Mimir's Head – by paying some kind of price to access its voice to gain power. But… A siren *devours*. So it likely has its own plans and is not helping her for any reason other than its own gain. Whatever its price is, it will be a steep price to pay, in the end."

Madge felt like she could be sick. She wasn't only up against her aunt – she was up against something darker and more sinister than she'd realized – and she'd felt it when she'd heard it singing… but worse of all was that now she had an image of its face in her head.

"What do you think the tsunami meant?" Giuliana asked, though Madge felt the sea nymph might know the answer.

Madge paused as she realized she somehow knew. And though it seemed strange, she said, "It was the end of a world."

14

Water

"It must be a miracle. What are you doing up so early Madgie-pie?" Grandpa Ollie said, lifting his head from the tidal charts he was studying next to the gurgling coffee pot.

"I want to come with you on your walk," she said in a gravelly voice, grabbing a to-go mug from the cupboard.

"We better get going then," he said, looking down at his watch.

"It's still on, then?" Madge grumbled.

"Yes, Pearl said if the weather held – and it's looking great out there," Grandpa Ollie said with a hint of surprise. "Something wrong? The Madge I know loves to sail."

"I'm just not looking forward to the Vala training with Pearl," Madge said as she squeezed through the sliding glass door, hit by a waft of cool, salty morning air. "You know, the vision stuff and Water Vala – stuff that will prove I've got all the other Saelfen talents that Merewif don't have. I'm basically going to be watched by a whole audience today, so no. I'm not looking forward to that part."

"I wouldn't call Max and Selene an audience—"

"There's a whole lot more coming than Max and Selene, and Pearl is an audience all by herself," Madge huffed, following Grandpa Ollie across the back deck to the top of the wooden steps that led down to the ocean.

"You're going to have to get used to an audience, kiddo," Grandpa Ollie said with little apology in his voice. "You'll feel better once we're out there."

The morning sun reflected off the ocean and what was left of the misty fog was still crawling along the sand. Madge scanned the beach for the MEI security detail. They were always there, always watching. By the time they reached the bottom of the steps, two of them were already following not far behind.

"That's getting really old," Madge complained as she turned to see the two bodies following them. "Where did they even come from?"

"Let's not talk about that right now. Let's just enjoy our walk," Grandpa Ollie said as he squeezed her shoulders in a sideways hug. "It's rare I get my Madgie to myself nowadays."

"I know… and there is something I need to talk to you about."

"Something important enough to get you out of bed this morning?"

"Yes. It's about Mom. Something she was working on."

Grandpa Ollie cast a glance behind his shoulder to make sure their bodyguards were out of earshot before he said, "Let me guess. Merlin?" he asked, raising bushy white brows skyward.

"She told you?"

"She told me a little."

"Grandpa! Why didn't you tell me? You said you didn't know what she'd been up to!"

"I said I didn't know her *plan*," Grandpa Ollie corrected her with a finger in the air. "And I don't. But I could say the same to you – why haven't you told me yet?"

"Grandpa, come on, what did she tell you?"

"Very little. She didn't let me in on much. But what I can tell you is what this whole Merlin business was doing to her. It was her obsession, finding a way to become – to transform. To be accepted as queen."

"Obviously, you know more than just a little!"

"You know to be careful with this information, right?" Grandpa Ollie asked as he took another glance behind him.

"Yes, I know. I haven't told a soul but you. Not even Ash."

"But why does it matter? You have the ability to transform already. You don't need to convince the Council of that, like she did."

"But others need it."

"You're saying others need the ability to transform? Why would anyone need that?"

"Apparently that's the whole reason she was trying to uncover this Merlin stuff – otherwise she wouldn't have pursued it. Not if it was for her purpose alone."

"She did tell me that what she was doing was for all her kind," Grandpa Ollie said after a pause. "But I thought she meant by her being queen – not because anyone needed the ability to transform besides her."

"If any Merewif could transform, it would negate the whole campaign Viviane is on, or any Saelfen that thinks the pure-bloodlines are in danger of being bred out. It would have been the ultimate proving ground to the Council, too. For me as their heir as well," Madge said, looking up at Grandpa Ollie whose brow was knit deeply in thought – and shock.

"You don't need anything but *you* to prove yourself."

"Thanks Grandpa. Problem is I have to figure out how she planned to do it. And once I do – I think only then will the cuffs return to me. Or so the sea nymph seems to think, so there is that."

"They'll return to you – and the sea nymph is right. It's probably all a part of some wild plan Rachel had," Grandpa Ollie said, shaking his head. "Rachel always had a plan."

"But she didn't tell you anything about Merlin's spell? Ingredients, perhaps?"

"The only thing she told me was that she'd thought Merlin's transformation spell was the answer to her becoming Queen. She said she'd had a vision, but I don't know what it was."

"Giuliana – the sea nymph said not all Merewif have the ability to have visions. What does that mean? Like, psychic abilities or how does that work? I'd love to know seeing I'll be tested on this today," Madge said, rolling her eyes.

"It's not psychic. Your grandma told me you can't just grab visions from the ether. They'd come because they are meant to, like a gift, and left from familial bonds."

"From ancestors?"

"Yes. Your mother had never had visions before, though. She always had uncanny intuition – just like your Grandma, but apparently when she was pregnant with you, she started having very strong visions, which is a very different thing from a gut feeling. But they were from your father's ancestors. She said it was because she was pregnant with you."

"*Because* she was pregnant with me? Giuliana – the sea nymph – mentioned she was pregnant when she had the vision about Merlin. But how was it *because* of me?"

"Like I said – visions come from familial bonds, and this vision was from your father's ancestors – that's not her bloodline. In fact, it happened before she even knew she was pregnant with you. She was probably five weeks along when your parents went for a night swim in Mexico. They'd been down there for a while – taking an extended honeymoon so to speak, hiding out from the mayhem up here that ensued after they eloped."

"But how did she know they weren't *her* ancestors?"

"I'm actually not sure. But at first she thought it was the cuff she wore and that somehow Merlin had enchanted them and sent a vision that way."

"Wait." Madge stopped in her tracks, sand whipping beneath her rubber boots as she stopped to face Grandpa Ollie with wide eyes. "If ancestors or familial bonds send visions – and you're saying Merlin sent one to my mom – does that mean *the Merlin* is my ancestor?"

"Your fascination with all things Camelot might not just be coincidental," Grandpa Ollie said, his face cracking into a rare, wide smile as he watched Madge maniacally jump up and down with excitement, until another look of shock and realization spread across her face, this time that had her gripping onto his elbow.

"But if Merlin was… Don't tell me King Arthur – and, and Guinevere – were Saelfen?"

"Yes, Guinevere and Arthur, according to your mom, were indeed Saelfen—" Grandpa Ollie said as Madge squealed in a pitch that had him grabbing his ears, "but there are quite a few historical figures and rulers that were. And are, even today."

"I hadn't even considered that!" Madge exclaimed, trying to reign herself back in when she noticed Grandpa Ollie glance behind them once more at the security detail still following. "So why can we only get visions from ancestors? Are you sure Merlin is my ancestor?"

"Your mom explained to me that those with the sight can leave messages, and that the messages are suspended in time until they are plucked out by someone who shares their blood – or their DNA. Visions reside in the blood, is what she told me."

"Blood," Madge said flatly, remembering the words in Merlin's scroll as she followed Grandpa Ollie who looked down at his watch and turned back around.

"Don't you be getting as obsessed as she was with this whole thing," Grandpa Ollie said, grabbing onto Madge's shoulders as his face crumpled in worry. "No matter how important it may seem – don't let it ruin your happiness in the meantime, like it did for her. You have a solid plan without all this Merlin business – I think making your mom's plan your plan B is the best route, if you ask me. Let Nico and the SI worry about Viviane."

"Nico and the *what?*"

"The SI. Saelfen Intelligence."

"*Oh*. I don't think I have a choice there, Grandpa," Madge said, smiling weakly.

"Life is nothing but the choices we make," he said with a defiant shake of his head.

"That and a little bit of destiny thrown in the mix?" Madge said with a wave of her hand towards the now sparkling ocean. "Your words, not mine!"

The small, rustic docks along the Skipanon Waterway were dominated by weathered fishing boats, so the immaculate sixty-foot Catamaran with MEI decaled on the stern along with *Marine Ecology Institute* along the sides, stood out like a hawk in a henhouse. With two stories of teak decks, crisp white cushions and steps off the stern to get in the water by, it seemed like the kind of boat that was meant to float around warmer, turquoise waters and white sandy beaches. Not in the wild, cold, tumultuous waters of the Pacific Northwest.

"Does everyone who belongs to MEI know how to sail?" Madge asked as she followed Selene and Max up the winding staircase that led to the top deck, affording a lofty view of the water and decks below, where Nico readied the main sail with two of his security personnel as the boat turned port onto the wide expanse of the sparkling Columbia River. The Astoria Bridge was behind them, spanning more than four miles across, trussed high enough off the water for ships to sail under. "I hadn't expected Nico and his team to know how to crew a sailing vessel."

"Pretty much – it's kind of a criterion to be employed by MEI, seeing we spend so much time out on boats for research and what not," Selene said, kicking off her loafers as they reached the top step.

"With exception of Pearl," Max said with a crooked grin as they reached the top, where the Regent was sat with large sunglasses. "She loves to sail but refuses to touch anything."

"Quite right, I'm a happy laissez-faire passenger, and shamelessly so," Pearl said with a graceful lift of her eyebrow as she bit into an olive from the toothpick in her martini glass.

Grandpa Ollie was at the helm, his back to the others who sat in spacious, cushioned bench seating behind him. Robert was snoozing already, and Dan and Christine were passing out cans of soda, wearing matching MEI blue windbreakers.

Everyone was here. Her *audience*.

By the time she sat down, the main sail had been flapped open to the wind and Grandpa Ollie cut the engine, the wind and water filling her ears. "That's my favorite part," Madge said to Selene who was filling her plate with crackers and cheese. "When you come out of the marina and cut engine, and there's nothing but the sound of the wind and the water."

"Ugh, you sound like Max," Selene said, lifting a chin in the air. "I like it, too, but I prefer the groan and rumble and speed of a powerboat."

Max's warm brown eyes met hers, and Madge felt her cheeks go hot despite the cold, November air rushing around her face and whipping her hair everywhere.

"I think anyone who likes to sail loves that," he shrugged, looking away as if he were as embarrassed as she was.

"Whatever. You two nerds are a lot alike, like it or not," Selene said, plunking a cracker piled high with cheese into her mouth.

"*Nerd?*" Max's face was purple.

"Please don't fight you two, not today," Christine complained as she handed Max a can of grape soda. "Sorry, Madge. These two fight constantly! They were raised together, and Selene is the sister Max never had, but sorely needed."

Sister?

"Oh, please! She needs an *older* brother more than I need a sister—"

"What, so you can scare off every guy I try to date?"

"No. So I can scare off every *jerk* you *do* date!"

"My job would be a lot harder without you, Max," Robert

said, popping an eye open and smirking. Apparently, he wasn't totally asleep.

"Don't encourage him, Dad," Selene said, throwing a cracker at Robert's chest.

Madge's stomach sank, like a stone plunging to the ocean floor. Had she been reading them all wrong – all this time? Max wasn't secretly in love with Selene, but protective. Brotherly. And, she knew from Ash's brother, who this year had gone away to college – sometimes brotherly protectiveness was worse than the fatherly kind.

Madge couldn't help but stare a little at Max now – seeing him in a new light. Protective. Not jealous. Not entirely a jerk characteristic after all.

"Listen up, everyone," Grandpa Ollie spoke over his shoulder. "We are crossing the Columbia River Bar, which is a notoriously rough crossing. Thanks to the calm water and southerly winds today, we plan on crossing it and anchoring just past Cape Disappointment."

"What makes it so dangerous? Rocks?" Selene asked, removing her sunglasses and squinting into the distance. "I don't see any."

"It's the water," Dan answered. "There are three major water forces at the bar, and it makes for quite a clash and some fairly large waves to contend with."

"Lucky for us we're all swimmers," Selene said as she flashed a smile at Madge. "I mean – apart from Ollie, of course. No offense!"

"None taken," Grandpa Ollie said with a chuckle.

"There's the ocean's current, plus the ebb and current of this huge Columbia River we are on now. You can see the strong currents we are riding on here, and that all clashes with the

WATER

pounding ocean swells powering through two jetties. It's a tornado of water coming together," Dan said as he gestured wildly with his hands.

"It's my duty to get us through it today," Grandpa Ollie said, adjusting the helm again. "All I ask is that you all keep your footing and do as I say upon the passage. Good swimmers or not, I'd rather not put on a show for the good people that watch the pass. Other than that, I expect we'll have smooth sailing today. If you look ahead, you'll see even that ship there needs help crossing this thing," he added, pointing towards a pilot boat, dwarfed alongside a bright orange cargo ship that carried huge pieces of timber as it navigated towards the bar.

"Well, we aren't out here for a pleasure sail," Pearl said, clapping her hands together as she sat forward in her seat and faced Madge. "Did you finish reading the material that Kento gave you?"

"Yes, just yesterday," Madge answered as her stomach tightened.

"And what did you learn about Air Vala in relation to the other elements?"

"It's the foundation of all the four elements. Energy."

"While air is the foundation, or the *energy* we draw from, Water Vala is the *conduit*, as it's what helps conduct the energy."

"It's the base ingredient in potions," Selene chimed in. "Not that I get to do anything with those, no human blood and all. Unlike you. Saelfen and witch, best of *both* worlds."

"Right! Only witches brew potions," Madge said, lifting her chin proudly into the air.

"Yes, water is the Universal Solvent," Selene said, smiling widely. "In potions and in many other ways, so by learning your abilities with water, it will help you flow into your other abilities—"

"Think of electricity in water, or a hair dryer in a bathtub," Pearl said with a wave of her hand. "You lot are overcomplicating it. It's a conduit in that way. Simple. Now, let's eat."

They gorged themselves on cold cheese and mayo sandwiches and orange soda, until the banks of the river widened. And not long after they finished gorging themselves on cookies, a black and white lighthouse poked up from the green headland on the starboard side.

"Cape Disappointment," Dan announced. "Not far from the bar now, as you can see."

White, crested caps crashed where the Columbia River met the Pacific. It didn't look like much from further back – but the closer they got, Madge realized, the bigger they actually were.

"Here we go – everyone stay seated – no bathroom breaks!" Grandpa Ollie said, his eyes sparkling as he squared his shoulders over the helm, turning the engine on to help power through it. As they hit the first wave, Madge felt her stomach tickle as the bow bucked up and crashed back down – and tickled worse as she exchanged a glance with Max, whose eyes were sparkling with excitement.

The sixty-foot catamaran part sailed, part *surfed* through the crashing waves, pushed in every direction, as Grandpa Ollie constantly readjusted the helm to maintain his course. Water thrashed against its sides, swirling and splaying across the decks in frequent outbursts.

"Tacking starboard!" Grandpa Ollie called out, as after a final downward dive of the dual hulled vessel, they surfed past the tempestuous bar – and with a wide turn north up the Pacific, wind filled the sails, and the catamaran was on a steadier course.

"Well done, Ollie!" Dan said as he stood up and clapped him on the shoulder. "Just a little further north and we'll anchor in," he said as he pointed to the lighthouse, which stood on a rocky bluff, in front of tall pines and a higher green bluff that rose up behind it. It was a breathtaking sight to behold so close to shore, especially seeing the weather was holding up and the glittering ocean reflected the blue, sunlit sky.

It was a perfect day for a swim. The ocean was joyful, and Madge felt in the pit of her stomach: more likely to reveal her secrets. Pearl had talked of the basics of Water Vala – but nothing yet on the bigger question lingering in Madge's mind. Merlin, and visions.

"Let's not waste peak sunlight!" Dan said, ushering Madge up from her seat and from her daydreaming. "Go ahead and use the head below deck, starboard side. Time to suit up, *lunita*."

"What?" Madge asked, her cheeks burning.

"Max has been calling you that," Dan answered with a shrug and a huge, knowing smile.

"I said it once," Max said, his cheeks turning a deep shade of purple.

"Come on, follow me," Selene said, breezing past in her perfect khakis and white knit sweater. "Time to suit up."

"I can't decide if he's making fun of me or…" Madge said, following Selene down the stairs and onto the top deck.

"Don't worry about it. He means it affectionately. *Obviously*," Selene said as she led Madge through a spacious galley, where bananas were swinging from a hook above the sink, and bright sunshine bounced off the white countertops, blinding her eyes.

"Obviously? How is that affectionate?"

"Little moon? It's cute," Selene said, cocking a smile. Madge felt an excited feeling gurgling in her stomach at the thought that the nickname was meant to be cute, and not offensive. She'd been getting it all wrong this far.

"Where do we get changed?" Madge asked, changing the subject.

"Just through there," Selene said, pointing down yet another small set of steps. "There's a wet suit on the bed."

The steps were narrow, and to the right a door had been left open, hooked to the wall, revealing a large bed where a royal blue wet suit was splayed across the bed next to a neatly folded towel. As Madge shut the door behind her, she was thankful for the large mirror hanging from behind it, especially after she noticed the wet suit, with a white MEI logo on the front, was long sleeved, but the pants ended mid-thigh, and she'd have to reveal her skinny, chalky legs.

Lunita. Little moon.

She rarely wore shorts, even at home. Now she had an audience not only to what her Vala would look like in the water – but, worse of all, an audience to her moon-white legs.

She held on extra tight to the beach towel wrapped around her waist as she made her way back up the steps to the cockpit, battling the November wind that threatened to blow it away.

"Anchor is set!" Grandpa Ollie said, his eyes flashing excitedly.

"You know, we might see some pretty cool things out there today," Dan said as he watched the shoreline with binoculars. "There are anemones out here like you've never seen. All hosts of starfish, spiny starfish, and sunflower starfish to name a couple off the top of my head. And we might see *un pulpo*. Octopus."

"Eastern Reds – those are out here. I've…" Madge stopped herself. No one here knew about her past night swims – especially not Grandpa. "I've, uh, read a lot about them."

"*Nice*, Madge. You know your ocean life," Dan said as he lowered his binoculars, handing them to Nico. "You're right. Shoreline is clear."

"Nico will stay up here, keeping an eye on things," Pearl said as she stood before Madge in a full wetsuit – one that covered her legs. "A few from the team are already out scouting in the water. We are good to go," she said, raising a manicured thumb in the air towards Nico, who nodded silently. 'Chop-chop, make your way to the lower deck stern, everyone."

Selene grabbed Madge by the hand. "Come on – you're getting in with us," she said, her white-blonde hair back in a tight French braid.

Selene pulled Madge down the stairs as they followed Max, turning left towards the bow instead of right, towards the stern.

"She said stern—"

"We are jumping from the bow," Max said, rushing over the lower deck towards the dual bows, past large windows revealing the spacious galley and saloon.

"They can walk down the little stairs of the stern, but *this* is the best way to get in," Selene said, pointing to the white trampoline netting on the foredeck, strung between the hulls over open water.

"We jump in at the same time," Max said, holding out his hand for Madge to grab it.

"All three of us," Selene added with a nod, keeping hold of

Madge's other hand.

She had to let go of her towel and grab Max's hand, and she stood blinking back at him, until she felt Selene rip it from her waist.

"It isn't that cold, and you'll warm up once we're in the water, princess."

Madge's cheeks heated as she took Max's warm hand. He held onto hers with a surprising grip, and thankfully didn't glance at her white legs even once, but instead stared down at the water, rolling and splashing below them.

Madge stared at it, too. The deep blue, the swells, raising the boat up and down—

And before Madge was ready—

"JUMP!" Selene screamed, and she hardly had time to move her feet before she was being pulled by both hands.

The initial shock of hitting the frigid water took her breath away – but as her skin hardened and scales rose like goosebumps up and down her body, and the sudden length and propulsion of her fins, the temperature felt normal as she rose to the surface to catch her breath.

And immediately as she surfaced, Max's face was close – *too close*.

Madge could hardly catch her breath by the way he stared back at her, his long lashes wet, those full lips dripping with ocean water… and coppery scales faded up his neck and stopped just under his jaw. It was a moment frozen in time, seeing one of her kind – him, up and close in the water with her. And those eyes – they were brighter, sharper, somehow. Magnetic—

She shoved back and away, playfully dousing his face with water.

"You two didn't wait for me to jump!"

"Oh, *honey*. There are much better ways to splash water. Watch this," Selene said, and before Madge could blink, Selene *threw* water at Max. Not a splash with an arm, but a torrent of water that rose beneath her palms and hit Max square in the face.

"So that's how you want to play?" Max said with a small laugh. "You know better—"

"Alright you three, come join us," Pearl's voice said, reaching Madge's ears like she was *right next to them*. Madge swiveled around in the water – but Pearl was nowhere near the bows of the massive, dual hull boat.

She was, in fact, about two hundred yards away.

"How did she…" Madge asked, startled.

"That's *wæterstefn*," Max said as turned over onto his back and began to back paddle – and Madge's breath hitched as she saw his fins skim along the surface, propelling him with ease and not so much as a splash. "Pearl used water particles to carry her voice to us. It means *water voice* in the old language – some can send their voice for miles."

"Is it – common? I mean…" Madge said, remembering with a shiver the voice on the wind that night she transformed for the first time – how Ash had heard it too, in the rain that pelted the windows of her car.

"No. It's a rare talent, and she likes to show off. Come on, let's go," Selene said, disappearing underwater.

Madge followed behind Max, wondering whose voice was on the wind that night and what it meant. Likely her aunt, or maybe the Daed who followed her when she took her night swim. They must have known about her longer than anyone knew. But how?

"Hey, Madgie!" Grandpa Ollie called out at her, pulling her from her thoughts as she backpaddled past where he was leaning over the port side of the boat. His face was alight in wonder. Madge waved back, smiling widely. She wondered how he must feel – seeing her in mer-form. He'd probably seen Grandma in this form plenty of times, but she'd died long ago. She arrived at the buoy feeling more light-hearted than ever about capturing a vision from an ancestor when she thought of her Grandma – as she felt, somehow, the love and Vala passed down between generations… Passed through bloodlines, she realized, remembering that visions were captured and passed on in the blood in the same way.

They reached Dan, Christine, and Pearl, all circled and bobbing in the water like surfers waiting for a wave, around what appeared to be an orange buoy.

"Okay, everyone," Christine said as she held onto the buoy. "For security reasons, we are going to stick to the orange buoy so Nico and his guys can keep an eye on us. No wandering off, okay?" she said, looking pointedly at Selene. "And if some humans happen upon us, fins and scales go away, okay, Madge?"

"Got it," Madge said, nodding her head as she watched all the heads bobbing up and down in the water, staring at her. And she couldn't help but gawk at them all – everyone's eyes were different out here. Pearl's sparkled like brown sugar with an underlying amber color that Madge had never noticed before. Selene's were as blue and iridescent as the ocean itself, and Christine's seemed to reflect the azure sky above them. Madge wondered what her own eyes looked like, making a mental note to bring a mirror next time.

"Now for the fun," Pearl said, snapping her attention towards Madge. "Let's show Madge how Saelfen communicate underwater. Duck under everyone!"

They propelled hardly a foot under, where shafts of golden light danced on their heads as they floated effortlessly in a circle. Madge watched with wide eyes as she beheld all the coppery scales and billowing, iridescent tail fins, tipped with an opaque, fleshy pink at the ends, moving and flowing them to keep in one spot. And she was marveling at just how much paler Selene's hair was underwater – as if that were possible – when Christine's voice rang in her mind.

Hello!

Madge flinched and gaped at Christine—

Her mouth wasn't moving – but Madge heard her voice again.

Your turn, Madge. Just speak with your mind and think of your intended audience.

Madge gaped at Christine, and all the others who were watching and waiting for her to try. But she wasn't nervous – because this all felt so *natural*, floating with them all, underwater in a circle in mer-form, speaking into each other's minds.

Go on – just speak, like you do in your own mind, but will it towards us...

Max's voice said in her mind as he reached out and squeezed her hand.

Finally, Madge squeezed back – and then—

Um... Can you hear this?

Max nodded – but the others still had vacant expressions.

Yes, I can hear you. Can the others?

No one else moved or replied.

You have to direct to all of us. Try it again.

Madge looked at everyone in turn, and said—

Okay... I'm speaking to everyone now. Is it working?

Pearl smiled and gave a thumb's up, as Madge heard her voice say—

Well done, let's get some air everyone.

When she surfaced now – after the very first exercise, Madge's senses were on *fire*.

Just like when she'd gotten stuck in the ravine – her skin was tingling everywhere.

But more than that, she could hear the surf hitting the sand on shore – and she felt things lurking in the depths below, as she had done on her very first swim.

"Our bodies are made up of around sixty percent water. Much like the amount of ocean covering the earth," Pearl said as she waved her hand towards the Pacific. "I'm sure without hardly any effort on your part, that you're feeling the power it provides surging through you."

Madge nodded. "That night I swam – I was pulled to some blue whales. It was like on instinct. And right now – I hear… everything. It's crystal clear…"

"That's something we can even do as a pod," Pearl said with a nod, "Together we could, if we wanted, home in on an energy or life source and be pulled towards it. But not today. We want to focus with our limited time on whether or not you have the ability to access visions."

Madge felt her stomach tighten. "Already?"

"Any other kind of Water Vala can be done without floating in an ocean, or some other source of water," Pearl said, grabbing water in her palm that formed into a ball and hovered over her palm. "Moving water like so, using voice carry as I did earlier – shoving it into someone's face like Max did. Or even affecting the *mood* of water, for example – all that can be done with your feet planted on the ground. Some visions can be accessed with a bowl, too – but the best way, the most powerful way to see things – is here. Submerged."

"Okay, let's all head back. This part will just be you and Pearl," Christine said with a tight smile as she looked apprehensively at Madge. "Food will be ready when you're done."

"Good luck" Max said, looking at her with eyes that looked like a harvest moon – more orange than brown, and with an almost imperceptible glow.

"Thanks," Madge replied, barely able to get the word out.

One by one, fins flopped up and away. And in what seemed like seconds, she saw them clambering onto the stern steps of the yacht, bobbing up and down against a blue sky. Pearl faced Madge as she touched the middle of her forehead. Her finger felt cold – and she felt something awaken within her as Pearl let go.

"What's it like?" Madge asked, her voice trembling slightly.

"Once it comes into your mind's eye, it plays… like a dream."

"So… things just… appear? Like our voices underwater, maybe?"

"Actually, that's an excellent comparison, and yes. Much like that. Simply open your mind – focus on receiving it."

"This isn't like a séance, is it?"

"Nothing like a séance, we don't speak to the dead, and they don't speak to us. It's a visual message left behind while they were living. That's why we call it a vision – or the sight."

"Do you think – I'd never considered this until now – but what if my mother or father left me one?"

Pearl smiled sadly and shrugged. "Ready to find out?"

Her heart was racing. If they had left her one, would she be able to share it?

"So – what do we do? How do I do this?"

"One word, from what I hear, you are familiar with. *Inlīht*. The one you used to help Max. The other word is *steorra*. Which means, in a way, a path to the stars through the blood. That one you say twice – I think it's done that way for emphasis. It's what calls the vision from your blood. *Inlīht* simply illuminates it and allows it to play."

"Okay… so I say inlīht – and then steorra, twice?"

"No," Pearl shook her head. "Say steorra twice first, to call it – and then inlīht, to illuminate the vision and allow it to play. Simply float underwater, and say in your mind's eye, *steorra, steorra, inlīht.*"

"Okay," Madge said, biting her lip. "Do I have to go inside my Vala to do this?" Madge hadn't told Pearl she was able to do so yet, successfully without getting stuck, with help from Giuliana. Because too many questions as to why she was accessing her Vala in the vaults would emerge, not to mention the fact she wasn't supposed to do it at all yet.

"No, not out here. You're basically floating in a well of energy, so all you do is float. Meditate for a moment, close your eyes, and recite the incantation. But make sure to try and keep your head clear before you call it. Then you wait and see."

"Got it," Madge answered, as a strange calm came over her. "I'm ready."

"Brilliant," Pearl said, her warm amber-brown eyes shining. "I'll be waiting here so you can concentrate. Follow the chain on this buoy down as far as you like – but don't let go."

Madge nodded before she ducked under, following the buoy

chain down as far as she could go while still able to see Pearl's tail fins.

Floating in place, she kept ahold of the chain – and pictured her mother's tome – the drawing. Madge hoped whatever she found, the mystery of the tree – the woman, the fruit, that monster – that all of it would be answered.

Keep your head clear, Madge reminded herself.

Putting the drawing out of her mind, she focused on the energy of the ocean and its constant inertia, the slight ebbing of current moving her hair around her head… The beating of her heart, the sounds echoing in the depths beneath her…

Her skin began to tingle wildly… Like it was burning.

She quickly squeezed her eyes shut and spoke the incantation within herself as she remembered what the words meant, what she was asking them to do… Calling on her blood.

Steorra, steorra, inlīht!

And like a flash of lightning in a dark sky, a scene illuminated.

She was snorkeling – a mask tight on her face and breathing through a mouthpiece. The water was clear and bathtub warm and white sand and colorful fish darted around coral reefs.

This was it. She was doing it – this was indeed someone else's memory.

Rising from the turquoise shallows, the heat of the sun on her back, she looked over to someone. It was her dad. *Russ.*

She felt a stab to her chest as she knew she was having a vision her mother sent. Her chin began to wobble – and though the ocean carried her tears, she felt them as the vision held.

Her mother ducked back underwater – and the scene began to darken and change as a different vision flashed and rammed through. A feeling came over her… something very old, powerful – like the space between the stars.

A cold, metallic tang rose in her mouth – like she'd been running away from something – it tasted of fear and adrenaline –

The same vision that her mother had… Swimming in Mexico, unaware she was pregnant yet – was the same one fading into her own mind. *The vision meant for her in the first place.*

Wet earth, fog, the smell of sulfur and salt…

Merlin.

It was dark, and cold, and mist hung in the forest of oaks around his peripheral vision as he looked down at a gnarled, wooden wand in a wooden box. He closed it and sealed it in a larger ornately pounded metal box, heart pounding, and placed it into a bucket to be lowered into a well to be hid. The light of a flickering torch lit the top of the well, but it couldn't be seen how far down it went. A flare of light flew overhead… then another, and another.

Arrows flamed and burst in the air all around.

A beautiful face appeared before him. This woman was ancient, wearing a plain gown and headdress. She was panicked. "Merlin," she sobbed. "Run!"

"No!" A young voice answered. "He'll never stop until we are both dead."

The woman turned her head and looked at him, as though she could see Madge instead of Merlin as though she were suddenly a ghost upon the scene.

"You must take it to Eressëa. It's the only way," she said, removing the metal box from the well. "GO!" she screamed, as a flaming arrow rammed into her back.

Darkness misted over, as the vision threatened to fade.

Madge concentrated as the last flicker of it held.

"I can carry you – if we make it to the ocean and use the wand, you can transform and heal yourself – and we can be away from here. Please! You must try!"

Madge heard a thud as the body of the woman hit the muddy, soft earth next to him. And in the night sky, stars twinkled beyond thick oak branches sprawled overhead, and the still fiery onslaught of arrows.

Madge opened her eyes and burst to the surface.

Her mother was after a wand.

15

Out of Sight

Madge was bone tired.

The visions had taken their toll, but it was more than that. Her heart felt sad.

Seeing her father for the first time in what felt like in real time – not a picture or a video but what felt like her own eyes… and feeling what her mother had felt, full of life and love and happiness, had made her feel the loss of her parents in a different way than she ever had before. She'd always wished she could have known or remembered them. But somehow, she did remember a *feeling* of them. Like tiny shards of a grainy, faded, and tattered dream.

A dream that was now in focus. Sharper, and more painful.

She'd cried her eyes out when she told Grandpa about the vision the minute they walked in the front door. He'd listened to every word, and, she knew, had spent a lot of effort biting back his own tears at the memory her mother had sent Madge.

But she left the part out about the wand being hidden in Eressëa… *The Old World*.

She had told him about the tree – with a siren hidden within it that her mother drew. But that was before the vision. The one where Merlin seemed to be going to Eressëa to hide it. And seeing Giuliana had mentioned that Eressëa was where the tree was, and the dreadful siren that guarded it, Madge didn't have the heart to say the words out loud yet that that wand and tree were likely in the Old World because getting there was impossible.

It was in another world, or realm, and her kind had been cast out of it. It would be just as likely for someone to travel to the Garden of Eden. So, instead, Madge simply huffed that she had no idea how to get to the tree or where it was, which was true, in part.

"Maybe it's fashioned from one of its branches. Maybe it's the tree, wherever it is, that's magical," Grandpa Ollie said, preparing a coffee for the night watch.

"Either way, it's likely guarded by a siren," Madge said, sighing deeply. "It's impossible, Grandpa."

"Don't jump to conclusions. You have questions, but no real answers. Not yet," he said, slipping out the back sliding door to bring the coffee when the phone rang. It was her cousin.

"I hope Ollie doesn't mind me calling so late," Selene said.

"It's okay," Madge said, glancing at the clock. It was only nine. "What's up?"

"Are you alone? I mean can your Grandpa hear you?"

"No. I mean yes. I am alone, and he can't hear me."

"I just wanted to check on you. When you got out of the water you… Well, you seemed different. But you said you didn't see anything."

"I think I'll try again sometime." Madge cleared her throat. She wondered how many more times she'd have to lie.

"You were down there for a while."

"I was trying to focus. It was a lot of information for one day." Madge stopped short – she didn't want to keep going, to dig the lie any deeper than she had to. An awkward pause ensued before Selene said anything again.

"I just feel like – I feel like we haven't gotten to know each other yet. So… I was thinking it's time you and I had that swim. Just the two of us. *Cousins*."

"Sure…" Madge said, glancing over her shoulder to make sure Grandpa Ollie was still outside. "When?"

"Tomorrow. You're ditching school with me."

"*Tomorrow*? In the daytime? Ditch school?"

"School is the only place we are allowed to be where you aren't watched. So, we ditch and slip under their noses that way. It's the only way. Trust me, I've thought about it."

Madge drummed her fingers on the countertop and thought hard. What kind of trouble would she be in if she went along with this? Perhaps Grandpa would understand?

"Hello?"

"Sorry," Madge said, biting back the words she knew she was about to say. She knew he would be disappointed, but she wanted this time with her cousin… and the ocean had been calling her, and she hadn't been able to answer it. She needed this, if only for a day. "Let's do it."

"Awesome!" Selene screeched. "Meet at the Bear Paw?"

"Seven a.m.?"

"Perfect. Oh, and Madge, don't tell Max."

The ocean was an angry display of white caps this morning, and the tops of the trees were swaying, and rain blew sideways against her windshield as she pulled into town.

Maybe Selene would change her mind, rather than go out

into *that*. Madge hoped not.

The Bear Paw was busy, but thankfully Selene was already sat at a table near the window, her white-blonde hair pulled back in a loose braid under a teal blue beret.

"What do you think – about this weather?" Madge asked, sitting down to the Black Bear Latte Selene slid across the table to her.

"The ocean kicks up more energy in a storm," Selene said, smiling devilishly. "It's actually my favorite kind of weather to swim in. Makes for empty beaches, too."

"Perfect," Madge said, mirroring that smile. She couldn't ask for better weather to suit her mood, anyway.

"Is that Ash?" Selene asked, pointing to the brown Honda parking outside the café.

"I told her to meet us here – it's okay if she knows, right?"

Selene nodded, considering. "She can tell Max you stayed home today," Selene said, waving and smiling at Ash as she squeezed through the door and out of the blustering wind.

"I have a lot to tell you," Ash said, sliding in next to Madge as she removed her bright orange puffer jacket and wool bucket cap. "I got in trouble this weekend. First time in forever since I've actually been grounded."

"Welcome to the club," Selene said, waving her hand in the air. "I've been grounded since summer. With no end in sight."

"What happened?" Madge asked. "Your parents never ground you. For anything."

"I went to a party. I told my parents I was going to your house. They found out."

"Speaking of doing things we aren't supposed to," Selene said, leaning conspiratorially across the table, "we need your help today to keep Madge from being grounded, too."

"I'm listening," Ash said with a small, wicked smile.

Swapping jackets and hats with Ash worked like a charm, and Selene and Madge made it to the trailhead without being followed.

The secluded hike down to Crescent Beach wound through old growth forest, along steep windswept bluffs, until it wound down again through the trees along a narrow trail, opening onto the beach which was shaped like a crescent moon between two headlands.

The sand was pristine, not a footprint in sight. Cold wind and sand bit their faces as they headed towards the surf. Madge felt jubilant. She hadn't been out in it – just to be in it, since the first night she'd learned what she was. "Ready?" Madge asked, her face spread wide in a smile.

"Run straight into the water – and wade past those rock boulders before you transform," Selene said, hiding their bags behind a large piece of driftwood as she pointed towards the large basalt outcropping poking up like dragon's teeth from the water. "Because you never know if someone is watching. Go!"

They sprinted from the tree line, across wind-blown sand, and sloshing into the frigid ocean, which was contending with the rocks in a display of angry foam that swirled and splashed around their legs as if trying to shove them back to shore. They pushed on until they hit a dip in the sand – and before Madge could brace herself, icy water rushed into her wetsuit.

It took more effort than she'd realized not to allow the transformation, and the water was colder, much colder knowing she'd barely notice it if she could. Her feet were like ice.

"It is *freezing*!" Madge complained, paddling like a dog above water to keep her neck and face out of the water. "Come on, we are alone—"

"Don't!" Selene screeched, grabbing onto Madge's wrist and pulling her around a wall of rock... just as a wave crashed over her head, soaking her skull—

And just in time.

Her body took over instantly, skin hardening and becoming scales and fins where her icy numb feet had been. It took a minute to gather her breath, to relax her muscles.

"Just breathe," Selene said, relaxing in the water on her back so her pale blonde hair splayed around her face.

"I am. *Now*," Madge laughed, exhilaration filling her belly as the rush and hum of the ocean and storm coursed through her. This was more than a tingling – it was almost electric. "I'm feeling it right now... The *storm*."

Selene angled her head at Madge, her eyes glowing. "Swimming in a storm is – it's like lightning in your veins."

"Your eyes – our eyes – they change in the water, don't they?"

Selene nodded her head. "I forget you don't know all the little nuances that happen with the transformation. Yours are a lot greener in the middle – like a vivid, rainforest green, and the brown bits are like... dark honey – and then there is a bluish green rim around the edge."

"Don't laugh, but I brought a mirror. I was curious!" Madge said, pulling a small mirror from a hidden pocket in her wetsuit.

"You have a mirror with you?" Selene laughed, shaking her head.

It was hard to see her reflection in a wet mirror, but she could see well enough. It was hard to believe those were her eyes staring back, and just as Selene had described them.

"So... Where we off to?" Madge asked, snapping the mirror shut and putting it away.

Madge scanned the white caps disappearing into the horizon as the sound of the crashing surf pounded in her ears, watching her cousin do the same from the corner of her eye.

"What was it – on your solo swim – that you were pulled towards again?"

"A pod of blue whales. Why?"

"Let's swim to whatever pulls us. As a two-person pod."

"How do we do that?" Madge asked, her eyes growing wide with excitement.

"Same way you did it on your own. I'll show you. We'll connect underwater," Selene said, turning towards Madge as her expression turned serious. "Oh – and one more thing. Stay with me at all times. Just in case, okay?"

"Yeah, about that. What if—"

"No what-ifs, not right now. Let's go," Selene said, not waiting for a response as she disappeared with a flash of her tail fins below water.

Madge shoved the *what-ifs* from her mind, took a deep breath and submerged.

Selene's pale hair swirled around her as she swam in place, as if listening for something.

Feel that? Just focus on the energy around you. You'll feel it...

Selene looked into Madge's face and waited. Madge felt the water – the usual ebb and flow of the swelling tides more of a swirl and ripple with the storm – and she felt the hidden depths again, the little creatures... Until she felt a spark. A pull

– similar to what she'd felt when she'd followed it unwittingly before.

What is it?

Madge asked, her face erupting into a smile.

Let's find out. Come on, stay with me!

Madge had to swim hard to keep on Selene's flank. She swam with her arms taut, pale hair streaming behind her, and Madge matched her move for move as they turned and propelled through the water, at times twirling and jumping as they surfaced for air, pulled by that spark, getting stronger and stronger as they followed it.

It was *nirvana*, and Madge was lost in it, all worries vanished from her mind. Ditching school, possibly getting caught and disappointing Grandpa... Winning the Council. A wand and a tree. Her aunt and the siren relic she carried and its voice. Not a hint rested on her mind.

They swam on until she could feel a slight difference in the water. Madge remembered that feeling from her first swim – and she knew they were on the continental shelf as she felt the depth drop beneath her where the ocean's bottom plunged many fathoms farther down. But she felt something *else*, too—

There!

Selene pointed left as she halted and floated in place.

Some distance away, floating in the distance—

Orcas!

A whole pod of them, with distinct black and white markings and a dorsal fin.

That's not an Orca. The tail is too small.

Madge looked more closely. They were different – the tail was different. They were smaller, for starters, and even the dorsal fin was much shorter and had a white tip. The dorsal fin on an Orca was tall and black.

Okay, kid who was raised at a Marine Ecological Institute. What are they?

Dall's Porpoises. They're friendly, let's go!

Madge followed Selene – who approached the pod carefully, moving much slower this time, until they were swimming alongside them.

Concentrate on their energy – which is nothing like an Orca. What do you feel?

Madge swam alongside the porpoise nearest her, who was eyeing her just as curiously as she was it. It had a squat head, and its mouth looked like it was upturned into a smile. The porpoise felt...

Gentle.

Madge stretched her hand out and softly touched its dorsal fin. Entranced by the sweet nature and connection Madge felt with *her* – somehow Madge knew she was a female – she willed her voice to the porpoise.

Hello.

Instantly she called back in light chirps and clicks. Madge felt like her heart could explode with sheer exhilaration and joy that she'd just communicated with one, and she looked wildly around for her cousin, wondering and hoping she'd heard it, too.

Tell me you heard that! She spoke to me!

Madge twirled around and around – but she didn't see Selene anywhere – and Selene wasn't answering.

Selene?

As if the pod sensed something wrong, they dispersed and swam away – like they were fleeing from something. And they were fast. Gone so quickly that Madge hardly had time to think about following – that maybe Selene was still with them...

Or maybe... Panic began to settle in.

Maybe she'd just gone up for air – and that's why she wasn't answering... Fear tightened her chest as she ascended to the surface, swirling and bubbling with the storm...

No sign of a coppery scale anywhere.

Madge surfaced, whipped by wind and pelted with rain as she swiveled around and around in the rolling ocean. Searching every white cap in sight, wishing one of them was instead the white-blonde head of her cousin...

"Selene!" Madge screamed, though her voice was swallowed by the storm.

She must have swum off with the porpoises... Thinking she was following, too.

Madge submerged again, hoping to home in on their energy again and find them – when instantly a voice screamed in her mind—

Madge!

Madge heard her just as she felt a rush come upon her from behind.

Selene sped towards her – with a terrified look on her face. She too, like the porpoises moments ago, was fleeing from something.

Go! GO! Stay with me!

Madge followed without question as terror rose in her stomach, the sea swallowing the tears that wanted to come from her eyes. She swam as hard as she could, trying not to think of what may be following them or even wanting to ask Selene what it was when—

What do we have here?

Madge's blood froze. It was not Selene's voice that hissed inside her mind just now.

Black figures sped into her peripheral vision. For a split second she hoped it was the porpoises, but she knew better.

Madge chanced a glance to her right –

Black scales, long dark hair, and a cocky grin back at Madge as she swam alongside her almost with *ease*.

Daeds?

Madge asked Selene who swam on her left.

You bank left – and get out of here! I'll take care of her!

A burst of white shocked through the water from Selene's hands – and the dark haired Daed twisted and banked deeper – and they were gone.

Madge swam hard and banked left…

Selene! I can't—

She'll be fine. No one will harm my daughter.

Her voice entered Madge's mind just as her figure did from Madge's peripheral vision – blonde hair. Dark scales.

Madge felt like ice was filling her veins as she recognized that face—

Her *aunt*. The one who murdered her parents. And who wanted to do the same to her.

Viviane smiled wickedly as she shot past, when Madge noticed she had a bag slung across her back….

Mimir's Head.

Madge banked right –– her mind racing wildly as she recalled Selene saying she'd carried it in the water before – when Viviane had found her that day, too. What were they thinking?

Selene shot back onto her flank, the dark haired Daed on

her tail – and another one, too.

Leave her alone!

Selene's voice screeched in her mind just as Madge came almost face to face with a younger looking, male Daed—

Better run while you can, witch.

His voice whispered in Madge's mind, just as he shot in and grabbed Selene's arm, the dark-haired woman on the other. And before Madge knew what to do, they were dragging Selene swiftly through the water towards Viviane – who had a number of other Daeds flanking her, behind her. But Madge didn't bother counting bodies because that wasn't the worse part.

It was the golden head she held in front of her.

Its horrible face gleamed in the water, and Madge froze as terror seized every muscle. Snakes crowned its head, and it looked exactly like the face from the drawing in the tree, except covered in gold and lifeless. Or so Madge thought, until she swore she saw the snakes *move*.

Everything felt like it was going in slow motion, as she watched helplessly as Selene was dragged towards it.

What are you doing to her?

Madge demanded, willing her voice to her aunt—

But her aunt didn't answer her. Nothing but a cackle filled Madge's mind.

Hearing it filled Madge's whole body with rage, beginning in her belly, spreading until her whole body crackled with it, until her scales felt like they would burn… Until she felt her blood turn to ice and heat, until the crackling surged and erupted from inside her, knocking her back several feet in the water as it shot from her hands—

And a massive ball, the size of Madge's own head, of

crackling white and blue sparked and hurled towards Viviane. *Towards that ghastly head.*

Madge barely had time to register Viviane's wide-eyed horror before a red burst of energy fizzed like fireworks hitting water, as it collided with the ball of blue-white flame and exploded in a cloud of froth and bubble.

And in the midst of the maelstrom – before her eyes adjusted to the water around her, bubbling like seltzer in a glass – she felt an iron grip clamp her wrists.

Greek fire. Impressive.

The man who was at her car that day – Malcolm. He stared at her with sharp blue eyes; the threat behind them like a blade to her throat. Madge thrashed and thrashed against his grip, but it did no good—

Stop struggling, princess. Malcolm could snap your little neck if I told him to.

Viviane's voice was cold and commanding.

What do you want? Why are you trying to hurt your own daughter?

Madge willed her voice into all their minds but stared at her aunt.

Viviane didn't answer – her expression was stone cold as she stared back at Madge with empty eyes. As she turned her attention to her daughter, no longer fighting and limp as she faced Mimir's Head. And like lightning, one of the golden snakes struck Selene on the neck.

Madge felt like the bottom of the very earth was dropping out.

Selene's blood formed a small ribbon in the water, and the world started to spin.

Madge squeezed her eyes shut, unable to take any more,

consciousness slipping away…

Next thing she knew – she could be dreaming it – but her wrists were free.

Madge! Come on, they're gone.

Selene? It was Selene's voice.

She gently grasped Madge's hand and led her to the surface. Warmth emanated from Selene's palm – and Madge knew her cousin was doing something to help stop the vertigo in her mind and body that was still spinning out of control, so much so Madge wouldn't have known which way was up.

But she could feel eyes from the deep watching her… like a pair of jaws would rise up and swallow her whole at any moment.

16

Murmuring Madness

Madge and Selene hadn't stopped running until they'd gotten to the car. Selene had been inconsolable the whole ride home, grasping at the wound on her neck.

She'd been bitten... by a *relic* – if that's what this thing even was.

Madge ran after Selene through the side of the Institute, up the stairs and into safety of her room, where Selene seemed to grow worse by the second. Worse of all, she'd mumbled something about *a voice singing in her head*.

"Selene, I'm going to go get help—"

"Why would she do this to me?" Selene wailed, grasping a picture she'd fished from her bedside table. A woman with blonde hair and a million-dollar smile held a bald, blue eyed baby girl. Viviane. Before she'd... turned. She was sunny – and looked happy.

Gulping against the panic lodged in her throat, Madge asked, "what does it sound like?"

"It whispers... *And sings and sings.* And then... whispers

things again."

"In a language you don't understand... beautiful, but scares you at the same time?" Madge asked as she gently moved Selene's hair from her neck. Her cousin vaguely nodded as Madge beheld two slightly raised marks, beginning to scab over.

"This might be poisonous. I'll get Kento – or Pearl," Madge breathed, making to get up.

"Cetus," Selene's voice rasped, as her hand curled around Madge's wrist. "Cetus is in the night sky now—" Selene began before she stopped short, her attention diverted behind Madge.

"Cetus?" Madge asked as a chill walked up her spine. "Is that its name?"

"It's a constellation," Max breathed, stepping through the door behind them, followed by Ash who looked extremely uncomfortable to barge into Selene's room.

"We came to find you – so we can switch cars back," Ash said with a nervous shrug.

"What happened?" Max demanded, gaping at Selene.

"Cetus shines on the water at night, and the gate is open..." Selene said as she stared at Madge with wild eyes. "For you."

"Did she take something?" Max asked Madge, whispering loudly as he checked the door behind him as if someone might be listening.

"No! We just went for a swim. But we ran into Viviane—"

"What?" Max said, doing his best not to yell. "Are you both *crazy*?"

"She had the stolen relic and the snakes on its head bit her," Madge said, as the weight of all that had happened began to settle in her chest, causing her chin to wobble and her hands to shake. "I think she's in the siren's thrall," Madge breathed, barely able to say the words out loud.

"I'm never going into the ocean again!" Ash gasped, grasping onto Max's arm.

"Siren's thrall?" Max repeated in a slow drawl, dropping to his knees. "The relic *bit* her?"

"I saw the snakes move with my own eyes. Look," Madge said as she held back Selene's hair from her neck. "And now its voice is in her head, whispering things, and she's hearing the same singing I heard."

"How did you witness this – and get away? Why would they hurt Selene and not you?" Max asked, turning his burning eyes on Madge.

"That's what I thought, too, but—"

"Did it bite *you*?" Max asked Madge as his eyes widened in fear, as he reached out and moved her hair from her neck—

"No," Madge said, grasping his hand. "They let us go. But whatever it's done to her – Viviane did it on purpose."

"She wants me to be one of them," Selene yelped, her shoulders shaking.

"I'll get Kento—"

"NO!" Selene grabbed Max's wrist and beseeched him with panicked eyes. "You need to listen. He can't help me. No one can. It's on the other side."

"What's on the other side?" Madge asked, feeling her heart thunder in her ears.

"The Lost Isle. It said the fruit I need to heal is there."

Madge felt blood drain from her face. "The Lost Isle?" Madge asked, though she already knew the answer that was coming. The tree. The fruit. The siren on the *other side*.

"It's where we came from," Max said. "The Old World."

"Eressëa," Madge said, feeling like she was going to be sick. "Giuliana – the sea nymph, mentioned sirens guard a tree there – because its fruit is the only cure to their bite. The bite of a siren. The siren's thrall – I went to her with questions after what happened to me."

"But if she told you about Eressëa, you'd know it's impossible to go there—"

"It's not impossible for her, Morgaine's descendant," Selene said as she pointed a finger at Madge, then moved it to point at the darkening sky outside. "She has to go while Cetus shines above the gate, just as Morgaine did. It says it over… and over… and over again."

"Morgaine?" Madge asked. "The sorceress, renowned in Camelot?

"Hold up. There's a gate to the Old World? To Eressëa?" Max asked, waving away Madge's awe that Morgaine was a part of the picture coming together now.

Selene nodded with hollow eyes.

Madge's breath hitched in her chest. She'd save questions about Arthurian legends and history for later – "Did it say where to find this gate?"

"No," Selene said as she shook her head. "Just that you have to go through it while Cetus shines in the night sky."

"The water nymph might know something," Max said as he looked over at Madge as though a great idea hit him. "We were taught – it's been said that sea nymphs guard the gate to the Old World. So, she might know…"

Giuliana knew? That there was a way there – or might be, even? But had failed to mention it? "Seriously?" Madge asked, standing to her feet. "I'll go ask her. You get Kento—"

"Wait!" Ash interrupted. "How am I the only one who

thinks this sounds like a trap?"

"Is it, Selene?" Max asked, trying to keep his voice gentle.

"I don't know," Selene whimpered, casting her gaze to look up at Madge.

"Well, there's only one way to find out," Madge said, standing to leave. She was angry. At Viviane, for doing this to her own daughter. At the sea nymph, who she thought she could trust… At herself, for lying to Max and Grandpa and everyone – if she hadn't gone…

"How didn't you think about this – I mean, you *knew* Viviane can supposedly find you, using blood Vala. And she can find Selene, too. What were you thinking?" Max asked as Madge stood by the door, frozen and stung by his words, by the angry expression on his face.

"It's my fault," Selene croaked, "It was my idea."

"It's not your fault, cousin," Madge said, shaking her head.

"It's both your faults," Max said, his voice cold.

"I'm sorry that we lied to you," Madge said, facing him as hot tears started to form in her eyes. "But maybe I don't want to trust someone who accepts a ride home from me so he can spy on me, and control me like everyone else," Madge said, sweeping out into the hallway before the tears started to fall.

17

Morgaine

Madge had every intention of going straight to Giuliana, but the minute she descended the steps into the hidden pools below the atrium, there was a stillness that hung in the air – and a whisper that waited to be heard. Heavy steam rose from the water, filling the cavernous space with an eerie mist that breathed onto her face, beckoning her to get in.

Morgaine.

The name had sung over and over in her mind as she ran through the halls of the Institute, through the backyard, through the hidden hatch in the atrium and down the dark, steep steps that led to the hidden pools, until she'd slammed to a stop at the bottom, met by a curtain of mist.

Madge crept forward as steamy tendrils swirled around her – and the second she stepped forward her belly started to tingle – as if to tell her there was *more*. Another vision – from her ancestor, Morgaine. She could feel it pulling at her mind, its whisper in the water surrounding her, waiting to be grabbed up from the ether, waiting behind the curtain of mist. She could feel it like a sigh not yet loosed… A sigh over a thousand years old that held a message – and all she had to do was draw back the curtain.

Madge shook with anticipation as she stared at the glowing water before her.

This could be the only way to help her cousin…

To finally unravel what her mother was trying to do – to get to the Old World. And perhaps she'd arm herself with her own answers before she picked a bone with the sea nymph.

Venturing all the way to the back of the pools near the entrance to the vault and the cascading water that hid the door, as deep as she could go into the mists, Madge slipped into the warm, saltwater pool. She was readying her breath and senses, about to duck under when she felt like she was being watched. Someone or something was *here*.

She turned slowly around, and screamed as a figure walked slowly through the steam towards her—

"It's just me!" Max called out. "Want to tell me why you're swimming in your jeans?"

"What are you doing following me?" Madge said, ignoring his question.

"I… wanted to apologize," Max said, stopping at the edge of the pool.

Madge looked up at him, even though she wanted to hide her eyes that were likely red from crying. "For what? Telling the truth?"

"For saying things that hurt and didn't help. And I don't spy on you, for the record."

"So you followed me down here to tell me you're sorry?" Madge said, smiling a little.

Max shrugged, searching her face. "Why are you in the

pool? I thought you were going to see the nymph."

"I need to access a vision. From Morgaine."

"I thought you couldn't..."

"I lied. *Again*," Madge said with a helpless shrug. "My mother painted a vision she had – at least I believe it was a vision, and it involved something she was working on to become queen... something I was asked to keep secret until the time came. I did have a vision in the ocean that day – but it wasn't the one my mother painted – it was from a different ancestor, one who I believe also may have travelled to the Old World. But after what Selene just told me – that *Morgaine* is my ancestor – I realize now that what she painted was Morgaine's vision. Who if I am correct and what my mother painted was what I think it is – then she too, was bit – by a siren. So, if I am to help Selene, I need to access that vision."

"Whoa – *wait*. I'm getting in," Max said as he plopped into the pool and waded towards Madge, his brows knit together as he tried to piece together what Madge was saying. "So... Who is this lady? You sound like you know who this descendent Morgaine is—"

"Morgaine of Camelot."

Max stopped before her, wiping a wet hand over his face as if trying to clear his thoughts. "Camelot? As in Knights of the Round Table and all of that?"

Madge nodded as she tried to keep her attention away from the wet t-shirt clinging to his sculpted chest. "And Merlin, too – his was the vision I had in the ocean that day."

Max stared back at her with raised brows. "As in Merlin the *Wizard*."

Madge nodded. "Yes, that one."

"Okay... Don't tell me she was looking for the Sacred Cup

or whatever it is?"

"No – no cup," Madge said, remaining serious. "His quest was for a wand, not a cup. One that he hid in the Old World and that allows a Merewif to transform. And my mom's plan – the one no one knew about – was to retrieve that wand. And it so happens that is where the only thing that will cure Selene is – fruit from the Tree of Life. The only cure for a siren's thrall."

"Wait. Stop," Max said, putting warm hands on both of her shoulders as he stepped even closer. His smell – the wind on the ocean – and the way he was looking at her made her knees weak. "This smells all wrong. Your mom wanted to go there – that's where she must have gone to when she was murdered, along with your dad. And now Viviane is trying to get *you* to go."

"It's the only way to help Selene. And I need some answers – I'm not going anywhere, not yet. I just need to get ahold of Morgaine's vision – if it exists at all."

Max let go of her shoulders but didn't back away. "Fine. I'll be waiting here."

He was so close. All she'd have to do is lift her eyes – and there would be a kiss, waiting to be had. She could feel it. And it surprised her – how much she wanted it. But she couldn't do it – not right now. Instead, she nodded, casting her gaze down as she waded towards the deep end of the pool before she had the courage to look at him again. "I'm glad you're here," she said, stopping at the deep end. "Um, I'll be right back, I guess."

"Hurry up," Max said, frowning deeply and biting into his bottom lip.

Madge nodded her head.

Then she took a deep breath and plunged her head underwater. Transforming as she swam deeper, she focused her mind away from Max's wet shirt and full lips – and onto the vision she sought... *Morgaine. Tree. Eressëa...*

But as she propelled with her fins, floating in the deepest part of the pool, she was distracted by something burning on her chest.

Her necklace.

She pulled the stone that had held her Vala but had been clear since the day it was released, in front of her face. It was hot to the touch, even underwater, but the perplexing part was that it now glowed within – with red and orange *flames*. She stared at it, wondering what it could mean, when her mind flashed.

She saw fire. *Torch* fire.

Madge was inside the mind of the person who sent the vision, just like last time.

And no incantation needed this time, apparently.

She stood, barefooted, the hem of her long dress brushing her ankles, near the bottom of a narrow sea cove, banked by steep cliffs, where water slid from mossy rock into a small pool before cascading down into the crashing surf. She stared down at her image in the pool of water. Her face pale and hard to make out, her hair long and dark, the fiery reflection of the torch she held in her hand quivering on the water. Her breath misted in the air before her – it was so cold it could only be winter, and she wore a heavy fur around her shoulders.

"Morgaine! Wait!" A woman's voice called out behind her. Morgaine turned back onto the rocky trail and picked up her pace – just a short distance to the water's edge. All that stood before her was crashing water and a short swim to the dark mouth of a sea cave, the cliffs around it reflecting the light of a pale moon, now high on the horizon.

Madge's heart pounded along with the heart of Morgaine as if they were one body. Madge felt what *she* felt. The cold beneath her feet. The sharp anticipation of what lay ahead.

She turned before she jumped into the freezing surf to see a woman who stood behind her, the torch she carried reflecting off her golden hair and the golden crown circling her head. Madge knew without a second thought that this was the infamous Guinevere.

As she was the sun, Morgaine was the moon.

"You don't have to do this! Morgaine, please – just listen to me. Arthur will bend his will – I can talk to him!"

Morgaine dove.

Her body hit the frigid water, drowning out whatever the golden lady had to say. Madge felt fear, regret, and anger in Morgaine as her skin grew hard with scales, and her legs powered towards the cave, driven by her tail fins.

She took a glance back. The cliffs of Camelot shone under the moonlight, the castle citadel lit by torch fire, bathing its turrets, grounds and banners, pale against the dark sky and host of stars beyond. Madge knew that somehow Morgaine saw the constellation Cetus up there, *somewhere*.

Pushing forward, she swam with the tide and was swallowed by the mouth of the cave.

It was almost perfect darkness within minutes, as the entrance disappeared. Her mer-vision barely sufficed and Morgaine had to feel her way through as she swam fast and hard, skimming rocks and shallows, until she could make out the exit to the cave, lit faintly by a sparkling, moonlit ocean on the other side.

Her heart quickened as she saw two watery figures floated on either side of the exit...

Sea nymphs!

Just as soon as she had noticed they were there, a torrent of water rose and swirled violently, filling the space that used to be the exit and the moonlit sea beyond with what she knew was a gate to Eressëa. The nymphs were letting her through after all.

In a quivering breath, Morgaine steeled herself as she plunged herself into it.

And in a brief second of pain – Madge wasn't sure *what* she felt as she squeezed through – she rose from the water.

On the other side.

Brilliant sunlight blinded her eyes. The sea she'd left behind was tumultuous and dark, but here, it was calm, and clear as glass.

The sea cave and pale rock met with a tall, white stone wall that reached to the heavens. She could neither see the end of it upwards, nor the length of the thing. But she could make out the gates – just barely. Their gold color reflecting in the sunlight, and to its right side, was a huge expanse of green that reached up and up and *up*–

The tree. The *Treoliffruma*.

As she craned her neck skyward, trying to see past a narrow fringe of mist and cloud, she noticed winged creatures flew high overhead in a breathtaking span of dark wings and golden armor, glinting in the sunlight. Morgaine bit back a scream as fear and trepidation reached her core – and then she heard them *singing*.

It wasn't the sight of them that took her breath away now, but the haunting chorus of their voices. And as they sang together, their song seemed to echo from all directions... yet she felt their call lure and pull her to a particular direction – away from where she tried to swim. Away from the gates and the *tree*. The Treoliffruma, which Morgaine now set her gaze upon.

She gritted her teeth and steeled her will – she knew she had to shut them out somehow, so she tore pieces of cloth from the hem of her dress and stuffed her ears with it, then plunged into the glassy sea as far down as she could. Even now, their voices were muffled, but she could *still* hear them. It took all her will power to keep towards the gates, their golden reflection easy to make out even as she swam low and skimmed the brilliant white sand beneath her.

Morgaine knew by instinct to be quiet – so when she reached the shallows and rose from the water, she moved as noiselessly and slowly as possible – almost reverently, even, the golden gates no more than a glint in her peripheral vision.

The Tree of Life was bigger than any tree she'd ever seen or begun to imagine. The top, wherever it stretched, was hidden in the mist and cloud that clung to the white walls of the fortress, its trunk was as wide as the castle of Camelot itself.

And swirling in that mist and cloud above the tree were the winged creatures, so high up they looked like nothing more than huge birds – but she knew better, as they were still singing their haunting chorus. There were so many of them. And she was still horribly exposed here.

Morgaine held her breath – just one more step until she could be hidden beneath its green shade, under its mighty bows heavy with red fruit.

And in one long stride, she swept her body beneath it,

crouching low as she let go of her breath. She was shaking and almost dizzy with relief as she stood up to her full height. The voices had stopped, too. It was as if their call couldn't penetrate here.

The light beneath seemed to glow... and the fruit was the most perfect and beautiful fruit she'd ever seen. Morgaine dragged her eyes to the twisting roots that angled up from the rock and between sand and wisps of long sea grass.

Her eyes stopped on something hidden in a crook. *Merlin's box*.

Morgaine had come for the wand.

No, Guinevere couldn't stop her from this. She'd come here knowing the dangers she'd face. She knew because Merlin had warned her as much and she also knew from the deafening singing that had only momentarily ago been echoing all around her and reverberating in her mind. But if she didn't do this, her life would be endangered in her own kingdom, along with everyone else she knew and loved within it. This was the only way to raise a Saelfen army large enough to contend with the Saxons – whose Saelfen legions far outweighed theirs.

The fact that Arthur's first son wasn't actually his – but was a half-blooded Merewif, was no longer of any importance if they didn't have a kingdom for him to inherit. There was no whisper of it anyway, not after the transformation – regardless of his dark hair. The wand could unseat him – could even lead towards his exile – but none of it mattered now.

And she was so close... only feet away from grabbing it.

But as Morgaine crept towards it, a voice reached her ears, and this one was *closer* than any of the others had been before, followed by a great rustling in the tree above her head.

She looked slowly up as her blood ran cold: high up in its branches a winged woman with a serpentine tale sat and sang. Its melody rang in her ears until she thought she'd go mad with it, and every fiber of her knew she needed to flee… and yet Morgaine stood frozen, unable to take her eyes off the thing.

Its black wings were relaxed behind it, the bottoms draping far down into sharp points, and its wing tops arched high above its head, framing the beautiful face of a woman. Yet only the upper half of her was, her bottom half a black serpentine tail wound all the way down the tree, tipped by a golden rattle. Her upper body was slender and muscular, every inch covered in golden armor, and her head covered in a tall, ornate head piece, pointed at the top. But her eyes could not hide what she was: they were as black as an abyss.

And looking straight at her.

And the singing that had once filled her ears stopped, and the silence this time, for a heartbeat, was *deafening*.

"What do we have here?" she hissed, as she uncoiled her tail from around the tree, spread her great wings, and swooped down in a rush of air and shadow.

Standing up on her tail like a cobra before Morgaine, she assessed her with her dark abysmal eyes, until her red lips curled up into a feral smile, revealing sharp teeth, as she stared down at the box Morgaine was only feet away from. She picked up the box with lazy interest, her hand tipped with sharp, golden claws, as she drawled, "I hear the sing from the tree. A part of it has returned?"

Morgaine found herself answering though she didn't want to utter a word. "A piece of it that my people have held on to since we were cast out, fashioned into a *wand*. A fool brought it here to hide it, and I've come to retrieve it."

"It hums with a *different* power, the essence of the tree mixed with something *else*. What does this wand do?" the winged creature said as she examined the metal box, not knowing it was a box at all, Morgaine realized. Otherwise she would have opened it. Indeed, the thing didn't know what a wand was, either.

Morgaine wanted to flee – she didn't want to commune with the creature before her, but she couldn't turn away from it. It was as if her very will had been taken from her in its presence. And she found herself answering her again, despite her greatest efforts not to. "Our Queen used it on her bastard son so that the King may not find out she would birth him a half-blood child that is not his. It gifts this child the power to transform, to have the same gifts as a *true blood*. Saelfen blood!" Morgaine said as her chest heaved with terror.

"Secrets loosed are delicious indeed," the creature said through a smile, in a flash of pointed teeth, her eyes dark and *hungry*. "I have no use for this wand," she said, throwing the box to the ground. "But a Saelfen I have not tasted for quite some time. Not since your kind were banished, and we have been stuck here to rot. Do you know who I am?"

Morgaine was shaking like a leaf. "Not who – but I know what you *are*."

"What am I?" She spoke with a deathly calm through bared teeth as she removed her helmet, revealing a crown of snakes, hissing and angling towards her.

"Siren. *Daedscua*," Morgaine said, and then spat at the ground before her as she reached for her chest, pulling up a necklace with a large blue stone hanging from it. "And I will not answer your call!" Morgaine screeched as she held the stone before her, a protective amulet that she had thought would work against the siren. But before she could react, it moved like lightening, and struck Morgaine, sending her body flying.

And as she fell to the ground, her body twisting and propelling until she finally slammed into the water – the first thing she felt was that her wrist was burning... and bleeding.

She'd been bit, on the wrist, just like in the picture her mother drew.

As fast as a whip, the siren coiled her tail around Morgaine's arm and pulled her up out of the water to stand before her. "Try now to resist me, you *fool*. I am Lilith, Siren *Queen*."

Morgaine had nothing to lose – she could almost see her life flashing before her, as Lilith looked down upon her with the greatest darkness in her eyes that Morgaine had ever beheld. It swallowed everything... light, hope...

"I could never resist you, your highness," Morgaine said as she secretly drew a great, heavy sword she had kept hidden under her dress skirts at her side. "And I shall not try!"

And in one swipe she cleaved Lilith's head from her body.

As Lilith's head rolled over, its face transformed from beautiful to hideous, its mouth wide open as it screeched through pointed teeth. Her body capsized and writhed on the ground, as its arms frantically searched for its head. Morgaine batted the still screaming head away from the body with the blade of the sword, knowing she wouldn't get a second chance if the body reunited with it. As she did so, she stepped backwards and out of the shade of the tree and away from the giant tail that was slithering and slapping the ground, searching for Morgaine, perhaps to coil her up and never let her go...

But what happened next sent goosebumps all the way up to the crown of her head.

A host of screams and screeches filled the sky, as if in answer to the same screeching call that their queen, Lilith had just loosed. Morgaine looked up and could see the winged sirens had begun to circle like vultures, more quickly and in tighter circles, making their way down.

They were coming.

She was about to turn and run – and swim away – when Lilith's voice filled her mind.

Return my head and I will help you and share with you the secrets of the universe.

And just as she heard it and was about to cut and run – something writhed and slapped in the water – and Morgaine almost jumped out of her skin as she saw Lilith's head, floating in the water behind her... but it had turned to *gold*.

Morgaine looked up at the body – but it had gone still and still lay beneath the tree.

"If this is true, tell me a secret I do not yet know. Tell me how to leave here *alive!*"

Your bite will forever connect you to me, whether you take me or not. My voice will echo ceaselessly in your mind, until you grow mad with it or do my bidding. Your scales will turn black and you will meet your end if I will it. But if you return me to my body, I will leave you in peace. I will command my legion to do the same.

"Sirens do nothing if not lie! The fruit from the tree will heal me. As for you, you are coming with me. But only your head. I will use your voice to weave my own spells, and you shall do as you say in the hopes that someday I may return you to your body here, in Eressëa."

Morgaine again ripped cloth from the hem of her skirts and used it to cover Lilith's golden head, for though the face didn't move, she didn't trust the snakes not to. She then picked a piece of crimson fruit from the tree, and almost dropped it due to its surprising weight. It was unlike any fruit she'd ever held before, its husk felt hard and sparkled like a gemstone.

When Morgaine swam away, she took one last look to see Lilith's headless body on shore… but it was no longer there… But… She released a gasp.

In her hurry, she'd left the *wand*.

But she couldn't go back. Not now. The screeching had stopped, but the sing of the sirens vibrated in her skull. This time a powerful, desperate call that screamed in her ears as they exploded in the air, like a giant flock of crows, coming for her.

Morgaine ducked back under and swam with every ounce of power she had. She hoped it was enough to get to the cave more swiftly than the sirens could fly, though their voices seemed to pull her back towards them, like a magnet. It was like running against the wind in a storm.

Reaching the mouth of the cave – feeling at any moment a claw would reach out and snatch at her or tear into her flesh – she slammed into the wall of water that rose to meet her… just in time.

And just as Morgaine erupted back into her world – Madge came to.

Shock and terror pounded through her, and she barely could open her eyes before she erupted out of the pool for a desperate breath of air.

18

Jonah's Whale

"I can accept the fact that you're a mermaid," Ash said, closing the lid of the toilet seat and plopping down while Madge changed out of her wet clothes, "but I can't believe, still, that you have an evil aunt that carries around a severed siren's head – it sounds like... *Medusa*."

"Siren *queen*. And according to Giuliana, it has its own plans. It has no intention of helping Viviane – not without helping itself. I don't know why it's trying to get me there – but its reasons and plans can't be good. But it's still the only way to help her," Madge said, staring back at Ash with hollow, defeated eyes.

"Well... If Morgaine and Merlin made it in and back again, you can, too."

"They're... legendary. And I'm so new to this. To my *Vala*. To all of it," Madge said, dread filling her belly. "But... I feel like I've already been there. I've seen what to do – and hopefully what not to do. Only thing left to do is find out where Camelot actually stood, so I can find the cove and the cave she travelled through."

"You mean in *England*?"

"Yes," Madge said, sighing. Madge loved all things Camelot, but she'd never thought to find out an actual location or if it were even known. Somehow, even the thought of knowing its whereabouts felt like a beckoning call to sure peril as if finding the historical site of legend would make this all real. If it weren't for the fact that Selene had been bitten by the serpents crowning the head of the siren queen, she wouldn't even think to go to Eressëa and face those *things*. At least not anytime soon – even if it did mean stopping her aunt – or possibly getting the cuffs and fulfilling her mother's dying wishes.

Every inch of the worst nightmares she ever had in her entire life could be summed up in the eyes of that creature. How on earth was she going to face it? Not on earth, apparently. But somewhere else, she mused, jumping at the knock on the door.

"You two okay in there?" Grandpa Ollie said through the crack in the door. "Everyone is waiting in Pearl's office."

"Coming," Madge said, opening the door and walking out to face Grandpa Ollie. He looked tired and worried, which didn't help her feel any better about what she squared her shoulders to ask him. "Grandpa, what do you know about the constellation, Cetus?"

"On that note, I'm going to get going," Ash said, grabbing her backpack and heading for the door. "Good luck – call me!"

"The Whale," he said as he held onto the stair banister, lifting his white brows in the air as he watched Ash hurry out the front door. "What's all this about? Don't you remember the stories I told you about this one as a kid?"

Madge shook her head. "I remember the dippers and Orion's Belt – and now that you mention a whale – I vaguely remember something. But not really."

"Can this wait? Everyone is waiting—"

"It's important, Grandpa."

"You've kept everyone waiting long enough. But I'll tell you as we head towards her office then," he said, starting up the stairs. "Some know it as the whale from the Bible – the one that Jonah was inside. But to the ancient Greeks it was Cetus. The sea monster Princess Andromeda was to be sacrificed to."

"Sea Monster? What kind?"

"I've read it being described like a serpent."

"Seriously?" Madge squeaked, causing Grandpa Ollie to swivel around to look at her with wide eyes. How fitting that she was to traverse to the Old World under a constellation of what looked like a serpent, to face a siren-demon with the tail of one. And Lilith was rather like a sea-monster serpent when Madge thought about it.

"What is this about, Madge?" he asked impatiently.

"Sorry – it's just… I only need to know when it is out – or visible, that is?"

"Well – right now, as a matter of fact," Grandpa Ollie said, heading back up the stairs with gusto. "Cetus is a huge constellation, but it's only fully visible in the early winter."

His answer left Madge feeling dizzy as they paused at the top of the stairs. "Visible from where? You mean visible anywhere in the Northern Hemisphere, right?"

"Correct. Now, you going to tell me what this is all about? I suppose something to do with your mother's vision and who knows what?" Grandpa Ollie whispered loudly, checking behind his shoulder to Pearl's office door, which opened suddenly.

"Ready?" Dr. Hiromi said, peeking his head out. "We're all here—"

"I need a minute with Madge. We'll be right there," Grandpa Ollie grumbled back.

"Yes, Grandpa." Madge said when Pearl's office door had shut again. "Promise if I tell you, you'll let me do what needs to be done. In fact, I'll need you in my corner when I talk about this with Pearl." Madge searched Grandpa Ollie's face. It was a storm of thought as he frowned and drummed his fingers on the banister.

"That's not how this works, young lady. But I can tell you that if it were your mother's intention that you do what needs to be done, I cannot say I would stop you. But that depends."

"It's exactly to do with what Mom and Dad were trying to do – and what she knew I would have to do, too, I *think*. But now it's also what I have to do to help Selene."

"You *think*? If you're thinking of travelling to the cave where your parents died, you can think again. They didn't find the wand there. No one has – and I don't think you will, either."

"It's not hidden in the cave, but I have to go *through* that cave, Grandpa. There's a gate to the place our kind came from—"

"Stop right there," he said, his face hard. "That's not happening, for starters, and even if I were to allow it, they won't," he said, pointing to Pearl's office door.

"Selene was bitten today, by the severed head of a siren. I saw it with my own eyes. And I saw it beheaded in a vision just now – when it was flesh, before it turned to gold," Madge said, watching Grandpa Ollie's face drain of color. "That bite has her in the thrall of the most evil, darkest thing you can imagine – and if I don't go there and get fruit from the Tree of Life, there's no helping her."

"If this is all true," Grandpa Ollie said as his face went ashy and he finally unfolded his arms, "Pearl wouldn't deny you if it really is the only way. Then they could go with you and you'd be safe."

"But what if it is true and they still don't let me go?"

"Did you learn nothing today – out there in the water, vulnerable, by yourself?" Grandpa Ollie said, his face pained. "If your mom and dad had let their advisors help them – or just security in general – they might be here today."

"But isn't that the point? They went in secret because of the reason they were going. They wouldn't have gotten approval."

"They wouldn't have, but you will," he said with a stubborn shake of his head. "Rachel and Russ, your parents, were going for a wand. Not fruit from a tree. The circumstances are entirely different."

"Not only that!" Madge said, snapping her fingers as a realization struck her. "Grandpa – the wand – it discredits a long line of royals! And so-called pure bloods!"

"What? How?"

"My vision – Morgaine revealed that Arthur's heir wasn't full blooded – wasn't *his*. The wand was used to transform him, then hidden by Merlin... where no one could ever find it."

"That would mean..." Grandpa Ollie paused, his eyes lighting with understanding. "That other royals had human blood all along – could even have been Kings or Queens. Many won't like that. They won't like that at *all*. In fact, I wouldn't mention the wand just yet. Just the fruit – it's the reason you'd be allowed to go, after all," Grandpa Ollie said, touching his nose to imply this was their little secret.

"So… this means you'll let me go?" Madge said as her heart thundered in her chest.

"If they let you, and provide security, I'll let you. And if you can prove nothing bad will happen… Otherwise the answer is a resounding and unwavering no."

"Can't I demand it? I mean, I'm the… *princess*… right?" Madge said, cringing.

"Not quite. You have a lot more rules to abide by than most, unfortunately. You'll have to use your powers of persuasion."

"One more thing, before we go in there… Where exactly is it – the cave – Camelot?"

"Tintagel, England. The castle is nothing but ruins now and sits high up on rocky bluffs right on the ocean. The cave is below it. It's a sea cave, when the tide is low you can walk inside it, when the tide is high you can paddle through it, and it goes all the way through—"

"I know what it looks like, from my vision – just not where it actually was."

"Anyway, it's in Cornwall, and that's quite a drive from London. Tickets won't be cheap this time of year."

"Well let's hope the Institute will pay for it, Grandpa."

"Oh, they will. Now that's one area where you can snap your fingers."

19

Treaties & Promises

Madge had not yet been inside Pearl's office.

It was cold and smelled like cinnamon. Paintings crowded the walls, some modern, some classic, and lace doilies were placed under porcelain horse figurines and antique teacups. Pearl stood before the cracked window, letting the winter air inside, where she drank tea from a delicate China cup.

"Tea? I find it satisfies *far* better than coffee on a day like this," Pearl said as she gestured towards a rosewood tea table, covered with China, cookies and finger sandwiches.

"I didn't know you had a cat," Madge said, smiling down at the tabby winding between her ankles.

"Yes, Mr. Bojangles. He's my sweetie."

"Mr. Bojangles is a big fella. Not fat, just… big," Grandpa Ollie said, scratching under his neck, to which the cat lifted his chin approvingly for.

"How is Selene?" Madge asked as she sat down, turning to Dr. Hiromi.

"She's sedated. But before that – she was spouting some

pretty wild things."

"All of which are *true*," Madge said, cringing under Pearl's glare as she said it.

"So Mimir's Head is, according to you two, a siren's head? Is that right?" Pearl asked, sitting down at her desk without taking her eyes off Madge.

"Yes," Madge answered weakly. "And it bit Selene. The snakes on its head did, I mean-"

"And the only way to help her is to get the fruit from the Treoliffruma," Pearl said as she raised an eyebrow, her voice full of irritation and disbelief. "And that means travelling through to the Old World, under a constellation – or so she told Robert."

"It *is* the head of a siren – I've seen it."

"You saw her bitten by something – a snake. Describe what else this golden, *lifeless* head has done to make you believe that it's actually the lopped-off head of a siren."

Madge blinked back at Pearl whose eyes held no warmth as she waited for an answer. She hadn't prepared herself for the possibility that they wouldn't *believe* her. "I – well… That day in the ocean – I had a vision, but I didn't want to tell you—"

"Oh, I am afraid that was quite obvious," Pearl said, waving a hand in the air. "Your eyes said everything when you came up from the water – but what does that have to do with what you saw today, when Selene was bit?"

"Okay, so – I had another vision. Just now – before I came here. In the pools…" Madge said, her voice trailing. It was hard to muster the words of what she'd just seen. To explain everything – if she even *could* explain everything: her mother's work, where she needed to go, what she needed to do to help Selene.

"I'm listening," Pearl said, impatience biting her tone.

"It was a vision from my ancestor, who traversed to the Old World," Madge answered, her voice and her knees shaking as she beheld the wide-eyed expression that Dr. Hiromi and Pearl shared. "Where she chopped off the head of a siren, which turned its head to gold. Its body still lives – *it* still lives. She brought its head back because it promised to reveal the secrets of the universe if she reunited its body to it. It's the same head Viviane stole, and it speaks to her now, too. And to Selene. And it's the same voice I heard, as we all thought it might be."

No one spoke for a few moments, until Pearl smoothed her hair back with her hand and narrowed her eyes at Madge. "No reliable, true account exists other than one possible legend of someone getting there. One more regarded as a cautionary tale. But you say you saw your ancestor do it? And you're sure about this?"

"Yes," Madge nodded, holding her chin high though her heart was racing.

"And the part you're leaving out – or apparently what Selene says, is that you need to go to the Old World now too, under the constellation Cetus. Are we getting this right?"

"What's with the interrogation tactics on my granddaughter, Pearl?" Grandpa Ollie huffed, folding his arms as he locked eyes with Pearl.

"Your granddaughter, with all due respect, could have lost her life today. Selene is hurt, and there are some pretty big stories being spun – and it's my job to get it straight. Or don't you agree? Would you rather me molly coddle her? Shall I pretend as though the acts they pulled today are of no coincidence?" Pearl spoke with a lethal calm.

"I'm not denying any of it, *with all due respect*," Grandpa Ollie answered with equal calm, not flinching from her. "But you can get to the point here, that's all I am saying."

"I'm trying to get her to the point!" Pearl spat, finally ruffled. "What is the point here, Madge? Do spit it out!"

Madge felt heat rise to her cheeks as a fire grew in her belly. "According to Giuliana, fruit from the tree is the only thing to cure the thrall of a siren. The bite. Selene's *bite* has her under its thrall and that's why she can hear its voice now. And there is no cure, and it will only get worse… And I have some ideas about that but – yes. I do need to traverse to the Old World and yes, I did see it, and yes, I know I'm in trouble and we did something very stupid out there today. But I still need to fix it, and I am the only one who can."

"Do you want to know another stupid thing?" Pearl asked, bridging her fingers under her chin. "Making promises you cannot *possibly* keep."

"What promises have I made that I can't keep?" Madge asked, her stomach sinking.

"A better question is what secrets are you keeping to meet those promises? Your parents kept secrets, the biggest one I thought was you and your ability to transform even though you're a Merewif. But Rachel didn't keep the secret from me that your father intended to travel to the Old World. She just didn't tell me for *what*. And they left to do just that, without telling anyone – without listening to wise Council – for a quest that got them murdered."

"Why has no one told *me* any of this?" Madge said when she found the words to speak. "I'm not the only one keeping secrets!"

"It simply hadn't come up yet," Pearl said, taken aback.

"What was she seeking from the Old World, pray tell? And why is it that now you have to go there – because Selene was bitten? This seems a strange coincidence, does it not?"

"It was part of her plan – to be accepted as Queen. She believed something was there that would allow her to transform – to become Saelfen."

"What was it? Does the fruit do that, too?" Dr. Hiromi asked, unable to hide the shock and excitement from his face.

"No – not the fruit. What it is I cannot say, and I won't say, so please don't try to make me," Madge said, shaking her head. "And it doesn't matter right now. All that matters is that I am the only one who can help Selene."

"I suppose you won't say for the same reasons your mother wouldn't say, and if you haven't learnt a lesson from them by now, I don't know what can help you," Pearl said, shoving away from her desk and facing the window. "Now, if I am getting this right, you believe you are… special, somehow, and that you're the *only* one who can go through to the Old World."

"Not *special*, no. But it's my ancestral right, somehow. My mother had those visions because of me. Because she was pregnant with *me*," Madge said, doing her best to keep her voice steady. "Those visions she had – they were meant for me, waiting in *my* blood. Visions that for some reason skipped generations – and are now in my lap. And yes, all of this has come to a head after my cousin was bit. So, coincidence or not – it's time to fulfill my destiny."

"Destiny?" Pearl said as she cracked a grin. "Why yours and no one else's? Do you think others, besides your parents, have not tried and failed?"

"I know there is a gate and that it's protected by sea nymphs.

There is a way to get there, if allowed to pass. Merlin and Morgaine both traversed there and back again – my ancestors were both allowed to go."

"Merlin? You've done your homework – Morgaine is indeed the legendary figure that *traversed*. But Merlin? What exactly makes you believe that?"

"Morgaine sent the vision I had today, and she is my ancestor. So is Merlin, and he sent me a vision, too. And as I've been told, visions are memories – so it has to be real."

"Morgaine is *your* ancestor? But why wouldn't anyone of her line have received the vision – why now?"

"That's the point I've been trying to make. It was meant for me. It called to me in the pools just now. I was on my way to see Giuliana – but then I got... sidetracked. I could feel it pulling at me through the mists."

"Mists?" Pearl asked, her pupils narrowing. "In the pools?"

"Yes. Ask Max, he was there when I went under."

"But for what purpose? I am here, as *your* Regent, trying to help you, as I tried to help your parents! If we don't have trust moving forward, we have nothing," Pearl said, her face grave. "It can't be your ancestors foresaw your cousin getting bit – and went through all this trouble to help her. So why is it *your* destiny to go to Eressëa?"

Madge looked at Grandpa Ollie, who nodded and said, "If you want the proper backing and support, she needs to know. *Everything*."

Madge bit her lip. "Fine," she said, throwing her hands up. He was right. Keeping secrets now would get her nowhere – and Selene needed her help and she needed it now.

Madge hardly came up for air. Every detail of her mother's plans. How Merlin had crafted a wand from the Treoliffruma that would allow a Merewif to transform, and that somewhere in the royal line, it had already been done. What she'd seen in her visions – Lilith – and how and why Morgaine had brought the head back.

And when she was done, it was Grandpa Ollie who spoke first.

"Lilith?" Grandpa Ollie breathed, his face drawn. "She sent a vision to warn you of the dangers of this thing, by the sounds of it! Not to entice you to go there!"

"Whatever the reasons the visions were sent Grandpa, mom knew the risks, too, and she left this for me… It proves that our kind will not die out due to breeding with humans. Merewifs – like me – can have full Saelfen abilities. *Vala will not die*. We will not fade but will be stronger in the end," Madge finished, watching Pearl carefully who still had not uttered a word.

"I'd rather you renounce all of this – live a *normal* life. Elect someone else!"

"You know we've explored all of those options already, Ollie," Pearl said finally, sitting forward in her chair. "Even if Madge stood down and *gave* it to Viviane, Madge would never be safe – she'd always be a threat. Any new royal taking the seat would be target B to target A – Madge. Viviane would *always* seek her out. And forget trying to hide her on your own – not now that Viviane can find her. On your own, without our royal protection?"

Grandpa Ollie huffed and looked over at Madge with vacant, fearful eyes. "So, we stick to the original plan, she stays here and will convince the Council on her own terms."

"Grandpa! What about Selene?"

"*That*," Pearl agreed, casting her gaze to Madge. "And another hard point. The Arthurian royals had a son that was half-human. If we could prove it, this could change everything in our war against Viviane and the Daedscuan, on so many levels..." Pearl said as her eyes grew distant, before shaking her head. "But I still can't get behind you on this."

Blood ran from Madge's face. "I don't understand. You just said it yourself – the wand could stop the war with the Daeds! But more importantly, what about Selene?"

Madge's question was met with silence. Mr. Bojangles purred loudly, oblivious to the tension in the room, as rain started misting the window.

"Sedatives can only work for so long," Dr. Hiromi said, letting go of a deep breath. "We tried healing her mind, but nothing is working."

"I think it's a Daed transformation," Madge said, her hands forming into fists.

"We fear the same," Dr. Hiromi said, more to Pearl than anyone.

"If I back you on this – this wild plan of yours – I'll lose all credibility," Pearl's eyes were shining. "No one will believe you. You're teetering on the edge of a knife as it is. Not to mention where the gate is located – do you know where it is?"

Madge nodded her head. "Camelot. England. The first realm."

"Correct. The last thing we want is to tell the Royals in the first realm what you are planning to do. The last thing we want is for them to meddle in all of this, I assure you."

"But you are a royal of the first realm – you couldn't pull some weight somehow? This is the only way to—"

"Stop." Pearl held up a hand in the air with raised eyebrows. "You don't understand. You cannot enlist the first realm in this. Think of them as an enemy – just as big of an enemy as your Aunt Viviane."

"Then we need to go under the guise of some other business!" Madge pleaded, though her voice had gone three octaves higher than usual.

"We will stick to the plan we already have as it's the only one that doesn't risk your life – and the lives of others, I might add – and that assures a favorable outcome!" Pearl shrieked. "You will continue your training and win the Council majority as previously discussed. There will be no going to the Old World and risking *your* life due to the Selene's bad choices!"

"This is NOT her fault! It was both our decision to go out there today!" Madge shrieked back, kicking herself up from her chair as it went sliding behind her. "And I will do this! I will help her, with or without your permission!"

"Madge!" Grandpa Ollie yelped as he stared at her in disbelief, his bushy brows pushing into his forehead.

"I'm *sorry*," Madge said, lowering her voice. "But she's my cousin and I am the only one who can help her. How can I be a leader if I'm not allowed to make my own choices? And why does no one seem to care what happens to Selene?"

"I care a great deal for Selene," Pearl said, her voice hoarse. "I've helped raise her, and I've been in her life a lot longer than you have. So don't think for a second that I don't care!"

Madge was taken aback by the genuine hurt that flashed in Pearl's face. "Then why won't you find a way for me to do this?"

"The Royal cuffs haven't even returned to you yet. The Council won't back you no matter what I say until that happens. And that includes the first realm and any dealings with them."

"Why can't we go without their permission?"

"Because once they find out we entered their realm, their domain, and went through to the Old World without it, we would be in violation of important treaties between realms," Pearl's face fell as she paused before what was said next. "And... Your father and mother did the very thing you are suggesting. It did not end well for them."

"What is that supposed to mean?" Madge asked, feeling like the wind had been knocked out of her.

"We have reason to believe the first realm may have tipped off your aunt," Dr. Hiromi said. "I know this is another detail you hadn't been told – but please know it was our intention to fill you in on everything in due time. I'm sorry you're learning about it this way."

Dr. Hiromi's voice rang in Madge's ears as the weight of what he said seemed to fall onto her shoulders, shoving her down. It made it hard to breathe. "And you're worried about violating a treaty with them?" Madge screamed, unable to stop her emotions from boiling over now. Hot tears filled her eyes and her face flushed crimson. "Why does it matter if I have the cuffs if they don't intend to let me on the Council regardless?"

"It's a conversation I've already had with my brother who happens to be the sitting king of the first realm," Pearl said, her expression growing wary. "He refuses to speak with you, acknowledge you or even *talk* about you until at the very least the royal cuffs return to you. If you want to help your cousin, I suggest you continue training and find a way to get them to find their way to you. Otherwise, my hands are tied, and I am not going to authorize or support violating a treaty with them, making a fragile situation all the more fragile. That would ruin your chances with the Council altogether."

"But what about Selene? The constellation—"

"Yes, I know – Cetus. It's only in the winter sky for so long so you have a short window if you want to pursue this. Let's hope and pray you do what needs to be done to get the cuffs to return to you – and soon. And in the meantime, we will find ways to help Selene."

"Dr. Hiromi just said they can't do much—"

"They had a whole half hour to figure something out."

"We have a local healer in town, well versed in Earth Vala," Dr. Hiromi said, his expression unconvincing. "I plan to work with her to find ways to help Selene. She's your English teacher. Wanda Whaling."

"What?" Madge screeched. "Mrs. *Whaling*?"

"Yes. The one and only English teacher you have. Now, get the cuffs, and we will revisit this," Pearl said, standing from her chair, letting it be known that the meeting was over. "For now, Kento and I have to make some phone calls."

"I can't understand why my parents left this to me," Madge said, standing from her chair and letting the tears fall as her hands balled into fists. "Knowing not only the Council would be against me, but apparently this *Regent* they left in control would make things impossible, too?" She ignored the hot, angry tears streaming down her face as Pearl looked back at her in shock. "I mean – they must have *known*! You didn't help *them*. And they didn't ask for it either because you wouldn't give it! If you'd have listened to them or been *willing* – maybe they wouldn't have kept all these secrets from you. Maybe they'd still be here today. A broken treaty, maybe, but they'd be alive. Think about that when you're lying awake tonight, worrying about how to help Selene." Madge had never felt so hollow and angry in her life. She let it be written in her face as she looked at Pearl, then turned away and walked out the door.

20

The Keeper

Madge ran.

Down the stairs, ignoring her Grandpa's calling out as he asked her where she was off to. Ran without as much as a glance at Ash, who sat by the fireplace in the common room, as she hurried out the back. She sprinted across the pavement stones, slick and wet with rain –

And when she fell, she fell hard.

Max's sweats now had a mud-soaked tear in the knee – and her palms, where they hit the ground to break her fall, were grated raw. She couldn't bring herself to get up off the soggy ground, the fall seeming to break her completely... Sobs ripped past her throat as she rolled over onto the cold and wet ground, letting it soak her through... as she let the pain and loss fill her chest like a water faucet had simply been turned on.

"Are you okay?" Ash yelped, running out the back door towards her. Apparently, Madge looked as bad as she felt, judging from Ash's expression as she knelt beside her in the wet grass. "What happened?"

"I fell," Madge answered, wiping her face with a dirty sleeve. "I thought you left?"

"I came back. You still have my car keys. So... I take it the meeting didn't go well?"

"Nope," Madge sniffed as Ash helped hoist her from the ground, her palms smarting against Ash's warm, dry hands.

"Okay... So where are you off to in such a hurry? Your car is the other way."

"I have a bone to pick with the nymph."

"I thought you already—"

"No," Madge said, brushing blades of grass from her hands. "Not that it matters anyway! They all pretend to want to help, but in reality, no one cares. Not really."

"So..."

"So, they won't let me go. And apparently the royal leaders in the first realm hated my parents as much as they hate me and could have had a hand in having them killed," Madge sputtered as the tears continued streaming. "And there is some stupid treaty I can't violate – and a whole host of other things. *I can't go.* They won't let me. Selene – she'll be..." Madge fought to breathe against the lump in her throat as Ash grabbed her in a tight hug and let her cry.

Madge withdrew, smiling weakly at her best friend. "I've got to talk to the nymph while I'm still good and angry. Fill you in on everything later?"

"I'll wait here," Ash said, wide eyed. "Good luck."

Madge opened the door to the warm and earthy atrium and closed it behind her, waving one last time at Ash.

But someone was already inside, judging by the clinking of glass and the whispers.

Clearing the bushy row of greenery that lined the walkway,

she found—

"Mrs. Whaling? Hazel?" Madge gasped, surprised to find them here. *Already.* With countless books and tomes sprawled out over the table, and a silver bowl, filled with water.

"Madge," Mrs. Whaling said, eyes wide. "I didn't expect you."

"I'm on my way to the vaults…" Madge said, her eyes sliding to the hatch door hidden beneath the table. "I don't mean to interrupt."

"Oh! We are in your way."

"No – that's okay. I'm just glad you're here, and that you might be able to help?"

Mrs. Whaling nodded. "You heard?"

"Yes. Dr. Hiromi said you were – one of us. And that you'd help Selene."

"I'll try," she said, her mouth set in a thin line. "Earth Vala is not exactly straight forward. And what has happened – it's well, unprecedented."

"If anyone can do something to help her, my Mom can," Hazel said with nothing but stone-cold conviction in her big blue eyes. *If only.*

"Is this Earth Vala?" Madge asked, limping forward.

"Yes. Want to watch?"

"If that's okay…"

Wanda Whaling nodded, then stood before the bowl and closed her eyes for a moment. "I declare I am salt and light," she said, sprinkling salt into the bowl as though she were salting a dish. The minute the salt hit, the water shimmered and flashed brightly. She then grabbed a long-stemmed plant, with a broad head full of small, white flowers from the table, and rubbed it between her palms, letting the tiny petals fall into the bowl. "Elderflower, shine bright against the fight! Cleanse the smudge of spreading blight!" she commanded, as wisps and tendrils of smoke rose gently from the crushed petals as they hit the surface of the water shimmering inside. "Lavender, quench the sting of the siren's bite, soothe and protect with a mother's might," she chanted as she added sprigs of lavender in the same manner as she'd done with the elderflower. The room felt *still* – as if even the plants were holding their breath, as Madge was, watching her English teacher in wonder. "Mugwort, ward against the stalking fright, calm the mind and keep her spirit alight," Wanda said with a shiver as the words fell from her mouth.

Madge felt a shiver walk up her spine, too. Maybe this *would* work? Maybe finding a cure for a siren's thrall simply hadn't been discovered yet – seeing Siren's bites were about as rare as travelling through space and time into another dimension.

"Bind and protect with malachite!" Mrs. Whaling finished, sprinkling a green, gritty powder into the bowl, sending a puff of cloud above it that sparked like lightning in a storm and immediately dissipated.

"Pour that into the vials, please Hazel," Mrs. Whaling said, wiping her hands on the apron she wore as she looked up at Madge.

"Do you think it will work?" Madge asked, studying the swirling liquid Hazel poured carefully into vials through a glass funnel.

"We will try everything," Mrs. Whaling said, her blue eyes soft.

"Truthfully?" Madge asked, knowing she was holding something back.

"Okay, well... I doubt it," she replied, her shoulders sagging.

"Plants... there's always a remedy for a poison. Often, where stinging nettles grow, a plant remedy grows nearby. But this – a siren's bite and thrall... I don't know that a cure exists in our world. But we can try."

Madge felt her stomach sink further as every last shred of hope burned away like paper in a flame. Pearl's promises – Kento's – even Mrs. Whaling's – their intentions might be good. But it was not going to help. Nothing would.

"All done," Hazel said, corking a vial closed. "We can get out of your way now."

The mists were gone. Madge stood by the pool she'd erupted from only an hour or so ago – and wished it had been the gate she'd feared it was when she woke from the vision. The one she felt was still open behind her, a host of siren's ready to claw at her skin, her hair. But it wasn't. If it were, she'd go through it – right here, right now. Despite the risks.

She turned away, and walked behind the falls to the hidden keypad, entered the code and slipped past the grating rock wall into the vault.

"The woman in the water – Morgaine, was *bitten!*" she screamed before the stone wall had even ground shut – before her eyes registered the floating sea nymph coming towards her. "Did you know? Like all the other things you knew and didn't tell me?"

Giuliana looked at Madge with wide, indigo eyes. "Did you have another vision?"

"Yes, one that showed me sea nymphs guard the gates to Eressëa, where fruit from the Treoliffruma hangs out, waiting to be picked, and where my ancestor Merlin hid the wand. You knew, didn't you?" Madge screeched, her hands in fists.

"I'm a keeper of secrets, Princess. That means I keep them and don't give them up unless instructed, or unless the seeker figures out the secret itself to begin with. Even then—"

"Don't call me princess! I'm beginning to *hate* it!"

"Your mother was selective in what she told me – and she was gone during much of the time she unraveled those visions."

"Visions? You knew she had more than one. You *knew*!"

"She came very briefly to deliver some things to my possession and gave me a very limited story as to what she was after – but very specific instructions as to what to do with you. She didn't explain the second vision – I was in the dark about that as much as you."

"But you knew she intended to go to the Old World to get the wand. Didn't you?"

"Why don't you tell me what is going on? You're extremely upset."

"Does the name Lilith mean anything to you?" Madge began, arms flailing as Giuliana's indigo eyes widened fully.

"*Sit*. Tell me everything."

Madge didn't want to – but she did as she was told. Especially when it appeared Giuliana might know who Lilith was – seeing the mention of the siren queen's name had the nymph's hair rising all around her head, her essence like a storm. As Madge recounted what she'd seen in her vision, Giuliana was very still throughout and listened to every word without so much as a blink.

Madge didn't cry when she got to the hard parts. The ones where she wasn't allowed to go – to help her cousin. The treaty. The first realm and their probable part in her parent's demise.

"So, that's it. And now they're working on an earthly cure – above us, as we speak, even. But that won't help her, will it?"

Giuliana shook her head. "It's a supernatural enemy, and it requires a supernatural cure."

"It's impossible," Madge breathed, feeling like she could vomit all over the floor. "I'm not allowed to go without the cuffs, and you said the cuffs wouldn't return until I unravel my mother's work!"

Giuliana drew closer to Madge until Madge could feel the minty chill of her presence on the tip of her nose. "Which you have done." Giuliana said through a smile.

"I haven't," Madge said, her brows knitting together. "I can't go."

"You unraveled what she was after – the clues she left you. All of it," Giuliana said, grabbing Madge unexpectedly by the wrists as an icy sensation went straight to the bone—

"What are you doing?" Madge yelped, staring into Giuliana's wide eyes, unable to sink back any farther in the chair away from her. Terror, that's what Madge felt. What was happening? Giuliana's expression was so jubilant it was almost *maniacal*. "Let me go!"

A laughing tinkled in Madge's ears. "Your parents said to only give these to you when you absolutely, desperately needed them—"

Madge's wrists were free. She flailed from her chair—

But there was still a cold grip on her wrists, as if Giuliana still held them… but as her palms hit the floor, met with the clang of metal – *and the glint of something silvery* – Madge gasped. She couldn't take in what she was seeing—

"Because the cuffs would tune the Council in to you and comes with a host of its own problems… But I believe that desperate time has come."

Madge blinked down at her wrists... *The cuffs?*

Silver wound around each wrist, identical with rough moonstone in the center. A scream erupted from her throat, and she said, "You had them – all along?"

Giuliana nodded, her dark hair trailing around her ivory face. "It was your father's idea to make me the Keeper. I was the one they would return to if something were to happen to your mom and dad. When the cuffs returned to me.... I knew. You could say I was the first to know."

"The *Keeper*? But why?" Madge said, still sat on the cold, hard floor as she gaped at her wrists. "They wanted me to win the Council – and I need the cuffs to do it – so why on earth hide them from me until – what was the word – I *desperately* needed them?"

"The cuffs tune you into the Council, and the Council to you, even if you aren't officially linked to them. They didn't want you to feel that weight until due time, nor did they want the Council weighing in on you until you had time to find your feet... And your fins."

As Giuliana said it, Madge felt it. An electricity pulsed through her – starting from the wrists. And something beckoned at her mind. "I feel something..."

"It will take time to home into it, and they to you," Giuliana said, helping Madge up from the floor at last. "But what else do you feel, now that you have what you need, to do what you said was impossible?"

Madge smiled at Giuliana as hope sprang from her belly. Feelings danced and swirled through her in ways she'd never imagined – even the feeling in her knee intensified, the once numb wobbly kneecap now stinging and smarting like new.

And then Madge did something she never thought she would do.

She pounced on Giuliana, wrapping the watery nymph in a hug that felt like a plunge in the ocean. "You've been watching me all along, haven't you?" she whispered.

"I'm the Keeper of Secrets, Guardian of the Vaults – but most of all, a Guardian to you, too. And yes, I've been there. Watching you. You were never alone."

Madge felt a lump grow in her throat. That minty, calming feeling – knowing someone was watching her – she was right. It was Giuliana.

"I wish you could come with me. To the other side."

"Alas, I cannot. I may be a source of Vala, but there are things I cannot do. And I am not omnipotent, and often my work… let's just say it requires I take a step back, sometimes."

"Any advice for my journey to the other side?"

"Go undetected as much as you can. Don't be lured by their voices – stuff your ears and block them out. They would have you lured to their island – what your kind's legends call a *Singastein*. There they would feed from your soul for a thousand years or more. No matter the pull or what good feelings you have – do *not* go. Resolve to go to the tree and come back immediately."

"That's what I thought," Madge said, biting her lip as her body flushed with a new wave of nerves all over again.

"But… Madge…" Giuliana said – and her eyes alarmed Madge. They were a storm of worry and fear – and warning. "If you see a headless body, get out of there. *Flee*. You do not want to cross Lilith's path."

21

The Academy

Madge had never been in a helicopter before.

Now, less than twelve hours after showing Pearl the royal cuffs wound around each of her wrists, she was sitting in the back of one. Piloted by Nico, Grandpa Ollie in the passenger seat, they flew over the San Juan Islands, a wild archipelago tucked into a vast inlet from the Pacific between Washington and Canada. With everything that had happened in the last twenty-four hours, she half wondered if she dreamed seeing the islands dotting the silvery expanse beneath her, soft in the early morning light.

Nico had hardly spoken a word to Madge since last night, when she'd rushed into Pearl's office in mud-soaked sweats, wearing the royal cuffs. He stood staring at her, jaw clenched, arms crossed tightly as she explained everything to Pearl, seemingly unimpressed that the cuffs had magically returned – and downright angry with her by his expression. Apparently, he wasn't going to forgive her anytime soon for slipping under his nose and going for a swim – and all the mayhem that now ensued because of it. But though his attitude hadn't changed much towards her this morning, he seemed to be laughing and carrying on with Grandpa Ollie just fine.

"The way she casually sipped her tea while she spoke to the King of the first realm – that woman is truly formidable," Grandpa Ollie said, his voice coming in through the speaker on Madge's helmet.

"She treated him like the petulant brother to her that he is. Apparently, she was the one who used to call him Rufus the Dufus!" Nico said, laughing heartily. "I'd have paid to have been a fly on the wall – to have seen *Dufus'* face when she called and woke him at four a.m. his time."

"Whatever she's got on him – he couldn't tell her no."

"She's always thinking steps ahead, one way or another. Our realm owes her a lot. If it weren't for her…"

Madge was beginning to understand what all the fuss over Pearl was about. Pearl had picked up the phone and called Rufus, her brother and king of the first realm, almost immediately after she'd seen the cuffs. In a matter of minutes, it was decided that Madge would be going to England on Christmas Eve, because that was the best and only time that Rufus and his family could accommodate them. Because, apparently, Madge wouldn't just be going to England – but she'd be *hosted* by Rufus and the royal family themselves.

Immediately Pearl had a laundry list of to-dos before her trip abroad, starting with "first thing in the morning," a briefing would be arranged at "the Academy," which Madge was still wrapping her head around what this place actually was, tucked away on a private, remote island.

"So – how big is this Academy – or this island we are going to?" Madge asked, one of the first and only questions she'd been brave enough to ask of Nico that morning.

"Something over five hundred acres," Nico answered. "Big enough to house the SI's largest and most sophisticated training grounds in the eighth realm."

"And is it true the US government is aware of what it's used for?"

"A handful of members in the US government are, yes, though most are Saelfen themselves and cooperate within our intelligence community as well."

"You'll be meeting one of their big wigs today, Madgie," Grandpa Ollie said.

"And the team we'll be taking with us to England. Sadly, Pearl won't be coming with us. She has to stay behind as Regent, especially while the princess goes abroad. But besides the Riveras, Robert and Selene, Dufus has agreed to me bringing a few of my best new recruits."

Madge felt her stomach drop. The Riveras were coming. *Max*.

"These new recruits belong to the Academy?" Grandpa Ollie asked.

Nico nodded. "All graduates. And you'll be meeting them shortly because there she is," Nico said, pointing to a long island below them. "The one that looks like the Loch Ness Monster, or some say a sauropod. *Sans Legs*."

Madge's stomach flip-flopped with excitement as the island loomed beneath them – and it really did look like a dinosaur, or a Loch Ness Monster. The eastern end resembled a rounded head, and a long neck connected to a hilly, wider expanse, with a short tail at the western end.

"And that's the Academy," Nico said, pointing to a M-shaped building on its head – which as they drew near, looked more like a castle or a chateau than a training compound.

"That's *it*?" Madge gasped, staring at the massive construction of limestone, dark, shingled rooftops and spires.

"Looks like Georgetown!" Grandpa Ollie said, clapping his hands together with excitement. "Your parents used to come here on occasion – but... I had no *idea*."

It was perched atop a grassy, domed hill, crowded by tall green pines, and fringed in barren rock where it met the Salish Sea. But the entire southern side of the island was oddly sparse – mostly grass and rock, with a scant spattering of oaks and firs.

"Where are the training grounds – the tents and obstacle courses?" Grandpa Ollie asked, his bulbous helmet swiveling every which way as they made to land.

"All hidden. Sixty thousand square-feet inside and bunkers underground – and they've got everything. Medical triage which includes Vala training as well as modern applications, three Olympic sized pools, tracks with obstacle courses, a VOC – I mean a Vehicle Operations Center... And my personal favorite, the weapons, sword and tactics training arena."

Grandpa Ollie whistled. "That's a lot to hide underground!"

"All the realms operate in some form or another underground, away from satellite imagery, or anything flying over."

The blades were still whirling as they stepped onto the landing before the grassy hill, topped by the chateau-like Academy, where a tall, barrel-chested Polynesian looking man, his hair pulled back in a ponytail, waited to escort them. He wore a tight black t-shirt, exposing his tattooed forearms, and cargo pants.

"Mr. Kekoa – meet Madge Ferriter, and her grandfather, Ollie Ronning," Nico said as Mr. Kekoa wrapped a giant hand around hers. "Thanks for meeting us on such short notice."

"My duty and pleasure, sir," he said, smiling widely. "I have the great honor of being your tour guide today. Please, follow me."

Mr. Kekoa led them up the wide stone steps that paved the way to the front doors of the looming Academy. When the helicopter blades stopped whirling, there was nothing but the sound of birdsong and distant surf. It was almost too quiet for the gargantuan looking building in front of them. No one was out here – anywhere on the grounds. It seemed... empty.

"Where is everyone?" Madge asked, peering into the looming forests surrounding them.

"Inside. We do everything inside and underground," Mr. Kekoa answered. "But we won't be seeing much of it today, unfortunately."

"Just one bunker, a briefing, and meeting the team," Nico agreed as they approached tall, double doors flanked on each side by security personnel who nodded quietly as they summited the final steps. "No one here knows we are visiting or who you are, apart from the folks expecting us, of course. You'll appear nothing more than a prospective student of the Academy."

"Otherwise, you'd have had countless folks out here trying to catch a glimpse of you," Mr. Kekoa whispered, winking at Madge. "The long-lost princess."

"Well, I'm glad then," Madge stammered. She hadn't thought of that – people she'd never met, anxious to meet her – gawking at her, even... And as they stepped through the doors, she was even more glad no one would know who she was. There were people *everywhere*.

The entryway was large and open, with stairways extending

in every direction. A garden courtyard, in the middle of the grand entry and enclosed in glass, flooded the space with natural light. People in white lab coats swept up and down the stairs and corridors, others in business attire.

"That's our little Garden of Eden – the herbs and plants grown here are used for the magical triage unit," Mr. Kekoa said to them, pointing at the lush garden courtyard before he swept left, straight towards an elevator at the end of the hallway. "Mostly this place houses offices and sleeping accommodations. A few libraries and quite a few labs. Some of the most talented witches and wizards come here to develop ways to help and protect the realm."

"Your necklace was crafted here – or invented, shall I say," Grandpa Ollie said as they all paused in front of a gleaming elevator.

"Seriously?" Madge asked, palming the now clear stone that hung around her neck.

"What does her necklace do?" Mr. Kekoa asked, sliding a card in a reader near the elevator as it slid open.

"A *Giesting*," Nico answered, sending Mr. Kekoa's face into a look of shock.

"A what?" Madge asked through knit brows.

"A *Giesting* means your Vala was exiled from you. It's the word we use for the stone enchantment that takes it away."

"Why was her Vala taken away?" Mr. Kekoa asked, his voice barely above a whisper.

"It was hidden to keep her safe," Nico answered, stepping into the open elevator.

"Enchanting the stone strips witches or wizards of their Vala if they misuse it," Grandpa Ollie explained as they all followed inside, and the doors closed.

"To be returned if and when appropriate," Nico added. "It's not one we use often."

"I think she enchanted it do more than just take my Vala away," Madge said quietly, remembering how only yesterday it turned white hot before her vision Morgaine sent.

"Your necklace did take some tweaking," Grandpa Ollie said with a nod of his head. "Your mother did imbue it with other protective qualities. The spell to make your Vala return on your sixteenth birthday was not an easy one, nor anything that had been done before."

"Rachel was well known in the labs here. She was one of the most talented to grace these halls in our lifetime, that's for sure," Mr. Kekoa said, placing his palm into a reader and jarring the elevator into action. "Maybe someday we can say the same of you, princess."

Madge felt heat rise to her cheeks as her stomach lifted into her chest. "I'd have a lot of catching up to do," she said with a less than optimistic shrug. "But I can't wait to hear about the things she did while she visited here."

"Next time we'll take the stairs. I don't like elevators," Grandpa Ollie said, his face white as he grasped Madge's shoulders.

"That'd be a lot of stairs. This bunker is one hundred twenty feet down," Mr. Kekoa said absentmindedly, causing Grandpa Ollie's grasp to tighten even more. "But we're almost there," he added quickly.

The smell of earth permeated the elevator, and in a matter of seconds, the doors slid open.

And Madge's jaw dropped open with it.

They stepped out onto a rough metal bridge, high up from a host of operations below that was about as long as a couple of football fields put together, where Saelfen trained in the Olympic sized pools on one side, and on the other, countless bodies sparred on an open field. Some threw various types of Vala from their hands – some crackling with light, some seemingly invisible – and all the while their opponent deflecting, while others trained in swordplay and martial arts. Their sparring crashed, crackled and echoed throughout the huge, cavernous space, backed by the thundering sound of a forty-foot waterfall that gushed out of a crevasse and fed into another pool below.

"This is where the SSO train and operate – the Saelfen Special Operations," Mr. Kekoa said with a proudly raised chin. "Where your man Nico here graduated some years ago."

"Some years ago is right. Let's not say how many," Nico said with a grin.

"These men and women show high Vala capability as well as physically," Mr. Kekoa continued, heading to their left, where the bridge wrapped all the way to the back of the compound and ended by the waterfall. "But we are going into the most secure space of all on this entire island. Behind the waterfall there."

"Of course we are," Madge said with a shake of her head, thinking of the waterfall that hid the opening to the vaults at the institute. The metal bridge hugged the rock walls, wending over the pools where Saelfen were sparring in the same fashion they were on the field. Shocks of light erupted below water, and some above, as flashes of copper scales and powerful tail fins moved so swiftly it was hard for Madge to track.

"Apart from the soundproof interior, the waterfall is an extra sound-proof precaution," Mr. Kekoa said as a loud crack, like a lightning bolt, struck in the confines of the cave. Both Madge and Grandpa Ollie ducked, as if the ceiling would start coming down – but Nico and Mr. Kekoa kept walking, as if it were nothing out of the ordinary.

"Sorry," Mr. Kekoa said, stifling a laugh as he glanced back at them over his shoulder. "It does get loud in here – another reason a soundproof interior is appropriate when they are down here training."

"What was that?" Grandpa Ollie asked, his face still pale.

"A demonstration of sword conduction. The SSO have a special sword they historically use. It's what the triton is fashioned after. The three prong allows for those with that particular gift to conduct a more intense burst – kind of like a wand, if you will."

"Are wands common, then? I haven't seen any," Madge said, hiding the shiver that ran up her spine at his mention of one, remembering the wand she would soon be after as well.

"Common enough – but used rarely. You'll see one soon enough. Maybe even make one yourself," Mr. Kekoa said, stopping in front of the heavy metal door at the end of the walkway.

"I hope so," Madge said, sharing a look with Grandpa Ollie.

"Everyone is waiting inside – so if we're all ready, let's go in," he said, getting an okay nod from Nico before placing his eye inside a small metal box near the door.

"A biometric iris scan and voice recognition are required to enter," Nico said as the metal door slowly slid open.

Madge was thankful Grandpa Ollie stood by her, a warm hand on her shoulder as three people stood up from a large square table in the middle of the plain, cold space, lit by fluorescent lighting. Several monitors filled the back wall, and low-lying counters and shelves wrapped around the exterior. "Welcome to SI headquarters, princess," said a middle-aged man with a flat top haircut and a wide jaw. His voice was boisterous and raspy, like a man who yelled too much, and his face was ruddy and red. "I'm Daryl Hannover. But please just call me Daryl."

"Hi," Madge squeaked as she shook his dry, calloused hand. "I'm Madge."

"I know who you are," he chuckled before finally releasing her hand. "Welcome, everyone. Please, take a seat."

"Took you a minute to get here, Elta," joked a tall blonde woman, wearing shorts that showed off legs the size of tree trunks as she rounded the table to greet them. "Did he talk your ears off? He couldn't eat breakfast he was so excited to meet you."

"We came straight here," Mr. Kokoa answered, his face flushing purple again.

"She's just jealous, Elta. She was pacing the room minutes ago," said a man with dark skin and green eyes who stood and clapped Mr. Kekoa on the back.

"Clare, Terrance, meet Ollie and Madge," Nico said, rolling his eyes. "Two of my new recruits who will be joining us to England. But where is Sam?"

"Sam is earning his sword today as an official inductee of the SSO," Daryl said, resuming his seat. "One of four of the twenty-five that tried. We'll have to start without him."

"All of us are on limited time," Nico said, nodding in agreement as they all took a seat at the table. "Daryl here specializes in foreign intel for the US government. Luckily he could meet with us on such short notice."

"I had to cancel some meetings," he said with a shrug. "But

this is important. My sources say the first realm is already up to foul play now that you're coming," Daryl said as he slid a file folder over to Nico. "That's all the intel we have on them – based on prior information as to their cooperation with the Daeds."

"Rufus intends to tip off the Daeds again, is that it?"

"You mean how they tipped off Viviane when my parents went to their realm?" Madge said, sharing a shocked look with Grandpa Ollie who ripped the file from Nico's hands.

"How did they find out my daughter and son in law were in the country, if it was secret from even our own people?" Grandpa Ollie asked, locking eyes with Daryl.

"A shop owner told someone, who told another someone, and news got back to the royals who then, we have good reason to believe, told Viviane. Reports say via the former Regent Malcolm, who we know was keeping in constant contact with them in one way or another."

"I'd love to get my hands on that guy," Nico said with lethal calm, his jaw feathering.

"I'd pay to see that happen. And if only you could do the same to Dufus," Daryl said, his face growing redder than before as his expression turned grave. "I had an informant call me at three a.m. this morning. Apparently, Rufus the Dufus intends to not only keep your visit completely secret to their realm – hence the reason he chose Christmas, because that allots his family private time without interference of other officials and what not – but also to provide extremely limited security. By all counts, Nico – you know what this points to."

Nico shook his head, his expression hard. "Why am I not surprised?"

Daryl slid another folder his way. "That's the complete

phone transcript of my conversation with my in-guy. That will need to stay here – but go ahead and take a look."

"Let me get this straight," Grandpa Ollie said, glancing at the phone transcripts in Nico's hands. "They've likely already tipped off Viviane. And they want to keep my granddaughter's visit secret – and provide little security – so that she'll be as vulnerable as they can allow."

"I'd bet all my stocks on it," Daryl answered as he leaned over the table onto his elbows. "But you needn't worry about that. We are always one step ahead of them."

A smirk spread across Nico's face. "You're sending your own guys."

Daryl smiled widely through perfect white teeth. "You're only allowed to bring three – but we're sending over an entire stealth team. You'll be covered, and your granddaughter will be kept safe. Our best team will be on it."

"Doesn't that violate certain treaties?" Nico asked carefully.

"There are loopholes. We are acting without official permission or command, either from the Regent, the princess, or yourself as their head of security."

"Thank you," Grandpa Ollie said, his eyes shining as Daryl nodded simply back at him.

Madge was glad Grandpa Ollie was relieved, but she almost felt worse than ever about the trip. "It's not even been twenty-four hours since it was decided that I'd go, and they're already doing this? They're partially responsible for my parent's death, and apparently have no remorse for it, and plan to do the same to me?" Madge asked as angry adrenaline shocked her body, causing her lips to quiver and her voice to shake. "And if the Daeds get involved," Madge paused and swallowed past fear rising in her throat, "will your team be enough?"

"Oh, honey," Clare said with a giggle and a snort. "Hell yeah they will—"

"I'm here, sorry I'm late!" interrupted a tall and lanky young man with fiery red hair who stepped through the metal door already sliding shut behind him.

"Everyone, this is Sam," Nico said.

Sam carried the SSO sword – which did look more like a trident – proudly over his left shoulder. It was half his size, with one main blade down the middle, but the prongs on the hilt were nearly as long as the main blade.

"Congratulations, Sam!" Nico said, as Sam took a seat between Clare and Terrance who were clapping him on the back. Sam's smile lit up his whole, freckled face.

"Thanks, y'all," he said, his eyes widening as he looked across the table at Madge, then to Nico. "I was about to lose it when we recited the creed."

"The SSO recites an old creed for graduation when they receive the sword," Nico drawled, his eyes shining, "I think the princess should know what you vow. Why don't you recite it for her?"

Sam's face turned as red as his hair. "Seriously?"

"I'd like to hear it too, if you don't mind," Daryl agreed with a nod.

"Okay," Sam said, the embarrassment disappearing from his face as his expression grew hard. He sat tall in his chair, and looking straight at Madge, he began.

"I am a warrior of the eighth realm. I am selfless, righteous, and courageous. I am a guardian and protector of life, especially those defenseless and too weak to defend themselves. My right eye is the sun and my left the moon, ever watchful, never letting down my guard. I am one with the water, the air, the land and all its elements. I will never compromise my mission. I am a soldier of the SSO, and I will defend our realm with honor, until the day I die."

Loud applause echoed through the cold room as he finished with his head bowed.

Madge's eyes were watering as she clapped with them. The way he'd said it – with fire in his eyes and *conviction* – she believed every word, as if he'd branded them onto her heart.

"The Daeds won't stand a chance," Grandpa Ollie said.

"This is the creed they all take – *we* all take, to protect the realm and protect you," Nico said hoarsely, the room growing so silent you could hear a pin drop. "And we mean every word, live by every word. I hope it has inspired you to never squander it again."

"I won't," Madge breathed, tears brimming her eyes. And she meant it.

22

The Help

Madge pressed her forehead against the cold window as the small passenger plane began its descent past grey clouds and towards the Cornish coastline. Shafts of golden light broke through in pockets, illuminating the rolling countryside in glimpses of bright green.

A voice came over the intercom, pulling Grandpa Ollie from his sleep as he ripped a final snore and popped his head forward. He'd been sawing logs with his mouth wide open the whole way from London.

"Welcome to Newquay. Local temperature is six degrees and windy. There's a chance of snow and ice tonight so please be careful in your travels. Happy Christmas! It's been a pleasure serving you."

"Six degrees?" Madge gasped.

"Celsius," Grandpa Ollie said, wiping sleep from his face. "That's around forty degrees Fahrenheit. Not much different than the weather we left back home."

But Madge could feel the cold in her bones. The plane was

freezing the entire way across the Atlantic, and the passenger plane was equally cold.

Or maybe it was just nerves.

It had been a hefty last couple of weeks leading up to Christmas. Rufus, Pearl's brother, was *barely* compliant, and seeming to do all he could to make them feel uncomfortable about their visit. Apparently, Rufus' previous Christmas plans had been interrupted, and because this *unprecedented* visit must be kept a secret, London, where they traditionally spent Christmas, was no longer an option. They'd be spending the holiday at their cottage in Cornwall – away from the masses, and close to Tintagel, where Madge would be travelling through Merlin's Cave.

"Christmas in England is the best," Pearl had said over and over the past weeks. "And though my brother doesn't particularly want you there, he has promised to make it a special and warm occasion. He'll treat you as the royal guest that you are. But if he doesn't…" And then Pearl had let them in on Rufus the Dufus' little secret. The one that Pearl had held over his head in order to get them here. "Feel free to hint at it should he decide to be the tyrant that he is," Pearl had advised Madge and Grandpa Ollie. "But do not leak this to *anyone*. If his dirty little secret gets out, all of this planning and any compliance on his part goes out the window."

"I wonder if we'll meet the Nanny?" Madge whispered in Grandpa Ollie's ear as the plane taxied on the small, country runway. "You know, the one Rufus was so fond of."

"Somehow I doubt she'll be making an appearance," he answered, shaking his head.

"I wonder if his wife knows – or knew – or whatever."

"Either she's too naïve to see it, or really doesn't give a

damn," Grandpa Ollie said through a big yawn. "I don't particularly care. To think we'll have to sit up and talk with these people when all I'll want to do is ring their necks. I'm just ready for a whiskey and a clean bed."

"It's only three o'clock, Grandpa."

"It is way past my bedtime back home, and it's Christmas Eve. And now that I think of it, I'd rather a Scotch. I'll bet *Dufus* has good Scotch!"

Madge peeked across the aisle at Selene, who was still asleep on her father's shoulder though the plane had just taxied to a stop. The concoction Mrs. Whaling made had worked at first, but then they'd had to come up with stronger and stronger serums. She had dark circles under her eyes, and she was hardly eating, and often the best the serum was the one to get her to sleep. Though apparently the voice would sometimes even reach her there.

The sooner she could get through to the Old World and back, the better – and seeing her cousin this way had been distraction enough to fend off the swirling fears and what ifs. But now that they were minutes away from meeting her enemies – it was becoming all too real.

As they departed the steps of the passenger plane, they were met by cold, biting wind. A short walk across the tarmac and through a small building, and they were already walking out the front doors. They were the only arriving flight into the small, unremarkable airport – so the idling, white Range Rovers, with the gruff looking men in front, could only be for them.

Madge's stomach twisted.

"Looks like they sent the prince to pick us up," Max said, sidling up to Madge as he scrunched up his nose. "Just look at that dude. Look at his hair! *Fancy*."

Madge barked a laugh. "He looks older than Nineteen."

"Nah, he looks about that to me," Terrance said, holding back a laugh with his fist over his mouth. "You should see the intel we got on this kid. He's got a different girl every week! Player thinks he's all that and a bag of chips."

But Madge could see why, though she didn't say so out loud. He looked like a blonde runway model. Tall, and well-dressed in a long black pea coat with the collar turned up and a scarf knotted neatly around his neck, framing a perfectly angular face.

"Good luck, he's coming towards you," Max muttered, slinking off with Terrance.

Madge's cheeks flushed as Prince Norbert approached, bowing ever so slightly as he stopped in front of her. Madge blinked back at him. He looked nothing like a *Norbert*. "You must be Madge," he said as his golden eyes assessed her, his hands remaining behind his back.

"And you must be Norbert."

"Please, call me Bert," he said, his lips puckering.

"Pearl has told me a lot about you," Madge said, trying to ignore Sam and Terrance, who she could see were giggling from the corner of her eye.

"*Auntie*. I'm sure she has," he said, nodding his head gently at Grandpa Ollie and Nico who appeared at Madge's side. "Why don't we all save further introductions for our final destination at the cottage and be on our way, shall we? Thomas will collect your things," Bert said, turning on his heels before Grandpa Ollie could speak a word.

"What a little snot!" Grandpa Ollie said, folding his arms as the prince climbed into one of the awaiting vehicles.

"Grandpa!" Madge hissed, hoping Norbert – or *Bert* – hadn't heard him.

"You two can ride with us," said a stout, middle-aged man with a protruding belly and a rough accent who took ahold of Madge's luggage. "I'm Thomas, by the way," he added, smiling through a set of crooked teeth as he tipped his houndstooth cap.

"Much obliged, Thomas," Nico said, offering a small smile. "Max, Christine, Dan and Clare are in the car behind us, Sam, Terrance, Robert and Selene in front. Let's go."

"You first, miss," Thomas said, holding the back door open for Madge as she slid into the middle of the soft leather seat. Nico climbed in on one side and Grandpa Ollie on the other.

It was all happening so fast... So fast, it was making her feel dizzy. Denial, her cold and comfortable friend these past weeks, didn't seem to be present now. For the first time since her feet had touched ground in England, Madge allowed herself to absorb the fact she was really, finally *here*. She wished she could feel excited instead of dizzy with numb anxiety.

"Right, welcome to England!" Thomas said, as they drove away from the small airport on what felt like the wrong side of the road and driving from the wrong side of the car.

They drove small, narrow streets through rolling green hillside, dotted with fluffy sheep, past quaint stone and thatched villages lit up for Christmas in the growing dusk, until finally they turned onto a road that followed along sheer cliffs that dropped into the Celtic Sea. Thomas and Grandpa Ollie had been chatting up a storm the whole way, seemingly instant friends.

"Not far now," Thomas said, turning onto an even narrower country lane, its hills and fields crisscrossed with low, stone walls. "Ready for some good English Ale, I'd reckon!"

"And whiskey!" Grandpa Ollie chuckled.

"Oh yes, they'll be plenty o' that!" Thomas chuckled hoarsely back.

"I hope you're all hungry. Thomas' wife is an excellent cook," Bert said, speaking for the first time since they'd left the airport. "And she's coordinated the whole thing. Sleeping arrangements, food, everything."

"We were thrilled when we heard you'd be here, spending Christmas with us. It's an honor, really. You've been making headlines around these parts, princess."

"Me?" Madge said, feeling her chest heave. "*Headlines?*"

"Of *course*. All the realms have been anticipating your return, but you'll find us Brits love a good gossip, especially within the magical communities. And seeing Auntie Pearl has been keeping you under lock and key – it leaves a lot of room for hearsay, I'm afraid."

"Do you mean to say news of her visit has spread?" Nico asked, masking his steely expression with as calm of a voice as he could muster.

"No, no, no!" Norbert said, turning towards Nico with wide eyes. "Only Thomas and Rosie, his wife – and the other two drivers, whom are their *sons*, by the way. They are the only family that knows, a very loyal family to us and our closest employees. There may be a lot of talk about her – but they all think she's back home in America, I can assure you."

"Not to worry – we are big fans of you lot an' you're safe with us," Thomas said, locking eyes with Nico in the rearview mirror. Nico only nodded in thanks before looking away.

They lurched down a steep, windy hill, where they could see the sun setting behind thick tufts of clouds, barely a stretch of red and orange in a darkening sky. "You can see the cottage just there, through the trees!" Thomas said, pointing towards what could be made out as twinkling lights through sprawling, bare oak branches before they finally took a sharp turn, past a weathered stone fence and into a long gravel driveway.

The two-story cottage was bigger than Madge had imagined. It was cut from the same weathered, grey stone popular to the area, and glowed in the twilight with festive golden lights, every light in every window on and gleaming. Madge lingered a few moments in the car with Grandpa Ollie, wanting one word with him alone before she stepped out there, moments away from meeting Rufus and Margaret.

She rubbed sweaty palms on her jeans as Grandpa Ollie looked at her sidelong. "You okay, kiddo?"

"You'll be nice, as we discussed, right Grandpa?"

"Yes. I'll leave strangling the old fool to death to my imagination.

"And?"

"And I won't confront him for his dirty dealings with Viviane and the Daeds. But I won't shake his hand or tell him Merry Christmas, or anything like that whatsoever."

"Me neither. I don't think I can fake it *that* much."

One by one the cars arrived, and as everyone filed out, they all gathered silently in the driveway, gaping up at the Christmas postcard perfect cottage, the smell of chimney smoke and hay stinging their nostrils in the cold winter air.

"Looks like snow," Max said, appearing at Madge's side, looking up at the thick, pink clouds overhead.

"We may have a white Christmas!" Thomas said, whisking

by as he carried armfuls of luggage past them.

"I don't know which part I'm more nervous about. Walking into that house – or the thought of passing through a gate into another world," Madge said, smiling weakly. Her knees felt like they would buckle.

"His bark is worse than his bite," Norbert said, standing silently behind them, having heard what Madge had just said. "You'll find ignoring him helps. I always do. Follow me, I'll show you in."

"You ready?" Max asked her, turning warm brown eyes towards her in a way that made her forget everything – even if just for a moment.

Madge shook her head – *no*. She wasn't ready.

But no sooner had Madge's leaden feet stepped onto the stone veranda, than Thomas appeared from the front door, followed by a rotund woman wearing an apron who practically bounced up and down as she approached. Her bright eyes lit up when she looked into Madge's face. "Welcome! I'm Rosie – Thomas' better half. I've been beside meself for weeks, I can't believe you're *finally* here! Come in, out of the cold," she said, grabbing Madge's hand and pulling her inside the entry hall.

Rich brown wainscoting lined the walls beneath paintings hanging in gilded frames, and leaden windows were warmed by thickly woven curtains. A polished oak stairway curved around the back of the entryway, decked with crimson bows and boughs of evergreen. The entrance was crowded in a matter of seconds, voices and laughter bouncing excitedly off the walls.

"If you need anything at all," Rosie said, keeping close to Madge whose knees were still shaking, "You just let me know.

Tea, a hot water bottle, anything."

"Thank you," Madge said quietly, smiling up at the warmth in Rosie's face.

Rosie beamed down at her, about to open her mouth to say something else – when suddenly her smile faded at something over Madge's shoulder. Madge knew before turning around who had entered the crowded entryway.

He was tall and slender, and his hair a silvery gray, much like Pearl's. He wore a silk neck scarf, and his face was grim – disinterested, sneering, and hard. Everyone seemed to notice the King of the first realm was now present, as all the excited chitter-chatter faded away to an awkward silence, and all eyes were on him. He didn't flinch – but instead smiled smugly and stood before them with his chin and nose in the air, as if he'd expected this kind of attention every time he walked into a room.

"I'd like someone to cover my Porsche straight away, it's going to snow," he said to Thomas before turning on his heels towards Madge, ignoring everyone else. "Welcome, and Happy Christmas. I'm Rufus," he said, with a forced smile that didn't reach his eyes, not giving her a chance to respond before he turned away from her again. "We can manage introductions after Rosie shows you all to your rooms. Let them know what time to be down for cocktail hour and dinner, Rosie. Norbert, would you come here please? I'd like to speak with you."

Norbert's cheeks flushed. "Call me Bert, Dad," he said, stomping off after him.

And just like that, before any of them could utter a word, Rufus the *Dufus* left the same way he'd come in, and no one wore a deeper frown at his back than Rosie.

The room Rosie had brought her to was the grandest she'd ever laid eyes on, let alone the fact that it was hers and she had it all to herself. It had its own bathroom with a clawfoot soaking tub which she'd just spent a good half hour in, and the giant canopy bed faced leaded, diamond paned, arched windows which spanned just an inch from the floor, revealing big tufts of gently falling snow outside.

"Look at this room!" Selene gasped as she waltzed in and dumped an armful of dresses, makeup and jewelry on Madge's bed. "Not fair."

Madge huffed a laugh. "You can sleep in here later if you want. You're a *savior*. My nerves are shot. I have no idea how I'm supposed to dress to impress my enemies."

"Enemies? They're not your enemies unless you decide to make them yours," Selene said, arching a brow at her as she arranged dresses across the bed. "In other words – pretend to like them, reel them in, make them like you, if even just a little. And then when it's time, kick 'em to the curb. Keep your friends close and your enemies closer."

"You look good," Madge said unable to stop the expression of disbelief from her voice as she gaped at her cousin. Selene had color in her cheeks – and more light in her eyes than she'd had since she'd been bitten. "I mean – you always do – but you know what I mean – you…"

Selene turned to face her – a shadow flickering across her face. "It's okay, Madge. You're allowed to say I look like crap these days, because I know I have and…" Selene shrugged, turning back towards the dresses on the bed, as she raised one up to look at it. "Rosie gave me a tonic – and insisted I drink it in front of her the minute I got to my room. It felt like – like warm cocoa after freezing in the snow." Selene faced her with big, blue eyes rimmed with emotion. "I could feel it warm me from the inside the minute I gulped it down."

Madge could barely speak past the lump in her throat. "That woman is…"

"Amazing," Selene said, finishing her sentence as she let a tear fall from her cheek. "I feel… *awake*. The other tincture Mrs. Whaling made worked, but it made me foggy and tired all the time. This is – it's just *so* much better."

Madge couldn't help the tears brimming in her own eyes, and she wiped them quickly away with the soft sleeve of her robe before Selene could see them. "I think we need to find a way to bring her home with us!"

"She said it won't wear off until morning, but that it won't keep me from sleeping. I told her she needs to give me the recipe – and she said I'd have to get it from a local witch who won't likely give it up," Selene said, and then laughed. Actually *laughed*. "Well, I told her this local witch can just *try me*."

"Oh boy," Madge said with a slight roll of her eyes. "Watch out witch!"

"And Norbert – he's dashing, isn't he? He hasn't even looked my way – *yet…*" Selene said as she held a knee-high, velvet burgundy dress before herself in the mirror.

"Ugh, that name. No wonder he doesn't like to go by it. But what about Tristan?"

"We aren't – we haven't talked much in these past weeks," Selene said, shrugging sadly.

"Well in that case… Of *course* he'll be looking at you," Madge said, holding up a particularly short, black dress. "But – I can't wear anything like… I hope you brought me something *longer*. I'm not showing off my horrible white legs to these people!"

"Give me a little credit. I think I know you a little better than that," Selene said as she picked up a long, silky emerald dress and held it before her. "You're the visiting princess. You need to outdo everyone in the room. This is a wide V-neck, so we'll be showing off your shoulders. And this color will bring out some of that green in your eyes, and compliment your pasty, white skin."

"Gee, thanks!" Madge said, slapping Selene's shoulder playfully. "I'm used to wearing flannel pajamas and watching Christmas movies in front of a fire and gorging myself on pie and cookies. Not dressing like I'm going to prom."

"Get used to it. Your life is different now, princess."

Dinner was in the Great Hall, where a long table had been festively set on one side, and a handsome sitting room on the other, where everyone gathered in front of a huge fireplace. Exposed beams painted black in Tudor style curved overhead in the vaulted ceiling where an enormous, ornate chandelier hung in the middle of the hall.

Rufus' wife, Margaret, had stolen Madge's attention the minute she'd entered the Great Hall. She wore an elaborate, couture black dress and an ornate diamond necklace around her neck that seemed to match the sparkle in her icy blue eyes. Eyes that assessed Madge in a quick sweep from head to toe as she beelined straight towards her.

"I'm Queen Margaret, and you must be Madge," Margaret said, smiling through ruby red lips as she lifted her champagne flute in the air, sliding her free arm through Madge's. "But, please, call me Margaret. From one *royal* to another," she said as they passed Rufus to sit by the blazing fire so he could hear, and not surprisingly at all, he stiffened upon hearing it.

"Thank you – for having us. For taking us on such short

notice," Madge said, doing her best to sink into her seat gracefully, glad to be free of Margaret's bony, awkward arm.

"Oh, please. We had plenty of time," Margaret said, waving a jeweled hand in the air.

"You look divine," Grandpa Ollie said as Madge felt his hand on her shoulder.

"Selene brought me the dress," Madge said quietly, looking up at his rosier than usual expression.

Grandpa Ollie nodded his head enthusiastically. "I'm going for a refill," he said, raising a near empty glass in his hand as he raised his white, bushy brows towards Margaret.

"Your grandfather is adorable," Margaret said as she waved Rosie over who carried a silver tray of hors d'oeuvres. "Now, I must hear all about *you*, Madge Ferriter. You're causing quite a stir amongst the Council," she said as she inclined her chin at the royal cuffs Madge wore on each wrist. "Especially since you put those on."

"Sounds like I've been doing that since day one," Madge said, grabbing up a stuffed mushroom as she shared a quick smile with Rosie.

Margaret took a long swig from her champagne glass. "Can you blame us?"

"Margaret you are suffocating the girl," Rufus interrupted as he appeared beside her high-backed chair, draping his arm over it. "Give her a chance to chew her food."

"Us girls are getting to know each other – off with you," Margaret said with a wave of her hand, as if to scatter a dog from her feet.

"Oh, no – it's okay—"

"How are we doing over here?" Selene asked, taking a seat next to Madge, swooping in the minute she noticed Rufus had sauntered over.

"You must be Selene. You look so much like – well. You look well... Considering," Margaret said, arching a brow. Madge's stomach roiled – how dare she—

But Selene could handle herself just fine. "Considering I got bitten by an ancient siren that my lunatic mother likes to carry around?" Selene said, smiling sarcastically as she cocked a head at Margaret and managed a small laugh. "And yes, I am aware that I look like her. I hear you two used to be close friends."

Margaret waved her champagne flute in the air in a silent touché. "You're alike in more ways than one. You certainly have her spirit."

"Before it was murdering and dark, maybe," Selene said, shrugging her shoulders as if nothing Margaret said could bother her. "Hear from her lately?"

Rufus cleared his throat and choked on his drink, and Margaret's eyes widened. "Of course not."

"As long as we're on... touchy subjects – Princess Madge, do you know *anything* about this passage you intend to take in..." Rufus checked his watch, "less than nineteen hours from now?"

Madge felt a slight pressure on her ribs from Selene's elbow. Everyone seemed to drop conversation, turning their faces towards her, seeing Rufus had announced his question for everyone to hear. Madge felt her ears go hot.

"I know enough." Madge did her best to look Rufus square in his steely eyes. "But I won't bore you with details – much you probably already know from your own research and attempts in crossing through."

Rufus' face paled. "We have surveyed the passage. We have

tried to speak to the nymphs, but they won't let us anywhere near it. They won't speak to us. They won't answer our questions. They are hostile indeed."

"Aren't they all?" Nico said, appearing at Madge's side. "If you're trying to scare her, she's already well acquainted with one."

Rufus paled. "So my sister says."

"And who will you be sending tomorrow to escort her through the cave?" Nico didn't blink as he stared Rufus down.

"Me," Norbert said, raising a half empty pint glass in the air. "And two of our own."

"Three. Just three." Nico's jaw feathered as he threw a muscled arm around the back of the couch, sinking back further into his seat as he continued to stare Rufus down.

Whatever Nico was doing, though Rufus did his best to frown deeply back at him, he was nonetheless more fidgety than before. "I think the princess has a sizeable entourage as it is, seeing the idea is to swim so close to shore and maintain any level of secrecy."

"I see," Nico said with lethal calm as his eyes narrowed up at Norbert.

"Sorry to interrupt," Rosie said, leaning over to pick up discarded plates. "Princess, you asked to see the tea potion before dinner. If I could borrow you for a few minutes, I'll show you, if you'd like?"

Madge blinked up at Rosie who was staring intently into her face. She had no idea what Rosie was talking about – but something in her expression told Madge to play along. "Oh, uh – yes. Sure, that'd be great," Madge said, sliding up from her seat.

"Dinner on soon, Rosie dear?" Margaret asked, arching a

brow.

"Yes, it will be served at eight o'clock on the dot, mum. We won't be a minute."

Madge followed Rosie down a bare hallway, and through a swinging door that led to the kitchens with windows open to the back garden. The smell of fresh baked bread and gravy hung in the air.

"Listen," Rosie said, turning quickly on her heels as she checked the kitchen to make sure they were alone. "I heard what they were tellin' ya, and I wasn't sure we'd get another moment this evening—"

The door swung open, and Rosie gasped and jumped—

"Just me," Thomas said, carrying in a tray of discarded food.

"Oh, you gave me a heart attack, Thomas!" Rosie said with her hand over her heart. "They were telling her about how they're only sending Norbert and two of their security team tomorrow, and I wanted to reassure her that she'll be safe tomorrow – to let her in a little."

"I figured as much – oh!" Thomas said, as the door swung open again and slammed into his back—

"Sorry!" Grandpa Ollie said as he shouldered through the door and into the kitchen. "I saw you bring my niece through here—"

"No, no – I'm glad you're here," Rosie said, patting his arm. "What we are about to tell you stays here. But I want you to know she'll be safe tomorrow."

"What's this all about?" Grandpa Ollie said, looking between Thomas and Rosie.

"They're only sending Norbert and two of their guys with us tomorrow," Madge said, as Rosie led them further away from the door and to the small table sat in front of a blazing hearth.

"And while we know that's less than what you'd anticipated, Thomas and I may have overstepped a little and made some of our own arrangements yesterday," Rosie said quietly, wringing her hands together as her face turned crimson.

"They wouldn't let their precious Norbert go along with – with so little protection if they weren't in cahoots with those black-scaled, murderin' Daeds!" Thomas whispered hoarsely, his eyes darting towards the door.

Madge sank into a chair and felt Grandpa Ollie's hand settle on her shoulder. "We assumed as much already," he said. "When they wouldn't let us bring more than three of our own guys – not including Nico, of course."

"I am surprised you're letting her go – under the circumstances," Rosie said, shaking her head and patting Grandpa Ollie's hand. "I can't imagine how you must be feeling."

"I have to keep reminding myself that kids barely a year older than her fought in the war. I was seventeen when I enlisted, just after the bombing of Pearl Harbor – with my parent's consent, of course. They let me do the right thing, so I have to let her. And if anyone can do this, she can."

Madge felt a shudder roll down her spine as the look of conviction in Grandpa Ollie's eyes fixed on her face. It was hard to imagine her sweet, stubborn Grandpa going off to war – in a different country – at just a year older than she was now. He would have been Max's age.

"But still…" Grandpa Ollie continued, shaking his head. "I'm fighting the urge to stop it all – especially if what you say is true."

"Well not to worry," Thomas said, sharing a nod with Rosie, "as we've assembled a whole mass of people – Merewif kind mostly, who *secretly* know she's here."

"You did what?" Grandpa Ollie gasped through wide eyes.

"We know her being here is no secret to the Daeds – so we figured…" Rosie shrugged as her face grew serious. "We may not have jobs tomorrow, but what she stands for – what's at stake, is more important than our bloomin' jobs."

"We'll be assembled and ready come time if need be," Thomas agreed.

"But how? If you're assembling Merewif – they can't… I'll be in the water," Madge said, her stomach so tight she felt nauseous. Though she'd been told the Daeds likely knew she was here – now it seemed impossibly true… The Daedscuan *knew*. And they'd likely be there tomorrow, at some point or another.

"We'll be on lookout from above – on the cliffs," Rosie said, pointing a finger in the air.

"But… Won't you be a bit far away if they meet us in the water?"

"Oh, we have our ways, princess. I assure you," Thomas said, touching his nose. "There's a whole lot of us folk turning out, too. We circulate news between our kind. The first day you made front page – when Rosie and I heard you came back – well, it caused quite a stir—"

"Front page?" Grandpa Ollie said, "You mean a *newspaper*?"

Thomas nodded. "Yes sir. Folks are eager to help the half-blood. They want to see one of our kind on the throne. It's a change for a better future – for all of us. The newspaper is how we got word out so quickly."

"Okay, but a newspaper? That's not exactly flying under the radar," Grandpa Ollie said, knitting his bushy brows together. "And if the first realm wants this to remain a secret, how—"

"It's not a newspaper you buy from a stand on the street," Thomas said as he fished a parchment from his coat jacket. "Here, 'ave a look." Thomas opened a piece of thick, wide paper before them – but nothing was on it.

"It's a blank piece of paper."

"It's bewitched," Rosie said with a giggle, snagging the parchment from him. "These are printed using a bewitched ink. Only those with this," she continued, fishing a vile from her apron, uncorking it and letting a single drop fall onto the page, "can read it."

Madge's eyes widened at the print on the page, its artistic rendering colorfully separated between gilded columns. "I'm on front page again, apparently," she said, eyeing her name within a subtitle beneath an old picture of her parents and a heading that read "Call to Action."

Grandpa Ollie snagged the paper, his mouth open. "Where'd you get this picture—"

The door to the kitchen squeaked open and Thomas grabbed at it with lightning reflexes, hiding it quickly behind his back—

But it was just Thomas and Rosie's oldest son, peeking his head through with a wide-eyed expression. "Queen Margaret is about to leave her chair—"

"Oh! Look at the time! Go, go – dinner is on in five minutes. Lots to do!" Rosie said as she bustled over to the stove, Thomas on her heels.

23

Droplets of Mist

Sweeping, grassy bluffs hung over the Celtic Sea, frozen with patches of snow where the ruins poked up from the jagged headland. Madge waited with Max by the footpath that led to the castle ruins as the rest of her entourage were still unloading and going over last-minute details.

"You okay?" Max asked Madge, who was shivering and shuffling side to side on her feet as freezing wind whipped her hair across her face.

"It's freezing out here," Madge lied, trying to ignore his warm brown eyes. She couldn't bear to look at him right now – nor any of them for that matter – and to witness their pitied, scared expressions. Though the wind was frigid – she knew the trembling from head to foot was due to the fact she was going to be traversing to *another world* in a short time from now. A world riddled with creatures worse than anything she could have imagined could ever be real, whose voices alone were perilous. If they didn't run into the Daeds who were likely out there in the water first, waiting to ambush them.

"That's not what I was asking," he said, turning towards her and stepping closer—

"I'm anything but okay, Max," Madge said, the truth coming out in a bitten tone.

"I'm sorry," he said, his brows raising, "I didn't mean—"

"No, *I'm* sorry. If it weren't for me and Selene, none of us would be here today, facing who knows how many Daeds and who knows what else out there," Madge said, the lump in her throat seeming to widen. "I don't know what's worse. What's on the other side, or the thought of something bad happening to anyone out here, risking their necks."

Madge felt a gloved hand squeeze her own, and she turned to see Max's eyes searching her face – his expression so desperate it made her chest ache. "You are the princess, so people have to risk their necks for you. And if anyone is at fault, it's your aunt."

Madge bit her lip and shook her head as she let him continue to stare into her face. The feeling was electric, and she wanted to savor this moment. The unspoken truth of what may or may not be between them before going to the other side. And possibly not making it back. "I'm glad you're here," she breathed, shocked at the words that came out of her mouth.

"I'm glad I'm here too. I'm glad I got to see you last night in that dress," Max said, his cheeks flushing slightly and his voice barely above a whisper.

"That – *that* was all Selene's doing," Madge stammered, unable to stop the grin from spreading across her face.

"Green is your color. She didn't wear the dress, you did. You looked beautiful, *lunita*," Max said, pinching her chin. His touch was electric, and her cheeks were on fire—

"The stones that stand today are actually from a thirteenth-century castle," Norbert said, appearing behind them with

Selene as he swept a hand across the landscape and ruins a short distance away. "Constructed on site here because it was believed this is where the mystical Camelot once stood. Though any archaeological evidence of Camelot is long gone, and it's still disputed where it stood, but our kind *know*. You can feel it. It's in the air."

"Let's go take a closer look, shall we, *Norbert*?" Selene said, smiling flirtatiously at him, grabbing his hand as they walked around Max and Madge as if they had been nothing more than a rock or a bush in their path.

"She can't help herself," Max said, shaking his head, watching them walk away.

"Come on. Cut her some slack. She could use a little distraction. We *all* could."

"*Alright*. Let's go check it out too, then. The rest of them will catch up."

The castle ruins were a skeletal stone labyrinth, teetering on the edge of a towering bluff before continuing to the other side of a sharp ravine and onto a tall, bulbous peninsula narrowly connecting at the bottom. Madge and Max wandered in comfortable, awed silence – stopping finally on a rocky bluff. Frozen sea mist stung their faces as they stood on the edge, and looking wearily below, Madge could make out the steps that led down to the mouth of the cave.

"That's the way down…" Madge said, a shiver crawling up her spine as she pointed at the steps winding down a pathway far below. "In my vision it was different. It was nighttime… The moon was full and the only light on the path. There weren't steps, either – but the trail was muddy and worn."

"Well, I can say one thing. Norbert is right. You can feel the magic in this place."

Madge nodded her head and smiled. Camelot was saturated in the ground and suspended in the air that whipped through her hair, in every droplet of ocean mist that touched her face. And like before in her vision – she felt the lure of the cave, pulling at her with an invisible string.

"We're all here," Nico said, jarring Madge from her daydream. She swiveled around, taking in all the somber faces gathered quietly behind her, watching her warily... or rather even *expectantly*, as if she were supposed to say something meaningful. But nothing – not even hello screeched past her lips – especially as she beheld Grandpa Ollie, who'd been particularly quiet and graver than usual today. Downright sad, even. And his expression was worse than ever now.

"I'll see you down there," Madge said, grasping Max's elbow before she wandered up to Grandpa Ollie who watched her with an almost vacant expression.

"Madge, you'll follow behind me," Clare said, her eyes sharp and blue and more focused than ever. "Let's do this."

Madge felt her stomach do somersaults – and her feet felt like lead. There was no more time for distraction or denial. The horizon was already smoldering orange and red in the swiftly falling dusk, and they were headed down *that trail*.

Grandpa Ollie squeezed onto her shoulder. "Come on. I'm coming with you every step of the way, until the damned water hits my knees."

Madge bit back her tears – and the sheer terror filling her belly. It made it worse, almost, that she could feel Grandpa Ollie – always the strong one – trembling as he held her shoulder. "Grandpa... that water is *freezing*. Don't you dare. It's not exactly summer out here."

"Since when did you get so bossy?" he said, huffing a laugh.

"I don't want you getting sick."

"You're worried right now about *me* getting sick?" he said, shaking his head.

"I'm worried about everyone out here," she breathed, past the growing lump in her throat.

"The only one anyone should be worrying about is you. These folks can all take care of themselves. And I talked to Nico – he talked to Mr. Hannover – they've got their eyes on the cove and are all hidden out there, keeping an eye out for the Daeds. We shouldn't have any run ins with them today. And Thomas said their cadre of volunteers would be arriving just after dark and watching from up above, with me."

"That's a relief." Madge nodded her head in reassurance more to herself than anything. If they were lucky, maybe they wouldn't even run into the Daeds after all.

There were so many steps down, down, down…

And what felt like a blink of an eye and yet also felt like it took forever, they rounded a corner, and when she was able to see past Clare's square shoulders, she could make out Merlin's Cave, yawning below in the fading light.

Seeing it caused her to slam into an invisible wall, as her heart pounded in her chest.

The lure of something inside it was stronger than ever now. And somehow, it felt as if the gate was already wide open. As if dark, giant wings of demon-sirens might explode from the mouth of the cave at any moment.

Grandpa Ollie seemed to sense her fear, and grasped her hand tightly with his big, calloused fingers. She didn't dare look up at his face. At his trembling chin, at the tears gathering beneath his bushy white eyebrows as he gently pulled her the rest of the way down the path.

All too soon they stepped beneath the shadow of the tall bluffs, not far now from the high tide's edge where half of the team was already waiting. She felt her palms go sweaty as they passed the same stream she'd seen in her vision, cascading down the hill and into the sand below. Madge turned just before they reached the bottom, and looked back up the trail, and at the cliffs, glowing in the fading sunset. It looked so different now, from her vision. The skeletal gray ruins barely visible from down below, where once Camelot's citadel had gleamed in the torchlight like a resplendent crown on the head of the cliff side, a vigilant, ever watchful eye on the sea below.

Madge turned back around to see Grandpa Ollie watching her with sad, large eyes.

"You sure you're ready for this?" he asked as he searched her face for even a shadow of doubt. "Just say the word if not."

"I'm more ready than I'll ever be, Grandpa," Madge said as she crashed into his chest, feeling hot tears spill from her eyes without warning.

"Then why are you crying?" he asked as she could feel the whole inside of him shaking.

"Because I love you, Grandpa," Madge breathed, and then grabbing onto her necklace, said, "And because… that's where Mom and Dad…"

"I know," he said, breathing in the top of her head as she could hear him biting back a sob. "I know. I can hardly stand to be here."

She pulled away from him and steeled herself, remembering she had to be strong – if not for anyone else, then for him.

"Promise me one thing," Grandpa Ollie said in perhaps the

grimmest expression Madge had ever seen on his face. "If your cuffs burn because danger has turned her eyes to you, you *run*. Or swim, do whatever you have to do, just get out of there. Even if you didn't get the fruit, or the wand, don't risk it."

"That's an easy promise," she said with a smile. And she meant it, though she didn't promise him something she knew she couldn't be sure to keep. "But it won't come to that."

Grandpa Ollie's face fell completely as his eyes flooded over with tears. "You're my world, Madgie-pie. Do what you need to do and make sure you make it back, that's all I ask."

When Madge finally released his hand, turning to face Merlin's Cave, it felt like she'd ripped her soul from its last shred of warmth and safety.

24

Merlin's Cave

The stars hadn't emerged yet – but Cetus was up there, somewhere.

They were all here, floating in the mouth of the cave in the now growing dark, and Madge felt a strange pulse of energy as she entered it, which continued to swirl around her in the shallow waters, swelling up and down with the tide.

"All clear," Nico said. Madge gaped at the SSO sword he carried, the smooth metal dimly reflecting the dying light off the water. Sam, Terrance and Clare all carried them, too. Nico stared blankly at the dark mouth of the cave. "I'll lead—"

"You don't have to do this!" Selene screeched suddenly, flinging her arms around Madge's neck. "I can't… I couldn't live with myself if… this is all my fault!" Her vivid blue eyes were wide. *Pitiful.*

"This is not your fault, Selene," Madge said, feeling a twisting in her gut. So many somber faces stared back at her, bobbing on the water. Waiting for her to say *more*.

"You can't help who your family is, who your parents are. If anyone knows that, I do," Norbert said almost too quietly.

"Ultimately it is Viviane's fault, but Selene *and* Madge share the responsibility of their actions equally," Nico said, his voice uncharacteristically gentle despite the harsh truth. "But she's right. If you want to change your mind, right now would be the time to speak up."

"Stop it, everyone, please," Madge said, shaking her head. "I'm meant to be here. There is no other way, no waiting – we are *here*. It doesn't matter whose fault it is, not anymore."

Madge shared a long look with her cousin. Her vivid blue eyes were spilling with tears. "I can – the potion Rosie gave me—"

"Will only work for so long. You need the fruit, and I'm going to go in and get it." Madge was surprised at the words tumbling from her mouth, and at the resolute emotion that sent her voice quaking. "Maybe it's because we are here – where my parents were… But I *need* to do this. It's my destiny – for a lot of reasons. And I'm ready," she finished, looking to Nico.

Nico stared quietly back at her for a moment, with surprise and pride in his eyes. "You triple checked your supplies?" he asked, referring to the items he'd insisted she take along with her to the other side. For once, she was happy with his mission essential, get it done attitude.

"Yes, and Clare checked again, too."

"Okay. Stay in formation, everyone. Let's go."

Nico had the foresight to ask what the terrain in Eressëa was like, so she could be outfitted into a full body suit that blended in, making her less likely to be seen. It was decided white was the best color: it was the color of the sand in its glassy sea, and the walls that stretched forever upwards. She carried a matching white cap to hide her hair, a few pairs of ear plugs, a flask of water, a protein bar, a roll of paracord and a diver's knife, strapped to her calf. It wasn't a sword like Morgaine had carried – but it would have to do.

One by one they filed in, as rehearsed so many times before today. Terrance was on the other side of the cave already, monitoring the other side. Nico led the way, followed by Dan and Christine, who Madge followed behind with Max. She was glad for his soothing, familiar presence. Her Uncle Robert was here, too – though he'd been quieter than ever in the past weeks since his daughter had been bitten. As if he'd been holding his breath. Norbert swam with his personal security just behind Selene and Robert, who were followed finally by Clare and Terrance, taking up the rear in case anyone followed them into the cave.

As they swam the shallows between rocks and the constant tides rolling through, Madge had time to feel the energy coursing through it – the pull of what she was heading towards stronger than ever. She also finally had time to think – to *feel*. She'd not had a moment to herself these past weeks – no time to absorb the reality of it all.

She knew that lingering fear should be what she felt the most – but it was shoved so far back now. First by the grim feeling of the fact she was swimming in the very place her parents were murdered, but most of all for the goodbye to Grandpa. The thought of him watching her swim into the same cave he knew he'd lost his daughter to weighed heavier than any of it.

Still, the swirling pulse of energy coursed around her in the water – getting stronger and stronger… Until the water felt deeper, and the tide intensified again. And before she knew it, they came to a halt, and terror slammed into her chest, making it hard to breathe.

Max floated by her side, yet she was barely aware of him squeezing her hand, or his intense expression as he searched her face. She could only stare at the end of the cave—

"They're waiting." Christine smiled sadly as she reached for Madge's cheek.

Madge refocused her dizzy eyes towards the other mouth of the cave, and a chill ran up her spine. She could make out two luminous figures – undoubtedly the sea nymphs – by the exit to the sea beyond, now sparkling with the light of the rising moon and stars.

"Here we go," Madge croaked, as a fire burned in the pit of her stomach.

"Stay *safe*. We love you," Christine said softly. She leaned in and kissed Madge's forehead before letting go and swimming behind Madge, as Nico, and all the others who'd swam in front of her now did, silently placing a hand on Madge's shoulder as they passed. And as each of them passed her, the silence of the cave swallowed her whole… and she felt… *numb*.

But Max lingered. His face was gently lit by his coppery scales, reflecting the amber brown in his eyes like the flame in a candle. And as she met his eyes, the numb feeling she'd had melted away, replaced by a sharp jolt that brought her back to earth. "I wish I could come with you," he whispered, squeezing her hand tightly. She wrapped him in a hug, nestling her nose in his neck, not caring what anyone else saw or thought for once.

"I'm not going to say goodbye. Just see you soon," she said, finally releasing him as she cast her gaze finally back at the others.

"We will be here, waiting. If you come back through and no

one is here, get out," Nico warned for the millionth time. He'd gone over this scenario more times than she could count.

"And don't take fourteen years this time. We need you back here," Uncle Robert said, who was holding onto his daughter Selene who was sobbing on his shoulder. It was all Madge needed to see and hear to give her the courage to turn back around – and swim away.

25

A Taste of Blood

The nymphs were identical. And agitated.

Their long, fiery red hair splayed in the air around them as they rose from the water and floated in the air before her. Madge was glad she'd already gotten to know Giuliana – and experienced the terror of meeting these creatures before. Otherwise, she'd have surely swum away by now. One was terrifying enough – but two—

"Who are you?" asked the one on the right, her eyes flashing with impending doom.

"And, pray tell, *what* are you?" asked the one on the left, who seemed to be sniffing the air in front of her, as if Madge gave off some kind of smell only they could detect.

"Um… I'm Madge. I'm Morgaine's descendant. She sent me a—"

"Very well, hold out your hand," the one on the right said, as they both approached Madge in an angry dance of watery light.

Madge did as she was asked, though her hand shook so much she could hardly hold it up.

The one on the right reached out and grasped her by the wrist – and Madge noticed with no small horror that her thumb nail was long and sharp, with a point at the end – and before Madge could process what was intended with her hand, she felt a hard prick. She tried to pull away – but she was held fast and watched helplessly as the first one lifted her finger to its mouth.

To taste her blood.

Pulling away, her wild, fiery eyes seemed to settle, and her hair fell onto her shoulders.

But something in her expression remained feral. Lethal.

Madge watched helplessly as the other nymph approached, her expression unreadable when she reached for Madge's hand—

Madge flinched and squeezed her eyes shut as her fingers brushed the tops of her own.

And finally opened her eyes when she felt a minty, calming feeling spread through her hand, like the deepest fathoms of the ocean... And her hand was released.

There wasn't any sign of a mark left behind – the prick was gone.

"Thank you," Madge breathed, finally exhaling the air she'd bottled up inside her chest.

"Once you go through, we cannot help you," said the nymph on the right, with a grim and almost indifferent expression. "If you bring anything back with you, we cannot help you. Our business is only to guard the gate from *this* side. Do you understand?"

Madge felt a wave or relief for a moment – she'd passed and would be granted permission to pass – but her breath hitched at the second part. A warning? "What does that mean, you can't help me if... I bring anything back?"

"Your ancestor brought something back, did she not? You intend to go and retrieve something, too. We are not permitted to help you, but only to open the gate."

Something was wrong. Was she walking into a trap after all? "Who ordered that? Someone from here? Viviane? Another royal?"

"Neither humans nor Saelfen nor any kind you'd find here can command us!" the nymph on the right spoke again, her eyes flashing angrily. "Neither could there be any kind of *bargain* with things from this world that would beg us to do anything other than what we are here to do."

The one on the left waved a hand in the air. "There are greater things at work in the Universe, princess. Yet nothing greater at the same time. But we don't expect you to understand that any more than you can fathom eternity. We are here to do our small part, nothing more."

"Enough questions and unfathomable, murky answers, sister," the one on the right said, taking her place on the opposite side of the cave entrance from her calmer twin. "The gate will open for you alone again as you come back through."

Madge wanted to object – to say she could understand—

But in the blink of an eye, their shimmering figures began to swell, and water spread from them, at first like ink spilling on a page before it began to swirl and eddy all around them... and the light from the moon and the stars beyond shone through them – as if their essence had thinned... until finally, the water in the cave began to *rise*.

"Get ready, princess," the nymph on the right commanded.

All of Madge's courage wilted upon hearing it, as she realized she was about to go through the gate. She felt neither an inch of numb, nor a splinter of denial, nor did she feel empowered now in any way whatsoever. Nothing but sheer terror now filled her belly as she watched the water continue to rise – filling the cave entrance… And the wall of water churned, and churned and churned—

"Everything you need is inside you. Godspeed," the twin on the left said as a way of goodbye – as if to say, *time to go now*.

The water was a deafening roar and a swirling mass of white foam.

The gate was here, it was ready. It was time.

Madge's body was tingling so fiercely it was burning her up from the inside out, and her heart felt like it was going to break out of her chest it was pounding so hard. Wading before this gate – the tornado of water so strong that it made it hard to breath, and that now pounded with energy so deep and fathomless it made her head hurt – made her feel like she was standing at the top of the tallest mountain, ready to jump off and be carried into nothing but the wind.

"Don't hesitate!" One of the twin nymph's commanding voice said above the pounding roar. "It only makes it worse. Go, now."

Breathless, and terrified to what felt like the point of death – Madge lunged into the swirling gate.

A thousand needles of water shoved her in every direction as she was flipped and whirled, and she couldn't tell which way was up or down.

And when she felt like she'd pass out from lack of air and the pain of the passage…

She came out the other side.

26

Breathe, See, Hear

Madge exploded up from the water, gasping for air and straining to see. And just like in her vision, she wasn't met by moonlight. The sun was high above in a perfect, azure sky, and the sea was perfectly calm and as clear as glass.

But it was all blurry.

It was taking so long to catch her breath – like her lungs had been squeezed through a vice grip from the passage – and worst of all, her eyesight wasn't adjusting to take in her surroundings… to know if anything drew near or to see what was out there…

She waded on her back, fighting to take a deep breath, her throat straining to take in air…

Until slowly – painfully slowly, she was able to breathe somewhat normally – and after blinking several times, her vision sharpened. Focused.

And as her eyes focused, sound came crashing in – she hadn't realized until now it had been muted to begin with, and a deep chill froze her to the core.

That eerie, beautiful singing...

The *pull*.

Her head was swimming – dizzy with the sound – unable to focus on anything but the singing pulling her... As if she were falling and couldn't stop herself.

Her wrist burned – and she was able to drag her eyes to the royal cuffs.

Glowing red.

Her stomach tightened – she needed to block them out – before they found her. Before they tasted her fear, the pull too tight to get away—

It took every effort of mind and will to find the zipper on her mesh bag – her hands shook and fumbled, as she fished around to find a pair of ear plugs. Her fingers closed around a small, plastic bag – and tearing it open, she couldn't get the soft foam into her ears fast enough – that line was pulling tighter and tighter...

One, two.

Deep breath. She ducked her head under, letting the water wash over her – letting the sound fade away to a chilly, uncomfortable sound in the back of her skull – but at least one she could deal with. She could think again. And her wrists no longer burned with warning.

Rising to the surface again, Madge took a deep breath...

And finally, took it all in—

Eressëa. It felt old – and otherworldly. It sang to her blood in equal parts awe and terror.

And though she *remembered* all of it from her vision, it was more surreal, here in person, than her imagination had allowed. Like she'd watched the whole thing as a movie – whereas now, she was living and breathing in the real thing.

And it felt far. Wherever it was – it *was* a different world. She even felt she shouldn't be here – at least not in this form.

The rock surrounding the cave behind her angled and rose up, and up, and up and up, farther than the eye could see, like looking at the horizon of the ocean as it seemed to curve in somehow, until it met the smooth white, gleaming stone of Eressëa. It too, reached as high as the heavens, and seemed entirely insurmountable. And likely it was.

Her eyes trailed along its walls, stretching on and on to her right, until she could make out the glint of the golden gates…

And immediately to its right stood the *Treoliffruma*.

A wall of green that reached up, and up, and up…

And her eyes darted to movement high above it–

Circling, black figures. *Sirens*.

Nothing could have prepared her for the way it felt to see them – even as far away as they were and nothing more than large black dots like far away planes in the sky. And as if by simply beholding them, their voices rang with a renewed push in her ears. But instead of a pull, she felt terror and darkness and foreboding sing through her blood.

Madge shuddered to think – if she hadn't had the ear plugs…

Because hearing their singing here – in person, was different also than the vision had allowed. Like voices echoing in a cave, the vibrations of their voices circled and ebbed around inside her skull, sending the hair on her head to prickle. Fathomless femininity and beauty were bottled in their voices – a promise of finding beauty, finding something ethereal, something magnificent, something…

But all of it… Tainted. Lies. Allure and deception – that's what Sirens were. Like Lilith, hidden behind something beautiful. Something disguised.

Dragging her eyes away from their dark, swirling figures – Madge squinted to see in the distance to where she remembered the Singasteinn must have been. The place they purportedly lured you to, according to Giuliana – and in the great expanse she could barely make it out... but it was there. A small, rocky outcrop of an island, covered with countless dark forms. If she hadn't known better, she would have thought she simply saw large, winged birds. Though the very sight of it made her eyeballs ache and burn and made her skin itch and pull towards it like it was a gigantic, magnetic force. Their winged forms traveled up and down from it, in constant lines back and forth from where they circled higher and higher above and towards the endless, gleaming walls of Eressëa, as though constantly seeking a way over and inside.

Heat again singed her wrists—

The cuffs.

The stones inside were now a deep, crimson red.

Red as the fruit... *Fruit from the tree.*

How long had she been staring at those winged demons in the distance? How long had she lost focus as to why she was here?

Red was a warning.

She needed to get underwater – get in, get out, she reminded herself.

Shoving her hair into the white skull cap, she took extra care to pile her hair over her ears to block out their sound even more. And finally, as she took several deep breaths – readying her lungs for ducking under the glassy surface – she eyed the Treoliffruma and the glinting, golden gate one last time, took a final deep breath into her lungs, and ducked under.

It took mere seconds as she dove as deep as she could to realize just how grating and horribly irresistible the siren-song had been. For as the water muted their voices just that much more, to where she wondered if she could hear them at all or if it was just her imagination, the relief she felt as the water soothed and eased her mind was like running cold water over a burn.

Her head again clear and focused, Madge swam as low as possible, fighting the urge to move too quickly, as that would disturb the sand and sea creatures and might bring attention to her, or so Nico had advised. But as she swam the sea in this otherworldly realm, she was surprised to see that every manner of sea creature was beneath her, though none familiar to what she'd ever seen before. She wondered if further away – far out to sea – there might be actual sea monsters, like Cetus, burrowing in its depths…

The swell here was gentle, if not barely there. But most of all, Madge noticed the *energy* here felt different. It was not the pounding Pacific but something else entirely. The sea here felt fathomless somehow. Madge noticed depth when she swam the Pacific – and could sense it, but here there was no bottom. And the strangest feeling of all was that swimming in its waters felt like tiptoeing past a sleeping giant. Its energy was there, but it wasn't awake. Like a dormant volcano, waiting for its time, its deep power vibrated and hummed and rippled the sand beneath her.

And, she noticed, the same feeling hovered over the breath of the water, as the sandy bottom she swam rose up gently into the beginning of the shallows.

Sand gave way to rocks, and massive roots—

The Treoliffruma.

She swam just a bit further – until she noticed she swam beneath the shade of its branches reaching over the water.

Now was the most terrifying moment of all.

Emerging from the safety of the water, somewhere beneath the tree, where the voices would reach her ears again—

And where she'd last seen, in her vision, the headless body of Lilith.

Madge rose as stealthily as she could, just like Nico had trained her to do, only letting her eyes surface, crouching on her on her hands and knees in the sand, with her tail fins swaying behind her in the shallows as she tried to behold the massive tree in front of her.

Up close, she was awestruck at the length and girth of its boughs, let alone its width stretching as far as a city block. Beneath the shade, the Treoliffruma seemed to glow with green energy – and a surge of adrenaline surged up Madge's spine as she at last beheld its flawless, perfect fruit. Oddly, the fruit was small in comparison to the colossal tree – no bigger than a pomegranate, or a large apple—

And then her breath hitched. It was quiet in its shade – too quiet.

She'd been so enchanted by the Tree and its fruit that she'd failed to realize it.

The voices hadn't reached her ears – in fact, not a whole lot of sound reached her ears at all. It was a sweet, strange, magical silence.

And then she remembered Morgaine had experienced the same thing – there was no singing beneath the tree. But she did remember that silence had been broken by Lilith's lone-voice, hanging above her head on one of the boughs –

and with a shock and a shudder, Madge searched within its branches...

Its boughs were heavy with fruit, a dance of light and shadow... but she saw nothing. Not a tail, not a flash or glint of golden armor.

Finally, she pulled her mer-form away, her fins receding to bare feet, until finally she stood and stepped slowly and carefully through the water, towards the grassy banks.

Climbing over webs of large, crisscrossing roots, she stepped as lithely and as quietly as she could – aiming to find ground where she could reach a piece of fruit—

And perhaps be lucky enough to find Merlin's wand.

The further beneath the tree she crept, the more the fruit glistened like rubies in the dappled sunlight, glittering and reflecting off the white, crystalline walls of Eressëa.

Finally, her feet stepped into deep, powdery sand before touching the tender, cool grass beneath its shade, and immediately as she did so, she noticed the air was filled with a sweet and musky smell... like a strange combination of maple syrup, strawberries, and peat moss.

The scent was so intoxicating, her mouth watered—

And as she reached for the lowest piece of gleaming fruit in her proximity, she froze.

Her hand had not yet reached the tree or so much as touched a piece of fruit let alone tug at it... and yet something moved within it, rustling the very branch she'd reached for.

With a heavier rustle, something heavy dropped with a thud.

Do not jump – do not move quickly – breathe through your nose—

Hopefully, all of Nico's tiresome stealth training would help her right now, though her chest was heaving so hard it was hard to breathe *quietly*... The silence too loud – apart from the sound of a *rattle*.

Slowly, she turned her head.

This had to be what a heart attack felt like.

Cupping her own hands over her mouth to hold back a scream, Madge tried not to let her knees completely buckle beneath her as terror ripped through her body as though a ghost had run straight through her. She couldn't have run if she'd tried.

The black tail of a humongous serpent snapped and thudded on the ground again – as the rest of the thing was all too quickly coming *down*.

Every bone in her body *wanted* to flee – but she didn't have time to turn and run or even process what was happening by the time the body of the thing slammed to the ground.

Its black, taught wings were still spread from the fall, hiding its upper half—

Until they dropped, spiking their sharp points into the ground behind her, revealing polished golden armor right down to sharp-tipped clawed fingers, so long they looked more like a dragon's talons—

And she lacked a head.

27

Pluck, Rattle, Burn

How could something so hideous – so evil – exist within this life-giving tree?

Its green, life-giving light still reflected and touched everything beneath it – apart from the scales on that tail. It seemed to repulse it, to push it away.

Now was the time to run. But her cuffs weren't yet burning – Lilith hadn't sensed her.

Yet.

Madge's throat tightened to the point she felt she could suffocate – and a shock of adrenaline hit her so hard she felt she could fall to her knees… But a gleaming piece of fruit was there, staring her in the face, within arm's reach—

Pluck.

Madge cringed as the branch quivered – the fruit was heavy. Far heavier than it looked – and she hadn't anticipated the branch to shiver upon releasing it—

Rattle.

Lilith's tail rattled, ever so slightly…

And her demon, black-scaled body stiffened and froze, the

nub of her torn neck angling towards her as if there were an invisible head attached, turning to look.

Burn.

The cuffs were warning her now, the stones within swirling like a black abysmal storm.

Lilith's tail slithered, the large rattle on the end of her tail angling—

And just as Madge was about to leap away, her heart pounding in her throat so hard she thought surely the monster in front of her could hear it – she was hit by the spray of sand from a massive wind, as Lilith arched up and beat her massive, black wings, and rose steadily, driving more sand and wind – until she shot up into the air and out of sight...

As Madge rubbed sand from her eyes, she looked to see where Lilith had gone – but the massive branches of the Treoliffruma stretched too far, and Lilith was nowhere in sight...

She could see sirens in the distance, still forming a steady line between their *Singasteinn* and the air somewhere high above – but for now, all was silent again.

Madge's knees finally buckled, and she fell to the ground as her chest heaved...

Yes, this was what a heart attack must feel like – she couldn't breathe, couldn't move—

She managed to lift her head slightly, turning her dizzy gaze to the glassy, turquoise sea, until she was able to focus on the sandy ground beneath her palms...

At the piece of fruit lying by her hand.

Stand up! Run, swim!

Impervious in her panicked state to notice the cuffs warning her, again.

She'd no sooner secured the fruit within the bag at her waist than the hairs stood on the back of her neck. She didn't even look down at the cuffs as slowly, she removed the knife strapped to her thigh...

THUD.

It was directly behind her.

Her wrists burned so much now she wanted to tear the cuffs off, and every hair on her body prickled as she slowly turned...

To face Lilith.

She was much closer this time... Too close.

The headless siren-queen stood erect and tall, her armored claws stiff and open and blocking Madge's path to the water with her black wings spread wide. Though her golden armor was polished and bright, it did not outdo or somehow even *outshine* the scales on her thick, long tail – twice the size of her torso – gleaming ebony and darker than the night sky, seeming to swallow any light or anything near it.

What was left of Lilith's neck wormed around, turning Madge's already burning, terrified stomach almost sour. And before Madge had time to move, or think what to do, Lilith's voice whispered and hissed in her mind.

Pathetic, little worm... Want to know how I sing to your dear cousin?

Without further warning, Lilith's haunting voice sang in Madge's mind, bringing her to her knees in angst and pain – as if the sound were burning her from the inside out—

Madge clenched her jaw, fighting with every ounce of strength to think past it, past the burning, past the sound echoing inside her skull so much every inch of her hurt—

And though she wanted to move, the burning was met by a

crippling fear, seeping into her bones like a cold flood—

Her whole body, mind – everything was fire and ice all at once...

But something at her neck burned with a new sensation—

The necklace.

Its heat was a different sort, moving in shocks and waves up and down her spine.

Madge's mind found a sliver of focus – and in it was one question:

How did Lilith know who she was?

Madge struggled to her feet. "What do you mean, singing to my cousin? How do you know who I am?" She said, though her voice quivered and shook, and she knew she should be running and not talking to this thing—

My head and my body are eternally connected, worm, *for I am an immortal creature.*

Lilith's voice hissed in her mind – and she knew... The siren queen had been expecting her. Trap – this was a trap. Madge backed away a step –

But Lilith's hideous voice growled in her skull. *You cannot run from me, worm, and if I wanted you dead, I would have killed you by now. It was you I wanted all along. I want to make you an offer—*

"NO!" Madge screamed, as her fear rose to boiling anger—

Instinct took over.

Before Madge knew what she was doing, she was lifting her hands before her, and a ball of white-hot light flashed so brightly she had to squeeze her eyes shut as it shot from her hands—

Hitting the monster square in the chest, exploding across her armor, raising and slamming her flailing body to the ground as her rattle at the end of her tail shook violently.

Madge sprinted for the water, leaping over a high root—

And the next thing she knew she was coming down, hard.

Her toe bled from the impact, but she'd caught herself enough to keep her cheek from slamming into the sand... and she was about to bounce back up to keep running when her eyes registered something metallic, held in the nook of the branch she'd tripped over, hidden in the tall grass around it...

A metal box... *The metal box.* Merlin's wand!

Lilith's screeching reached her ears as she scrambled to reach the box – and grasping it in her hands, she took off on the ground running again—

Fighting against the deafening screams piercing and stabbing in her mind, echoing and bouncing and slamming inside her skull to the point of physical pain.

As her feet hit the glassy sea, she could feel the wind from Lilith's wings, could see the shadow approaching from behind – and as she sloshed through the water, she heard the answering call of the sirens up above reach her ears.

She didn't even have to look up to know.

They were coming...

In circles and droves... circling down, down, down.

28

Squall

Madge dove headfirst.

She willed her Vala to propel her forward as she sliced through the water. She wasn't sure if it was sheer terror or her Vala that rippled and tingled and burned throughout her body, her core, her bones, her skin.

Despite being under the water – which blocked out their voices before, but this time – she could hear them. Their shrieking screams were barely muted. They must be close... But she didn't dare look up or behind to see how close.

Pushing and pushing, her chest feeling like it would explode, she got past the shallows and cut through deeper water, moving as fast as her Vala and fins would allow, focusing on nothing but what was in front—

Until their shadows began to creep in on all sides of her peripheral vision...

One shadow inching in *front* of her as if directly over her—

Madge pushed harder, towards a shelf on the seafloor that went deeper–

The drop off, just a breath away...

But just as Madge curved her body to move down further into the depths, she felt a sharp slice tear into her calf, leaving a lingering burning sensation that ripped through her leg. And Lilith's voice laughed in her mind – its sound distant, but seeming to slow her down – to slow her Vala that helped cut through the water—

Onspen!

Madge pushed the word through her core, shoving away the fog of the laughing echoing in her mind, and the fear that attempted to cripple and slow her down…

A shock hit the crown of her head, surging to her fins… and her focus became sharp. But the most curious feeling of all was that the cuffs seemed to help her, as waves and surges of power vibrated against her wrists, filling her with a renewed push and a deeper Vala than she'd felt before, moving her along at a pace her mind could barely register.

Time itself didn't seem to exist as she propelled forward – there was no space in her mind now, no thought, but breaching the gap between the rest of this glassy sea and the gate—

Until she could feel a pull of something else—

The gate.

It was close.

Dread filled her belly. She'd have to rise above the water to get through it…

Hopefully, it would open quickly enough for her to barrel through it unscathed.

It was there – right before her now—

Madge set her jaw, and gritted her teeth so hard she thought her teeth might break—

And vaulted from the water.

Air filled her lungs, and she screamed as she plunged forward. She was high in the air, higher than she'd ever leapt—

And mercifully, she was barreling towards a wall of swirling, thrashing water...

Keeping her eye on the pounding vortex before her, feeling as if sharp, golden talons might rip her to shreds any second – she slammed headfirst into the gate so hard it felt like she'd hit hard ground.

The passage pierced every part of her, pins and needles shooting and slicing at her skin, her head throbbing as pounding water filled her ears until she thought it would burst—

Until... Despite the racking pain... She felt something *else*. *Something was in here with her.*

In the dark, rushing gateway between worlds, she felt something long and scaly, something not from her own body, slide past her legs... then past her face—

And Madge was spit from the gate and back into Merlin's Cave.

But she didn't have time to register the terror of what it was – what had been in there with her – not as her body was still thrashing through pounding water, toppling over and over again, hitting rocks, slamming past the walls of the cave, her body like a ragdoll as she was driven by a great surge of water...

As if a tsunami was thrusting her through the entire length of the cave.

Madge kicked, and kicked and kicked, and battled the water and swam harder, trying to avoid the bone crushing rocks as her chest tightened from lack of air.

But as she kicked – she noticed something was latched to

her calf—

Terror made a fresh ripple through her body, making her even more desperate for air – but she couldn't find a way up–

Because there wasn't one.

Finally, when her chest was so tight, she thought she was going to fill her lungs with water, she saw light at the end of the tunnel…

Flashes of it.

Lightening.

Much like she'd seen that day beneath the ground in the Academy—

It cracked and surged through the still thrashing water again and again, and through a particularly bright flash, as the water lit up, she saw an image that made her heart skid to a halt—

The headless body of Lilith clung to her with a clawed hand.

With the last breath of power she had, Madge summoned the same ball of burning fire she used on her aunt: *Greek Fire.*

Lilith was knocked back and away—

And Madge didn't stop as she pushed up, and up…

Until she felt a hand grab hers – she went to shake it away—

Max. He was pulling her up—

Until she finally broke to the surface, with a desperate gasp, right into the middle of a battle where even the sea was angry.

"Are you okay?" Max screamed, his voice carried away by wind, the crackle of lightning—

Madge nodded as lightning kept flashing everywhere. In the water, and in the sky—

Bursts of energy shot down like cannon fire from the clifftops.

The Merewif Cadre— Thomas and Rosie had stayed true to their word.

Madge tried to breathe past the fire in her lungs—

"Max – Lilith – she's here," she shrieked as tears filled her eyes.

"Where? Here? In our world?" He asked before his eyes shot suddenly off to the side—

Madge swiveled around in the water, ready to fight whatever drew near—

"Madge! Max!" Nico howled, holding his sword above the water as it glowed white hot with electricity. "Stay with me!"

Lightning shot from his sword, blazing past the darkness as it slammed into the water, just missing a Daed coming straight for them—

"She's here!" Malcolm roared, banking right—

Nico aimed his trident-sword – and the bolt of lightning struck and lit up a gargantuan wave, rising out of the water like a hand—

"SQUAAAALLLL!" Nico shrieked.

Max grasped Madge's arm with wide, panicked eyes.

"Swim deep, away from shore!" Nico shouted to them, just as Madge could feel a powerful current pulling beneath her fins – the water pulling back and back and joining the wall of water – it would be on them in seconds—

She prepared to duck under and do as Nico asked, feeling Max pulling on her to start swimming – but she couldn't peel her eyes away as continued shocks of light flashed within its crest, revealing bodies suspended and tumbling inside – lit again and again as they battled each other even as the sea attempted to dump them against the rocky bluffs—

And a large serpentine tail, tipped by a golden rattle snaked through it.

Lilith.

Her headless body shot up, wings spread wide, just as the wall of water slammed down.

Madge couldn't tell what happened next – and she couldn't gauge which way was up or down, let alone which direction to swim – so she pushed against the water, though her body was rolled around and around and around—

And Max held her tightly, his arms wrapped around her – and she held him too, their bodies slamming into rocks and sand—

They pushed harder, away from the sea bottom—

Until the water began to swell and sway again, finally pulling back out to sea...

They slammed into a sea wall, and Max was deposited to a rocky ledge, unconscious. Madge clung and clawed at the sea wall as thrashing surf continued to slap her body – and her bleeding, torn calf burned in the cold night air. She held tightly, looking for a way down or up or otherwise—

"Max!" Madge tried to scream, but she could barely rasp it out—

Until she noticed something was behind her.

On a rocky ledge between the cove and the bulbous peninsula—wide, dark wings flapped and whooshed... And she had Viviane, unconscious, in her golden-clad arms, whom she now dropped unceremoniously to the rocky ground as she dug around in a bag...

And pulled something out, letting the bag drop to the ground, empty.

Long, golden talons wrapped around Mimir's Head, glinting in the moonlight as Lilith raised it above her worming neck—

And before Madge's eyes, its frozen, golden face melted...

And was alive again, *reattached*.

Its horrid, ghastly expression peeled back – and faded into the imitation of a beautiful face – pale skin, red lips – but the black, abysmal eyes remained unchanged…

And looking right at Madge.

Viviane struggled to rise – her blonde hair plastered on her face, on her hands and knees— until Lilith turned and swooped over her.

The snakes crowning her head lashed out, biting Viviane over and over again…

Until the siren queen threw her head back and screamed—

A blood-curling, shrieking call that sounded like a thousand voices reverberated through the cove, as rocks crumbled and fell from overhead.

Madge could barely breathe, her arms burning and straining as tears burned hot in her eyes, watching helplessly as Lilith scooped a collapsed and lifeless Viviane in her arms again.

Then slowly, like a predator hunting prey – she turned her head towards Madge.

Her red lips were spread wide in a show of spiked teeth as she slowly arched her body up on her giant snake tail – rising high enough to reach the height Madge clung to on the rock wall as she slithered towards her—

And a small rush of minty wind touched her neck.

Giuliana.

She appeared, like a dance of blue, white northern lights – and floated by Madge.

"Don't move," she commanded, her arms spread wide as she watched Lilith, her hair spread high, her eyes a blazing fire, like a cobra ready to strike.

But Madge felt she could fall any minute, her heart lodged

in her throat, and she searched the rocky ledge beneath her frantically, looking for a place to jump and land to get to Max, whose unconscious body was dangerously close to the edge—

Just as an agony, pain-filled scream filled her ears and jarred her body.

Lilith was screaming.

Light-filled balls of energy vaulted from the cliff tops, one after the other in a steady stream, slinging again and again into Lilith's back, exploding across her wings—

Landing dangerously close to Madge, close to Max – the ocean splashing up in hisses of angry foam—

The Merewif cadre couldn't see her. Couldn't see *Max*.

"Stop! We are down here!" Madge screamed, but her voice was lost in the surf.

"I'm here, child!' Giuliana said as she moved closer, her face right up next to Madge as the kiss of mint hit her nose and cheeks. "I've got you. Be still."

"Max – help him—" Madge sobbed.

"He's okay – I've got you—"

Lilith shrieked again, her mouth open in a wide display as electricity flashed and zapped between her sharp teeth, her eyes looking as though they would bulge from their sockets—

And lightning struck now from the water, too, and crashed into the rock beside Lilith…

In the blink of an eye, in a breath of space between vaulting light—

Lilith's wings exploded up and away…

With Viviane, lifeless in her arms, like a bird of prey carrying a fish.

29

Awakening

Madge awoke with a start when she heard something collapse to the ground outside her window.

As her eyes widened, for a split second she expected to see the view from her bay window – back in her room at home – waking from a bad dream. Maybe Grandpa Ollie was dropping things in the kitchen, brewing coffee and frying eggs.

But that was snow outside the leaded, arched windows—

The Cottage. England.

It was all real.

Everything hurt. Her head, her arms and wrists, but most of all her calf as she attempted to lift her legs from the covers and hissed in pain.

The sky was dark with rain, melting the crusted, frozen snow that now shed from the roof by the window and collapsed to the ground. She breathed a sigh of relief as she realized that's what she'd heard moments ago – not the body of a giant snake-siren-demon landing outside...

One that had carried Selene's mother away.

Madge glanced over at Selene who had finally cried herself to sleep in the early hours of the morning. So far, her cousin had down right refused to eat the fruit, seeing she'd been so hysterically upset about witnessing her mother carried off by a winged demon.

Not that they'd have had time to push the matter with all the mayhem that ensued after the battle and the squall. The cottage had been in an uproar – injuries being tended to, the local Royals making matters worse by screaming in anger that things weren't handled as they should have been...

Madge limped over to her suitcase, hissing again at the pain that tore through her leg and threatened to drop her to the floor, rough stitches catching against the inside of her pajamas.

Rosie had been up half the night, stitching and healing and doing everything she could to help them. For now, they still had their jobs – because no one had yet reported the mysterious balls of light and energy that had come from the cliff tops. And if they hadn't been there...

Madge suppressed a shudder.

She might not be here if it weren't for them.

Besides Max's concussion, most everyone had an injury of some form or another and had poured into the Cottage in droves to share news and receive medical care. But the most intensive so far was Christine, who was still unconscious when they'd brought her back. Nico's shoulder had been crushed. Terrance, Clare, and Sam were still in pursuit of the Daeds and hadn't reported back by the time Madge had finally been forced to get to bed.

And that was the worst part.

Lilith was out there, somewhere. And Terrance, Clare, and Sam – and maybe the other stealth team that had been there – where were they? Had they found her? Was Viviane alive?

Madge fumbled in her suitcase, peeling back a hidden compartment until her fingers grazed the thick, hard skin of the fruit.

And next to it was the ancient, metal box. Merlin's wand.

Madge glanced behind her to make sure Selene was still asleep before she snuck a peek at the box she'd hidden in her suitcase. The outer metal box was thin and had been pounded artfully with a Saelfen figure down the middle, and runes adorning its edges. Inside was the smaller, simply carved wooden box which held the wand inside it, wrapped in cloth.

She was surprised at how small the wand was. She'd imagined it would have at least been the length of her forearm, but it was half of that. It was slightly bent and looked something like an old crone's finger, with a few gnarls and knots along the way, and the wood was both brown and silver at the same time. It had been smoothed down and was somehow preserved remarkably well, for as ancient as it was; and the scent of peat moss, strawberries and maple syrup could vaguely be detected when she held it to her nose.

The scent of the Treoliffruma.

Maybe it was as immortal as the tree itself? She had no idea how to use it yet, but she'd figure that out later. And for now, it would remain a secret until she did.

What mattered now was the fruit – and healing Selene. And if Lilith were still out there – would one piece be enough?

"What are you doing up? You need to rest!" Rosie clucked at her as she pulled out a chair by the small table which sat near the open fireplace. "Sit down. I don't want you putting pressure on those stitches."

"I wanted to see what you want to do with this before the rest of the house wakes up," Madge said as she sat down with a thud, placing the heavy fruit on the table.

"Help yourself to a scone – breakfast isn't ready yet," Rosie said, sliding a tray of the golden, round pastries in front of her as she frowned at the gleaming fruit. "Clotted cream is on the table. Make sure you layer it on thick. We're famous for it here in Cornwall. We'll talk about this fruit after you get something in your belly."

"Here, have a look a' that!" Thomas said, sliding a large piece of parchment across the table to Madge. *The enchanted newspaper.* Madge shoved a bite of warm, soft scone into her mouth, piled high with the sweet, cold and tangy, clotted cream that she slathered over with a smear of strawberry preserves, and grabbed up the thick paper into her hands.

"Squall in Camelot, Daedscuan on the Run?" she managed to choke out through a mouth full. "It's already in the papers?"

"You saw all those people on the bluffs last night. One of them was a local journalist."

"She works fast, and news travels even faster," Thomas said as he slid a steaming mug of tea towards Madge. "I added milk and sugar for you."

"*American Princess brings a siren back with her…*" Madge read aloud from the subtitle, before blinking up at Thomas whose face seemed to lose all color. "How – *what?*"

"Keep reading. You'll love the next part," Rosie said with a roll of her eyes.

"*The Princess called the Siren by name, none other than the Lilith, Queen of the Sirens, loosed in the New World. Lilith's headless body reunited with her head, which was held as an ancient relic by the Americans in the eighth realm for centuries, the legendary Mimir's Head, the relic responsible for creating the Daedscuan. Seemingly lifeless, it was anything but: the serpents on its head bit and infused its prey with a dark Vala unlike anything our kind have ever seen..."*

Madge grumbled, piling more cream and preserves onto her scone. "This isn't going to help me win the Council. And she wrote it, so it sounds like – like it's my fault Lilith is here! Does it not mention *why* I went through? Does it mention the fruit?"

"She writes with a particular flair – and people love that but – let me see that," Rosie said, grabbing up the paper in her flour covered hands. *"We await news on whether or not the fruit from the Treoliffruma will actually heal her cousin, Viviane's daughter, who was lured by her mother and bit by the head and is in now in danger of becoming a Daed. Viviane's whereabouts and whether she is alive, or dead, are unknown. Most believe she is still alive, else the Siren Queen, Lilith, would not have carried her away. We caution everyone to take care in the days and weeks to come. Intelligence and forces from all the Nine Realms will work together to stamp out this problem as soon as possible. See Mathilda Conway in Tregatta for protective amulets and charms."*

"She's always pushing Mathilda's—"

Rosie stopped short as the kitchen door swung open.

"Time to get packing," Nico said angrily as he poked his head in, his arm in a sling. His face was black and blue, and he had a cut on his cheekbone.

"What happened?" Rosie asked, folding the newspaper, and putting it in her apron.

"We are being ordered to leave within the hour – before

people wake up and read that paper. Rufus is furious."

"You've got to be joking," Thomas said as he shook his head. "Unbelievable!"

"What did they expect – you can't keep an ancient siren queen loosed on our world exactly a secret!" Rosie's face flushed red, and she pointed a wooden spoon at Nico. "With you in the shape you're in and the princess and – Christine definitely isn't well enough yet to move!"

Thomas rose a fist in the air, "You should stick that Trident up his royal—"

"Thomas!" Rosie interrupted as she slapped his arm. "Don't!"

"What about Selene?" Madge said, twisting in her chair to look at Nico.

"We have to be gone within the hour," Nico said, shrugging. "Maybe we can call Pearl."

Madge felt a fire rise in her belly. "And Sam, Clare – and Terrance?"

"They're safe. The stealth team – I don't know. But they don't report to me."

"That sick girl is eating that fruit before you go anywhere. So yes, call Pearl," Rosie said, her eyes flashing. "Thomas, grab me down that cutting board there, please. And sharpen my paring knife," Rosie said as her lips set into a hard line.

"With all due respect, we can't go against royal orders," Nico said, frowning. "If you want to do that while we pack – we can give it to her on the plane..."

"You cannot feed that to her on a public plane. What if she has an adverse reaction to it?"

Nico shrugged, splaying his hands in the air. "I'll call Pearl."

"You know what?" Madge said, standing from the table, her

calve barking in pain. "*No*. Bring Selene here, please. And Max. We are doing this now. We can apologize later or call Pearl – but we are doing this now."

Nico's eyes were wide. "Whatever you say, princess."

"The husk is hard, but the inside is soft," Rosie said, wiping her hands on her apron. "I cut just a small piece for now," she said, holding up a piece to Selene.

Selene's face was paler than ever as she shrank back from it. "I don't think I can," she said, her eyes darting towards the kitchen door.

"Of course you can," Madge said as her brow knit together.

"The thought of it makes me want to vomit!" Selene said, taking a step away—

"You're going to eat it, even if we all have to hold you down," Max said, nodding at Nico who barricaded the kitchen door just as Selene turned on her heels, as if to run away.

"Selene!" Madge said with disbelief in her voice. "You do realize what we all went through to get this, right?"

Selene shook her head, backing into a counter as if she'd rather scale the wall. "It… it doesn't want *it*," Selene hissed as she pointed with a shaking hand at the piece of fruit Rosie still held aloft in her hand.

"I see," Rosie said, removing her apron and arching a brow. "Nico, Max, sit her down—"

"NO!" Selene screeched, stamping her feet as Nico drew near—

"Stop thrashing, I don't want to hurt your wrist," Max said through clenched teeth.

"What's wrong with her?" Madge asked as her heart pounded in her chest.

"I'll tell you," Rosie said, pulling a chair away from the table and to the middle of the floor. "That siren has its claws into her more potently than ever now. That venom is – it's acting like a *living* thing inside her. And in a way, it is, really. We're going to have to force this down her gullet and hope it's not too late."

Selene threw her head back and laughed. "Try to make me, I dare you," she said, baring her teeth at Rosie.

"Nico, Max – the two of you, help her into that chair," Rosie said, lifting her chin.

Selene flailed as Max grabbed one arm, Nico the other – and screamed and kicked—

"Don't hurt her—"

A sound screeched and echoed off the kitchen walls that almost stopped Madge's heart.

The screech and call of the siren was coming from Selene's mouth, her eyes rolling back into her head as she dug her heels into the ground—

"That – that sound!" Madge gasped. "It's the siren's call – she's calling Lilith!"

Nico and Max wrestled Selene into a chair—

Thomas tried to hold her feet, and got a swift kick on the chin—

"Help me get this in her mouth!" Rosie said, her eyes wide. "Hold her head!"

Madge jumped forward and grabbed onto her cousin's head. She was wet and clammy and frantic – and Madge bit back tears as she tried to hold her head still.

"Hold it still – don't worry about hurting her, it's better than the alternative!" Rosie said, chasing Selene's screeching mouth with the morsel of red fruit—

Robert burst into the kitchen. "What is going on here? Let her go!"

"Daddy!" Selene screamed as she kicked her feet in the air, Thomas holding his gushing nose now, almost sending her flying backwards in the chair—

Robert lunged – but Madge stood in his way, just in time. "No – the thrall has gotten worse – we have to get her to eat this!"

"Daddy!" Selene screamed, "They're hurting me! Make them let me go!"

"No," Madge said, holding her hand out for her uncle to stay put. "We need to get her to eat the fruit and she's – something inside her is resisting."

"If you try to force her, she'll choke!" Robert said, stepping forward again—

"If she doesn't eat this now, we may lose her forever," Rosie said, as Robert stilled. "You hold her head, then. And lock that bloody door."

Madge watched in horror as Selene went into fits of panic. She thrashed and kicked to where four grown men struggled to hold down her arms, legs, and head. Prying her jaw open was the hardest part to watch as tears streamed down her almost unrecognizable face…

Until finally, Rosie dropped the fruit inside her mouth – and clamped her jaw back shut.

Selene choked – and flailed harder—

"Let her go! She can't breathe!" Robert hollered, pushing everyone away as Selene writhed and kicked until she fell to the ground—

Madge scrambled onto the kitchen floor with her – not caring if she got kicked, punched, or scratched, cradling

Selene's head as she continued to spasm...

"Let them be – let it take root inside her," Rosie said, holding her arms out to give them space on the kitchen floor.

"I've got you. I've got you..." Madge breathed, hot tears flooding her face as she gently held Selene to her, watching as her head turned from side to side, her chest heaving, her eyes squeezed shut... Silent eyes watched. Seconds felt like an eternity...

Until Selene's body went limp.

Madge shook her by the shoulders. "Selene? SELENE!"

"What's happened? What's wrong with her?" Robert asked as he knelt beside her, his face ghostly pale. "Selene?"

Rosie was on the ground now too – examining her face, her gums, and under her eyelids, until she pulled her hands away suddenly. "Shock her heart," Rosie mumbled, as she checked her pulse, her eyes going wide. "Did you hear me? Shock her heart!"

There was a ringing in Madge's ears –

"What do you mean, shock her heart?" Robert bellowed, "What's wrong with her? What did you do!" he went to grab Selene up – but Madge stopped him.

"NO!" Madge said, knowing what she had to do, her mind flashing back to Max when he had his head in her lap, unconscious and hurt. Selene was in far worse shape, but Madge knew she had to try. "Move away," Madge rasped, hovering over her as she held one hand over Selene's blonde, sweat drenched head, and one over her heart. Just as she'd done with Max.

"Madge – don't!" Max shrieked. But Madge ignored him.

"Stand. *Back*," Madge snapped.

Her skin broke out in a raging, itching tingle – until she

couldn't hear anything but her own pulse thundering in her ears. She held her breath... And heat rose from her stomach, spreading through her chest and arms until her hands were hot with it.

"Inlīht!" Madge screeched, feeling her throat vibrate with the urgency that exploded from inside as white-hot energy pushed from her fingertips—

Selene's chest rose, slamming into Madge's hands, before falling again and slamming into the hard kitchen floor...

Pain.

Radiating through Madge's hands—

Then darkness... cold and complete... swept through her blood, through her mind.

And a loud screech filled her skull so fiercely that she fell backwards and screamed, and screamed and screamed, holding her head in her hands as if to try and block the *singing*.

She vaguely felt warm hands touching her – and words she couldn't make out being mumbled, but she couldn't respond. Her entire body was racked with pain and anguish, as something horrible, dark and lifeless battled inside, rattling in the halls of her being...

Hardly aware of anything but the beating of her own heart, vaguely she noticed someone pull her up off the floor, onto her feet. Fear and grief smashed into her gut in nauseous waves, until she was spilling the contents of her belly on the floor.

Madge!" Selene's rasping scream pleaded in her ears...

Selene.

"Stop!" Madge heard Rosie's voice now.

Strong arms held her up, rubbing her back as she collapsed into a chair, sweat dripping down her brow. Her vision began to clear – and Selene's face was inches from her own—

"Are you okay?" she pleaded, her face strained and tear streaked.

Madge felt Selene's small, cold hands grab onto her own… and the pain and joy of it overwhelmed her into fits and wails of tears, as she slid off the chair onto her knees. "You're back," Madge managed to croak to Selene, who was now on the kitchen floor with her, hugging her tightly around the shoulders.

30

Foreweard

"Okay, so – I have to light the first luminary and then release it when, exactly?" Madge asked with a frown as Selene arranged Ash's hair into a neat half up-do. Selene's bathroom was a mess of hairspray, curling irons and hairpins – and makeup covering the counter.

"Pearl explained all of this," Selene answered through a bobby pin clenched in her front teeth, flashing an exasperated look at Ash in the mirror. "Hold still. I swear you two are like feral cats that don't like a bath." Selene twisted her hair again and pinned it. "Tonight is the biggest celebration of the year and literally the only purely Saelfen celebration we have. It's imperative you look your best, princess."

Madge couldn't believe how fast the fruit had acted. Selene's skin and eyes held no shred of evidence that she'd been poisoned by an ancient demon just days ago, and her old personality wasn't struggling an inch, either.

"This piece about how to track and kill a siren is garbage," Madge said, folding the bewitched Cannon Beach Chronicle back up and throwing it on the counter. She'd tracked the

Chronicle down the day after they'd arrived back home, painfully curious as to what everyone was saying about the whole thing and if they were blaming her for it all, too. "We aren't even sure she *can* be killed."

"Why not?" Ash asked, turning towards Madge with wide eyes. Ever since Ash had heard there was a literal, real life monster on the loose she had been having a hard time sleeping.

"She's immortal. Her head was severed for thousands of years and yet she's not dead. Captured and put back is more likely – and I don't even want to think about how we'd do that. So maybe captured and killed and detained…"

"I'm just relieved my mom is alive," Selene said with a shake of her head. "Even if she is still with that thing."

"Wait, when did you find that out?" Ash screeched, earning a slap on the shoulder from Selene to remain still.

"Today. Nico's team confirmed," Madge said with a deep sigh. "No one knows what shape she's in other than that, though."

"I wonder what she's like now, seeing you said it was like being demon possessed," Ash said with a shudder.

Selene shrugged. "I don't know, but half of what she's done – I don't know if it was her, or that thing inside her. I'd say if you're a Daed, you can't be acting of your own will. I wasn't. And I wasn't even a Daed yet."

"We may never know," Madge said, meeting Selene's eyes in the bathroom mirror. "But Nico and his team apprehended two of them, and Dr. Hiromi will be feeding them some of the fruit so see if it heals them and then maybe they'll cooperate enough to answer some questions."

"Ick. Isn't that fruit like a week old?" Ash asked.

"Rosie was able to preserve it. With a spell. But we only have so much of it – and who knows how many she has bitten by now."

"I'm fed up with monster talk!" Ash squeaked, grimacing as Selene pushed a pin too hard into her scalp. "Does every mermaid get together require this much primping and dressing up?"

"Well… Yes. More or less," Selene said, smirking. "But with good reason. For example, tonight – *Foreweard* – it's the biggest celebration we have. It's been around since – well forever. It's a celebration of the New World, New Hope and New Promise," Selene said as she secured a towel around Madge's shoulders so she could do her hair. "When our kind finally embraced this new place, and realized we were here for a reason – this holiday came about. And that is a reason to get dressed and looking our best, don't you think? Especially when you'll be the center of attention at the start?"

Madge cringed. Tonight was their biggest celebration of the year – and all eyes would be on her, some familiar and many not. "Remind me again… I light the luminary when everyone starts to sing, or when they finish the hymn?"

"When they start to sing, and you make it to end of the aisle—"

"UGH," Madge huffed, her cheeks reddening. "Why do I have to walk the aisle like a bride at a wedding? Why can't I just wait at the front? I hate that!"

"The point is to be singing while we watch the luminaries sweep up into the sky. And you walk the aisle because it is *tradition*. Queens do it upon inauguration – it won't be the first or the last time you do it, so—"

"Get used to it, princess. I know, I know." Madge looked

down at her dress. It was midnight blue, to match the velvet cloaks that everyone was required to wear, as per tradition. "Are you sure we won't look like some cult having a séance or something weird outside?"

"We've never had a problem," Selene said, rolling her eyes. "You know how well… connected we are. It's New Year's Eve. A lot of people throw parties."

The *Foreweard* celebration had been set up at Indian Beach, and indeed looked like a midnight fairy wedding was taking place. Silver lanterns glowed faintly at the ends of the rows, dimly lighting the aisle, and flaming torches were spiked into the sand, making it seem like a scene that probably looked incredibly similar had it even been a thousand years ago. An archway made of driftwood stood at the end, speckled by tiny, enchanted pricks of light that resembled floating fireflies or twinkling starlight, and strung with clusters of white baby's breath and sprigs of foxtail fern. And apart from the security team on duty, every person in attendance was wearing one of the midnight blue velvet cloaks, a tradition so closely followed that if anyone came without one, there were extras on hand to lend them.

Madge stood talking to Pearl and Nico, Grandpa Ollie at her side (who Madge thought looked hilarious in a hooded cloak, so much so she had to force herself to stop giggling at him) as they went over last-minute preparations.

"We're all in place, full eyes on the perimeter – if any winged demon zombie-snake-mermaids are overly confident enough to erupt out of the sky, we'll take 'em out," Nico said, chuckling. His face was still healing, and it would be a while until his shoulder would heal completely, but his eyes were as sharp as ever – and danced with a rare humor.

"I don't know what we'd do without you," Pearl said, patting him on his good shoulder.

"Me neither," he said as he stalked off into the night, his arm still in a sling, decked out in full gear with night-vision goggles on his head. "Good luck, *princess*," he called out behind him.

Madge felt her stomach tighten as she felt Pearl's sharp, brown eyes turn towards her.

"Here's the song – it's in bewitched ink so will light up in the dark so you can read it. Remember, you don't have to do much but sing along and light your luminary."

"There are a lot of people here," Madge complained. "What if I fall or something?"

Pearl clucked her tongue. "You'll be fine. And it's quite simple. Don't fall," Pearl answered with a rare giggle as she waved and walked away to find her seat.

Grandpa Ollie's warm, calloused hands wrapped around Madge's. "I'm going to go sit too, Madgie-pie. It's almost time," Grandpa Ollie said to her as he glanced down at his watch.

"I don't want to stand here by myself, Grandpa—"

"You won't be," he said, nodding his head at Max who approached from behind.

Madge felt her stomach flutter. Max looked incredible in his cloak. Taller, somehow, and mysterious, the firelight dancing in his eyes beneath its hood. Madge felt she must look the opposite, as she shuffled her feet in the sand and asked, "How stupid do I look in this thing?"

"You look perfect. And we're used to them. We wear them every year," he said with a small tug of his lips upward, as the clink of piano keys began to tinkle on the wind. He brushed her hand lightly. "That's my cue. You'll be fine. Just walk, one foot in front of the other."

Madge gulped, watching silently as Max took his seat. As she stood at the back, *alone*, and a soft melody rose steadily, keeping up with the swelling tides, the beating of her heart... and everyone – every single last Saelfen and Merewif were now sitting. Waiting for her.

"And that's *your* cue," Madge whispered to herself, taking her first step forward, her feet cold and bare in the freezing sand. She'd removed her shoes at the last minute – worried that they'd cause her to trip – and she was happy for the cold on her feet. It made her feel alive and grounded. *Left, Left, Left-right-left...* Madge recited the silent cadence, rallying the nerve and rhythm to walk the aisle – something Grandpa Ollie had thought of and taught her last minute.

Hooded figures turned to watch her approach, and Madge did her best not to rush past the flaming torches, continuing to recite the silent cadence as she walked, her breath steaming in the cold, gentle wind, as her midnight blue cloak swept over the sand. The ocean was spread before them like a sparkling blanket, and Madge grinned as she cast her gaze to the tidal pools that she'd fallen into not many months before. A moment that had changed her life forever.

New World, New Hope, and New Promise...

The words of Foreweard chanted in her mind now as she neared the end. As the slow, sweet, deep melody swelled like the ocean itself, rising in intensity with every step she took.

Piano, violin, cello—

And as she finally neared the end, and took a step towards the stage, voices began to sing as the deep boom of a bass drum joined its chorus.

"Foreweard, Foreweard, we must go... Foreweard, Foreweard, to the land unknown... Foreweard, Foreweard, the stars shine bright..."

As Madge lit the first luminary and released it, and hundreds of voices filled the night sky, the harmony of it all ignited in her chest and filled her with hope. And a warmth spread through her as she watched more luminaries join hers. A warmth that spread to her toes, warm even against the cold, winter sand... A warmth she couldn't explain.

Until her neck prickled, and a thought and a feeling shot through her chest.

Her parents were watching – she could feel it...

As if she could turn her head and see them standing there.

And she felt a part of her people, her kind, in a way she'd never felt until now as a fire ignited in her chest.

This was her course. This was her task, her destiny, her calling, she realized as her eyes stung, and she continued to stare up at the rising lights floating up into the night sky. No longer was it her mother's work, but hers. And no longer would she fight to save one person alone, but all of them. She couldn't – she wouldn't fail them. She felt it in her bones as hope replaced every ounce of fear she'd felt until now.

Lilith was out there, somewhere. The Council would have to work with her to bring her down – they'd have to accept her, at least for the battle they'd all have to face together. And judging by what her cuffs did for her on the other side – she felt every confidence they would. Because *someone* had helped her – had reached out through that void and lent her some powerful Vala when it mattered most.

"Foreweard, Foreweard, we sing this night. Foreweard, Foreweard, a new covenant unfolds. Foreweard, Foreweard,

we must be bold!"

Madge finally turned, thankful for the hood hiding the tears swelling in her eyes, as one by one, their entire host of luminaries swept over the dark, sparkling ocean, floating upwards towards the stars, filling the night sky with amber light.

Made in the USA
Las Vegas, NV
22 February 2024

86062681R00204